WADING THROUGH THE SHADOWS OF HEAVEN

WADING THROUGH THE SHADOWS OF HEAVEN

Kate Radtke

Wading through the Shadows of Heaven
Kate Radtke

Produced by Spoonbridge Press
Cover and interior design by Jason Craft, Crafticity LLC

First U.S. Edition, 2024

Print ISBN: 979-8-9904393-0-6
Ebook ISBN: 979-8-9904393-1-3

Printed in the U.S.A.

CHAPTER 1

My grandmother died the day of my ninth birthday. It was my first real experience with death, a matter that I seemed to think about more than the average nine-year-old. It often crept into my mind when I was alone at night, paralyzing me under my kitten-print comforter. After a few minutes of torment, I would force myself out of my bed and run to the comfort of my sleeping mother.

"What's wrong, Penny?" she would ask groggily as I slid into the opposite side of the bed.

"Can I sleep with you?"

"Sure. You OK?"

My head would relax into the pillow as I curled up under the sheets. "Yeah," I'd lie. "I just can't sleep."

She'd reach over and rub my back until I faded into the intangible world of my unconscious.

Despite my occasional death-related panic attacks, I was not terribly saddened by the news of my grandmother's passing. She wasn't the sweet and loving type of grandma who smothered you with hugs and butterscotch candies. Her approach to grandparenting was much more abrasive, and the only things she gave me were pinches under my arm if I forgot to take my shoes off in her house or put my elbows on the table during dinner. In her eyes, everything my older sister or I did wrong revealed our mother's poor parenting.

My grandma may not have had the warmest demeanor, but she did occasionally read me stories. They were always from the Bible, and with each one, it seemed I was supposed to be learning a lesson of some sort. But I had never been to church or learned much about religion, so I usually just got caught up in the adventures of each character. The fight between David and Goliath was my favorite. I asked each birthday and holiday for a slingshot so I could be prepared if I ever had to face a giant. And each time my mother refused, claiming I was too young. Luckily, my sister answered my wish. She secretly got me one for my eighth birthday. I'll never forget her sneaking into my room after my mom went to sleep and handing me the lumpy present wrapped in a paper bag. I tucked it behind my dresser out of sight so my mom wouldn't find it.

* * *

The call about my grandmother came in the morning. My mom had taken the day off from work for my birthday and was cooking French toast for breakfast. I sipped a mug of chocolate milk, pretending it was coffee, and watched cartoons on the little box TV above the refrigerator. When the phone rang, my mom set the spatula next to the stove and turned to answer. "Hello? Oh, Bobby, hi."

Bobby was my mom's younger brother by ten years. My mom was already out of the house when Bobby was my age, and he had succumbed to my grandmother's stern religious ways when he was young. I figured he was calling to wish me happy birthday, and because he felt it was his duty to check in and make sure I didn't get into trouble. There was still hope for me, unlike my rebellious older sister.

A few months ago, Amelia had dropped out of her senior year of high school to live with her twenty-year-old boyfriend. He had been at the house a few times, but he never stayed long. I didn't know him well enough to have an opinion, but my mom said he was bad news. She tried to stop Amelia from moving out, but that only made my sister more determined to do so. They'd gotten in a huge fight right before my sister left, which ended with her kicking a hole through her bedroom door and storming out of the house. They hadn't talked since.

I held my breath and hoped my mom didn't hand me the phone.

"Bobby, slow down—what happened?" Her brow tightened with concern, and she walked into the dining room to continue the call in private.

I exhaled a sigh of relief for having avoided an uncomfortable conversation, but my apprehension was immediately replaced with curiosity. What didn't she want me to hear? The dining room was separated from the kitchen by a short hallway. I flipped the burner on the stove and quietly walked closer to hear. If I was caught, I could just pretend to be grabbing a plate from the cupboard.

"Mm-hmm, mm-hmm . . . oh, no."

I could just barely make out what she was saying, but it was obviously bad news. My mind raced through the possibilities. Was it something with my sister? No, he wouldn't be the first to know. Maybe he was calling because he lost his job again and needed money. No, that didn't seem right either. My mom sounded too distressed for something that usual. It had to be something with my grandmother.

I lingered in the hallway, listening to a one-sided conversation, trying to fill in the holes. My mom was leaning on the dining room table trying to calm my uncle down. "Bobby, slow down. Where are you now?"

I pictured him in my grandmother's living room pacing back and forth clutching a rosary.

"Which hospital?"

She must be sick. My mental image skipped to her lying in a hospital bed and Uncle Bobby doing nervous laps around the room.

"I'll come right now."

I wondered if my mom would take me with her. Sometimes she tried to shelter me from things she felt were too "grown-up," even though I usually ended up finding out about them anyway, either from my sister or my eavesdropping habits. But I couldn't eavesdrop if I wasn't there. Hopefully I'd get to go.

The only times I'd ever been to the hospital were when I was born and when my sister would dislocate my shoulder. We'd play "windmill," where she would grab my hands and spin me around so fast my legs would fly out from under me, and my body would levitate horizontally to the ground. I always started out giggling uncontrollably, until my shoulder popped out of its socket and my laughter turned into wails. It happened so often that I eventually just learned how to pop it back into place on my own. My mother was happy to at least avoid the medical bills.

After a few more *mm-hmms*, I sensed that the conversation was winding down and quickly sat back at the kitchen table.

"We'll figure that out, just stay there." My mom made her way back to the phone receiver. She exhaled heavily. I pretended to watch cartoons, waiting for her to tell me what happened.

"That was your uncle." She eased herself into a chair to my left. "He was calling about Grandma Margery."

My head shifted from the TV to my mother. I was surprised to see she had been crying. Her eyes were still glossy with tears.

She reached out her hand and gently touched my arm. "Penny, your grandmother is in the hospital, but she isn't going to make it."

An awkward lump swelled in my throat. Not because I was upset, but because I had no idea how to react. My mother's sorrow had caught me completely off guard. It seemed like she expected me to start crying, but I could not muster any tears. I felt no sadness. I stared at her blankly, my mind fumbling for something to say. Finally, I managed to mumble, "What happened?"

"She had a stroke. She was rushed to the hospital, but it was too late. We have to meet Uncle Bobby." She let go of my arm and stood up. "Go put your shoes on."

I ran to the front hall, leaping over our cat, Henry. I *did* get to go! A spark of excitement rose in my stomach, but I shoved it back down. It seemed wrong to feel happy at a time like this. I grabbed my tennis shoes and slipped them onto my feet. My mother was waiting for me at the back door.

"Should we tell Amelia?" I asked as she closed the door behind me.

"We can't track her down right now." She jingled the keys aggressively in the lock.

We shuffled down the flight of stairs that led to the back hall. My mom rented out the lower half of the duplex to a pair of college-aged guys. One was a computer nerd who spent most of his free time playing video games, and the other worked third shift as a police dispatcher, so we didn't see them very much. We raced past their back door and out into the driveway. The summer heat had finally arrived, and the sun baked through my navy T-shirt.

"She's probably at Jimmy's," I suggested. My sister's boyfriend lived above Scottie's Pub, where he also bartended.

"Maybe, but we don't have time to check."

I slid into the front seat of our mint-green Volkswagen Beetle. The thick, sultry air trapped in the car immediately smothered me. I cranked my window down and gasped for air.

"But we could pick her up!" Hope filled my voice. I missed having Amelia around. She hadn't been home all summer. "Please, Mom?"

"We don't have time."

"It's just a few blocks away," I pleaded.

"Penelope Louise, this is no time to argue." Her harsh tone was not something I was used to. She cranked the key in the ignition and the car groaned to life. The tiny Beetle roared as it accelerated backward out of the driveway and onto the street.

My head darted toward the passenger's side window. I closed my eyes and let the warm summer air brush my face. It smelled of lilacs and freshly cut grass with a hint of steaming asphalt. My mom's moodiness made me uncomfortable, and I wished I were alone, outside riding my bike or playing basketball in the backyard.

Her relationship with my grandmother was anything but loving, so I was confused about why she was so upset. The divide began long before I was born, when my mom met my father and moved out. She was only eighteen. My dad proposed but refused to convert to Catholicism. Grandma Margery, in return, refused to attend the wedding. It would not be recognized by God, she believed; therefore, it would not be witnessed by her. "Nothing but a charade," she muttered repeatedly at various family functions.

For the first few years of their marriage, my grandmother was around for only the major events—when Amelia and I were born, Thanksgiving, Christmas, and birthdays. My mom didn't want to cut her completely out of our lives just because of their disagreements. But Grandma Margery's disapproval of my parents, my father in particular, loomed with each visit. It was obvious she blamed him for stealing my mother away from God. It created a tension that spread beyond the forced family interactions and permeated my parents' relationship. My dad was always a heavy drinker, but he started spending more time at the bar than at home. It became too much for my mom, and when I was four, she kicked him out. While my mother struggled to pull herself out of depression and raise two children, Grandma Margery preached how it was proof that a godless marriage could not endure, and my father was destined for Hell. She was delighted to have been "proven right" and my mother never forgave her.

Aside from the rumble of our car, the rest of the ten-minute trip was silent. I stared out the windshield, watching the ripples of heat rise off the road. If I looked far enough ahead, the road appeared to be wet. But the heat was full of deception, and the water disappeared before I could reach it.

We arrived at St. Charles Hospital and wound through the parking structure until we found a spot. The number 6 was in red on the dull concrete pillar near our car. I followed my mother down the ramp and into the elevator.

"Which floor is Uncle Bobby on?" I asked, waiting to press the button.

She reached over and hit the 1, making it glow a pale yellow. "We'll have to ask at the front desk." My mother sounded distracted.

I followed her off the elevator and through the two glass doors that parted as we approached. It felt like I was stepping inside a giant refrigerator. The bright florescent lighting bounced off the shiny white floor, and the chilled air smelled of stale cafeteria food and bleach. We walked up to the reception desk, and my mom began talking to the man behind the counter.

My attention wandered to the people roaming around the lobby and the hallway. An elderly woman in a baggy white gown staggered alone down the hallway behind me. Her weathered hands clasped the walker in front of her tightly. A lost expression hung morosely on her wrinkled face. To my left, a younger man, not much older than my mother, sat slouched in his wheelchair with a clear tube leading from his nose to a metal canister next to him. An attractive young woman with raven-black hair and a ruby stud in her nose stood behind him. She gently pushed him closer to the window that looked out to the hospital patio. Probably his daughter, I thought. At least he had someone, unlike the woman with the walker. I wondered if these people were going to die. The sullen atmosphere made me feel helpless.

"Penny?" My mom's hand brushed my back, pulling me from my gaze. "You OK?"

"Mm-hmm." I nodded.

"We have to take the orange elevators to the second floor."

We followed a path of orange diamonds to the elevator and stepped in. I pushed the button marked 2. "Is Grandma up there?"

"Her body is, honey, but her soul is no longer on this earth."

That was the first time I had ever heard my mother speak of a soul or anything having to do with religion. It seemed she'd held on to some of those beliefs her mother had enforced so militantly throughout her life.

The elevator doors parted, and we stepped out. The smell of antiseptic saturated the hallway and made my stomach uneasy. It also didn't help that my breakfast was still sitting in the pan on our stove at home. I traipsed behind my mother as she examined the signs on the wall. After a few turns, we entered another reception area.

The heavyset woman behind the counter looked up. Her eyes were underlined with dark circles. "How may I help you?"

"Hi." My mom forced a smile to be polite. "We're here for Margery Murray?"

"Your name and relation?" the woman rasped, not returning my mom's fake cheer.

"Louanne Marques. I'm her daughter."

The woman typed on her computer for a few seconds before answering. "OK, go on back to room 2101," she directed, handing my mom a plastic rectangle with a clip on it. "Make sure you return your visitor badge before leaving."

* * *

The room was smaller than I'd imagined and crowded with medical equipment. Two burgundy vinyl-upholstered chairs were crammed on one side of the bed, next to a large machine that was beeping steadily. Uncle Bobby sat in one of the chairs, hunched over on the hospital bed, holding my grandmother's hand. I didn't understand why she would be hooked up to that machine if she wasn't alive. Was my mother wrong? Had they found a way to fix her?

"Bobby, we're here." My mom rushed to his side. "How are you doing?"

He startled at the sound of my mom's voice, then turned to greet her. "God help me." His voice was weak with grief.

My mother sat down in the empty seat next to my uncle.

"I don't know what I'm going to do." His head collapsed into his hands. "I don't even know where to go now."

Uncle Bobby had lived with my grandmother in her small two-bedroom apartment ever since he lost his job at Wilson Family Roofing Company two years ago. Like my grandmother, he had a habit of pushing his religious beliefs on everyone, including customers. The last straw was when Bobby laid down in a customer's driveway reading the Bible in protest. The customer was trying to leave for work, but Bobby wanted to talk to him about God. Since the man refused, my uncle chose to block him from leaving. When Bobby returned to the office an hour later, he was fired before he even stepped through the door. My sister heard the entire fiasco because she was working at the office as a file clerk. I was only six at the time, but Amelia was never one to hide the truth from me. With no job and no savings, Uncle Bobby couldn't afford his rent and got kicked out of his apartment. My grandmother welcomed her son into her home with open arms, proud of his efforts to save the heathens from damnation. He'd lived there ever since.

"Can't you stay at Mom's still?" my mother suggested. "It's a nice apartment."

"I can't afford it."

Her head tilted back as if she were thrown off by what he said. "I thought you were working for that moving company. Doesn't that pay OK?"

"I'm not there anymore."

"Oh." Her response was terse with disappointment.

I was standing in the doorway listening to their conversation and staring at the lifeless lump of blankets on the bed that was my grandma.

A nurse appeared behind me. "I'm sorry, I don't mean to interrupt," she apologized as she brushed beside me to enter. "Dr. Krolly needs to speak to Mr. Murray for a moment."

Even though the nurse had asked for my uncle, my mother was the one who answered. "OK. Should we come into the hallway?"

"Sure, that will be fine."

My mother stood and led my uncle out of the room. "We'll be right back, honey. Just have a seat for now," she said as they passed me.

"OK," I responded timidly. I was hesitant to be alone with my grandmother. The room was silent except for the rhythmic beeping of the machine next to the bed. I inched toward one of the chairs. My grandma's face was slack and pale. Her eyes were shut, but I felt certain that any moment they would suddenly pop open. Goose bumps rose on my neck and arms. I sat down and watched the green electric line on the monitor jump with each beep until my mother returned.

After a few minutes that felt like hours, she walked into the room and slid into the chair next to me. "Penny, do you want to say anything to Grandma Margery?"

"I thought she was already gone."

"They used these machines to keep her body alive a little longer, honey, so we could have a chance to see her one last time and say goodbye." Her soft voice eased my apprehension, but my goose bumps remained. The brisk air of the hospital made me wish I had brought a sweatshirt.

"I don't know," I mumbled, shrugging.

"It's OK, you don't have to." Her hand lightly rubbed my back. "They'll be coming in soon to turn off the machines, so let me know if you change your mind."

I knew I wouldn't. Anything I could think of saying would be generic and forced. It seemed better to just say nothing.

A few minutes passed, and my uncle came in. A priest followed behind him, carrying various items in his hands. His long black tunic looked warm, and I wanted to use it as a blanket.

"Good afternoon, Louanne." He smiled sympathetically at my mother as he set his supplies on the small table next to the doorway. His face was slender but wrinkled, and his white hair circled his head like a halo. I wondered how he knew my mom's first name.

"Good afternoon, Father."

"Is this Penelope?" he remarked, stepping further into the room. "I haven't seen her since her baptism. She looks so grown-up."

Baptism? I never knew I was baptized.

My mother backed up so the priest could see me. "Yes. She just turned nine. Today is her birthday."

"Oh, Penny. I'm sorry this happened today of all days." They both turned their eyes to me.

This sudden attention on me made my cheeks warm. I looked to the floor and shifted out of his line of sight, leaning behind my mother.

"She's very shy." His eyes squinted with a smile.

My mother patted my back. "She certainly is."

I hated it when adults talked about me like I wasn't there. It made me feel smaller than I already was. My silence seemed to cue them to move on.

"I suppose we should get started," the priest announced.

My mother and uncle met him at the bedside. I remained sitting. Watching.

He grabbed a small glass bottle of holy water off the table.

"Let this water call to mind our baptism into Christ, who by his death and resurrection has redeemed us."

He sprinkled the water over Grandma Margery. "My dear friends, we are gathered here in the name of our Lord Jesus Christ who is present among us. As the gospels relate, the sick came to him for healing; he loves us so much that he died for our sake. Let us therefore commend our sick sister to the grace and power of Christ, that he may save her and raise her up."

It all sounded very scripted and emotionless to me. I didn't see the point. He continued with more lines and prayers. My mother and uncle joined in at times with rehearsed responses. Then he brought out a vial of oil, which he rubbed on my grandmother's forehead as he said a final blessing. The entire ritual seemed bizarre to me, and I was glad when it was over.

Once he finished, the priest stepped into the hallway to

get the doctor. My mom glanced over to me and extended her hand. "Penny, come stand next to me."

I stood and stepped beside my mother, unsure of what was going on.

"The doctor is going to come in soon to let your grandma pass on completely." Her voice was delicate and calm.

I didn't say anything back because, again, I didn't really know what to say.

A moment later, the priest returned with the doctor behind him. "Is it OK if we stand by the bed?" the priest asked Dr. Krolly.

"Of course." He stepped around us to turn off the beeping monitor. Then he moved around to the other side of the bed and took out a small vial of clear liquid.

I looked up at my uncle. His head was bowed, and his hand rested on my grandmother's forearm. The priest was next to him, clutching a silver cross close to his chest with both hands.

The doctor took a syringe and drew some of the liquid from the vial. "This is just a sedation to keep her muscles relaxed," he explained, injecting it into a tube connected to my grandma's arm. "I'm going to remove the ventilator, but she won't immediately pass on."

"How long does it take?" my mother asked warily.

"It varies with each patient. It can take a few minutes or hours, even days in some cases."

* * *

We stood around my grandmother's bed, waiting for and wanting her to die. It made me feel uneasy. Hoping for a person to die seemed wrong, and it didn't fit with anything I had been taught before. The next ten minutes seemed to expand beyond the normal restraints of a clock, like a rubber band stretched around an elephant. Time was funny like that. It was supposed to be constant, but it never seemed to obey the rules, speeding up or slowing down whenever it pleased.

It took much longer than ten minutes. My grandmother was unconscious but apparently still just as stubborn as ever. My mom awkwardly escorted us out of the room, not knowing what to do. The doctor said it could take hours.

Grandma Margery died at 10:12 p.m., the exact same time that I was born nine years ago to the day, in the same hospital.

CHAPTER 2

In the days that followed my grandmother's passing, Uncle Bobby was at our house a lot. He drove home with us from the hospital and never left. He and my mom were busy making funeral arrangements, and they both left me alone to do pretty much whatever I wanted, so it wasn't so bad. They were in the dining room trying to decide where to get flowers when the phone rang.

"Hello?" I answered.

"Hey, you want to ride our bikes to the river?" It was Edgar, the only friend I saw outside of school. We met in kindergarten and have been friends ever since.

"OK. Meet you by the baseball field?"

"Yeah."

"See you there." I hung up the phone. "Mom, I'm gonna ride my bike with Edgar," I hollered from the kitchen as I slid my shoes on.

"Where are you going?" she questioned.

"By the river."

"OK. But Penny, don't you two dare go in the water, it's not safe."

"I know, Mom. See you later." I headed for the back door.

"I don't know why you let her run off like that. She's going to turn out just like her sister," I heard Uncle Bobby lecture my mother as I pulled the door shut. His overbearing ways were beginning to surface, and I was glad to be leaving.

* * *

I barreled through the outside door and hurried over to the aluminum shed behind our house. It was where my mom kept all her gardening supplies and the lawn mower. It was also home to my basketballs, jump ropes, and bike. I grabbed the key out from under one of the bricks that lined the path, pushed it into the lock, and turned. The metal loop popped open. I pulled the key out and slid it into my pocket. My fingers clutched the flimsy plastic handle, and I yanked open the rusty door. Before entering, I banged on the door a couple of times with my hand to make sure the path was clear of mice, then quickly leaped in and wheeled out my bike. I didn't want to keep Edgar waiting because I knew his mom wouldn't let him stay out very long.

He was riding his bike on the baseball diamond when I arrived. A cloud of tan dirt trailed him around each base.

"Hey!" I shouted, rolling up behind the fence of one of the dugouts. "Where'd you hide your helmet?"

He sprinted toward me, then slammed on his brakes, his back tire swerving out to the side. "I shoved it in one of the bushes as soon as my mom was out of sight."

I smiled. "Race ya to the river?"

"Go!"

I pushed off the ground and began to pedal fervently toward the trail. Edgar cut me off at the turn onto the trail, nearly shoving me into a tree. I hit my brakes and leaned left to regain control. Both of us laughed at the possible collision as we sped down the narrow dirt path toward the river. I was close behind Edgar, looking for any opportunity to pass. Up ahead, the path widened for a small stretch. That was my chance. I pumped my legs vigorously to gain speed and shifted my weight so my bike would move slightly to the right. Edgar saw my opportunity too and was trying to take up as much of the path as he could. But I was agile and smaller than him. With one last burst of speed, I shot past on the right. My tires balanced precariously close to the edge of the path, which was bordered by a steep, rocky hill. Just before the path narrowed again, I shifted left and cut Edgar off. The river was only twenty-five yards away. He'd had no chance to pass, and I coasted to victory.

We both skidded to a stop at the small clearing at the river's edge. It served as a docking area for canoes, but we never saw anyone use it. I stepped off my bike and laid it on its side. "My legs burn."

"Mine too." Edgar set his bike next to mine. He bent to pick up a rock.

I walked toward the river and slid off my shoes. "I bet my uncle is worse than your mom," I commented as I peeled off my sweaty socks. I stepped into the cool water, my feet sinking into the muddy bottom.

"Maybe, but you don't live with him."

I rolled my eyes. "He's been staying at our house for the past week."

"Why?" Edgar questioned, flinging his rock into the water. It skipped three times before being sucked under.

"My grandma died."

"Oh." He paused. "Sorry."

"It's OK, we weren't close." I bent down and reached my hand into the water, trying to feel for a stone. "But my uncle lived with her, and now he has nowhere to go."

"You know my mom hardly lets me out of the house. And no sleepovers, not even at my cousins' house. And I go to church with her twice a week. How is your uncle worse?"

I shrugged. "I don't know. He just makes me uncomfortable."

"How?"

I rinsed off the stone in my hand and stood up. "He's just really religious, like my grandma was."

"Why is that bad? I'm religious." His head was bent as he examined the ground for another rock.

"He always pushes it on people. And he's kind of controlling."

"Don't you go to church?" Edgar said it like he assumed everybody went.

"No. My grandma tried to take me. And she told me stories from the Bible. But I don't think I'd like it." I turned and flung the stone into the river. It plunked immediately to the bottom.

"But aren't you afraid of going to Hell?"

I turned in his direction. "Why would I go to Hell?"

"God won't let you into Heaven if you don't believe in him." He stepped closer to me, still looking for a stone. "That's what they taught me in Sunday school."

"But I haven't done anything wrong. I've never even been in detention."

Edgar looked at me. "It doesn't matter."

"That's stupid." I bent down to pick up another stone.

We were both quiet for a second. I tossed the stone into the river, but it plopped just as quickly as my previous attempt.

"You're not very good at that," Edgar jested.

"Shut up." I used my hands to flick water in his direction, spattering his green-and-white striped T-shirt.

"Hey!" He stepped forward and reached into the water to splash me back.

I stooped down, trying to avoid the spray, and nearly lost my balance. My hand caught the ground, and I was able to regain my footing. "OK, truce!"

Edgar laughed. "My mom would never let me out of the house again if I came home with soaked clothes."

"Yeah, mine either. I promised her we wouldn't go in." I stepped out of the water.

He picked up a stone and walked over to stand next to me. "Here, try again."

I looked at him doubtfully but accepted the rock anyway.

"You gotta grab it with your pointer finger on the side and try to spin it when you let it go."

I positioned my finger carefully.

"And face sideways," he added.

I adjusted my mud-caked feet and prepared to throw. My arm reached back, and I paused for a second, thinking of Edgar's advice. With a slight exhale, I flung the stone toward the river. It bounced lightly across the surface of the water twice. "I did it!" I gasped.

"My dad taught me." Edgar spoke quietly. He didn't talk about his dad a lot. "Before he got sick, we'd always go camping at this lake up north."

"That sounds fun. I've never been camping." Part of me wished I had happy memories like those of my father. Edgar's dad had died a little over a year ago, after a long battle with cancer.

"How'd your grandma die?" He knelt and found a spot to sit that wasn't completely muddy.

"My mom said she had a stroke." I crouched down next to him in the dirt. "We saw her in the hospital."

"Was she awake?"

"No, she was hooked up to a bunch of machines." I tried to brush some of the dirt off my feet before pulling my socks on. "A priest came in and did a prayer or something, with holy water and weird oil, right before they took her off the machines."

"The last rites. They did the same thing for my dad." He shifted his legs, crossing one over the other out in front of him. "It prepares them for Heaven, and they say their last confession to ask God for forgiveness."

"What happens if someone dies before the priest comes?"

Edgar shrugged. "I don't know, they didn't teach that in Sunday school yet. I guess they're left for God's judgment."

"God seems mean."

"I guess, sometimes." He shrugged again.

I slid my shoes back on. Edgar had to be home soon. The sun was already starting to sink into the western horizon. I thought of science class when Mrs. Brown taught us about the solar system. She said that the sun isn't really moving, that it remains still as we move. I guess, like time, the sun setting was just another illusion to confuse me.

We hopped on our bikes and wound through the dirt path back to the baseball field.

"See ya tomorrow?" I asked as we slowed to go our separate ways.

"Not sure." Edgar turned left and headed off down the sidewalk. "I'll call you!" he hollered.

I turned right and headed home. The smell of burning charcoal and sizzling hamburgers drifted through the neighborhood. My stomach rumbled. I pedaled lazily down the block, hoping I could convince my mom to grill out for dinner.

As I turned onto our street, I noticed someone sitting on our front porch. It was Jimmy. That meant my sister was home! I hurried up the driveway and tossed my bike onto the back lawn. My legs bounded up the stairs and I burst through the door. My mom and Uncle Bobby were sitting at the kitchen table.

"Is Amelia here?" I questioned eagerly. Both of their faces were firm with anger, quickly extinguishing my excitement. I gently shut the back door. "What's wrong?"

My mother cleared her throat. "Penny, you forgot to lock the shed."

My hand moved down to feel the key in my pocket. "Sorry," I mumbled.

"You have to be more careful," my mother began calmly, but Uncle Bobby cut her off.

"Your carelessness got your mother's shed trashed and her things stolen!" he bellowed, rising from his chair and coming toward me. "Her gardening tools, which were your grandmother's, gone! Along with the lawnmower!" He still had the temper of an alcoholic even though he'd quit years ago.

"I said I'm sorry," I squeaked, backing up against the door.

"Sorry!" he roared. "Sorry doesn't replace anything!"

"Bobby, settle down. She didn't do it on purpose." My mother tried to interject, but she was too passive, like a lamb standing up to a lion.

He was inches away from me, towering over my scrawny four-foot frame. "Those gardening tools were priceless—a piece of your grandmother gone forever because of your stupidity! What are you going to do? Huh?"

My head drooped and I turned my eyes to the floor, not daring to look at him. I remained silent, hoping to turn invisible, or that my mom would save me.

"Don't disrespect me! Answer me!" His hand connected hard with my face, stinging my cheek and bringing tears to my eyes.

"Bobby, that's enough!" my mother screamed, finally coming to pull him back.

I ducked under them both and ran through the dining room and living room straight into my bedroom, whipping the door shut behind me. Guilt and anger coursed through me and spilled from my eyes. I dove onto the bed and buried my face in the pillow. Part of me felt terrible for forgetting to lock the shed and causing my mom's things to be stolen, but I was also mad. Mad at Uncle Bobby for hitting me, and mad at my mom for not stopping him. I rolled over onto my back and wiped the remaining tears from my eyes. My face ached where I was slapped. I sat up to examine it in the mirror above my bed. A rose-colored splotch slightly resembling a handprint spread across my left cheek. I wished I had some ice to put on it, but there was no way I was going back out there by him.

A soft thumping on my bedroom door distracted me. I hopped off the bed and opened the door a crack to let Henry in. His fluffy black fur condensed as he squeezed through the narrow gap. He immediately began purring and rubbing against my leg. I plopped down on the floor to pet him. He meowed softly and leaned forward to nuzzle my face. "You always know when something's wrong." I scratched behind his ears. "Hopefully Uncle Bobby leaves after the funeral."

From the floor, I caught a glimpse of the slingshot resting behind my dresser. I crawled over to grab it. "This might come in handy," I said softly to Henry, who had followed me to the dresser.

My hands fondled the slingshot as I imagined a heroic battle between me and my uncle. We were back in the time before electricity and houses, when everything was made of dirt and stone. I pictured him swinging laboriously as I dashed and dodged out of the way, hopping on top of a boulder. I would load a stone into the slingshot and take him out with one swift blow right between his eyes. He'd fall heavily to the ground, never to bother me again. I smiled and took a penny out of my basket of change. I loaded it into the slingshot and aimed at a cat poster that hung on the wall across the room. Picturing my uncle's face, I released the trigger and the penny shot across the room, straight into my target. My aim had gotten better.

As I returned the slingshot behind the dresser, I suddenly remembered Jimmy sitting on the porch. My anger vanished at the thought of seeing my sister. I crept over to my bedroom door and listened. My mom was arguing with Uncle Bobby in the kitchen, so the coast was clear. I scurried out of my bedroom and down the front hallway steps. Henry followed at my feet. The bitter smell of cigarette smoke wafted through the mail slot as I carefully lifted the metal flap. I bent to peek through. Jimmy was still sitting on the front steps, but he was alone. A cigarette burned between his fingers, and his knee bounced nervously up and down. I plugged my nose and kept my eyes focused through the door. No sign of Amelia yet.

Henry grew bored and found a sunny spot at the top of the stairs. I remained at my post, gazing through the slot. Jimmy extinguished the cigarette on the porch and flicked it to the sidewalk. As he reached to grab another from the pack, a car pulled up in front of the house. Amelia was in the passenger's seat. Her friend Jane was driving. I didn't understand what Jimmy was doing here alone, but I was happy to see my sister. She reached into the back seat to grab a duffle bag, then hugged Jane goodbye. They paused to talk for a moment, and I wished I could hear what was being said. Amelia nodded, then turned and stepped out of the car. As Jane drove off, I saw her stick up her middle finger at Jimmy. I wasn't sure exactly what it meant, but I knew it was like swearing. My sister walked toward the house, glaring at Jimmy the entire time. I wanted to run out and say hi to her, and my hand hovered on the doorknob.

"Get off my porch!" Amelia shouted.

My hand dropped from the doorknob. I knew my

sister's temper and that it was better to stay inside, behind the safety of the door.

"Let me explain." Jimmy rose from the step to face her.

"Get out of my way!"

He extended an arm out to touch her shoulder. "Please."

"Don't ever touch me again." Amelia shoved his arm away and tried to step around him.

Jimmy moved in front of her. "It's not what you think."

She jammed the duffel bag into his chest, forcing him backward and out of her way.

"You're not even gonna give me a chance to explain?"

"I said get away from me!"

He turned as she charged past him. "I made a mistake."

"Leave," she said firmly, but with more sadness than anger this time.

"Em, come on," he begged. Her back was to him.

She hesitated for a moment, then reached into her pocket to retrieve her front door key. "It's done."

I guided the metal flap down gently, careful not to make any noise, and raced back upstairs and into the living room. She'd be mad if she caught me spying on her. I leaped onto the couch and flicked on the TV.

My mom walked into the living room. Uncle Bobby stood in the doorway to the kitchen. He looked unsure about coming any closer. "Honey, are you OK?" my mom asked, sitting down in the brown recliner next to the couch.

I stared at the TV. "Mm-hmm."

Before my mom could say anything else, Amelia pushed through the front door. I was grateful for the distraction.

"Amelia?" My mother left the chair and stepped toward the door.

My sister pushed the door shut and dropped her bag to the floor. Her eyes were glossy, and she tried to avoid eye contact.

"Em, what happened?" My mom rushed to her.

"Can I stay here?"

My mom wrapped her arms around her. "This is your home."

Amelia's head sunk into my mom's shoulder as her body heaved with sobs.

My eyes reflected concern, but inside, my heart beamed with the thought of having my sister home again.

CHAPTER 3

The day before my grandmother's funeral, my mom was in a frenzy. She had been cleaning the house incessantly since six o'clock in the morning. My great-uncle Theodore, who was my grandpa's brother, would be staying with us. He was flying in today, and there were only a few hours before we had to meet him at the airport. Other relatives I had never met or even heard of would also be in town to say their last goodbyes to Grandma Margery. The stress of it all was wearing on my mother.

She was behind the couch in the living room, armed with dusting spray and a rag. Her chestnut-brown hair was clipped behind her head, but a few frazzled strands had fallen loose and whirled messily around her face. "Penny, you need to straighten your room, and take the sheets off your bed so you can put new ones on for Uncle Theo."

"OK." My response was muffled by the huge bite of sandwich I had just crammed in my mouth. I was sitting on the living room floor eating my lunch. Henry was next to me, trying to steal each bite I took. He shoved his way onto my plate and grabbed a scrap of turkey that fell off my sandwich. I quickly pushed him back as he swallowed the meat. He flanked me, trying a sneak attack from the other side, but I stuck my knee out to block him.

"Penny, let's go, we're running out of time," my mother urged.

"I'm going." I stuck the last bite of sandwich in my mouth and pushed myself off the carpet.

Henry sat licking the crumbs off my plate, his fluffy black tail curled behind him.

"The sheets are on the piano bench."

"OK." I slid the plate away from Henry and set it on the coffee table, then wandered into my mom's bedroom to get the fresh sheets. I checked the wooden pendulum clock that swung rhythmically above the piano. It was 2:34 p.m. We had to meet Uncle Theo at the airport at 5:00, which meant my mom would have us leave the house at 3:30. It wasn't that far of a drive, but she'd rather arrive thirty minutes too early than be a minute late. I hugged the stack of sheets with both arms and headed to my room.

Uncle Theo was the closest thing I had to a grandfather. I never had the chance to meet my grandpa on my dad's side, and my mom's dad had died from cancer when she was twenty. We didn't see Uncle Theo very often, but he sent us frequent letters and cards, in addition to the ones he sent for birthdays or Christmas. And he always made sure to include pictures and stories detailing his latest fishing adventure. I was looking forward to his visit and didn't mind giving up my bedroom for him. It also meant I'd have an excuse to have a sleepover in my sister's room.

I dropped the sheets at the foot of my bed. My room was overflowing with stuffed animals. A variety of fuzzy creatures filled the shelves, my dresser, and the top of my TV. I collected the ones strewn across my bed and shoved them into the closet. That would have to do. Next, I tore the dirty sheets off my bed and added them to the pile of dirty clothes that lay behind my door. By the time I was done remaking the bed, my mom was calling to me from the back door.

"Come on, girls, traffic might be bad, and I don't want to be late."

I quickly wadded up all the dirty laundry from behind my door.

"Amelia, did you hear me?" She was outside my sister's bedroom door.

Amelia had locked herself in her room since she returned. Periodically, my mom would go in there to check on her, but the door was always closed, so I couldn't hear what they were saying. It was obvious that she was upset about Jimmy, and I had seen enough on TV and in movies to recognize that he had broken her heart. Love wasn't something I really understood, but from what I observed, it seemed awful. I'd seen it dissolve things that had once seemed absolute, make people doubt everything they thought was right, and turn logic into complete nonsense. Love could make someone risk everything with no guarantee of happiness. It was viciously unfair, and I wanted nothing to do with it.

While my mom tried to coax Amelia out of her haze of depression, I hurried to her room and dropped the dirty laundry on the floor. Henry was sleeping on the bed in a blanket of sun. I reached to scratch the top of his head. His eyes squinted open lazily.

"See ya later." I gave him one last scratch, then headed to the back door.

My mom was still at Amelia's bedroom. "Honey, it will be good for you to get out of the house. You need a distraction."

I slipped my shoes on and sat down at the kitchen table.

"And we're going to dinner after we pick up Uncle Theo. It would be nice if you came." She had opened the door just enough to lean her head in. "What do you think?"

"Fine, I'll come," my sister conceded. Her bed squeaked as she moved to get up.

My mom entered the kitchen. "Penny, are you all ready?"

"Yep."

"And the bed is made?" she questioned, grabbing her purse and keys.

I nodded.

"Good."

A moment later, Amelia appeared. Her tousled hair and puffy eyes were glaring evidence of her inner distress. Though she never was one to hide her emotions anyway.

"All right, let's go, girls." My mom herded us out of the house, and we set off toward the airport.

***

My mom's concerns about traffic were unfounded. The gruff little Beetle encountered zero resistance from other cars as we cruised down the highway. We reached the airport at 4:15 and spent forty-five minutes wandering around the main terminal. I tried to get my mom to buy me various items while we waited: a stuffed dog dressed like a pilot from the gift shop, a battery-operated airplane that flew in circles attached to a string, and a happy meal from McDonald's. But she refused each of my requests.

Luckily, Uncle Theo's flight was right on time. We stood outside concourse D and watched for him. A line of passengers began to file down the wide, brightly lit hallway, towing luggage and backpacks behind them. In the middle of the line, I spotted Uncle Theo. His portly stature and cue ball–like head made him stand out from the crowd. He wore large, square-rimmed glasses that rested softly on his round cheeks and had a tan duffel bag slung over his left shoulder. I couldn't wait to see what kind of souvenirs for us were packed in there!

The moment he saw us, a jolly smile stretched across his face. It made my heart feel warm. He broke away from the line and strode over to us.

"Look at you beautiful ladies!" he greeted. "Best welcome any man could hope for."

"Uncle Theo, it's good to see you too." My mother laughed and reached up to hug him.

"Amelia, how's life been treating you, darlin'?" Uncle Theo spoke with a slight Southern drawl, and I wondered if the way I talked sounded funny to him.

My sister just shrugged morosely.

"Must be takin' your grandma's death hard, huh." Uncle Theo turned to me. "What about you, little One-Cent?"

"Good." I smiled as he draped his arm around my shoulder and squeezed me into his side. "Did you bring us anything?"

"Penny! That's rude," my mom scolded.

Uncle Theo gave a deep chuckle. "Oh, Annie, let her be a kid." Then he winked at me and patted his duffle bag. "Of course I brought you something!"

My mom shook her head. "All right, let's get going."

"So, where's a fella go to get a hamburger round here?"

"We should go to Gilbert's!" I blurted.

"You are *not* eating ice cream for dinner." My mother knew my real intentions; ice cream was my favorite food.

Amelia came to my defense. "They do have hamburgers."

We approached the car, and my mom reached to open the trunk. "Gilbert's it is," Uncle Theo concurred, setting his bag in the back of the car.

My mom had no argument; she was outnumbered.

"Boy, I hope this thing can hold me." Uncle Theo chuckled again.

Amelia and I were already in the back seat as Uncle Theo crouched to get in. The car recoiled under his weight. It reminded me of the springy horse at the playground, and I smiled. We wound out of the airport parking garage and headed toward home.

* * *

We reached Gilbert's a little after 6:00 p.m. My mom parked in the back facing the empty field that all the kids cut across in the summer to get to the local pool. I stepped out onto the gravel parking lot and reached my arms up to stretch. The birds had all retired for the day, their energetic chatter now replaced by the hypnotic chirps of the evening crickets. That comforting rhythm always seemed to lull me into a trance. They made me want to sit outside on my front porch and just stare off into the distance, not alone but surrounded by their invisible presence, calling for me to surrender to the tranquility of the night.

I turned to follow my sister toward the front of the building. My mom and Uncle Theo were close behind. "Edgar's brother used to work here. He gave us free ice cream all the time," I remarked to Amelia.

"Didn't Matthew join the military right out of high school?"

"Yeah. His mom didn't want him to."

"She seems a little high-strung," Amelia commented as we rounded the corner of the building.

There was a family with their two young boys standing out front by the walk-up windows. Each boy had an ice cream cone the size of their head dripping down their arms. The mom pivoted between her two sons, frantically trying to catch the sticky mess with her napkin before it reached their clothes. The dad was at the counter getting more napkins.

A group of teenagers sat at another picnic table, throwing crumpled burger wrappers at each other and laughing. A girl with too much eyeshadow and blush shrieked and jumped off her boyfriend's lap. She shook the back of her blouse and an ice cube fell onto the pavement. "Punk!" she yelled. He laughed and grabbed her waist, pulling her back into him. They started kissing, sloppy and lustful, oblivious to the three other guys at the table with them. His hand began creeping up the girl's skirt, and she started kissing his neck.

Amelia rolled her eyes. "Let's go, Penny, before some-one gets pregnant."

I blushed instantly. I was just starting to understand how babies were made, from what I'd watched on TV and heard at school.

"Amelia!" my mother chastised, just as embarrassed as me.

"What?"

"Penny doesn't need to hear that!"

Uncle Theo stepped up to defend my sister. "I'm with Amelia—there's enough hormones flying around out here to sully the Virgin Mary. We better take shelter, quick."

Before my mother could respond, a high-pitched wail filled the air. One of the young boys had dropped his ice cream—splat—straight to the pavement. The mother tried to console him, explaining he could have more ice cream. But he was too focused on the melting glob that was no longer atop his cone that he didn't hear a word she was saying.

"I . . . I . . . I want m . . . my ice cream!"

"Them high school kids should be watching that," Uncle Theo added as we approached the entrance. "Get a glimpse of the consequences of their actions."

Amelia laughed, the first genuine laugh I'd heard from her in a long time. I pulled open the heavy glass door just as my mother let out a disapproving sigh. Sex was another one of those things that she didn't want me to know existed.

We walked up to the stainless-steel counter and were greeted by a freckle-faced teenager with a mouthful of braces. "What can I get you all tonight?"

We each took turns telling him our orders. Two ham-burgers, one cheeseburger, and one fish sandwich, all with fries. My mom promised that if I didn't get a milkshake with dinner, she'd buy me ice cream afterward, so I settled for a root beer.

"That'll be twenty-eight dollars and fifty-two cents," the cashier politely announced.

My mom opened her wallet, but Uncle Theo gently nudged her aside. "My treat tonight, put that away."

"Theo, no. You're our guest," my mom protested.

"And I'm also your elder, young lady, and I say your money is no good here tonight." Theo handed the cashier his money.

The boy looked apprehensively at my mother before grabbing it.

"I'm your elder too, young man, you don't need to look at her." Uncle Theo glanced down at me and winked. "Always remember, sometimes what may seem like a disadvantage, like me being an old geezer, can work in your favor if you play it right."

I nodded, not fully understanding what he meant.

"Here you go, sir." The cashier handed him his change and the receipt.

My mother finally returned her wallet to her scuffed black fanny pack that she used as a purse. "All right, old man," she teased. "You got dinner, but I'm getting dessert."

We waited for our beverages, then walked to a booth against the wall and squeezed in. I sat on the inside of Amelia, across from Uncle Theo. While we waited for our food, Theo told us one of his fantastic fishing stories.

"So, I'm sitting in this old Mexican cantina in Tampico. It's nine o'clock in the morning and already a hundred degrees, so I got an ice-cold beer in my hand and I'm talking up the bartender in my own broken cacophony of Spanish and English." My uncle leaned back in the booth, stretched out his arm, and grasped his soda like the beer in his story.

He continued. "The bartender is nodding, pretending

to understand me, when I look over and see this dark-haired senorita staring at me, smiling." He paused again and turned specifically toward Amelia and me. "Now, this is back when I was still young and had a lot more up here and a lot less down here," he said, first motioning to the top of his head and then rubbing his belly.

As he talked, I tried to picture a much younger and thinner Uncle Theo with the same magnetic smile and kind eyes. But it was hard for me to imagine him as an attractive man.

"So, I ask the bartender to put her next drink on my tab. After a few minutes, she comes over. She tells me her name—Sophia—and asks what I'm doing in Mexico. I ask what she's doing in a bar at nine in the morning. She laughs and says she works there, that her father owns it, and that the drink I just bought her was water. Her subtle aroma of lilac entices me, but it's her wit that completely captivates me."

I began to wonder if this was a fishing story or a love story. But I kept quiet and listened.

"We talk all morning, until her father comes in and glares at me for occupying his daughter's attention. She says she better get back to work, but I, many beers in, place my hand on hers and insist that she stay a little longer. I assure her that it will be OK and I'll talk to her father, who by now is starting to walk over toward us." Uncle Theo paused again and took a sip of his soda. "Before he reaches us, she takes my hand and yanks me toward the back door, yelling something in Spanish to her father. He yells back angrily, I imagine something along the lines of 'get that gringo out of here.'"

"What's a gringo?" I asked.

Amelia answered, "It's what they call Americans."

Uncle Theo continued, "We stand in the doorway, and

she tells me I better leave before her father gets mad and goes for his gun. I ignore the severity of her warning and kiss her. I beg to see her again, tell her I'll cook her dinner, fresh-caught fish and wine. She finally agrees. I kiss her once more before she pushes me out the door, closing it behind me."

At this point in my uncle's story, a server arrived with our food, and I worried we'd have to wait to hear the rest until after dinner. But luckily, he grabbed his burger and continued in between bites.

"I end up hooking up with these local fishermen who do daily trips for a living and know the best spots and lures and whatnot. They were a funny bunch. Esteban was a talker and didn't seem to take any notice of the fact that I barely understood one word he was saying. He carried on an entire conversation with me, laughing and patting me on the shoulder like I knew what was going on. Fabian was short, burly, and sported a silky black eye patch. I'm pretty sure it was just for show, though, because when I met him, it was on his right eye, and halfway through the trip it switched to his left. Enrique completed the trio. He didn't say much, but he was the levelheaded mediator between the other two. Esteban and Fabian would start to disagree, and it would escalate; soon their cheeks would be red with anger, and they would flail their arms to emphasize every word, and just before they came to blows, Enrique would step in. This happened about every thirty minutes but became more frequent as the beer bottles began to pile up. Enrique was the voice of reason, or the tie-breaker vote.

"They were entertaining, to say the least. Between their broken English and my broken Spanish, we made a go of it. For the most part, I just watched and followed directions, which was easy because talk ain't really a necessity when you're fishing. They really knew all the tricks.

Within the first hour, we caught four flounder, which was surprising because these guys weren't the most patient, and flounder can be very cunning. It was all kinda surreal, like something out of a fairy tale. Well, at first at least. We reached late afternoon, and I began to wonder when we'd head back to shore. I was growing anxious thinking of Sophia waiting for me. I made an attempt at asking Enrique when we were heading back, but as he was trying to figure out what I was saying, we got a bite that shook me off my feet. 'Aleta amarilla!' Esteban yelled. My brain struggled to understand. *Yellow*, I knew that much. Then it hit me—*yellowfin*! We had to be at least fifteen miles out to hook a yellowfin, and they were fierce fighters. A yellowfin would be a once-in-a-lifetime catch. My heart pumped with excitement.

"As expected, the fish gave us hell. It wasn't until the sun began to set that I realized Sophia was already waiting for me, and we were hours from shore. By the time I got to her, it was well past midnight. I knocked on her door, waited a few minutes, then knocked again. A half hour probably went by, me pacing back and forth, until the door finally opened. I gazed eagerly at the door awaiting Sophia's face. I was met with whiskey breath, a five o'clock shadow, and the stubby nose of a well-worn thirty-eight revolver. Despite my certain death, I began to argue with him to let me see Sophia. Two words in and he shot a hole in the ground an inch away from my foot. I never saw her face again, never again smelled her lilac perfume. I had the catch of my life on that trip, but I lost it all due to that darn fish."

I had almost finished my burger by the time he ended his story. "You were actually shot!" I mumbled excitedly between bites.

My mom answered before Uncle Theo, "No honey, he wasn't shot."

"Darn close though," Theo replied.

It was quiet for a few seconds as everyone finished their food. My mom collected the empty sandwich wrappers and French fry containers.

"Penny, help me bring these to the garbage and we can go get dessert."

I took one last sip of my soda and slid out of the booth, excited for ice cream.

"Anyone else want a scoop?" my mom asked as I collected the trash on the table.

"Oh, I probably shouldn't," Uncle Theo said, placing one hand on his belly. "But I could kick the bucket tomorrow, so I'll take a scoop of chocolate in a waffle cone, please."

Amelia just shook her head.

"All right, one scoop of chocolate for the old man," my mother joked.

I followed her to the garbage can. Just as we stepped up to the counter, her cell phone rang. She pulled it out of the side pocket in her purse and flipped it open. "Hi, Bobby, is everything OK?"

I cringed. She walked away from the counter, leaving me in ice cream limbo. As I waited, I could overhear Amelia talking to Uncle Theo.

"Do you regret it?" she asked. Her head drooped as she played with the straw in her soda cup. "Like, she was the one, and you lost her."

I was caught off guard by Amelia's candor.

"Well, my dear, that's a very romantic perspective." He paused and took a sip of his soda. "And I may have believed that at one time. But I've lived long enough to realize that love is what you make it."

"What about soulmates, true love?" Amelia seemed to have lost her depression-induced silence, at least for a moment.

"True love exists, but it ain't the fairy tale people want to pretend it is. It ain't easy. The heart and the head can get into some fierce battles. But sometimes, no matter how much you want something or how hard you try, it's not meant to be."

That was obviously not what my sister wanted to hear, because she retreated into her silence and didn't say another word the entire ride home, where she immediately returned to her room and went to bed. On the bright side, I did enjoy a double hot fudge sundae in the car.

CHAPTER 4

The funeral was different from what I'd pictured. I'd never been to one before, but I always imagined funerals as being very quiet and grim, with everyone silent out of sadness or respect, wiping their teary eyes on their black sleeves. I never thought it'd have tiny little sandwiches with the crusts cut off and endless trays of cheese and crackers. And cake! It was like a party. People were having conversations, even laughing at times. Amelia and I sat on a maroon vinyl couch against the wall. The room we were gathered in looked very similar to a living room, with end tables and coffee tables and floral curtains in the windows, except there was also a dead body.

We both had little plates of snacks spread out before us. Everyone around us was talking, and we were both listening intently to what they were saying. Uncle Theo was entertaining a small crowd with another fishing tale. His arms stretched wide as he described the mouth of a shark that tried to take a chunk out of the catch that he was reeling in.

My mom darted around from group to group, clearing empty glasses and crumpled napkins, greeting every person that walked through the door, asking people if they needed anything. She never stopped in one place for more than a minute. It was like she was playing the hostess, waiter, and busboy all in one in order to avoid any serious conversation.

"Louanne, your anxiety is starting to rub off on me, and I don't like it." Her cousin Theresa put a hand on my mom's shoulder to settle her. "Here, take this and go sit down for a little while." She handed her a wineglass filled to the brim with dark red liquid.

My mom began, "I don't think I should drink. I'll just—"

But Theresa cut her off. "If you don't drink it, I'm going to tell everyone about that time by the lake when you got too friendly with—"

"Teri May, don't you dare!" My mom glared.

"Then take this and come sit down."

"Fine." My mom clutched the wineglass reluctantly and followed Theresa to the main room where Amelia and I were sitting. My mom and her cousin had been close growing up. I was curious to hear the stories Theresa had of when they were young. I felt like there was a whole side to my mom that she kept a secret from me, a side that showed she was once young and rebellious like my sister.

The second my mom sat down, Edgar appeared in the entrance of the funeral home. He made his way into the sitting room where we were all gathered. His mother was right on his heels.

"Hi, Penny." He smiled, then turned to mom. "I'm sorry for your loss, Ms. Marques."

"Thank you, Edgar. I appreciate you coming."

Edgar's mom stepped forward. "Find peace knowing Margery was a woman of the Lord. She is with Him now."

It was meant to be reassuring, but to me, it felt hollow and presumptuous.

"Yes, I'm sure she is." My mom took a sip of her wine. "You have such a polite son, Evelyn. Thank you both for coming."

Edgar's mom sat down and began small talk. I looked at Amelia, then at Edgar, and the three of us stood up and walked into the hallway where the food was spread out.

"Sorry about my mom. I know you don't believe in that," Edgar said sincerely as he picked up a mini turkey sandwich.

"I don't know what I believe," I answered quickly. The truth had a way of just slipping out before you could catch it.

Amelia sighed. "I don't know what I believe either, but I do know if ghosts exist, there's no better place to look for them than a funeral home."

Edgar and I smiled at the thought.

"Come on, let's go explore this place. There's bound to be something creepy around here."

* * *

We followed my sister around, investigating all the stairwells and hallways of the funeral home and creating our own eerie stories to go with them. By the time we finished our exploration, there were the ghosts of two little orphan girls, a lonely old cat lady, and a wounded Civil War soldier with a peg leg, all sulking in the shadows. But as much as we tried, our imaginations only got us so far, and any rooms that looked remotely interesting were locked. We gave up and retreated back to the main gathering room.

When we returned, we saw that Uncle Theo had joined the group. He was telling stories from when he and my grandfather were kids. Grandpa Louie was Uncle Theo's younger brother. They were four years apart, but that didn't stop them from spending nearly every minute together.

Uncle Bobby was at the back of the room, pacing. I'd almost forgotten he was here. The three of us snuck past him and grabbed a seat next to Theresa. My mom was on her other side, holding a new, full glass of wine.

"Me and my buddy would climb up these tall skinny pine trees until they bent over and touched the ground. And we'd get Louie to climb onto the tip of it. He was easily convinced; at six years old, he was still very trusting. So, he wrapped his entire body around the end of the tree. We made sure he was holding on as tightly as he could before we slipped carefully off the tree and sent him flying forty feet into the air. He'd boomerang back and forth, and then when the tree finally settled, he'd shimmy his way down and ask for another ride."

His audience chuckled. My mom tipped her wineglass back until it was empty and stood up. She walked to the back of the room to refill it. As she reached for the bottle, Uncle Bobby stepped over and grabbed it.

"I can't believe this is how you behave at her funeral." He ripped the bottle out of my mom's hand. "And Theo goes on and on about Dad, but this isn't his funeral! This is Mom's time!"

My mom reacted without pause, grabbing the bottle back out of his hand. "Saint Margery kept a bottle of peach schnapps in her nightstand, so don't act like she never touched the stuff! Or like you haven't either for that matter." My mom took a swig straight from the bottle that she was holding. "And there's a reason that we're talking about Dad—because he was the only redeeming part of her life that exists! She was a mean, self-righteous, spiteful old woman who probably contributed to Dad's cancer!"

"Louanne—" Uncle Theo tried to interject, but Bobby cut him off.

"Don't you have any loyalty to the woman who raised you?"

"Oh. Let's talk about loyalty. Loyalty was not one of Mother's virtues." My mom took another swig of wine. "All that going to church, her time spent praying and confiding in the preacher about how distraught she was over Dad dying—it was all a hoax. She was sleeping with him. There are letters to prove it."

Uncle Bobby's face was red in anger. "How dare you speak of her that way!" His fists were clenched tight.

"It's the truth—you want to see the letters? Your mother dearest never showed them to you?"

"Louanne!" Uncle Theo roared, stepping between my mom and Uncle Bobby. I had never heard him raise his voice like that. "That's enough. You think your father would want this?"

My mom's anger subsided at the thought of her father. "No," she said, setting the wine bottle on the table. "He wouldn't."

Suddenly, the party atmosphere that I felt at the start of the funeral had disappeared and was replaced with a much more serious tone. I grew awkward and uncomfortable with the sudden tension. My instinct was to shut down when people became angry. I thought any movement or sound I made might make things worse, so I did my best to just blend into the background. I slunk back in between Edgar and Amelia.

My mom had retreated to the bathroom, Theresa on her tail. Uncle Bobby was sitting out front in his car, protesting the rest of what he viewed as the mockery that was his mother's funeral. Everyone else in the room was unsure of what to do. I looked to Amelia for guidance, but before she could make a move, Edgar's mother stood and walked toward us.

"Edgar, I think it's time for us to go." She took him by the hand and led him toward the door.

"Bye, Penny," he said before she pulled him from the room.

I was sad to see my friend go, and I felt like I had done something wrong to make his mother upset. Guilt seemed to be my default emotion in a lot of situations growing up, which made it exponentially more awful when I actually did something wrong.

Amelia had a mischievous smirk on her face. "Grandma Margery almost made it to the grave with that secret."

I looked up at her, somewhat confused.

"Let's go get some more cake before they take it away." She shoved me toward the food.

I broke into a smile and followed behind her.

* * *

The burial was soon to follow. Only immediate family accompanied the hearse to the cemetery. It was a small convoy. Amelia, Uncle Theo, and I rode with my mom. Theresa followed behind us in her silver Jetta, and Uncle Bobby brought up the rear in his rumbling, rusty Ford pickup. As they lowered the coffin into the ground, a deep sense of loneliness flooded over me. I wasn't close to my grandma, and I had gathered enough from my mom to realize she was far from the perfect person my uncle Bobby believed her to be. But I couldn't help but feel a deep sadness for her, imagining her body all alone, decaying, devoured by the earth. It was at that moment I decided I wanted anything but a burial when I died.

Most people are so uncomfortable being alone that even the introvert and recluse craves a connection to some living being in one form or another. Yet in death, there is no choice. Even if you are surrounded by people, they can't follow you to where you are going. You are ultimately alone. I think that's what terrified me most from a young age, what made me run into my mother's bedroom in the middle of the night. I had no control over it; one day, no matter what I did, I would end up like Grandma Margery. Alone, succumbing to darkness.

CHAPTER 5

I was relieved that the funeral was over. It finally felt like things could get back to normal. There were still a few weeks left in the summer, a few weeks of freedom before I had to go back to school. I looked forward to long bike rides, playing in the sprinkler, staying up late with Amelia playing games or watching movies, and sleeping in late with Henry snuggled up next to me. Uncle Theo was packing up his things in my bedroom. He was the only part of all this that I would miss. He created a sense of security and joy when he was around, like he had all the answers, and everything would be OK. He was also the only father figure I'd ever really had. I was too young when my dad left to have many memories with him. Our dad being gone affected Amelia much more. To me, it was just normal to not have a dad around, but my sister had him for twelve years of her life. There was no way I could ever imagine leaving my family. I felt like I should hate him, but I didn't know him enough to have any strong feelings one way or the other. Mostly I just didn't care.

Amelia and I were sitting in the living room watching *The Price Is Right* and bidding on the various items brought out by the Barbie-like models. Henry sat on my sister's lap, licking the butter that dripped off her bagel. The heat of summer had set in, and we were trying to talk our mom into putting the air conditioner in. It was tradition that on sweltering days, we would drape off our living room with sheets and close all the bedroom doors to contain the cold air. Our mom always tried to wait as long as she could before putting the old window unit in. She said it wasted too much energy and money. If it wasn't a forecasted high of 100 degrees, our chances of cool conditioned air would be slim.

Uncle Theo appeared from the bedroom wiping the sweat from his brow. "Louanne, don't make these girls melt. Embrace the luxury of modern technology."

"I would hardly argue that our hunk-of-junk air conditioner is modern technology." My mom peeked out from her bedroom. "Are you girls almost ready to go?"

Amelia and I both grunted. Neither a yes nor no, just an acknowledgment that my mom said something.

"Well, we have to leave in five minutes, so you better be ready." My mom seemed to have recovered from the previous day's drama or chose to just ignore it.

Uncle Theo was all set to go. He set his bag down in the doorway and took a seat next to me on the couch. "Old Bob is still doing this show, huh."

"Let's see what the lovely Tricia has for us today," Bob Barker responded from the TV. The model brought out a dark brown La-Z-Boy recliner. She ran her fingers along the upholstery, then sat down in the chair and reclined it back.

"Four hundred and fifty dollars!" I shouted.

Uncle Theo played along. "I'm going with six hundred."

Before we had a chance to see the winning bid, my mom came out of her bedroom and shut off the TV. "Let's go, we don't want Uncle Theo to be late."

We all marched down the back steps. One of our tenants was coming up the basement steps with a basket full of laundry. It was the computer nerd. He had large headphones over his ears with an attached headset microphone. My mom paused to let him through as she smiled and said hi. He nodded and then put his head down, staring at his laundry as he scurried through nervously.

"Odd fella," my Uncle Theo commented as our downstairs neighbor closed his door. Amelia and I laughed. We all continued outside and piled into the car. At least it had air conditioning. My mom started the engine, then reached into her purse and pulled out a bottle of ibuprofen.

"Want a glass of wine to wash that down?" Uncle Theo smirked.

My mom put the car in reverse and backed out of the driveway without a word.

* * *

We got to the airport two hours before my uncle's flight departed. After meandering around the gift shops and food court with no real purpose but to kill time, we walked him to his terminal to say our goodbyes. Amelia was first.

"It was really good to have you here, Uncle Theo."

"It was really good to be here, kid," Uncle Theo said, reaching his arm around her shoulders and pulling her to his side. "Hang in there. Sometimes you gotta throw back a few fish before you find the one worth keeping."

Amelia nodded and leaned in to him. She seemed to be finally moving past her broken heart with Uncle Theo's help.

He turned to me. "You keep your sister in line, kid. I think she's got a little of her mom's rebellious streak in her."

"I wish you could stay." My eyes darted to the ground.

"Well, I'll miss you gals too." He bent down and looked me right in the eye. "What do ya say you be my pen pal?"

My face lit up with a smile. "Yeah." I nodded eagerly.

He wrapped me up in a big bear hug.

Last but not least, he turned to my mom. "Annie, thanks for your hospitality."

"You were a bigger help the past few days than you know." My mom's voice was soft and a bit shaky. She was clearly overwhelmed by recent events. Her mother's death seemed to catch her off guard, like she didn't think it would affect her at all, and she didn't realize how much having Uncle Theo here was helping until just now.

Uncle Theo saw the emotion swelling in her eyes. "You'll be OK, you always have been." He embraced her in a hug.

While they were close, I could hear him whispering something to her. I turned my head in that direction and focused all my energy on listening to him. With my mom trying to shelter me from everything, I had gotten pretty good at snooping. Uncle Theo's voice was naturally deep, so his whisper still carried.

"You need to be careful with Bobby. I don't think he's in a good state of mind. I don't trust him, especially not around the girls."

My mom looked at him with skepticism. "I know he's a little extreme sometimes, but I think he's harmless."

My mind flashed to him slapping me across my face just days earlier. Why couldn't my mom see her brother for who he really was? If she made my dad leave, why couldn't she stand up to her brother? It made me angry.

"He's in AA now—he attends meetings at the church," my mom added.

Uncle Theo pleaded, "Louanne, please. Just watch him and let me know if you need anything."

"OK, I will," she conceded.

We said our last goodbyes and then watched Uncle Theo walk to his gate.

* * *

We made the drive home almost entirely in silence. Now that everything was over, we actually had time to process what had happened the past few days. The distractions were gone. I had always thought a funeral was the final part of a person's death, where you remembered them and said goodbye one last time and then went on to live your life. If only it were that simple. I'd grow to learn that the funeral was really only just the beginning. It was the time after all the busyness and planning, when all the people were done saying their condolences and all the family and friends had traveled back to where they came from. That's when you were truly confronted with your thoughts and emotions. That's when the grieving process really began.

I could already tell Amelia was sinking back into her lovesick depression. She checked the answering machine constantly, silently wishing Jimmy would call. It had only really been three days since their big fight on the porch. Amelia didn't talk to me about what happened, but I overheard her talking to my mom in between sobs, saying she'd found a message on his answering machine from another girl about what a great night she had and how good of a kisser he was. She'd packed her things and left while he was in the shower.

Feeling unwanted by the person you love is bad enough, but having them betray you for another is a pain that defies reason. Logically, you should hate them and want nothing to do with them, but in your heart, no matter how angry you are, you still wish that they would want you, that they would be madly in love with you and find a way to make everything better. One of the hardest lessons to learn is that no matter how much you love someone, sometimes you just have to walk away to save yourself.

As we pulled into the driveway, I saw Edgar sitting on the front porch. My heart lightened and a smile spread across my face. He was a welcome surprise. The second the car stopped, I opened the door and ran down the driveway to the front porch.

"Hey!" I shouted to him excitedly.

He didn't look happy.

"What's wrong?"

"My mom said I can't hang out with you anymore." He slouched on the stairs, picking at the paint that was peeling off the wood.

I sat down next to him. "What? What do you mean?"

"She was upset after the funeral yesterday, about the fight with your mom and Bobby. She said she doesn't want me around that."

"But that doesn't make sense. We're never even around them." The heaviness returned to my chest.

"I tried to tell her, but then she got upset and said we shouldn't be unsupervised." Edgar continued picking at the paint.

"What if I came over by you? Then she could know we were supervised or whatever."

"Penny, I don't know." His words were quiet, like he didn't really want me to hear. "I think she thinks you're a bad influence. Like because you don't go to church."

"That's bullshit." It just came out. I had never sworn before, but it didn't feel shameful like I thought it would.

Edgar didn't say anything. He just continued picking away at the paint.

My mind raced, trying desperately to come up with a solution. Edgar was my only friend and had been since we were five. None of this made sense. "What about when school starts? She can't keep us from seeing each other then!"

He turned his body toward me but kept his eyes focused on the porch. "She can. She did."

"What?"

"She put me in Catholic school."

My mind raced with so many thoughts and emotions,

but I couldn't think of anything to say. Nothing would make it better. So all I said was "Oh."

"I'm sorry, Penny." Edgar finally picked his head up and looked at me.

I looked away. I didn't want him to see my anger and sadness.

I tried not to have hate for his mother, but I could feel it thumping through my temples and settling in my jaw. I knew what it was because I had the same feeling when I thought of Uncle Bobby.

"See you around I guess," I muttered, trying to disguise my sadness.

It's strange how automatic it is for people to try to hide their pain, to appear unaffected by things that so clearly should hurt. Perhaps it's an innate defense mechanism to make your enemy think you're stronger than you really are. Even though Edgar wasn't my enemy, I turned away so he couldn't see how upset I was.

"Penny, say something. I don't want this." He had tears in his eyes. "But you know my mom."

"It's fine. Good luck at your new school." My heart sank to my stomach, but my words revealed no emotion. "Goodbye, Edgar."

I walked back down the driveway and in the back door. This was the first time I ever remember really feeling sadness. Not little-kid sadness, over a lost toy or bumped head. This was a pain with grown-up weight behind it, and I wasn't sure how to deal with it.

My mom was sitting at the kitchen table when I walked in. "Hey, honey, how's Edgar?"

"Fine." I rushed past her, not wanting her to see how upset I was.

She stood up to follow me. "Penny, what's wrong?"

"Nothing," I said, picking up Henry off the dining room table on my way to my bedroom.

"You can talk to me," my mom pleaded.

"It's nothing." I retreated to my bedroom and shut the door.

My mom sighed loudly. "These boys are not worth you girls shutting yourselves away!"

I sat in my room, hugging Henry and feeling guilty for the way I had treated Edgar and my mom. Amelia was also hiding away in her room, once again. My mom was desperate to help, but neither of us would let her.

CHAPTER 6

Eventually, Amelia and I pulled ourselves out of our funks and emerged from our rooms. We spent the last few weeks of summer doing everything and absolutely nothing at the same time. Our afternoons were spent rollerblading around the neighborhood or swimming at the public pool. We'd make sure to grease up with sunscreen to obtain maximum velocity down the slides. The ultimate goal was to go fast enough around the curve to splash the lifeguard sitting in the nearby stand. Our nights were spent playing board games or going to the twenty-four-hour Walmart just because we could. And of course, there were always movie marathons any given morning, noon, or night, usually things that weren't appropriate for me to watch, which made it even more fun. Most of the time we managed to stay out of trouble. But there were a few close calls.

One of those occasions was when we had the brilliant idea to take a mountain bike, ten feet of rope, and a pair of rollerblades to create a land version of waterskiing around our neighborhood. The problem we failed to think of is that pavement is a harsh substitute for water. But it was a hot summer day, where the heat rippled off the pavement, creating the illusion of puddles, so that was close enough for us. We often rollerbladed around the neighborhood together, creating obstacle courses in the church parking lot, going to the fountain near our mom's work and stripping off our sweaty socks to wade in the cool water, and then stopping at the Dairy Queen on our way home to get Blizzards. This time, though, we had a different idea.

I was sprawled out on the living room floor eating a super-soft pretzel hot out of the microwave and staring up at the TV. Amelia was curled up on the couch with Henry in her lap.

"Hey, we should go rollerblading," I suggested. Music from *The Price Is Right* played in the background as the next contestant came on down.

"I don't know, it's hot." My sister wasn't a fan of the heat. This would take some convincing.

"Please? We could get Dairy Queen. I saved up my allowance."

She finished her last bit of cinnamon toast with Henry licking up the crumbs. "Maybe. I'd rather ride bikes."

"My bike has a flat tire."

"How'd you do that?" she questioned.

I shrugged. I didn't know how it happened, but I suspected Uncle Bobby.

Amelia patted Henry on his head and set her plate on the table. "What if I pulled you behind my bike on your Rollerblades?"

My eyes lit up like it was the best idea I had ever heard. "OK!"

"Grab the bungees from the back hall." She scooted Henry off her lap. "I'll go get my bike out."

I jumped up and raced out the kitchen door into the back hall. There was a rusty beige metal storage cabinet that my mom kept all kinds of random items in—gardening supplies, wrenches, bug spray, WD-40, rope, and bungee cords. I opened one of the doors and began to search. The top shelf was too tall for me to see, but it didn't matter. A tangle of red bungee cords beamed at me from the bottom shelf. I grabbed all of them, and some rope just in case, and headed down the back stairs. The screen door hissed as I opened it to meet my sister in the backyard. I handed her the supplies.

"Perfect." She took them from my hands and began to secure the bungees to the back of her bike. Then she tied the rope to the bungees and stretched it out behind the bike. A ten-foot tail was laid out on the driveway. "Go grab your skates!"

A few minutes later, I returned with my Rollerblades strapped to my feet. I picked up the rope and created a loop to hold on to. Amelia hopped on her bike and slowly pedaled out of the driveway. I rolled carefully behind, holding the rope tight and keeping the slack off the ground. We turned out of the driveway and into the street.

"Let's just go around the block," she hollered back to me. "I'll start slow."

My fingers clenched the rope as it pulled taught. I had the benefit of being fearless in my youth, and I sped along with confidence. We made it around the block, and I was feeling pretty comfortable as we started our second lap. "You can go a little faster this time!" I hollered.

We cruised around the corner and I let the rope whip me into a wide turn. I shifted my weight to straighten back out. We made another short right as we approached the last block of the loop. It was the longest straightaway on the route, and slightly downhill. A smile lit up my face as I anticipated the burst of speed. I sunk back into the last turn, pulling my weight against the rope. My legs tensed as we accelerated. I leaned right to straighten myself out, but this time I leaned a little too far.

A parked car came out of nowhere, and its side-view mirror slammed straight into my shoulder. The rope was ripped from my hands. My skates lifted off the ground and I flew forward, skidding down the street on my stomach.

My body came to a stop a few yards from the car. Amelia set her bike on the side of the street and sprinted toward me.

"Are you OK?" she screamed.

I pushed myself to my knees, sobbing uncontrollably.

My sister bent down in front of me. "Come on, we gotta get out of the street." She began to help me to the curb. "Can you make it home?"

My head nodded up and down as I wailed.

Amelia collected the rope and bungee cords and got back on her bike. I skated behind with mopey and labored glides, as if my feet were pushing through maple syrup.

We made it to the front of the house and my sister assessed the damage. My knees were scuffed and the left one was bleeding a little, but it wasn't bad. My palms had tiny black pebbles engraved in them from the road, but most of it could be brushed off. My stomach is what had taken the brunt of the fall. A two-inch patch of flesh had been grated raw by the pavement, and it would require some type of first aid. I stood in front of Amelia with one hand holding my shirt up off my wound and the other wiping tears from my face.

"You're going to be OK," my sister consoled me. "It's just a big scrape, you'll be fine."

I took a deep breath, a little more composed. "What should we do? Mom is going to be mad."

"It's too big to hide, she'll see it for sure," Amelia answered.

My mind quickly came up with a cover. "I could tell her we were doing an obstacle course race and I tripped and fell."

"Yeah, that's good." She nodded.

By now, our mom was home, and she'd be expecting us upstairs soon. We made our way to the backyard and disassembled the bungee cords and rope. I took off my Rollerblades and set them in the back hall. Amelia hauled her bike inside and put the evidence back in the metal cabinet. Then we marched upstairs.

I opened the back door and stepped into the kitchen, expecting my mom to be waiting and ready to interrogate us. But she wasn't there. I made my way through the house into the living room. Amelia followed behind. My mom was in her room sorting through mail and talking to the cat.

I looked at my sister and quickly whipped up some more tears. Our mom heard us and rushed out of her room. "What happened!?" Her voice was filled with concern.

I was sitting on the brown recliner holding my shirt up. Tears trickled from the corners of my eyes. One of my talents I developed as the baby of the family was crying on command. Amelia stood in front of me as I explained our version of what happened.

"We were rollerblading and racing and I fell." I tried to sound as pathetic as possible.

"She was going for a record," my sister added.

"This is quite the scrape!" My mom examined me. "Amelia, go grab the iodine swabs and gauze from the bathroom. And medical tape."

My sister retrieved the medical supplies and handed them to our mom.

"So where was this race happening?" my mom questioned as she tore open one of the iodine swabs.

Amelia jumped in. "Over at Holy Rosary, in the parking lot." My mom knew we frequently went over there to skate because it was one of the smoothest surfaces we could find.

"I tripped on a crack and flew forward," I concurred, squinting as my mom rubbed the iodine on my wound.

"As long as you weren't in the street." My mom tore open a bandage to cover the abrasion and sealed it with medical tape. "OK, you're all set."

"Thanks," I answered quietly.

I glanced up at Amelia as my mom turned to throw away the garbage. Her eyes widened as she breathed a sigh of relief. We'd gotten away with it. I wouldn't be banned from Rollerblades for being too reckless, and my sister wouldn't be grounded for almost killing me.

CHAPTER 7

I lay in bed with my eyes shut, but my mind was running wild. It was the night before my first day back to school, and I was restless with anxiety. My legs squirmed like they were trying to break free from some sort of restraint. Any time I got close to being comfortable, something began to itch—my eyelid, the back of my knee, the inside of my nose. I was so frustrated I wanted to scream. If I could only break the endless stream of thoughts, I might be able to settle down. But it was impossible. I tried counting sheep, singing the words to the national anthem in my head, even listing all the foods I could think of that started with the letter P. No matter what, my mind always found its way back to worrying about something.

I started out thinking about Edgar and how he wouldn't be there on my first day of school. My anxiety swelled as I thought about how I was going into fourth grade, and in just two years I'd be in middle school, and then high school. Before I knew it, my life was rushing by and I was an adult. I imagined myself applying for colleges, then jobs, and I thought about how my days sleeping in my childhood bedroom were numbered. Before I could blink, I'd be an old woman. My mom and sister would die, and I would be completely alone. Then, eventually, I would die and fade into nothingness, into darkness. I would cease to exist.

The thought was too much for my nine-year-old brain to bear. My breaths became shallow. My heart pounded beneath my chest. Sheer terror consumed me. For a moment, I was trapped. Incapable of moving. But I managed to break free and jolted out of my bed. Moving was the only way to shake myself back to the comfort of being alive, back to a state of mind where I could ignore the reality of the human condition. I started toward my mom's room, humming a random tune, hoping the sound would pull my mind back from the grips of death. My hands clenched into nervous fists. My feet moved on instinct. Tunnel vision blinded me and I didn't see Henry dart in front of my path. He let out a loud screech that snapped me back to the present.

"Oh no, buddy, are you OK!?" I crouched down and picked him up. He started purring immediately, not one to hold grudges.

It was enough to give me the courage to go back to my own bedroom. Or at least enough to distract me from my grim fate. I crawled into bed with Henry curled up on the pillow next to my head. This was the first time I was able to pull myself out of the panic attacks that crept up in the middle of the night. All other nights since I was five years old, I would run into my mom's bedroom for comfort, most times never really telling my mom why I was upset. But this time, I was able to do it on my own, with a little help from Henry. The thought of death still disturbed me deeply, but I was able to ignore it for the moment and let myself believe it was a problem for the distant future. I let Henry's rhythmic purring lull me to sleep, my mind at peace, for now.

* * *

My mom stood in my doorway. "Sweetheart, it's time to get up."

Henry moved, I did not.

"First day of school, let's go," my mom said a little louder.

I grumbled something incoherent, then extended my arms and legs out in a big stretch.

"Come on, Penny, I'm not coming back in here." She walked over and put her hand on my shoulder, shaking it gently. "It's time for school."

My eyes opened. I pushed myself up and looked hazily at my mom. "Okayyyy, I'm up."

"Good, get going." My mom turned and walked out of the bedroom.

I sat up. As much as I was resisting waking up and hated that summer was over, I actually wasn't completely dreading school. I was a good student. Following directions was in my nature, and I did well academically. I didn't have a lot of friends, but I wasn't antisocial. I just kept to myself unless someone approached me. In the past, Edgar was there to help me build bridges with other kids, but this year would be different. Edgar would be in a different school. I didn't know if or when I would see him again. I pushed the thought to the back of my mind and climbed out of bed.

My outfit was already sitting out on the dresser. My favorite light pink tank top—a hand-me-down from Amelia—cutoff jean shorts that I cut myself, and a spiffy new pair of pink Converse. I got dressed and met my mom and sister in the kitchen for breakfast.

"Glad you made it." My mom smiled from behind her mug of coffee.

I didn't respond. I pulled a bowl from the cabinet and filled it with cereal.

Amelia passed me the milk. "Who's your teacher?"

"Ms. Jenkins," I answered, covering my cereal with milk.

"Ooooh, she's pretty tough, I think." Amelia had gone to the same elementary school, but that was seven years ago.

"Does Edgar have the same teacher?" my mom asked.

I stared down at my cereal. I hadn't told my mom about Edgar. I was trying so hard not to think about it. Maybe if I pretended it didn't bother me, then my sadness would go away. I hadn't yet learned that ignoring problems only prolongs your pain.

"Edgar is going to a Catholic school this year. His mom pulled him," Amelia answered for me.

"Oh, that's too bad." My mom squeezed my shoulder. "Hopefully you two can stay in touch. You can still see each other out of school."

I kept my head down, knowing that wouldn't be the case. Edgar was basically banned from seeing me.

"We can always go rollerblading if you get bored." Amelia smirked.

I tried not to smile but ended up breaking into a full-out laugh.

"What's so funny?" our mom asked. Which made us laugh even harder.

Our mom was not amused. "Finish your breakfast, Penny, we have to get going."

I picked my head up and looked at Amelia. "Hey, why are you up so early?" She was not naturally a morning person, and she had no reason to be up since she dropped out.

"I'm checking out an alternative school," she answered. "Mom's taking me after she drops you off."

"Oh, cool." I slurped down the rest of my cereal so I could finish getting ready.

* * *

My mom pulled up to the side of the chain-link fence that bordered the playground. "Do you know where to line up?"

"Yeah," I answered, grabbing my backpack and stepping out of the car.

"I took off work today. Do you want me to pick you up after school?" She leaned over from the driver's seat so she could see me.

I thought for a second. As much as I wanted to pretend to be grown-up, I still craved the comfort of dependence and would have plenty of other chances to walk home by myself.

"Sure," I answered.

"OK, I'll see you after school. Have a great first day, sweetheart! I love you!"

"Love you too." I swung the door shut and headed toward the playground. A subtle wave of homesickness rushed through me. I took a deep breath and shrugged it off. It was nothing new, but I had gotten better at managing it throughout the years. My first day of kindergarten wasn't quite as smooth; I started crying the second my mom dropped me off. It lasted through story time, lunch, nap, play time, and almost up until the end of the day. Nothing and nobody could calm me down. Then I met Edgar. He crawled over to me under one of the tables with a toy car in hand. He pulled a Tootsie Roll from his pocket and stuck it on the car and rolled it over to me. From that moment on, we were best friends.

I walked through the gate and scanned the crowd for a familiar face. Most of the other kids in my class took the bus to school. It had been that way since K-5. That's one of the reasons Edgar and I bonded. We both lived in the neighborhood and were "walkers." We were also two of the only non-black students in our grade, which never occurred to me as a dividing factor. But it was. Edgar was Hispanic and seemed to fit in a little better than me, maybe just because he was naturally more outgoing. I was the nerdy tomboy that everyone wanted to cheat off of and have on their kickball team, but no one really wanted to be my friend, except Edgar. Now, since he changed schools, I'd have to build my own bridges.

I spotted Jasmine by the basketball court. Her long, thick, black braid swung behind her as she shot a free throw. Every day, her hair was pulled back in that braid. It was her trademark. I made my way toward the court. Jasmine was someone that I was only "school friends" with. We hung out at lunch and recess, but never outside of school. There were a few other kids that I had that relationship with, but I never felt completely comfortable around them and kept up a defense. This was partly due to my reserved personality, but also because I was different. I didn't naturally fit in with most of my classmates. Beyond skin color, I lived in a different neighborhood, came from a different background, a different culture, and had different interests. It all created an unspoken divide. And even though I got along with everyone, or tried to, I would never be completely accepted. Living in different neighborhoods was like living in different worlds when you're a kid.

Sports were always a way for me to make connections. Jasmine was athletic and competitive, which is one of the reasons we got along, and also one of the reasons we didn't. Every now and then we got into fierce battles on the basketball court. She was more aggressive than me, but I didn't back down. And afterward, we were always able to let it go. As I approached her, she passed me the basketball.

"Hey," she said plainly.

I caught the ball and dropped my backpack. "Hey."

We played one-on-one until the bell rang, then grabbed our bags and raced into line. Our competition shifted from the court to a running race. We both skidded to a stop by the door at the same time.

"Rematch at lunch?" I puffed, out of breath.

Jasmine smiled. "You're on."

The rest of our class joined the line behind us. There was an energy that buzzed across the entire playground. Kids reuniting with friends they hadn't seen all summer, showing off new shoes and backpack accessories. Younger kids desperately clinging to their parents, wailing uncontrollably. The quiet, nervous ones anxiously pivoting from foot to foot while staring down at the pavement.

Ms. Jenkins appeared in the doorway and ushered us inside. She was a petite woman, slender almost to the point of looking frail. But there was nothing petite about her personality. Her no-nonsense attitude demanded respect from even the worst-behaved kids. I was nervous about having her as a teacher because I knew she was strict. I had also never had a black teacher before, so I felt like I would be even more of an outsider in class.

We hiked single file up to the second floor and began to put our things away in the coatroom.

"Good morning, fourth graders, I am Ms. Jenkins." Her voice was sharp, demanding attention, but not in a harsh way. "You will find this morning's instructions written on the blackboard. If you have lunch money, please bring it to me before you find your seat."

With pencils and notebooks in hand, I made my way into the classroom. Written on the board in long, flowy cursive were three instructions. 1—Find your assigned seat. They are alphabetical by first name. 2—Take out your writing notebook. 3—Silently write for twenty minutes about one of the best things that happened this summer.

Most kids had already found the name tag marking their seat, but I wandered around not seeing mine. I was hesitant to ask for help, so I double-backed through all the rows. Yolanda. Sharee. Thomas. Rashad. Monique. No Penny. My face grew red with embarrassment. I hated any attention on me, and now I was the only kid left standing in the middle of the classroom.

I started to hear whispers back and forth and just assumed they were directed at me. One clearly was. "White girl can't read."

"Kevin, you got something to say to the class? Or maybe to the principal? 'Cuz I can get him up here if you'd like," Ms. Jenkins snapped from the back of the class.

"Nuh-uh," Kevin responded with a smirk. He was a newer student to the school. Most of us had been here since K-5 and had developed somewhat of a community over the years, despite our differences.

"Well, you just let me know if you change your mind." Ms. Jenkins leaned forward in her desk and her eyes locked onto me. "Baby, what's the problem?"

I turned my body to face her. "I can't find my seat."

"Let's see here," she said as she walked around her desk. "Penny, right?"

I nodded sheepishly. "Mm-hmm."

She walked through the rows but came to the same conclusion as me. "I'm sorry, Penny, I seem to have forgotten your name tag. Let me get you a seat." She walked over to her desk and wrote my name on a new name tag. "Marcus, can you grab that empty desk back there and bring it over?"

"Sure, Ms. Jenkins." He quickly appeared next to me.

I smiled as he set it down. "Thanks."

"You're welcome." Marcus slid into his desk to my right.

I settled into my seat and sighed with relief. My concerns about Ms. Jenkins were dispelled within the first few minutes of class.

The rest of the morning went quickly. We had an assembly welcoming everyone back, then a math lesson before lunch. I had a rematch with Jasmine at recess, which ended with her jumping on my back as I tried to shoot a free throw and us wrestling on the ground over the ball until the bell rang. Art was our last class of the day. We learned the origin of dream catchers and how they were meant to represent spiderwebs because many Native American cultures saw spiders as a symbol of protection. I found it fascinating and couldn't wait to hang mine in my bedroom. Maybe it would keep some of my panic attacks at bay.

We shoved our things into our backpacks and stacked our chairs on top of our desks. All the bussers were called to line up first, then the walkers at the end. The dismissal bell rang, and Ms. Jenkins wished us a good evening as we raced out of the classroom.

"See you tomorrow," I yelled to Jasmine as she headed for the bus.

"See ya," she said, pulling her long braid out from under her backpack.

I turned and headed to the side street by the playground. My mom's Beetle was parked in the same spot she'd dropped me off, with Amelia in the front passenger's seat. A wave of comfort and safety rushed through me. It was the opposite of the homesickness I'd felt earlier, a feeling that only family and unconditional love could bring. I slid into the back seat and shut the door.

"How was your first day?" My mom turned around to face me. Her round oversize peach-tinted sunglasses covered most of her face.

"It was good." I fastened my seatbelt. "Really good, actually."

A huge smile spread across my mom's face. Not a fake mom smile where they pretend to be happy because they're playing the mom role. It was a genuine smile of joy. "Penny, that's great to hear! I know it's probably hard without Edgar. Did you have other friends to play with?"

"Yeah, Mom, I have other friends." A hint of irritation hung in my voice, partly because I didn't want to admit that Edgar was really my only friend.

Amelia sensed my snark and wasn't going to let me get away with it. "You get a new boyfriend to replace Edgar?"

"Ugh, he's not my boyfriend!" I huffed.

"Mm-hmm, sure he's not." My sister knew just how to push my buttons.

My mom intervened. "Well, I couldn't be happier. You had a great first day, and Amelia is all set to start at Grand View to get her diploma and has a new job. I think we should celebrate. Dairy Queen?"

"Amelia got a new job?" I questioned, then realized my mom had mentioned ice cream. "Dairy Queen? Yes!"

"I'm starting weekends at Bruegger's Bagels," Amelia answered.

My mom pulled away from the curb.

"Are we going to Dairy Queen?" I questioned aggressively, like an addict needing a fix.

"An M&M Blizzard sounds good to me," my sister added to help my cause.

"All right, ice cream it is!" My mom put her left signal on and turned into the strip mall that was home to Blockbuster, Pizza Hut, and Dairy Queen. As we got out of the car, I noticed a familiar bike parked in the bike rack. Edgar's. A twinge of excitement shot through me, but it was immediately extinguished by the thought of the last time we saw each other. I felt ashamed about how I reacted. We approached the glass door as Edgar and his older brother walked out. Our eyes locked and my stomach sank.

"Hey, Penny." He smiled.

Before I could respond, my mom jumped in, "Hey, Edgar, what a coincidence! Matthew, are you home now?"

"Hi, Ms. Marques. I'm just home on leave, wanted to surprise Edgar on his first day."

"Well, what a nice surprise. Are you here long?"

"For two weeks, then I head back to Arizona." He shifted his attention to me and my sister. "Hey, Penny, Amelia. How've you been?"

He was two years older than my sister, but they shared the same friend group in high school. "Matt, it's been a while." Amelia smiled. "I've been OK. Working on getting my life in order."

"Hey, the army's really good at helping with that, or so they say." He laughed.

My mom jumped in again. "Hey now, we just came for ice cream, not to be recruited."

I smirked at the idea of my sister in the army. She wasn't exactly one to take orders.

"Don't let us hold you up." Matthew stepped aside holding the door open. "Amelia, if you're free, we should catch up while I'm in town."

"Yeah, for sure." My sister was trying to play it cool, but I could tell she was excited.

Edgar and I looked at each other and rolled our eyes.

"Well, it was nice seeing you both." My mom stepped through the doorway.

"You too, enjoy," Matthew said. "And Amelia, I'll give you a call."

"Sounds good." She followed through the doorway behind my mom.

I lingered for a second. I didn't know what to say to Edgar, but I knew I had to say something.

He beat me to it. "Meet by the river on Friday? Three thirty?"

A huge smile spread across my face. "But I thought—"

"Matthew will cover for me," he explained, cutting me off.

"I'll be there!"

"See you then." Edgar turned and met his brother by the bike rack.

My face beamed with excitement as I walked in and met my mom and sister by the counter.

"Penny, what do you want?" my mom prompted.

For a brief moment, my mind blanked. I was so happy about meeting Edgar that I forgot all about ice cream. "Umm . . ."

"Penny, are you OK?" Amelia was understandably taken aback. I never hesitated about ice cream; it was a 24/7 obsession.

I robotically shouted out my usual order, "Large Butterfinger Blizzard!"

* * *

We took our ice cream outside and ate on the concrete stoop. The sun beat down, warming the cool breeze. Summer was barely hanging on. Soon the crisp autumn air would take over, bringing falling leaves and foggy breath. I ate my ice cream contently, not thinking of the future. It was a childhood luxury many take for granted. But even my mom and sister seemed consumed in the moment. We all sat silently, soaking up the sun and the creamy sweetness, without a care in the world.

CHAPTER 8

The second we pulled into the driveway, I saw Uncle Bobby's truck parked in my mom's spot.

"Ugh, what's he doing here." Amelia wasn't really asking. It was more just a statement of disappointment.

My mom pulled up behind the truck. "He's staying with us until he can get a place of his own." She took the keys out of the ignition and opened her door to get out.

Amelia and I didn't budge. We sat in silent disapproval, protesting.

"It's just for a little while," my mom tried to assuage us. "He's staying in the attic, so you won't even see him that much."

"Hmm." Amelia looked skeptical. "Do we get any say?"

"It will be fine. Just give him a chance." My mom avoided answering her question.

"Yeah. OK."

I sat in the back seat waiting to follow my sister's lead, not moving until she did.

My mom turned to look at me, then to Amelia. "I promise, he won't be here long. Now come on, let's go inside. This car isn't getting any cooler."

Amelia opened her door to get out, and I followed suit.

"Maybe some more ice cream would make us feel better about this." I thought it was worth a shot.

"Don't push your luck," my mom said, unlocking the back door. "I'm making tacos for dinner.

Once we got inside, I headed to my room to put my

school things away. I slung my backpack onto my bed. Henry trotted in behind me and jumped up to investigate. I unzipped my bag and took out the dream catcher. I scanned the room, trying to find the perfect place to hang it. Ideally, it would be directly over my bed for optimal protection. I walked into my mom's room, dream catcher in hand. "Do we have any nails?"

"What do you need nails for?"

"I want to hang this. We made them in school today."

She looked up from the pile of papers on her bed. "Oh. Hmm. I don't really want you pounding a hole in the wall. Can you find another way to hang it?"

"But it's supposed to protect me while I sleep," I pleaded. "It needs to be over my bed for that."

"Fine," my mom conceded. "The nails and hammer are in the drawers in the hallway. Let me know if you need help."

"OK!" As the youngest, I seemed to have a knack for getting my way.

I skipped out of my mom's room to the hallway by the kitchen. The first drawer I opened had various screwdrivers that I somehow knew the names of—hex key, Phillips, flathead—along with boxes of different-sized screws. None of what I needed. I pulled open another drawer. Bingo! A hammer lay surrounded by boxes of all sorts of nails. I grabbed one that looked like a good size and headed back to my bedroom.

Henry was waiting by my backpack. I stepped up onto the bed, and he let out an annoyed meow.

"Oh hush," I answered.

He circled in between my ankles, headbutting me with each pass.

I held the nail up to the wall with one hand and lined up the hammer with the other. If I wasn't careful, I might hit my thumb, or even worse, the wall. It'd be the last time my mom ever let me use any kind of tool on my own. I cautiously pounded the head of the nail, proud that I didn't miss once. It was sticking out just enough to catch the loop on the string. When I bent down to pick up the dream catcher, Henry let out another loud meow. He reached up with a paw and batted playfully at one of the feathers hanging from it.

"Hey!" I scolded and nudged him away with my foot.

His attention was easily redirected to the decorative plastic spiral that hung off the pull cord for my light. It was a fourth birthday present from one of my dad's friends, "Bob the Beard." Stars were scattered on each rung of the spiral that glowed in the dark. My own personal galaxy. One of the only memories I have of my dad is him helping me attach it to my light string, only a few weeks before he left. It's weird how we can cling to something painful, refusing to let it go because it's a reminder of a love that was once there.

I watched Henry stare at the dangling light cord for a moment, then returned to the task at hand. The dream catcher hung high enough that Henry couldn't reach it but close enough to ward off evil of any form. It looked perfect. I sat for a moment admiring my work.

My mom's voice pulled my attention away. "Penny, there's a letter for you here from Uncle Theo."

I jumped off the bed and ran into her room. "Where?"

"There, at the end of the bed."

Henry had followed me and jumped up on my mom's bed. He nuzzled my hand as I carefully tore open the envelope. I slid out a picture of Uncle Theo on a fishing boat with the pearl-blue ocean behind him. He was wearing a straw fishing hat with the strap hanging slackly underneath his chin. Brown tinted aviator sunglasses covered his eyes, and his arms were stretched wide holding one of the biggest and weirdest fish I had ever seen. From nose to tail, it was about as tall as my uncle. It had a long point that protruded from its mouth, and my first thought was that he'd caught a swordfish. But as I examined it more, I noticed its unusual back. It had a huge fin that expanded out at least three feet, like a big kite. I had no idea what kind of fish it was.

"Mom, look at this picture of Uncle Theo!" I handed her the photo, then unfolded his letter.

My mom studied the picture as I began to read:

> *Hey there, little One-Cent,*
>
> *How ya holding up? I caught that beauty off the coast of Belize. It's a sailfish, the fastest fish in the ocean! Harder than heck to catch, because they're so quick, and that long hard snout makes it tricky to hook 'em. And once they're hooked, boy do they put up a fight. I admire that in a fish. Anyway, that fella sure didn't disappoint. My guide, Anders, helped brace the pole as I reeled it in, slow and steady. My arms burned with every crank. After about ten minutes of fighting, I finally got him near the side of the boat. But it wasn't going to be that easy. He jumped and flailed like a maniac, trying to shake the hook loose. Anders said that we'd need at least one other person in the boat to help us if we expected to bring this guy in. I disagreed. I didn't come this far to give up, and at my age, I may never get another chance at a catch like this.*
>
> *My shaking muscles strained to guide the fish closer. It bucked and jerked and ended up flying*

right into the boat. Its sharp bill jabbed toward us like a sword out of control, attempting to skewer us like shish kebabs. Over 100 pounds of ferocity fighting for its life, looking to take at least one of us down with him. Anders managed to kick him out of the boat, swearing at me the entire time because I wouldn't let him cut the line. I remained calm, telling him there wasn't enough room in his boat for another person and this fish, so that was a moot point, and he better start thinking of how to bring this fish in with just the two of us. He jumped behind the boat wheel to steer us away from the fish, then jumped back over by me. I let it take a little line, then reeled it in a bit. We continued this game for a few minutes, seeing which one of us tired first. Luckily, it was him. I managed to get him within an arm's reach of the boat and instructed Anders to get ready to grab the bill. He swore at me again in protest. I told him to calm down and trust me.

Using all the fight I had left, I pulled the rod toward the fish's tail. This caused him to flip over onto his back, and he gave up. Anders quickly reached down and grabbed him and we both hauled him over the side of the boat. He flopped around a little on the deck of the boat but eventually accepted his defeat. Anders and I cheered, his arm draped around me as we each cracked open beers. That fish was something else. I got Anders to take the pic, and then told him he could keep the sucker, as long as I got just one meal from it.

We ventured back to shore and cut it up. He kept some for his family, but he sold most of it to the local market. And that night, he prepared two fat sailfish steaks over a charcoal firepit. I watched him coat them in oil and a mix of crushed spices. It was a work of art. He seared them for a few minutes on each side, then plopped them each on a plate next to a healthy serving of rice and beans. We said a brief thanks to that feisty demon of a fish for giving its life, then we dug in. It was one of the best meals I've ever eaten. Let me tell ya, Penn, there's something about eating a meal that you caught and prepared yourself. You feel a connection to life and death, and to nature, that you just can't get from going to the grocery store and making a box of frozen fish sticks. One of these days I'll take you gals out to catch something.

Well, I suppose I'll sign off for now. I expect a letter back from you telling me all the things going on with you gals! And hopefully I can plan another visit in the near future.

Until next time, kiddo,
Theo

I refolded the letter and set it on top of the envelope.

"That's some fish," my mom said, handing the picture back to me. "Did he say what kind it is?"

"A sailfish, the fastest fish in the ocean!" I said it with a sense of pride, like I was the one who'd caught it. "He said he wants to take us fishing sometime!"

"Oh did he. I'll talk to him to work out those details."

I returned the picture and letter to the envelope. "I'll ask him when. I'm gonna go write him back!" I skipped out of the room.

"After you pack your lunch for tomorrow," my mom instructed.

"OK!" I set the envelope on my dresser and headed to the kitchen. There was talking coming from my sister's room. She was on the phone with someone. I hovered in the hallway outside her door to try to figure out who it was.

She was laughing. "Yeah, well, I guess once you graduated the place really went downhill, so I stopped going . . . yep, exactly, it is your fault." She laughed again.

It must be Matthew, I thought. Henry trotted through the dining room, brushing against my leg before heading to Amelia's door. He began scratching and meowing at the door. My sister's voice grew louder as she walked over to let him in. I stepped into the kitchen and out of view.

"OK, I'll see you Friday . . . mm-hmm, OK, bye." She cracked the door and Henry scooted in.

Amelia had a date. The corner of my mouth raised into a smile at the thought. I was happy for my sister. Now that my snooping was complete, I grabbed the loaf of bread from the top of the refrigerator. We had to keep it where Henry couldn't get it. He was known for chewing a hole in the bag and trying to eat the entire loaf. He never succeeded, but he always managed to take at least one bite out of every piece of bread. I grabbed two pieces and plopped them down on the table.

My mom walked in just as I began to spread a big scoop of peanut butter onto one of the slices. She had a stack of mail that she set on the counter by the phone. All bills, I figured. I finished making my sandwich and slid it into a Ziploc baggie, then turned back toward the fridge to see what else I could put in my lunch.

My mom bent down and grabbed a large skillet from one of the cabinets. "Could you get the ground beef that's in the freezer?" she asked, setting the skillet on the stove.

"Sure." I reached into the freezer, pausing for a moment to enjoy the frigid air. It wasn't very hot out, but the afternoon sun baked into the kitchen, heating it to an uncomfortable temperature. I handed my mom the ground beef. "Can I open the windows? It's hot in here."

"Just not too wide, Henry will scratch the screens."

"He's in Amelia's room, it'll be OK," I argued, pushing the first window open wide.

My mom set the frozen meat on a plate in the microwave to defrost. "Fine, but we're closing it as soon as he comes out."

I gathered a few other items for my lunch—an apple, a baggie of potato chips, and a Little Debbie Zebra Cake—and tossed them into a brown paper bag along with my peanut butter sandwich. Then I walked to grab a marker from the cup of pens on the counter so I could write my name on the bag. I caught a glimpse of a name on one of the pieces of mail hiding beneath the stack: *Loren Marques*. It was my dad. I didn't think my mom had kept in touch with him since he left, but he had clearly sent her something. His name was in the upper left corner, where the return address went. I nudged the pile of mail to unveil his whole address, 2753 W Blue Spruce Dr., Peosta, IA. His family was from Iowa; he must've moved there after he left. I peeked over my shoulder to see if my mom was looking, but she was preoccupied with chopping an onion. I quickly grabbed a pen and a piece of scrap paper and wrote down his address. I glanced at the address written on the center of the envelope. It was my mom's name but not our home address. I slid the letter back under the pile of mail and tucked the paper into my pocket.

"I finished making my lunch," I announced, scribbling my name on the brown paper bag with a marker. "I'm going to go to my room and write my letter."

"OK. Dinner will be ready in an hour."

I paused in the hallway, debating whether or not to tell Amelia about what I'd seen. Maybe she would have a better idea of what might be going on. But she was just finally happy again, and I didn't want to do anything to mess that up. I continued to my bedroom and grabbed a notebook and pen.

"Dear Dad," I began to write.

It's Penny. I'm in 4th grade now. I don't really remember you very much. I think that makes it easier though, because then I have less to miss. Kinda like when Amelia got her kitten Vern for her 13th birthday but then a few days later he escaped through the back door and we found him in the street, hit by a car. She was so upset about it she sobbed the entire night. But I remember I wasn't that sad. I mean I felt bad, but more for Amelia. I think it's because we only had Vern for a few days, and I didn't get the chance to know him. Amelia was so protective and kept him with her almost everywhere she went, I didn't get to spend much time with him. That wasn't that long after you left. We got Henry after that. He's one of my best friends. Maybe I can find a picture of him to send you. He's got long black hair that gets on everything, no matter how many times Mom vacuums. Do you miss us? I think Amelia misses you, but she doesn't talk about it. What's your job? I want to be a veterinarian when I grow up. Or a detective. I've never been to Iowa. I've never really been anywhere. But Uncle Theo said he wants to take us fishing in the ocean! Do you talk to Mom a lot? She doesn't ever talk about you to us. I'm gonna go eat dinner now. You can write back if you want.

Sincerely,
Penny

I carefully tore the page out of the notebook and folded it in thirds. I didn't know yet if I was going to send it. There were many reasons I knew I shouldn't. If my mom found out, she would be furious. If Amelia found out, she might be upset I didn't tell her. And what if my dad didn't care enough to even respond? But what if he did care and missed us? I tucked the letter into the pocket in the back cover of my notebook and put my dad's address along with it. I decided to take a day to think about it. Maybe I could get more information first.

I headed to the kitchen and saw Uncle Bobby sitting at the table, drinking a beer. My stomach sank.

My mom was standing at the stove stirring the meat with a spatula. "Penny, perfect timing. Will you let your sister know dinner is ready?"

"Mm-hmm." I kept my head down and turned toward my sister's room. There was heavy metal music playing loudly, so I knocked hard on the door. "Amelia, dinner's done."

The music softened. "OK, I'll be right out."

I turned and headed back to the kitchen. Uncle Bobby tipped his beer back, emptying the last of its contents into his mouth.

"Penny, could you grab me another beer from the fridge?" he asked, setting the empty bottle on the table.

I hesitated and looked at my mom. "Could you grab the shredded cheese out of the fridge too, Penny?"

I silently went to the fridge and took out the cheese and a beer from the six-pack that was sitting on the bottom shelf. It had three beers left in it. I set them both on the table and sat down without a word.

"Thanks, kid," Uncle Bobby said, twisting open the bottle.

I didn't respond.

My mom turned to face me, still standing by the stove. "Do you want hard or soft shells?"

Amelia walked out just as she asked the question. "I want hard." Henry followed behind her.

"Me too," I answered.

Amelia stopped suddenly when she saw Uncle Bobby. "I thought you didn't drink," she said firmly. "Mom, I thought he didn't drink anymore."

"It's just tonight."

Amelia's face was frozen with doubt and anger. "What about at Grandma's funeral? You're just gonna forget about him yelling about the wine?"

"We were both in the wrong there, and he apologized." My mom turned the burner off on the stove. "He wanted to celebrate tonight."

"I got a job!" Uncle Bobby announced, raising his beer in the air, then slowly lowering it to his lips.

Amelia stood still in the doorway to the kitchen. I sat in the chair across from Uncle Bobby, watching timidly. I knew Amelia wouldn't back down easily, but I didn't fully comprehend the reason for her hostility toward Uncle Bobby's drinking. I felt like I was missing something.

My mom walked into the pantry and reappeared with the taco shells in hand. "Amelia, come on, have a seat. Dinner is done."

"I don't want to be here if he's drinking."

My mom set the shells on the table next to the chopped tomatoes and lettuce. "It's just tonight. We're all celebrating. Penny's first day, your new school, and Bobby's new job."

"Great!" she said sarcastically. "Let's all have a beer. Penny, grab one for you and me outta the fridge."

I looked up nervously, not sure what to do.

"Amelia, that's enough." My mom tried to put her foot down. "Have a seat and let's have a nice dinner together."

Uncle Bobby chimed in, "It's just a few beers, just tonight. Listen to your mom, let's eat."

Amelia rolled her eyes.

My mom made one last attempt. "Look, we can talk about this later, I promise. But for now, let's just eat dinner and try to have a nice night. Please."

Henry jumped up onto the windowsill. The window was still wide open from when I had opened it. His long hair blew in the breeze, and he closed his eyes to sniff the air. Amelia walked over and picked him up gently. She was always telling me not to let him sit there with the window open that wide because he could fall through the screen. She pushed the window down, holding Henry over her shoulder.

"Fine," she conceded, sitting in the chair to my right with Henry in her lap.

My mom scooped the seasoned taco meat into a glass dish with a cover and set it at the center of the table. "Oh, shoot, I forgot to heat these up in the oven," she said, grabbing the box of taco shells.

"It's all right, Annie, they'll be fine." Uncle Bobby took the box from her and began to peel away at the cardboard flap.

"Well, there's soft shells in the pantry if anyone wants them instead."

Uncle Bobby slid out the package of taco shells and set three on his plate. "This looks great, thanks for cooking." He handed the box to Amelia.

She begrudgingly accepted.

"Would anyone like to join me in a prayer before we eat?" Uncle Bobby looked around the table.

My mom was the only one to oblige him. "Sure, that would be nice."

They both bowed their heads and closed their eyes as Uncle Bobby thanked God for the food before us and asked him to bless us. I sat still and remained quiet. I didn't want to pray, but I was also trying to be respectful. Amelia proceeded to take shells out of the box and make her tacos, completely disregarding anything Uncle Bobby said. When he was done with his prayer, he took a sip of beer and began to fill his taco shells with meat.

"So Bobby, you wanna tell the girls about your new job?" My mom tried desperately to fill the uncomfortable silence as we dished up our food.

"It's nothing special. Dock work at Forward Trucking." He bit into his taco and continued to talk. "Driving the forklift and loading the trucks before they hit the road."

Amelia and I didn't pretend to care. Henry slowly inched his nose closer to Amelia's plate.

"But once I get a little money saved up, I can try to get my trucking license and find a place of my own."

"Well, I think that's great news," My mom responded in place of my and Amelia's silence. Her bubbly demeanor was trying to compensate for our obstinance. It only made things more awkward.

Henry made a quick move for one of the scraps of meat that fell out of Amelia's shell. She pulled him back onto her lap and continued eating.

Our mother continued, "Speaking of new jobs, Amelia, are you excited to start at Bruegger's?"

Amelia shrugged.

"Maybe you can bring home all the leftover bagels!" I answered for her.

My sister used to work at Rocky Rococo when she was sixteen and would bring home garbage bags full of leftover pizza from the end of the night. Our refrigerator was stocked full of super slices for months. She'd tried to give them to the homeless people behind the restaurant, but her manager wouldn't allow it. He said they could get food poisoning and sue. Amelia continued to do it until he threatened to fire her. That's when she started bringing most of the extras home. Her relationship with that manager never did improve, though, and she eventually quit.

"That reminds me of when you and Teri worked at Leo's Ice Cream Parlor." Uncle Bobby looked at my mom as he began assembling another taco.

"Oh my gosh, that was ages ago." My mom smiled. "I think I was about sixteen or seventeen that summer."

"Yeah, and I was six or seven."

I tried to picture Uncle Bobby as a kid, younger than me. I had never seen pictures of him or my mom when they were younger.

Uncle Bobby continued, "And I used to hang out on the floor behind the counter almost every day you worked."

"Mm-hmm, I remember you suckering me and Theresa into giving you scoops of ice cream until you'd tried every flavor twice."

Uncle Bobby smirked. "Well, I remember what you and Teri did Saturday nights after closing."

My mom's face turned bright red. "I don't think we should talk about that!"

"Oh, come on, it wasn't that bad, and it's your fault you brought me along."

I listened intently. This was a side of Uncle Bobby I had never seen before. It was playful, almost fun. Even Amelia looked at him with interest.

"Your mom here has a mischievous side to her." Uncle Bobby looked from me to Amelia. "She and our cousin Teri would clean out all of the old pails of ice cream at the end of the night and put all of the gross flavors into one container—you know, the bubblegum, blue moon, coffee, rum raisin, all those piled into one disgusting concoction.

Then they'd take an ice cream scoop and go to the bridge over Honey Creek Parkway. And they'd drop fat melting scoops on the cars that passed below."

My mom covered her face with her hand, but a smile hid behind it.

Uncle Bobby continued the story, "Then one time they let me do it and I landed the scoop right in some guy's open sunroof. He double-backed and tried to catch us, but we made it to the bike path and hid behind the bushes until we were sure the coast was clear. To this day, I think your mom and Teri are jealous they got outshot at their own game by a seven-year-old."

"Oh, please, you got lucky." My mom looked over at me and Amelia, then quickly added, "Besides, we shouldn't have been doing that to begin with."

Amelia smiled wide. "Well, I guess me and Penny will be given a free pass for all those times we threw hot McDonald's syrup packets at cars off the balcony."

My mom sighed and took a sip of water. "Hmm."

The heaviness that was present at the start of dinner was suddenly lifted. My reluctance about having Uncle Bobby stay with us eased a little. Maybe it would be good for him to be around us, I thought, cramming the last bite of my taco into my mouth and licking my fingers clean.

CHAPTER 9

The next morning, my mom woke me up a half hour earlier because she had to go to work for a meeting and wouldn't be able to drive me to school. She was an accountant at Schobke and Radler Law Firm. They specialized in personal injury and property law. I always envisioned that the majority of their job was fierce courtroom battles against other attorneys, with witness interrogations and secret evidence being revealed, and that the fate of the case was left up to a jury's decision. It was disappointing to learn that it was nothing like I'd seen on *Matlock*. Most cases never even made it to the courtroom.

My mom had worked there for over ten years and had gotten to know both attorneys well, though she seemed to get along with Jack Radler better. Every summer, we'd attend the company get-together at the Radler's lake cabin. "Lake cabin" was an understatement. It was a mansion. As you stepped inside, the foyer opened up into a ginormous room with a vault ceiling and a chandelier hanging down over the sitting area. To the left and right was a double staircase leading to the second floor, with so many rooms and hallways that you got lost just trying to find the bathroom. The house sat a good three hundred yards above the lake on a bluff, with a long stone staircase that led down through the woods to the water. On the way down was a small guesthouse with a screened-in porch, which they used as a staging area for all the snacks and beverages so people didn't have to make the trek all the way back up to the main house.

Despite the obvious wealth and opulence, the Radlers were some of the most down-to-earth and kind people I had ever met. They were always looking for ways to help people and never made you feel out of place. Mr. Radler even hired Amelia one summer to file client's cases in the back room at the law office. He paid her in cash, off the books, and let her make her own schedule. I'd go there with her sometimes to hang out and eat snacks from the lunch vending machines they had in the break room. The microwave rolls with butter were my favorite. I hoped that when I was old enough, I could take over and file the cases as my first job.

The second my mom called to me from my bedroom doorway, my eyes sprung open. I'd slept much better than the night before and was ready to start the day. Henry grumbled when I pulled my arm out from under him, but he didn't bother getting up. I looked over at my writing notebook that held the letter to my dad. A box of envelopes was sitting next to my dresser from thank-you cards I was forced to write after my birthday. I slid one out and tucked it inside the notebook, then shoved the notebook into my backpack. There was a mailbox on my route to and from school, but I hadn't yet decided whether I was going to send the letter. I slid my shoes on, slung my backpack over my shoulder, and headed to the kitchen.

"It looks like it might rain later." My mom was standing in front of the toaster spreading cream cheese on a bagel. "Do you want to bring an umbrella for the walk home?"

"Um." I thought, looking at the sun shining brightly with not a cloud in the sky, and also not wanting to be the nerd lugging around an umbrella. "No, I'll be OK."

"All right. Just remember I can't pick you up today."

"Mm-hmm," I mumbled, shoving a granola bar into my mouth. "Where's Amelia? Doesn't she have school?"

"Yeah, but she only has to go half days because she had enough credits before she dropped out."

"Oh." I finished chewing as I poured a cup of orange juice.

The clock on the kitchen wall read 6:50. I had about twenty minutes before I had to leave for school.

"Hey, Mom." I paused, thinking carefully about what I was going to say next. "Do you ever talk to Dad?"

Her brow immediately creased with concern. "What makes you ask that?"

I shrugged. "I don't know. I was just thinking about how he helped me hang the present from Bob the Beard, and it made me start to wonder about him." It wasn't a complete lie.

"Oh, honey, I'm sorry you've had to go through all of this. I don't know exactly how you feel, but I know how much I missed your grandpa Louie when he died."

"It's not that I miss Dad, I don't know. I guess I just wondered if you still talked to him because maybe I could get to know him, since he's not dead." I took a swig of my orange juice and tried to study my mom's face.

A slight smile of sympathy raised the corner of her mouth as she lowered herself into the chair next to me. "Penny, I understand you wanting to get to know your dad, but when he left here, it was what was best for you and Amelia, and me. I wish things had worked out differently, but that's the way it is."

She extended her hand to touch my arm. There was heartbreak in her eyes. I couldn't decide if her sadness was because she missed my dad or because she felt guilty about the effects his absence had on us. It was probably both. I stared down at her hand on my arm, contemplating every-thing she said and everything she seemed to be feeling. I had to know the truth.

"But if you were still in touch with him, maybe things could be different."

She gently squeezed my arm. "Honey, I don't think that's a good idea."

"But maybe if you just asked him, maybe we could meet, or—"

She cut me off. "No, Penny, I haven't talked to him since he left. It's not going to happen." Her voice was stern with agitation.

I pulled my arm away, angered by my mom's bold-faced lie. "OK." I didn't look at her.

"I'm really sorry, Penny." Her voice had softened.

"It's fine." I chugged the last of my orange juice and stood up to set my cup in the sink. "Do we have any stamps? I want to mail my letter to Uncle Theo on the way to school."

"Sure, sweetheart, they're in the top drawer of the china hutch."

* * *

I waited for my mom to leave for work, then took out the letter and tucked it into the envelope. I copied my dad's address onto the front and slapped a stamp on the up-per right-hand corner. If Mom didn't want to tell me the truth, I would find it out for myself. I stepped outside with the letter in hand. The thick, muggy air made my walk to school a little slower than usual. It didn't feel like Sep-tember weather. I passed the mailbox a block away from school and dropped the letter inside. By the time I made it to my coat hook, I was dripping sweat. I slung my back-pack off to reveal a huge sweat spot where it had been rest-ing. Peeling my wet shirt off my back, I walked into the classroom and sat down at my desk. Ms. Jenkins had all the windows open wide, but it did little to circulate the stagnant classroom air.

The morning dragged on incredibly slowly. The ripe smell of thirty sweaty fourth graders worsened with each passing minute. To make the day worse, Ms. Jenkins surprised us with a pop quiz on the multiplication tables we studied during math the previous day. Most teachers wouldn't give a quiz on the second day of school, but Ms. Jenkins wasn't most teachers. She believed in high expectations for all her students, and that life wasn't easy so her class wouldn't be either.

"You'll have two minutes to complete as many problems as possible." She stood at the front of the class holding a stack of quizzes. "Keep the paper face down until I instruct you to begin."

She counted out six and handed them to Adam in the front row. I tapped my pencil anxiously as my mind replayed the math flash cards that I studied with Jasmine yesterday. Marcus reached over to hand me a quiz. I set it face down and waited. Ms. Jenkins walked back over behind her desk. "Any questions before we begin?"

A few of my classmates shook their heads; most of us just sat quietly. Marcus looked over at me nervously.

"All right then. You may begin."

I quickly flipped my paper over and began writing. There were forty problems in total. I whipped through each row confidently. As I started the last row, I glanced over and saw Marcus staring blankly at his paper, his pencil motionless. I carefully slid my paper toward him on my desk. He scribbled rapidly as he copied my answers. He finished the last problem just as Ms. Jenkins called time.

"Turn your papers over, please, and write your name on the back." There was a whoosh throughout the room as everyone flipped their quizzes. "Monique, please collect them and set them on my desk."

"OK," Monique answered as she scrawled her name in long, flowy cursive on the back of her paper.

Ms. Jenkins stood up and walked over to the phone hanging on the wall next to the classroom doorway. She dialed and stepped into the hallway to talk but faced the classroom to keep an eye on us. Monique shuffled around the room collecting everyone's quiz. Rashad pulled his away right as she went to grab it. He held it playfully behind his back.

"Boy stop." She reached behind him and snatched it from his hand.

He laughed. "All right, all right," he said, putting his hands up to surrender.

Ms. Jenkins returned to the room and set the phone on the receiver. Monique handed her the stack of quizzes and walked back to her seat. We all waited eagerly for Ms. Jenkins to dismiss us for lunch. She stood by her desk sorting through the quizzes. Chatter started quietly, then spread through the room. She pulled two papers from the pile and put them at the top.

"We're not going anywhere until you all quiet down." The room was almost immediately silenced. "All right, back row, you can line up."

Ms. Jenkins proceeded to call each row. "If you have a cold lunch, don't forget to grab it from the coatroom."

She escorted us into the hallway. As I walked toward the doorway, I saw Mr. K, the vice principal, standing near the double doors that led to the main staircase. His eyes narrowed on me as I exited the classroom.

"Penny, I need to talk to you in my office," he said sternly.

A rush of adrenaline trembled in my gut. I felt my cheeks flush with embarrassment. My chest pounded frantically as if my heartbeat was replaced with an erratic drum solo.

Everyone watched as I stepped out of line and followed Mr. K to his office.

He used to be our third grade teacher last year before he got promoted to vice principal. He was like Ms. Jenkins in his no-nonsense approach, and he had a very strict discipline policy. If you broke a classroom rule, there would be consequences. But there was also a kind and funny side to him. He tried hard to build relationships with his students and often hung out on the playground during recess and played dodgeball or basketball with us, something no other teacher did. There was no doubt he cared, but your actions determined how he expressed it.

Mr. K had a bit of a temper, and very few made the mistake of getting on the wrong side of it. Everyone in my class remembers the day he hung Marcus out of the window by his ankles for talking back. We were on the first floor, but it still would have been a nine- or ten-foot drop. The whole class crowded around the window, waiting to see him fall. Marcus pleaded and apologized desperately until Mr. K pulled him back in. That memory sat heavy in my head as I followed Mr. K into the dimly lit hallway that led to his office. He paused, closed the hallway door, and didn't go any further.

"Penny, what were you thinking!" He towered over me.

I shrugged my shoulders timidly, unsure what he was talking about and too scared to ask. At least there were no windows in this hallway, I thought to myself.

"You don't have an answer? That's not gonna cut it!" His voice reverberated in the small space.

Tears immediately began to drip from my eyes. My chest heaved as I tried desperately to hold in my cry.

His face grew red with anger. "Penny, letting someone cheat off you is no better than cheating yourself. I really thought you were better than that!"

I broke into a full-out sob, but Mr. K took no mercy.

"What would your parents say if they found out?" he raged. "And you think you're helping Marcus?"

The tears rushed down my face. I was so upset I couldn't even form words. And the more I cried, the more embarrassed I became for not being able to stop, which made me cry even more. It was a hopeless cycle. I completely shut down in the face of his anger. Every word he yelled exploded into an indistinguishable mush of fury. I kept my head down and stared at my feet. Mr. K continued his bombardment for what seemed like an eternity. I wished I could shrink down and disappear. Finally, his voice lowered, and he asked, "Do you understand?"

I didn't hear him at first.

"Penny," he said, putting his hand on my shoulder, "take a breath."

I tried to pull myself together. My hands reached up to wipe the tears from my face. But I remained silent.

"You're a good kid. I don't want to see you in my office again."

I nodded and managed to squeak out an "OK" in between sniffles.

He patted me on the back. "Go eat your lunch and have fun at recess."

I nodded again but couldn't bring myself to look at him. I was afraid if I looked at him the wrong way, it would be my turn to dangle upside down out the window. To my relief, he walked me to the main hallway, then turned to go back to his office. I paused at the top of the staircase. Everyone would know I'd been crying. My face was red, and my eyes were puffy. I took a deep breath and wiped my face one more time to make sure it was dry, then pushed through the double doors and headed to the lunchroom.

The aroma of bananas and peanut butter sandwiches melded with the mock chicken legs and mashed potatoes they were serving for hot lunch. It created a unique smell that you could only find in a school cafeteria. Since I was late, I didn't have to wait in line. I stepped up to the lunch lady and handed her my milk ticket. "Chocolate, please."

She smiled and extended the carton of milk across the stainless-steel counter.

"Thanks," I said, grabbing the milk. I turned and scanned the tables, trying to locate where my class was sitting. The cafeteria was also our gymnasium and hosted our school concerts. Jasmine was at the far table right in front of the stage. She sat at an end seat sawing apart her mock chicken leg with a butter knife, and there was an open seat across from her. I walked over and set my lunch on the table. A few heads turned to look at me, but to my relief nobody said anything. No questions about what happened. No making fun of me. I slid down into the seat, keeping my eyes on my lunch.

"Hey," Jasmine said, scooping a bite of mashed potatoes.

I unfolded the paper bag and dumped out my lunch. "Hey."

* * *

Lunch went by quickly. Jasmine and I picked up a game of four square with a few of our classmates, but we were all called inside when it began to rain. It seemed my mom was right when she asked if I wanted an umbrella. By the time school was dismissed it was an all-out thunderstorm. Lightning flashed across the sky, with thunder booming three seconds later. The skies had opened into a steady downpour. Ms. Jenkins led us down to the main entrance and dismissed the bussers. They all raced across the playground and down the concrete stairs to their assigned bus. I paused at the doorway, giving myself a second to accept that I was going to get drenched.

"Get home safe now," Ms. Jenkins said as I stepped outside.

"Yes, ma'am." I headed across the playground. My shoulders scrunched up with my head tucked to the right. I was almost immediately soaked. As I stepped onto the sidewalk, I noticed a truck rumbling in front of me. Uncle Bobby.

He leaned across and cranked the passenger window down. "Hey, Penny! Hop in!"

I didn't think twice. I scurried over to his truck and jumped in, then quickly cranked the window back up.

"What a storm!" Uncle Bobby pulled open the glove box and handed me a wad of paper napkins. "Here, try to dry off a bit."

"Thanks." I wiped my face and arms.

We sat in silence for a few seconds. The fat raindrops pounded loudly against the metal hood of the truck.

"How was school?" he asked hesitantly, like he was unsure what to talk about.

I shrugged and looked out the passenger window, replaying the incident with Mr. K in my head. I didn't feel comfortable enough with Uncle Bobby to be open with him, especially about getting in trouble. I'd really only accepted the ride because it was only slightly better than getting washed away in the storm.

Uncle Bobby ground the car into first gear and pulled away from the curb. "What do you say we stop at Dairy Queen on our way home?"

My head whipped around to face him. "Yeah, OK." I tried to hide my excitement.

"Just don't tell your mom, she asked me to bring you straight home."

I nodded in agreement.

The short drive was made in silence. He could sense that I was guarded. Neither of us spoke until we reached the Dairy Queen parking lot.

"Run in and get us a couple of sundaes." He held out a crumpled five-dollar bill.

I grabbed the money and hopped out of the truck. I returned a minute later with two small hot fudge sundaes, each with crushed peanuts and a cherry on top. I handed him his sundae and reached into my pocket for his forty-seven cents of change.

"Keep it for your piggy bank." He took a spoonful of ice cream.

I was surprised by his generosity. "Thanks."

We sat in silence again for a few seconds, enjoying our sundaes and listening to the rain.

"So, how was school?" he asked again.

I stared down at my ice cream, debating whether to tell him about what happened. I swirled my spoon around a ribbon of hot fudge and brought it to my lips.

He pressed me some more. "You know, I got in trouble a time or two in grade school. Looked exactly the way you look right now."

I swallowed and glanced over at him. "I got caught letting someone cheat off my quiz." My eyes darted to my feet as I braced for him to yell at me.

"So, what happened?" There was no anger in his voice, only curiosity.

"I got called into the vice principal's office."

"Did he call your mom?"

I shook my head.

He scraped the bottom of his sundae cup with the spoon. "Well, then it's not such a big deal, right?"

"I guess." If there was anyone who I thought would make

me feel better, Uncle Bobby would've been last on the list. But talking to him actually did help. I started to feel less guilty and embarrassed about it all.

He tossed his empty cup behind my seat, then reached back into the glove box. "Don't worry about that vice principal. The only one you must fear is God." Uncle Bobby retrieved a book and held it in both of his hands near his chest.

I ignored his comment about God and continued eating my ice cream.

"Ask him for forgiveness and he will make things right in your heart." He extended the Bible toward me. "I want you to have this; it's helped me through some tough times."

I stared at the book like a deer in headlights, unsure what to do. Uncle Bobby was being nice, and I was scared one wrong move would ruin it and make him angry with me. I stuck my spoon in the cup and reached to take the Bible.

Uncle Bobby seemed pleased. "Take a look at it, there's some pretty good stories in there."

I thought about the stories Grandma Margery told me. I could tell my uncle that David beating Goliath was my favorite. The words formed on my tongue, but I washed them back down with a bite of ice cream. It felt better to keep it to myself for now. This was the best time I'd had with my uncle, and I thought bringing up my grandma might change his mood.

He turned the windshield wipers on full blast and pulled out of the parking lot. I unzipped my backpack and stuck the Bible inside. We rode the rest of the way home without talking, but it wasn't an uncomfortable silence. I savored the rest of my sundae, saving the cherry as my last bite. Bobby pulled into the driveway just as the rain began to let up.

"Toss that cup on the floor so we don't get busted by your mom," he said with a smirk.

I set the empty cup by my feet and smiled back at him. I don't know if I had ever smiled at Uncle Bobby before. He opened his door, and I grabbed my backpack to follow him into the house.

CHAPTER 10

S ince the first day of school was on a Wednesday, the weekend arrived quickly. But school couldn't go by fast enough. Friday was the day Edgar had told me to meet him! The second Ms. Jenkins dismissed us, I ran down the school steps and all the way home to get my bike. Edgar would be at the river in fifteen minutes. I pulled open the shed door and wheeled my bike out, making sure that this time I locked the door back up. Thankfully, my uncle had helped fix my flat tire, though I still suspected it was him that caused it. My mom wasn't home yet, so I ran upstairs to leave a note about where I was going. I heard music coming from Amelia's bedroom and peeked my head in.

"Hey, I'm gonna go meet Edgar down by the river. Can you tell Mom when she gets home?"

My sister looked up from the book she was reading. "Sure. What time will you be home?"

I shrugged.

"You better be home by five." Amelia took on the role of my parent sometimes. Now that I was getting older, it was starting to bug me.

"You're not Mom," I snipped.

She glared at me and didn't have to say a word.

I quickly surrendered. "I'll be home by five."

"Good."

I turned to leave, but she called after me, "Hey, I'm meeting Matthew later. Maybe if you and Edgar wanted to come with, you could get a couple extra hours of hanging out. I know you don't get to see him much anymore."

A smile spread across my face. "OK, yeah!"

"See you later." Amelia turned back to her book.

Edgar's mom could stop him from hanging out with me, but she no longer had that control over Matthew. It was a perfect idea to have Edgar and me come along with them. It was what my sister called "working within the gray area." I didn't really understand what she meant, but I liked being able to break the rules.

* * *

I raced downstairs and hopped onto my bike. It didn't take long to get to the dirt trail that led to the river. I bounced along, dodging the stumpy roots that stuck out of the ground. The opening to the river came into view and I saw Edgar's bike resting against a tree. He had already taken his shoes off and was wading in the muddy riverbank. I squeezed the brakes and slid to a stop next to his bike.

"Took ya long enough!" he teased.

I swung my leg over to get off my bike. "It's not my fault you're early."

He skimmed his hand over the surface, spraying me with water.

"Hey!" I danced backward, trying to avoid getting wet. We both chuckled, and I slid my shoes and socks off. "So, what'd you tell your mom?"

"She thinks I'm with Matthew at the basketball courts."

I stepped in next to him, tensing in the cool water. "Where's Matthew?"

"His friend Tomas picked him up and they're out running errands before his date with Amelia."

"I don't know if it's a date, she said we could go with."

Edgar picked up a stick and began tracing designs in the water. "Matthew didn't say anything to me."

"Oh." I scanned the water's edge for an available stick.

"I'll ask him when I get back."

I spotted a stick behind our bikes and sloshed over to grab it. We both stood spiraling our sticks in different patterns.

"So how do you like your new school?" I asked hesitantly, worried he was going to tell me he had made a new best friend.

"Man, it really sucks."

I felt relieved at first, until I saw the sadness on his face.

"I don't know anyone, and they have all these strict rules and routines, and I can't seem to get the hang of them. I mean, I'm used to religion and going to church, but this is a whole different level. I feel so out of place."

I knew exactly what he meant. I felt like I didn't belong in most places, aside from my family. "Did you tell your mom? Maybe she'd let you come back to Maryland."

He shook his head. "She said that it's for my own good and that I need to be pushed out of my comfort zone and went on and on about me getting closer to my faith and how I'd make lots of good Catholic friends."

As he spoke, I could hear the words coming out of his mother's mouth. I hated how unhappy he was, and I had to try to make it better. "It's only been a few days, maybe you'll get used to it and it won't be so bad."

He shook his head slowly. "I just wish I was back at Maryland with you."

"Me too."

A fish jumped in the distance, and both our heads whipped up to catch a glimpse. The only evidence left was the ripples as they circled out wider and wider, making their way toward us. It was mesmerizing to watch.

I reached my stick out and tried to touch the tiny waves. "Do you ever think things happen for a reason?"

"I think God always has a reason, even if we don't understand it." Edgar's answer seemed rehearsed, like he was repeating something he'd been told.

"But even if it's something bad? Like a person dying?"

"Like my dad." He said it softly, staring down at the water.

I immediately felt guilty for accidentally bringing up his father's death.

He picked his head up and looked at me. "It's OK, I think about it a lot."

"I don't understand how there could be a reason for your dad getting cancer."

"I think you have to have faith. My dad used to say, 'There are no coincidences. Everything happens for a reason, you just have to keep your eyes open.' In his own way, he was telling me to just have faith." Edgar spoke steadily, hiding any emotion, then his voice cracked and he turned away from me so I couldn't see his face. "It doesn't mean I don't miss him."

I didn't understand how he couldn't be angry with God for letting his father die. Religion didn't make sense to me, but I didn't question him about it. Instead, I tried to redirect the conversation back to my initial point. "When I think about my grandma's death, I don't really feel anything. I don't miss her." I looked at Edgar, but he was turned away, so I kept talking. "I mean, I don't like death in general, but the thing that upset me the most about her dying was that it brought Uncle Bobby around."

Edgar brought a hand up to wipe his face, then turned toward me.

"Lately, though, I've been thinking my grandma's death pushed him to us because it's what he needed, like it's actually a good thing for him to stay with us."

Edgar looked surprised. "I thought you hated your uncle."

"I did. But I don't know, he seems different now."

"He seemed pretty angry at the funeral, like he has kind of a mean streak."

"Yeah." I hadn't told Edgar about Uncle Bobby slapping me, but it seemed he'd already had a good idea of what my uncle was capable of. I blinked the memory away and continued, "But I think he's changed. He seems nicer. He even bought me ice cream the other day after school."

Edgar laughed. "If Freddy Krueger bought you ice cream, you'd say he seemed like a nice person."

"Shut up, I would not!" I laughed, smacking his stick with mine.

Last summer, when Edgar was still allowed to come over, we watched the entire Nightmare on Elm Street series with my sister. Probably part of the reason he was now forbidden from seeing me.

He backed up a step because the edges of his shorts were getting wet. "I saw your uncle the past few days when I was riding home from school. He was pulling out of this trucking place."

"He just got a job there. He works weird hours loading the semis or something."

Edgar nodded. "My uncle drives semis, all over to different states. He sleeps in his truck sometimes, and hotels."

"That sounds like a fun job." I stepped back so I was next to Edgar.

He smirked and looked me up and down.

"What?"

"I'm picturing you as a truck driver, with overalls and a beer belly."

"I would not have a belly!" I contended, shoving him on the shoulder.

Edgar lifted the end of his stick and tried to hit me with it. I swung my stick up to block it and we broke into an all-out sword fight. Water splashed wildly between us. Eventually, he knocked the stick out of my hand and chucked it into the distance.

"Surrender?" He pointed his stick at my chest.

I reached forward, trying to rip the stick from his hand. "Never!"

We began grappling in place, trying not to fall completely over into the water.

"OK, truce!" Edgar yelled. "I can't go home muddy!"

"You let go first," I demanded, not willing to give up.

"Fine." Edgar released his grip.

I held the stick up victoriously in the air. "Champion!"

Edgar pretended to punch me in the stomach, and I flinched, dropping the stick. It floated down the river until it was out of sight. Suddenly, another fish jumped, a little closer this time, followed immediately by a second and a third.

"Whoa! They're going crazy!" I was in awe.

"They're jumping at the flies. Me and my dad used to come here and fish for trout all the time."

It was Edgar who had shown me this spot when we started riding our bikes together. I never knew it was where he fished with his dad. "That's really cool. I've never been fishing before. Did you catch a lot?"

"My dad did. Some nights we'd come down here with our poles and a five-gallon bucket and walk home with dinner." He was gazing out across the river, like he was trying to look back in time. "My dad would walk in the front door announcing our success, and my mom would race out to greet him with a kiss and remind him to clean them out on the front porch. She hated picking fish guts out of the sink."

"Yuck. I don't blame her."

"Yeah." Edgar smiled. "She did like cooking them though. She'd plop the fillets in a pan on the stove, and my dad would dance around the kitchen retrieving spices as she called out what she needed. They'd toss them back and forth like a circus act. As soon as she was done sprinkling one seasoning in the pan, she'd toss it back to him and catch another."

"I can't picture your mom like that. She seems so . . . serious."

"She used to be different. Happy, I guess. My dad was her best friend—it's like she's a different person without him. And now she's terrified of anything happening to me or Matthew. You know how she doesn't let me do anything, and she barely leaves the house herself. Besides for work and church."

"I wish I could've known her before. And your dad."

We were both quiet for a moment, watching the current of the river and waiting for another fish to jump. A monarch butterfly flapped clumsily in front of us before landing on a flower near the riverbank. Soon it would begin its journey south to the mountains of Central Mexico. I read about it in a book from the library. She was the offspring of multiple generations who'd traveled nearly three thousand miles north, making it to where she was now. Amazingly, she would make that same distance, going south, in just one trip, one lifetime. She was a "super generation," living eight times longer than her predecessors. How did she know where to go? She couldn't have learned the route from following her parents, yet she would find it and join the millions of other monarchs from all over the country. They would end their journey resting on the exact trees that their great-great-grandparents were born on. The connection to their ancestors transcended death. I never knew any of my grandparents either, but I didn't feel any sort of connection to them. I was envious of the monarchs' ties to their past.

Edgar climbed out of the water and began to put his shoes back on. "I should get back, Matthew's gonna meet me at the courts."

"Yeah, I gotta be home for dinner."

We hopped on our bikes and rode together until the river trail ended.

I hollered to him as we split directions, "Maybe I'll see you later!"

"I'll try!" he yelled back as we both sped in opposite directions.

* * *

I pedaled quickly, not wanting to be late and hear about it from Amelia, or my mom . . . or Uncle Bobby, for that matter. As I approached the house, I saw my mom standing in the driveway. She was talking to someone, a man, and she didn't look happy. A flutter rose in my stomach. Was it my dad? Did he already get my letter and come to see me? I rode closer. It wasn't my dad. It was Jimmy.

"Please, Ms. Marques, will you tell her I need to talk to her? She's not answering any of my messages."

"I'm sorry, Jimmy, I don't think she wants to see you." My mom was sincere in her sympathy, but she stood firm.

I wondered how long he'd been here arguing with my mom. He looked distraught. His shoulders were slumped, his hair was a mess, and he couldn't seem to look my mom in the eyes. "Could you just tell her I'm here?"

I turned slowly into the driveway and rode past them without saying a word.

My mom turned to acknowledge me, then turned back

toward Jimmy. "I'll let her know you're here, but it's up to her if she comes down or not."

"Thank you." He ran a hand through his hair. "I'll wait here."

I shoved my bike into the shed and headed upstairs. Amelia was in her bedroom listening to music, completely unaware of the drama awaiting her outside. I grabbed a soda from the fridge and walked to the living room. A few seconds later, my mom walked through the back door and into my sister's room. I couldn't hear them talking, but a minute later, Amelia appeared and headed down the back steps. I carefully stepped out onto the balcony, making sure to guide the screen door shut so it didn't slam and blow my cover. I peeked over the railing to see Jimmy pacing back and forth in the driveway. He stopped abruptly when he saw Amelia.

"Em, hey, how are you?"

She stopped a good ten feet away from him. "Jimmy, what do you want?"

"I just needed to see you, to tell you I'm sorry for how things ended, and how hurt you were. I mean, we both played our parts, but I think maybe if I'd done things differently, I don't know." He stepped closer to her.

My sister didn't say anything, but she didn't move away either.

Jimmy took another step closer. "Do you miss me?"

She studied him for a moment. "Sure. Sometimes. Do you miss me?"

"Morethanyouknow." His answer was quick and jumbled, and he looked away as he said it.

Amelia's eyes locked onto his. "What?"

"More than you know." This time he said it slowly, enunciating each word.

Amelia was silent. Jimmy wasn't the type to admit he cared about anything, and it caught her off guard.

He filled the silence. "My sister asks about you. I think she likes you and is worried I'm going to be alone forever."

Amelia laughed. "Well, she has good taste."

"Yeah, she does." He moved next to my sister and reached his hand out to touch her waist. For a second, she hesitated, then pulled away.

"No." She took a step backward. "I started talking to someone else, I'm finally happy. Please respect that."

"Yeah." He retracted his hand and smirked. "You came out here to talk to me."

A short laugh escaped my sister's mouth. "Right. My mistake."

Jimmy turned and walked to his truck without another word. Amelia watched him go. I couldn't tell if she was sad or not, but I was glad she didn't let him back into her life. She seemed so much happier without him. She headed back down the driveway, and I made my way inside so she wouldn't know I was listening in.

"Oh, Penny, there you are." My mom appeared from her bedroom. "You got a *Cat Fancy* magazine in the mail, I set it on your bed."

"Yes!" My mom renewed my subscription for my birthday each year. I was going to add a *Dog Fancy* subscription to my Christmas list. It was a sorry replacement for an actual puppy, but I tried to stay somewhat realistic in my requests. I sprawled out on my bed with the magazine in front of me. On the cover was a sphynx cat posing in an arched position. It was one of those disturbing-looking hairless cats with wrinkly skin and big ears. Henry jumped up and traipsed across the page and meowed.

"Don't worry, you're way cuter." I patted him on the

head. I spent the next half hour paging through the magazine looking for fluffy kittens and reading an article about why it's bad to declaw your cat. The author said it was equivalent to cutting off part of a human's fingers.

"Yikes! Good thing we didn't do that to you." Henry purred loudly as I scratched his back. It almost masked the grumble of my empty stomach. I closed the magazine and walked to the kitchen. Amelia was sitting at the table eating a peanut butter sandwich.

"Where's Mom?"

My sister looked up. "She's out cutting the grass."

"Do you know what's for dinner? I'm starving." I scanned the pantry shelf for a snack.

"I don't know, she didn't say anything to me about dinner."

I opened a box of cereal and shoved a handful in my mouth. "Are you still meeting Matthew?" I spoke between crunching.

"After dinner, probably around seven thirty. Mom said we can take her car."

"I hope Edgar's mom is OK with him going out that late." My mom trusted Amelia to take care of me no matter what time it was, but Edgar's mom was a whole different story.

Amelia didn't seem to think it'd be a problem. "It's a Friday, and his brother's only in town for so long."

"Yeah, but you know how she is."

The back screen door slammed shut and I heard footsteps coming up the steps. They stopped in the back hall. My mom must be putting stuff away in the cabinet. I was too hungry to wait. I set the cereal box on the table and went to the back door to ask my mom about dinner. When I opened it, I saw Uncle Bobby searching through the metal cabinet. He was stumbling a bit and smelled like beer.

"Hey, Penny, can you find me a screwdriver? Your mom said there was one in here."

The open drawer in front of him had three different screwdrivers in plain sight. "They're right there." I pointed.

"Ha. There we go!" He grabbed a flathead. "Why aren't you out cutting the grass for your mom?"

Amelia answered for me, shouting from her chair at the kitchen table, "Why aren't you?"

"I'm going to work, just as soon as I get my truck open. Locked my dang keys in there."

Amelia laughed, which caused me to laugh.

"Something funny?" Bobby snapped. He had the same tone that he had the day I forgot to lock the shed. All the kindness from yesterday had vanished.

My mom walked up the back steps. "Bobby, did you find it?"

He held up the screwdriver. "You should get on your daughters about helping out around here."

"They have a list of chores they do." My mom reached down to brush grass off her ankles.

Uncle Bobby patted me on the shoulder, and I flinched. "Thanks for your help, kid." He passed my mom on the stairs.

"Let me know if you can't get it," she said as he walked outside.

I followed my mom into the kitchen. I was confused by my Uncle Bobby's attitude. He was unpredictable, and it made me uneasy.

"He's going to work?" Amelia questioned my mom.

"They need him to load the trucks for the morning. He was out eating dinner at Larry's Pub when they called."

"I think he was drinking his dinner."

"Amelia, he's fine, he said he just had one beer with

dinner. I asked him about it." My mom was irritated that Amelia was questioning her judgment. She would rather pretend everything was fine than have to face the problem and deal with potential conflict. It was too difficult for her to admit that there were issues with Uncle Bobby and his drinking. Kicking him out would be a major conflict, and she had already been through that once with our dad.

"What's for dinner? I'm starving." I changed the subject.

My mom grabbed the weekly neighborhood coupon flyer from the counter. "Takeout. See if you can find something in here you want."

* * *

Amelia and I argued over what to get. I wanted KFC, she wanted Cousins Subs. My mom sided with her because it was cheaper. I was OK with that because at least I could get French fries. We picked up our food and ate at a picnic table outside the restaurant. It would be one of the last nice evenings that you could comfortably enjoy a meal outside. As we ate, my mom asked us about school, how our days were, and if we had a lot of homework. We both gave the bare minimum answers, so she started talking about her work. She said Dick Schobke was thinking of retiring in a year, so they were talking about bringing in a new younger lawyer to apprentice and eventually take Schobke's spot when he retired. There seemed to be a disagreement on who to bring in. Schobke wanted to give the spot to his nephew, and Radler wanted to interview different candidates. My mom went on to talk about how arrogant Schobke was, how he treated her and the paralegals like they were second-class citizens, and that it would be a nice change of pace to have someone new. I listened carefully, enjoying the gossip.

My mom took a sip of her soda and looked at her watch. "Oh jeez, it's almost seven o'clock. What time are you supposed to meet Matthew?"

"Around seven thirty." Amelia shoved the last bite of her sandwich in her mouth and crumpled up the paper.

"Well, we better get going then, you don't want to be late."

"We gotta pick up Jane on the way too, her car is broken." She was still chewing.

I followed my mom and sister to the car, carrying my sleeve of French fries. I always believed in saving the best part of the meal for last. My mom began searching for her keys in her fanny pack. "That's too bad about Jane's car. Does she know what's wrong with it?"

"Matthew's gonna take a look at it tomorrow."

"Oh, does he know a lot about cars?" My mom sounded surprised.

"Yeah, he took auto mechanics sophomore year and has been into it ever since. He's a mechanic in the army."

My mom unlocked the car doors and we all climbed in. "Well, that's nice to have around. I think I'm due for an oil change." She slid her sunglasses on.

"Maa-umm." Amelia turned it into a two-syllable word with an annoyed teenager tone. "I doubt he wants to spend his leave fixing people's cars."

"Who said anything about him doing it? I was thinking he could teach you a few things and then you could change my oil."

Amelia rolled her eyes and ignored my mom's comment. "Come on, we're gonna be late."

I sat in the back seat munching on the remainder of my French fries and staring out the window. The sun was already beginning to set. Another reminder that summer was ending. I typically had an aversion to change, but I loved the different seasons. It was a change that was pre-dictable, and it gave me something to look forward to. I was ready for the crisp fall air, the crunch of leaves under-foot, being able to see your breath, and the excitement of the first flurries. There was a certain beauty in it all, from the hot thick days of summer to the subzero harsh winter days, and everything in between. The key was to embrace what you had no control over, which kids seemed to be better at.

Amelia reached to turn on the radio. "Groovin'" by the Rascals blasted through the speakers. "Oooh, I like this one!" I spoke up from the back. The oldies station was my favorite. I sang along loudly, "Life would be ecstasy, you and me and Leslie, groovin' . . ."

My mom and Amelia laughed loudly.

"What's so funny?" I questioned.

"It's you and me ENDLESSLY!"

I disregarded the critique and sang with confidence the whole way home.

CHAPTER 11

My mom pulled over in front of our house instead of into the driveway. "All right, girls." She turned the car off and handed my sister the keys. "Have fun, be safe."

Amelia reached to grab them. "Thanks, we will."

"And not too late."

They both opened their doors to get out. I crawled over into the front passenger's seat and cranked the window down. Our downstairs tenants were sitting out on the porch, and my mom chatted with them as she walked up the front steps. The police dispatcher had a cigarette in one hand and a beer in the other. The computer nerd was drinking a Mountain Dew. It was a rare sighting, both of them out in the daylight.

Amelia slid into the driver's seat and stuck the key into the ignition. "Buckle your seatbelt," she instructed.

I clicked my belt without protest. I was excited to be hanging out with her and her friends, and to see Edgar again. Amelia pulled away from the curb and we were on our way.

Jane had just moved out of her parents' house and into a studio apartment in the Riverwest neighborhood. Her parents had given her an ultimatum: stay home and go to college or get a job and move out. She had no idea what she wanted to study or even if she wanted to go to college. She thought it would be a waste of money and time, so she got a job waitressing at an upscale steak house down-town and moved into her tiny apartment. It was the type of neighborhood where you made sure to lock your doors

and check behind you, always paying a little extra attention to your surroundings. There were often shady char-
acters skulking in the shadows, but most turned out to
be harmless drunks. There was a dive bar on almost every
corner, tucked right into the heart of the residential neighborhood. But compared to other parts of the city, it was
relatively safe.

My sister turned onto North Avenue and headed across
the bridge. The atmosphere shifted the farther west we
traveled. The houses got a little more run-down with
each block. Within a few minutes, we pulled up in front
of Jane's apartment. It was above Sunshine Foods corner
store and across the street from Eagles Nest Pub. Out front
was a petite wrinkled lady with short bleach-blond hair
and a baggy white T-shirt that hung just above her knees.
She was hunched over, pounding a pack of Virginia Slims
cigarettes against her palm. I couldn't help but wonder if
she had somehow gotten shrunk down and that's why her
T-shirt didn't fit right.

Amelia shut the car off. "Wait here, I'm going to go buzz
her door to let her know we're outside.

"OK."

She opened her door and turned back to me before getting out. "Keep the doors locked and honk if you need me."

I nodded and watched my sister walk to the side of the
building. The lady out front had pulled one of her long,
slender cigarettes out of the pack and rested it in the corner of her mouth. She reached under her oversize T-shirt
and into her pajama pants to retrieve a lighter. It sparked
but failed to hold a flame.

"Shit!" she yelled, throwing the lighter to the ground.
Then she looked up and across the street toward Eagles
Nest Pub. "Hey, Tony!"

My head whipped around to see who she was talking to.

"Hey, Denise, how are you?" A rotund man with rosy cheeks and a bad comb-over was standing outside the bar smoking a cigarette.

Denise began walking over to him, her flip-flop sandals slapping with each step. "You got a light?" She was still shouting even though she was standing right next to him.

Tony pulled a lighter from his pocket and held it up to her cigarette.

"Thanks, Tony, you're a real lifesaver," she rasped, puffing on the end until it lit.

"Anytime, D." Tony pocketed the lighter.

Denise took a long, slow drag of smoke, like she had been underwater and that cigarette was a breath of fresh air.

As they stood outside talking and smoking, a boy about my age rode by on his bike with his younger brother trailing behind him. I began to wonder what it was like to live around here and imagined what it would be like if this were my life. I pictured myself walking to Sunshine Foods to get snacks after school instead of the Open Pantry by my house, and rollerblading up and down these streets, passing by Denise and Tony smoking their cigarettes on the corners, and the houses with broken windows and dirt-patched lawns. For some kids, this was normal, this was home, but I felt grateful it wasn't mine. Denise and Tony walked up the bar steps and opened the door. "Who Do You Love?" by George Thorogood blasted out of the opening until the door shut behind them.

When I turned back around in my seat, I saw Amelia and Jane walking toward the car. I stretched my body across and pulled up the locks on the driver's side and back passenger doors.

"So, he just showed up at your house?" Jane slid into the back seat and scooted all the way to the center so she could see my sister.

Amelia dropped into the driver's seat and started the car. "Yeah, he talked to my mom first. She's the one who told me he was outside."

Jane was getting filled in on the Jimmy situation. I listened like it was my first time hearing about it.

"What did he say?" Jane questioned intensely.

"He asked how I was doing and if I missed him."

"And? What did you say!" Jane was on the edge of the beige, synthetic leather car seat, leaning halfway into the front of the car.

"I don't know. I said yeah, sometimes."

"Amelia!"

"What! It was the truth." My sister defended her response.

Jane didn't approve. "Since when does a liar like him deserve the truth?"

"I know, I don't know." My sister seemed flustered. "But then I asked him if he missed me, and he said he did, he said he missed me more than I know."

"Big whoop. Too little too late."

Amelia paused like she was about to stick up for him but decided against it. "I told him I was talking to someone, and that I was happy."

"Good." Jane smacked loudly on a piece of gum. "You can't waste your time trying to change someone that doesn't wanna change, that's like the first rule of dating."

"I know, you're right. It's just easier said than done."

"Em, nobody said love was easy." She relaxed back into the seat. "So, what's up with you and Matthew?"

My ears perked up. This was my chance to get the inside scoop on my sister's relationship with Edgar's brother.

"We're just talking." Amelia kept her answer short.

Jane returned to her role of investigative reporter. "Sure.

Talking. What does that mean? Is he going to take you on a date? I know you had a thing for each other in high school."

"It means we're talking!" Amelia matched Jane's intensity for a moment, then took a breath. "He's stationed in Arizona, that's not exactly close. We're just taking things as they come. We're friends."

"Yeah, we'll see by the end of the night if you're still just friends."

Amelia pulled over to the side of the road then did a U-turn and parked. "You wanting something to happen doesn't mean it will. Project your wild imagination on someone else."

Jane grinned but remained surprisingly silent.

"Where are we going?" I finally spoke, convinced that I'd figured out all I would from that conversation.

"Bay View Park. Matthew said to meet him down by the beach."

Bay View Park was one of several parks along the coast of Lake Michigan. It was a few miles south from the bigger, more popular beaches, but on a typical hot summer afternoon or evening, it was always busy with activity. People riding their bikes or jogging along the path, couples playing fetch with their dogs in the big open field, and families hiking down to the beach for a cool dip in the lake. However, on this brisk, near-autumn evening, with the sun almost down, we were the only people in sight. The ambient lighting was enough to guide us down the long, winding path toward the beach, but I still wished we'd brought flashlights. I worried how we would find our way back to the car in the pitch black, but I kept it to myself. I didn't want to seem like a scared little kid. I stayed in between Amelia and Jane as we walked.

"He told you to meet him at the beach?" Jane questioned.

"Are you sure he didn't mean alone? That sounds like a date to me."

I started to think Jane might be right. Edgar also said it was a date, and that he didn't know anything about us tagging along.

"It's not a date," Amelia contended.

I began to picture Matthew waiting alone on the beach with a blanket spread out before him. There was a bouquet of roses in the middle, along with a bottle of wine and a burning candle. It seemed plausible in my nine-year-old mind, which had clearly absorbed too many romance scenes from TV and movies. I prepared myself to turn around and walk back up the path and have Jane drive me home while Amelia and Matthew spent a romantic night on the beach.

We rounded the last turn on the path. The beach was only about twenty-five yards away, and I could hear the rhythmic whooshing of the waves washing on the shore. There was a rumble of voices, but they were too far away for me to distinguish what was being said. Two dark outlines appeared as we got closer. Both adult sized. Disappointment sunk in my stomach; Edgar must be stuck at home with his mom.

"Go farther!" one of the voices shouted.

A glowing football flew through the darkness and bounced off the sand. It was retrieved by a smaller figure. "Bad throw!"

It was Edgar! Warmth spread up through my chest and released into a giant smile across my face. I picked up my pace and began speed-walking to the end of the path. Matthew and Tomas came into view, and Edgar zoomed toward them with the football tucked against his side. He zigged right and zagged left around them.

"Touchdown!" he yelled, spiking the football into the sand.

I sprinted over and scooped it up. "Fumble recovery!" I yelled, dashing down the beach in the opposite direction.

"Hey!" Edgar took a moment to realize who I was. "Penny!" He darted after me, hot on my heels.

My feet dug into the soft sand with each step, making it difficult to build up speed. I glanced over my shoulder just as Edgar wrapped an arm around my waist and tackled me to the ground. We both tumbled to the ground giggling uncontrollably.

"Yuck! I got sand in my mouth." I bent to the side, spitting profusely until most of it was gone.

"I got sand everywhere!" Edgar stood up and brushed off his arms and legs, then extended his hand to pull me up.

"I can't believe your mom let you come."

"I gotta be home by nine."

"That's not so bad." I tossed him the football and we started walking back toward the group.

Matthew and Tomas were crouched down digging through a backpack and Amelia and Jane peered over them.

"This looks like trouble." Jane stood next to Tomas with her arms crossed.

"You mean it looks like fun," Tomas corrected, reaching up to hand her something from the bag. "Here, take these, just sparklers, basically harmless."

"Oooh, I want one!" Edgar and I hovered by Jane. She picked open the flap on the box and stuck out two sparklers for us.

"What else is in that bag?" Amelia questioned.

Matthew looked up at her, smiling mischievously. He reached in and retrieved two long cardboard tubes and handed her one. "Roman candles."

"What do those do?"

Matthew stood up next to her. "Here, hold your arm out straight and just aim it where you want to shoot." He put his hand on her wrist and guided it into position.

"This isn't going to blow my fingers off or anything, is it?" she asked, tilting her head up toward him. She was looking into his eyes and her face was only an inch or so away from his.

"You trust me?"

She nodded.

"OK, ready?" He brought his lighter up to the end of the tube, sparking it to life, then quickly shifted the lighter to the tube in his hand so it did the same.

I watched eagerly. A few seconds later, red balls of flame shot out of the ends, one after another, each exploding into the night sky. Just as the last of the flames shot from the tubes, Tomas tossed a handful of firecrackers toward Jane only a few feet to her right. They popped rapidly as they fell to the ground.

Jane jumped and brought both hands up to her ears. "Tomas!"

"What?" He laughed.

"Give me that lighter." She lunged after him.

He dodged her and hid behind me and Edgar.

"Fine." She quickly gave up. "Just light our sparklers for us, ya big jerk."

Edgar and I held ours out straight as Tomas lit the ends. When he went to light Jane's, she reached to grab the lighter. He quickly hid it behind his back. While she struggled with him, bright sparks began to dance from the ends of our sticks. We waved them around in circles, jumping and dancing right along with them. The second they fizzled out, we immediately asked for more. Matthew set us up with two in each of our hands and lit them. This time we waved both our arms up and down and imagined we had flaming wings like a phoenix. Matthew and Amelia grabbed two more Roman candles from the bag and shot them into the air, this time aiming at the "No Lifeguard on Duty" sign, seeing who could hit it first.

Tomas spun past Jane and grabbed another handful of firecrackers. He held them up and threatened to detonate them next to her.

"OK, OK!" She skittered backward. "Just keep it away from me!"

Edgar and I spent the rest of the night twirling sparklers and watching everyone else shoot off Roman candles and firecrackers. Even Jane joined in. We were told we were too little for them, but we didn't care. The sparklers were good enough for us. Eventually, Matthew and Tomas began aiming at each other from across the beach, flaming balls exploding back and forth. Amelia and Jane joined us on the sidelines, laughing at how stupid they were and yelling that we weren't going to rush them to the hospital when they blew their faces off. Luckily, when they ran out of fireworks, they still had all digits and limbs intact and had avoided any major burns.

"It's almost nine. We should get going soon or I'll never hear the end of it from Mom." Matthew grabbed the backpack and walked over to where we were sitting.

Tomas had already taken a seat next to Jane and was taunting her with one last pack of firecrackers that he'd saved in his pocket. Matthew lowered himself in between Edgar and Amelia. We all sat quietly for a moment, staring up at the sky. It was a clear night, and despite the light from the city, you could see a decent number of stars. Amelia had told me once that looking into space was like looking into the past, since it took so long for light to travel to Earth. She said that if you looked through a telescope at distant galaxies, you could be looking back one hundred million years ago, when the dinosaurs were on Earth. It confused me, like what I was seeing wasn't real. Did that mean there could be other life-forms out there looking through a telescope at Earth and seeing dinosaurs? None of it made sense to me. But it was amazing.

It was a peaceful end to a night of explosions and excitement, until we saw a flashlight bobbing down the path. Tomas saw it first. "Hey, Matt, check that out." He spoke quietly.

All of us turned toward the light. We watched it for a few moments, keeping our bodies still as statues. A fuzzy voice crackled through a radio, too muffled to understand.

A man spoke in the distance. "Yeah, I'm checking it out, I'm almost down to the beach."

"Shit, cops." Matthew kept his voice low. "Follow me, stay low."

My heart began to race as I pictured us getting cuffed, tossed in the back of the squad car, and hauled off to jail. Edgar would never be allowed to leave his house again.

Amelia crouched behind Matthew, and I stayed close on her heels, with Edgar next to me and Jane and Tomas bringing up the rear. We crawled off the beach away from the path. Matthew led us up the steep bluff through the trees and brush. The cop was to our left on the paved path, but maybe fifty feet away. He shone his flashlight through the woods, and we froze.

"Lay flat," Matthew instructed.

I dropped to my stomach and tried to become one with the dirt. The flashlight beamed over us, and then the cop continued on the paved path to the beach.

Matthew continued up the slope. "Em, where's your car?"

"Parked at the top of the path."

Matthew nodded. He led us the rest of the way up the

hill but motioned for us to pause before we reached the top. He stayed crouched and slowly made his way to the sidewalk. He was scoping for other cops. The coast was clear. He waved us up. We reached the top and stood.

"Em, get your keys out, we gotta get your car outta here before that cop comes back up," Matthew instructed.

Amelia nodded and put a reassuring hand on my shoulder.

"Tomas, can you drive me home?" Jane asked. I wasn't sure if she was trying to set my sister up or if she had a thing for Tomas, maybe both.

Tomas agreed, "Sure, I'm parked around the corner."

"Let's get outta here," Matthew urged.

We split off, Tomas and Jane running to his car, and the rest of us hurrying to my mom's Beetle. Edgar and I scooted into the back, Amelia and Matthew jumped in the front, and we all quickly slammed the doors shut. Amelia started it up and sped off. We made it. I breathed a sigh of relief, happy that I wasn't going to have a criminal record at the age of nine.

* * *

When we pulled up to Edgar's house, the curtain in the front room cracked open. His mom peeked through, then let it fall back into place when she saw Edgar step out of the car. The clock on the dashboard read 9:01, but my mom had it set five minutes fast.

"Thanks for the ride. See ya, Penny."

I didn't know when I'd get another chance to see Edgar. Sadness crept in, invading the happiness of the night. I pushed it down, determined not to let it ruin my mood. "I had fun. Hope we can hang again soon."

"I'll find a way to sneak out." He smiled.

Matthew turned around from the front seat. "Tell Mom I'll be home later. I'm gonna go out with Amelia for a bit."

"OK, see you later." Edgar shut the door and walked up to the house.

* * *

Amelia and Matthew dropped me off in front of the house. They were heading to a bowling alley, and she said to tell my mom that she'd be home by midnight. I walked up the front steps and into the living room. Henry greeted me with a headbutt. I heard my mom laughing in the kitchen, then another voice. It was my mom's cousin, Theresa. I started walking out there to say hi and let my mom know I was home, but I stopped suddenly when I heard what Teri was saying.

"But seriously, Annie, how much longer are you going to have him secretly mail letters and money to my house? Maybe it's time to let him back into the girls' lives. It seems like he's trying."

I backed up slowly, making sure to avoid the creaking parts of the floor. Henry stayed by my side, and we settled into the brown recliner in the living room.

"I don't know." My mom paused. "He hasn't quit drinking."

"Bobby is drinking again, and you let him stay here." Teri was direct but not harsh.

"That's different."

"OK. How?" I was glad my aunt continued to press the issue.

"I'm just helping Bobby out until he gets back on his feet."

My mom didn't say it, but I think what she really meant is that it was different because my dad had hurt her in a way that my uncle never could.

Teri saw through my mother's response. "I know Loren wasn't the best husband, but he wasn't a bad father."

I heard the legs of a kitchen chair as it was being scooted out from under the table. One of them was on the move, hopefully not to the living room. I grabbed a magazine off the end table and pretended to read it.

"If we're talking about this, I'm going to need another bottle of wine." My mom opened the fridge, and a few moments later, I heard the pop of a cork. I set the magazine down, confident they were both staying put in the kitchen.

"Here, fill me up too." I heard the glass slide across the table.

I heard the *glug-glug-glug* of the wine being poured.

"Thanks." Teri paused to take a sip. "So. Back to what you were saying."

My mom laughed. "I don't believe I was saying anything."

"OK, let's recap: For the past two years, Loren has been sending letters and money to my house, every month, for you and the girls. And I was saying that it seems like he has been consistently trying and that maybe you should consider letting him see the girls, especially since you said Penny asked about him yesterday. And then you were saying?"

My dad had been sending letters to *us*, not just to my mom. My mind raced. What did they say? Why didn't my mom let us read them? I pulled myself from my endless spiral of questions so I could continue listening to their conversation.

"You make it sound so simple, to just let him back in. It's not." My mom sounded small, defeated.

Teri sighed. "Well. I can tell you that it won't get any easier if you keep ignoring it, hiding it."

My mom didn't have a response to counter what her cousin said, so she said nothing. I suspect she took this time to take a swig of wine.

"Annie, I'm on your side. I know how hard it was for you to do what you did, and when he moved so far away. I just don't want the girls to feel the consequences of the pain he caused you."

I silently begged for my mom to admit that Teri was right, and to call my dad and tell him he could come see us. My vague memories of him weren't enough. I never realized how much I actually wanted a father. It never seemed like a possibility.

"I just can't, not now, with everything that's happened this past month. It's too much."

My heart sank with disappointment. Realizing that my dad could be part of my life was like a door opening where there once was a wall. And my mom was blocking the doorway. Anger and sadness mixed into an uneasy knot in my stomach. I embraced Henry in a forced hug and pressed my face into his fluffy mane. He allowed it for about ten seconds and then squirmed out of my arms. As he jumped to the floor, I stood up and headed to the kitchen.

Teri greeted me with a warm smile. "Hey Penny."

"Hi, Aunt Teri." I smiled back at her, then headed to the pantry to grab a bag of potato chips.

My mom set her wineglass on the table. "Honey, how was your night? Did you have fun?"

"It was fine." I opened the fridge and grabbed a soda.

My mom seemed confused by my terse response. "Well . . . that's good. Where's Amelia?"

"She's out with Matthew, said she'll be home by midnight." I turned to leave the kitchen.

"Are you OK?" my mom called after me.

"I'm fine!" I hurried to the solitude of my bedroom and shut the door.

* * *

The rest of my night was spent paging through *Cat Fancy* magazines and eating potato chips. I refused to leave my bedroom until my mom went to bed. Around eleven o'clock, I heard her say goodbye to Theresa at the front door. She shut the door to the front hall, then hovered outside my bedroom.

"Goodnight, Penny, I love you." Her voice was muffled through the door.

I didn't respond, trying to prove a point of some sort.

A minute later, remorse crept up in my throat, and I felt bad for being rude to my mom. Part of me wanted to crawl into my mom's bed and say goodnight and let her know I wasn't mad at her. I didn't like thinking that she was upset, and that I had been mean to her. I stood with my hand on the doorknob, ready to open it and go tell her I was sorry. Then I saw the cardboard spiral galaxy hanging from my light cord, and the memory of my dad flashed through my mind. How many other memories could I have had if it weren't for my mom keeping him from me? Then I thought of how Edgar would give almost anything for another day with his dad, and mine was alive and trying to contact me. Resentment flooded through me. I removed my hand from the doorknob. As uncomfortable as it was, I was beginning to understand that sometimes conflict was necessary. I shut off my bedroom light and crawled under the covers.

CHAPTER 12

There was a scratching on the outside of my bedroom door. I rolled over in bed, keeping my eyes closed, not ready to give up the soft cloud of sleep that blanketed my consciousness. The scratching continued, higher up this time near the doorknob. It was followed by a loud yowl. I rolled over to my other side. "Henry, be quiet!"

He screamed at me again and continued scratching.

"Ugh, fine!" I hurried out of bed, trying not to lose any of my sleepiness. I cracked the door and Henry scooted in. We both crawled into my bed. He curled into the bend behind my legs and began purring loudly. I rubbed his fuzzy cheeks, then tucked the blanket up to my chin and relaxed my head into the pillow. A wave of sleep began to rock my body into a slumber. My mind walked the line between reality and the dream world, and a beach scene began to swirl before my eyes. The sun was shining bright and the wet sand squished between my toes as Edgar's mom and I walked to meet my sister at work. As we approached the bagel shop, which was, for some reason, located on the beach, I saw Amelia hugging Matthew as he cried.

Before I could figure out what was the matter, I was yanked awake by more scratching on my door. This time it was coming from inside my bedroom. I begrudgingly opened my eyes and lifted my head from my pillow. Henry hopped out of bed and wanted out of the room. I knew there was no use arguing with him, so I planted my feet on the floor and opened the door for him. There was no point in going back to bed now; my body thought it was time to wake up.

I peeked my head out to see if I could hear anyone. The clock on the living room wall read 8:15 a.m. It was too early for Amelia to be awake, but I suspected my mom was out of bed. A bolt of irritation shot through me when I remembered how she was keeping me from my father. I made my way to the kitchen. She was sitting at the kitchen table with a cup of coffee and the newspaper's crossword puzzle spread out before her. The TV was on, and a lady with a blond bob haircut and too much blush was interviewing another lady who was holding a puppy.

"So folks, if you are interested in Munchkin here or any of the other animals at Wildwood Animal Rescue, come visit Mindy and she can help you take home your new family member!" Her hair bobbed as she talked with too much enthusiasm.

If I wasn't still upset with my mom, I would have used this as an opportunity to try to convince her to let us get that puppy. Instead, I silently walked to the refrigerator and grabbed the carton of orange juice.

"Good morning." She picked her head up and smiled. "How'd you sleep?"

"Fine." I grabbed a cup from the cabinet and filled it with juice.

"I'm going to head to Kohl's this afternoon if you want to come along."

I shrugged and mumbled a lazy "I dunno" without opening my mouth.

My mom chose to ignore my moodiness. "OK, well, let me know."

I took my orange juice into the living room and turned on the TV. My fingers mindlessly flipped through the channels. I had to figure out what to do. I couldn't continue being mad at my mom forever, it was too exhausting. And there was no way I was going to miss out on a shopping trip to get new clothes. Should I write my dad another letter? He had to have gotten the first one by now. But I should probably give him some time to respond. Maybe it was time to fill Amelia in on what I knew. That would be my next move, I thought.

There was nothing on TV, so I flipped to the VCR and hit play. The opening scenes to the movie *Uncle Buck* began to play on the screen. I settled into the couch, more at ease now that I had a plan. Amelia would help me figure out what to do. I spent the rest of the morning reciting John Candy's lines along with him. It was my favorite movie, and I watched it at least once a week. The tape had been recorded off the TV, so during the commercial breaks, I'd run into the kitchen and grab a snack or refill my orange juice. On one of my dashes to grab another bowl of cereal, I decided to break the silence with my mom.

"I guess I'll go shopping with you later."

She was still working on her crossword puzzle, now with a bowl of yogurt in front of her. "OK, I'll see if your sister wants to come whenever she gets up."

I spilled the cereal into my bowl in a rush, picking up the stray pieces that fell onto the table and shoving them into my mouth.

"You in a hurry?"

"I gotta make it back before the commercials are over." I splashed milk over the cereal and tossed the carton back on the shelf in the fridge.

My mom rolled her eyes and hollered after me, "Just don't spill."

"I won't!" I quickly shuffled back to the living room. The milk sloshed dangerously close to the edges of the bowl, but I made it to the couch without spilling a drop. My luck ran out as I sunk into the cushion and cereal splattered across the armrest. I set my bowl on the coffee table and grabbed a wad of Kleenex to soak up my mess. There was a wet blotch, but it would quickly dry. The smell of sour milk was a problem for what I viewed as the distant future. I picked my bowl back up and spooned cereal into my mouth just as the "we now return you to the feature presentation" voice sounded, signaling that the commercials were over.

* * *

My sister walked into the living room just as the closing scene finished. John Candy's smiling face froze on the screen as he waved goodbye to his niece, and the credits flooded across the screen.

"You watched this again? What is that, the 596th time?" She lowered herself into the recliner to my right.

"Probably."

Henry strutted out from the kitchen and jumped up into her lap. "Lemme see the remote."

I reached across to hand it to her. "There's nothing on."

We were lost without *The Price is Right* on the weekends. Amelia flipped through the channels and stopped at an educational nature show. Elephants lumbered across a dusty dirt path somewhere in Africa. The babies swung their trunks clumsily and it was one of the cutest things I had ever seen. I was immediately hooked. The narrator explained how they typically traveled in herds of females and babies. This specific herd was visiting the spot where one of their members had died a year ago. The narrator said they may remain there for a day or even longer mourning the loss of their loved one. He went on to say that elephants often examined the bones of other dead elephants or even occasionally humans, but they oddly weren't interested in the bones of any other species. It was one of the strang-est things about them. The program continued to explain different facts about the magnificent gray creatures. They seemed so similar to humans, maybe even more fascinat-ing and compassionate in some ways.

I decided I wanted to meet an elephant in person, but not at the zoo where they were confined and sad. I wanted to meet one in its natural habitat.

Henry traipsed across the end table and began sniff-ing the wet milk spot. I pulled him into my lap, worried he would expose my spill. "Are you coming to Kohl's with us later?"

Amelia shook her head. "I gotta work, noon to eight."

"Bring me home some bagels!"

The doorbell rang, interrupting us. We looked at each other and both rose from our seats to investigate. I thought it might be Jimmy trying to beg his way back into my sis-ter's life again, but as we crept out to the front hall and peered down the steps, I realized I was wrong. Through the window, I saw Matthew's short brown hair sticking up. Amelia skipped down the stairs and opened the door. "Hey, what's up?" Her voice was high-pitched and joyful.

He smiled as she stepped into the doorway. "I was won-dering if you found my dog tags in your mom's car last night. I can't find them anywhere."

"Oh no. I didn't see them, but we can check." She stepped back. "Do you want to come in for a second while I grab the keys?"

"I don't want to cause you any trouble."

"It's no trouble, really." Amelia moved to the side to cre-ate an opening.

"OK, then sure." He stepped in and followed my sister up the stairs.

I waited for them at the top, worried that Matthew was

in big trouble. Losing dog tags in the army had to be a serious infraction. I pictured him getting yelled at by a commander as he was forced to do an endless number of push-ups. I imagined the commander would be shouting the entire time about how he was supposed to be responsible for guns and grenades and he couldn't even keep track of a chain around his neck and calling him a maggot and all other sorts of names. What if he got kicked out? Or worse, what if he got put in army jail? We had to find those dog tags.

"I'll get Mom's keys!" I announced as I turned and dashed toward the kitchen.

"It's really not that big of a deal." Matthew's voice barely registered. I was on a mission.

"Mom, we need your car keys." I charged into the kitchen.

She was standing at the counter writing a list. "Do you want any more granola bars from the grocery store? I wasn't sure if you liked that new kind."

"Mom, we need your car keys." I repeated my request, having no time for the frivolities of granola bars.

"They're on the key hook by the phone. What's going on?"

I marched over and grabbed them from the hook. Just as I retrieved them, Amelia and Matthew appeared.

"Hi, Ms. Marques, how are you?"

"Oh, Matthew, nice to see you. I'm doing fine. What brings you here this morning?"

He and Amelia had paused in the doorway in front of me. They were standing suspiciously close together, and his arm was stretched out behind her with his hand resting on the door frame.

"I lost my dog tags last night and wanted to check if they were in your car."

My mom set her pen down. "Oh no, I hope you find them."

The keys jingled as I switched hands and headed for the back door. Amelia and Matthew trailed slowly behind me, apparently not sharing my urgency.

"While you're down there, maybe you can show one of my daughters how to change my oil!" my mom called after us.

Amelia groaned in disapproval.

Matthew laughed. "What?"

"Just ignore her."

"I'd be happy to help while I'm home. Sounds like her car needs an oil change?"

I pushed through the screen door, holding it open for my sister to grab. "You don't have to spend your time off working on cars. You're already looking at Jane's this afternoon."

"It's not a problem. Maybe we can do it together."

I saw an opening to use this to my advantage. "Maybe you and Edgar could come do it!"

Amelia poked my side; she knew right where I was ticklish. "We'll see. We can talk about it when I get off later."

I unlocked the driver's side door and reached in to unlock the back door. We searched the car top to bottom but came up empty-handed.

Matthew stepped out into the driveway. "I bet they fell off in the woods."

My sister nodded. "Penny, you can stop looking, they're not in there."

"My hands are smaller, I can reach places you can't!" I shouted back.

I buried my hands deep in between the seat cushions and into all of the cracks and crevices, but all I found were sticky candy wrappers and a few dirty pennies. A frown spread across my face as I pictured Matthew's grim fate. I was so preoccupied with the problem before me I didn't hear Bobby's truck roaring down the driveway, a little too fast. Amelia screamed as she reached to drag me from the car by the back of my shirt. The truck screeched to halt, leaving a trail of black skid marks on the driveway. When Bobby shifted into park, he was only an inch from my mom's bumper.

Amelia was livid, almost foaming at the mouth. "You moron, you could've killed my sister! What is wrong with you!"

Matthew stepped in front of her to keep her from charging him.

Bobby opened the driver's side door and a beer can rolled out. He bent nonchalantly to pick it up and threw it in the back seat, then slammed the door shut. "What's got you all worked up?"

My eyes bounced back and forth between him and my sister, waiting for a fight to break out. Matthew held his ground, keeping a barrier between the two of them.

"You're an asshole." Amelia glared.

Bobby took a few steps forward, then paused at the front of his truck. "Does your mother know you talk like that?"

"I don't know, why don't you go get her and we can talk about how you almost hit her car with Penny inside."

He turned and took a long look at the tiny gap between his truck and my mother's car. "I didn't hit it. Now get out of my way, I just got off work and need to go to sleep."

My sister lunged toward him as he passed, but Matthew held her back. "That's not going to solve anything. Penny is safe. Let him go and we'll deal with it later."

Amelia backed off reluctantly.

Bobby smiled as if he'd just won the battle. "The head of every man is Christ; the head of every woman is man."

Matthew stepped in front of him at the bottom of the steps. His face was as close to Bobby's as the truck was to my mom's car, and he spoke quietly so I couldn't hear what he said. But Bobby didn't put up a fight. He turned and walked upstairs without another word.

Amelia touched my arm to get my attention. "Are you OK?"

I nodded.

Matthew walked over and stood next to my sister.

"I'm sorry about all that." Amelia rolled her eyes and shook her head as if to enunciate how ridiculous Bobby's behavior was.

"Nothing you need to apologize for."

She smiled. "What'd you say to him?"

"Peter 5:8."

Amelia and I looked at him like he was speaking a different language.

He laughed. "Be sober-minded and watchful, your adversary the devil prowls around like a roaring lion seeking someone to devour."

"Well, that's a fitting Bible verse."

"Yeah, I figured he wouldn't argue with that." Matthew reached for my sister's hand. "I should probably get going to look at Jane's car."

"And I have to get to work." She wove her fingers between his. "See you when I get off?"

"My mom wants to take me and Edgar to dinner and a movie. Used to be our Saturday-night tradition with our dad."

"Oh, that's nice."

Matthew nodded. "I'll let you know when we're done. If not tonight, tomorrow for sure?"

"Of course."

Matthew gave my sister a brief hug, then turned to walk

down the driveway. I followed my sister inside. Uncle Bobby's TV sermon could be heard from the attic as we passed through the back hall into the kitchen. I used to think Bobby used religion as a substitution for alcohol, but now that he was drinking again, I didn't know what to think.

* * *

The afternoon came quickly. My mom dropped Amelia off at work on her way to the grocery store. She had to move Bobby's truck to the street in order to get out of the driveway, but she conveniently didn't notice the tire marks on the concrete. Had the marks been left by me or Amelia, I don't think we would've gotten off as easily. After they left, I tried to get Henry to participate in an obstacle course I set up for him. The can opener was his starting gun, motivating him to jump over and through the obstacles. It started in the living room with a wall of pillows and ended in the kitchen with a maze of empty boxes he had to crawl through. Despite a generous reward of treats at the finish line, I only convinced him to run through it twice. He then retired to a sunny spot on the back of the couch.

My mom wouldn't be home for at least an hour. Since my only available friend was being stubborn and lazy, I made my way back outside. I grabbed the basketball from the corner of the shed and started to play my own version of Around the World. On my second attempt to make a free throw, Uncle Bobby appeared at the top of the back steps. My shot swished through the net, but I didn't celebrate. I stood frozen in place, worried that I was about to be yelled at for keeping him awake. The basketball bounced beneath the hoop and rolled to a stop in the grass.

"Nice shot, kid." Bobby lumbered down the steps and picked up the ball. "You mind if I shoot a few hoops with ya? I can't sleep."

I stared at him blankly; my mouth might have even been open in confusion. I never knew what to expect from my uncle. There seemed to be different versions of him, and I never knew which one I was going to get. I felt I had to tiptoe on thin ice until I figured out what kind of mood he was in. Apparently, at this moment, he wanted to be my friend.

"I'm sorry about earlier. I was just so tired. I barely made it home." He dribbled a few times, then took a shot. It bounced off the rim in my direction.

"It's OK." I grabbed the ball and passed it back to him.

"How about a game of Pig?"

I nodded and he passed the ball back to me.

"You start," he said, taking a step back.

I walked to the far corner of the court. My favorite shot. I bounced the ball a few times, squaring up my target, then shot. The ball rolled around the rim and then sunk through the basket.

"Good thing we didn't bet." Bobby smiled, retrieving the ball.

I smiled back. "Winner gets an ice cream sundae!"

"Hmm." He walked to the corner and shot. Swish. "So, you're gonna buy me an ice cream sundae?"

I walked to the free-throw line and did a bounce shot into the basket. "I think you're going to buy *me* a sundae."

Uncle Bobby walked to my spot and attempted the shot. The ball bounced off the backboard, hit the rim, then bounced off the pavement.

"P!" I shouted.

"You really got a lot of your mom in you." He laughed. "She never let me win at anything when we were kids."

I thought about Amelia; she never let me win either. "Were you close to my mom when you were little?"

"Yeah, until she moved out to be with your dad."

"Oh." I remembered how lonely I was when Amelia went to live with Jimmy, and there was a sudden unexpected connection between me and my uncle. I walked behind the basket and shot up and over. The ball hit a power line that drooped above the hoop and bounced off the top of the rim. "I'm sorry she left you."

Bobby grabbed the rebound and walked to the free-throw line. "It was OK, I had your grandma."

"Yeah, but she was so . . ." I stopped, knowing that what I was about to say would trigger my uncle.

"She was what?" He chucked the ball at the hoop with one arm, slamming it into the backboard.

"Nothing," I mumbled, afraid he was about to explode.

"Finish your thought." His tone was serious, but not mean, not yet at least.

It felt like a setup. I stood still and silent, scared that anything I said would be wrong. My mind raced to come up with something. She was so . . . mean? strict? hypocritical? unforgiving? No. I definitely couldn't tell the truth. Instead, I shrugged my shoulders. "I dunno, I guess I didn't know her that much."

Uncle Bobby nodded and took a step toward me. "Your grandmother was there for me when no one else was. She showed me the way to eternal life. And when the drink strayed me from that path, she helped bring me back. My faith has saved me, and I owe that to her."

I wanted to remind him that he had started drinking again but decided against it. Instead, I nodded and walked toward the basketball that was resting on the grass near the shed.

Uncle Bobby followed a few steps behind. "I want to show you that path, Penny. Your soul depends on it."

Uneasiness weakened my muscles, making me feel wobbly and slow. Religion on its own made me uncomfortable, but talking about it with my uncle was almost unbearable. He was so strong in his convictions that there was no room for any other viewpoint. I bent to pick up the basketball, fighting the urge to run away.

"You are on the path to Hell." He didn't say it with the innocence and concern that Edgar had when we had talked about Hell.

It felt like my uncle was accusing me of something terrible, and it made me nervous. I hugged the basketball and walked back to the pavement, refusing to look at him. I had no desire to finish the game, but I didn't know how to escape.

He stared at me but didn't speak.

I bounced the ball a few times, trying to fill the awkward silence. Just as I was about to shoot, my mom's Beetle turned into the driveway. She was my savior. I smiled and rolled the ball onto the grass. "I gotta help my mom carry groceries."

Bobby turned and disappeared into the house.

The trunk of my mom's car popped open as she stepped out of the driver's seat.

"Hey, Mom!" My greeting was overly welcoming, a drastic change from my attitude earlier.

"Hi, Penny." A confused look spread across her face. She could tell something was off, but she didn't question it.

I walked to the rear of the car. "I'll help you bring the groceries in."

* * *

By the time we unloaded the groceries, it was two o'clock in the afternoon. We ate a quick lunch and then headed to Kohl's, where we both rummaged through the clearance items. My mom found a few bath towels and a pair of new socks. I filled the rest of the space in the cart with a couple of T-shirts, a pair of shoes, an elephant stuffed animal, and a jacket that wasn't from the clearance rack. I knew I was pushing my luck with the jacket, but I figured there was no harm in trying. On our way up to the checkout, my mom surveyed the cart.

"The jacket's on sale," I said, conveniently leaving out the price.

"OK, but it's going to be part of your Christmas present."

That was just her way of justifying buying it for me. We both knew it was only September and I would be wearing that jacket to school by October. She would still ask me to write out a Christmas list in a couple of months, and I would have plenty of things to add to it.

As we drove home, the last little bit of anger that I was holding on to chipped away. My mom may not have been truthful about my dad, and I was still determined to figure out what was going on, but I couldn't let it ruin our relationship. She was the only parent I had at the moment, and she was a good mom.

CHAPTER 13

I was in the kitchen looking for a snack when Amelia walked in, cradling a bouquet of red and white roses.

I poked my head out of the pantry. "What's the occasion?"

"Matthew stopped by my work when he was done with Jane's car."

"For your one-week anniversary?" I teased, making kissing noises with my lips.

"Shut up, no. Just because. He stopped by to say sorry that he couldn't hang tonight."

"Oh, yeah, the movie night with Edgar and their mom."

Amelia reached for a vase from the cabinet and began to fill it with water. "It's nice they all do that together."

"Yeah. Edgar said his mom wasn't always so . . ."

"Uptight?" She finished my sentence.

"Yeah. She was different before their dad died." I wondered if my mom was different before our dad left. I couldn't remember.

Amelia reached for the scissors. "It wasn't that long ago. It makes sense she'd still be sad."

"But Matthew and Edgar seem fine."

"Yeah, maybe. But it's different, losing your best friend, your other half or whatever you want to call it. I think it leaves you with a hollow space that you don't know how to fill, that you don't even really want to fill."

"I guess, but losing your dad can't be much easier."

She leaned over the garbage can to trim the rose stems.

"I dunno. Everyone reacts differently, and kids are usually more resilient."

I nodded, not sure exactly what *resilient* meant.

Amelia slid the roses into the vase and set them on the kitchen table. "Wanna play a game? I don't feel like studying."

"OK!" I darted to the game shelf in the dining room and came back with Guess Who? and The Game of Life. "Which one?"

She glanced over her shoulder to see the choices. "Life."

I set it on the table and took the cardboard top off. "I hope I get ten babies this time!"

On top of getting the most money, our goal was to have so many kids that you needed a second car to hold them. I set the game board on the table and picked out the orange car.

Amelia set the vase of flowers on the stove and slid into a seat at the table. She reached into the box for her blue car.

We finished setting up the game just as our mom walked into the kitchen. "Ooh, those are pretty flowers. Where'd they come from?"

"Matthew stopped by my work earlier." Amelia spun and the arrow landed on the 5.

"Well, that was awfully nice of him."

"Yeah." My sister pushed the board closer to me so I could reach the spinner.

I spun and landed on the 3, not high enough. "You go first," I said, sliding the board back toward her.

"All right, I'm heading to go over to Theresa's for a little bit." My mom slung her fanny pack around her shoulder and reached for her keys. "What are your plans for tonight?"

I deferred to Amelia.

"We're just hanging here."

"OK. I should be home by eleven at the latest. Call me if you need anything."

"OK," My sister and I answered in unison as our mom walked out the back door.

Amelia spun and moved her car four squares along the *go to college* path on the board, then read the space out loud: "Start a part-time job, collect five thousand dollars."

I handed her money from the bank, then took my turn. I moved my car two spaces and read the square: "Buy books, pay five thousand dollars. Ugh, no fair!" I deposited a $5,000 bill in the bank.

"Well, have you ever heard the saying 'life's not fair'?"

I rolled my eyes and stood up to search for snacks in the pantry.

"Make some popcorn!" Amelia instructed. "I think Mom got the homestyle kind."

I retrieved a bag and began to unwrap the plastic. The homestyle kind was the best, especially with a cold can of Mountain Dew. I stuck the bag in the microwave and hit the popcorn button. "Hey, do you ever wish that you could see Dad again?"

Amelia looked up from the game. "What's got you thinking about that?"

"I saw a piece of mail from him addressed to Mom, I dunno what was in it. But it got me thinking about him, and then with Edgar losing his dad, it all made me start to wish that Dad wasn't completely cut out of our life."

The popping from the microwave was the only sound for a moment as Amelia thought about how to respond. "Did you ask Mom about it?"

"Yeah, she lied and said that she hadn't had contact with Dad. I didn't tell her I saw the mail."

"I can't believe she lied."

"Yeah, I know." I debated telling my sister about the

letter I wrote to our dad, but I decided to gauge her response first. The microwave beeped loudly as the last few kernels popped.

"I would've just confronted Mom and told her what I saw. But that's me."

I shrugged my shoulders and went to grab a bowl to dump the popcorn in.

"How much do you remember about Dad, like when he still lived here?" Amelia questioned.

"Not a lot." I set the bowl of popcorn on the table and slid back into my chair. "And what I do remember is all in bits and pieces. I don't really have any memories of him and Mom together, except when they'd take me to Barkley's Café before K-4 sometimes."

"He drank a lot, Penny."

"So." I shoved a handful of popcorn into my mouth.

"No, like that was all he did. He worked at the bar and lived at the bar. He sold it after he and Mom got divorced. Maybe if he'd sold it before, they'd still be together."

"I didn't even know he owned a bar. I mean I guess part of me remembers him being there all the time, but I thought he was just a bartender or something."

"He got it a year after I was born, I think. It was a problem as long as I can remember, but it got really bad after you were born. He started to spend more time there than at home. Mom would call up there to see what time he'd be home, but the answer was always ten minutes, which really meant a couple of hours. And when he did finally come home, he was always drunk. She eventually just stopped asking. Toward the end, I think she actually preferred him to stay away. It was better to just act like he didn't live here."

I was surprised at how little I actually knew about my parents' history. "I kind of remember them fighting sometimes. I thought it was about Grandma Margery."

"That's how it'd usually start. But when he drank, you never quite knew what you'd get. He could have a temper as bad as Bobby sometimes."

"Really?"

"Yeah, and you know how Mom hates confrontation. She just shut down and tried to avoid him."

I didn't like this new version of my dad. "Was he always mean to her?"

"No, he wasn't always mean, and there were good times. But it was the drinking, it made you have to walk on eggshells around him, and ultimately he chose it over us."

"But the bar was his work. He had to be up there, right?" I grasped at any kind of redemption for my dad.

"Not as much as he was. And he didn't have to drink."

"So, he was a bad dad?" I felt crushed. My image of the kind father who helped me hang my present from Bob the Beard was shattered.

"Penny, it's not that simple. He wasn't a bad dad, when he was around. He was a bad husband and an alcoholic."

"What if he's changed, like if he quit drinking and wants to be a part of our life? Wouldn't you want him to be around?"

"Honestly, I don't know. He left our family long before Mom kicked him out."

I nodded and looked down at the game board, trying to hide my disappointment.

It was clear that Amelia was hesitant to let our dad back into her life. I didn't think it was a good idea to tell her about the letter I sent, at least not until I heard back from him and got a better idea what he was like. Our dad's past flaws weren't enough for me to give up my hope of knowing him, especially if he was reaching out. We switched to a different topic of conversation as we finished our game of Life. Amelia ended up a doctor living in a split-level, and I was a police officer living in a beachside mansion. Neither of us had enough kids to need a second car, so we were both losers according to our rules.

* * *

Bobby's car roared into the driveway Sunday afternoon. A few moments later, he appeared in the kitchen carrying a white bakery bag of fresh rolls and a plastic container of hot ham. "I got lunch for everyone from Nina's Bakery."

"Thanks, Bobby, that looks great." My mom took the ham and rolls from her brother's hands and set them on the kitchen table. "How was Sunday's service?"

Bobby took a seat next to Amelia at the table. "It was good. Pastor Brown talked about how important it is to follow the word of Christ when you find yourself struggling. He said it's during your most difficult times that the devil is testing you, and it is only through Christ that you can be saved and obtain eternal salvation."

"Well, that sounds like a good sermon."

Amelia and I looked at each other, speaking a silent language through our eyes. We were annoyed by our mother's response, but we weren't sure if she was just saying it to appease Uncle Bobby or if she really believed it.

"It really was. You should come with me next week, all three of you."

"Maybe we will." My mom set a stack of paper plates on the center of the table.

I cringed at the thought of my mom dragging us to church with Uncle Bobby. Surprisingly, Amelia chose to ignore the comment completely. She kept her head down, focusing on the Sunday crossword puzzle in front of her. She was trying to fill in the gaps my mom had missed. I grabbed a plate from the stack and set a giant fluffy bakery roll on it. If this was some type of bribe to get us to go to church with him, Uncle Bobby might actually win me over. I loved fresh bread as much as I loved ice cream. I grabbed a thin slice of ham from the container and shoved it into the center of my roll. My sandwich was 99 percent bread.

"Do you want any mustard?" My uncle extended the bottle out to me.

"No thanks."

He set the bottle down and looked at my sandwich quizzically. "Don't you want more ham?"

I shook my head and took a huge bite of the roll. My shoulders did a happy dance back and forth as I chewed.

Amelia looked up at me and rolled her eyes, then turned her attention to our mom. "You're not going anywhere, right?"

"Not that I can think of, just staying around here and getting this place cleaned up a bit."

"OK, good. Matthew is on his way over to change your oil."

My mom's face lit up with a smile. "Well isn't he just the nicest young man. Make sure you have him come in for some ham and rolls."

Amelia nodded and pushed her chair out. "Edgar is coming with him."

She said it so nonchalantly I almost didn't catch it. "Wait, his mom is letting him come over?"

Edgar was barely allowed over here even when we were still able to hang out. I could hardly believe his mom had changed her mind now.

"Yeah, Matthew said he needed help and wanted to spend time with his brother."

"That's awesome!"

Amelia disappeared into her bedroom to change out of her pajamas, and I finished the last few bites of my sandwich. When the doorbell rang, I jumped out of my seat.

"I'll get it!" Amelia and I shouted at the same time. She was still in her bedroom as I raced down the front steps.

I flung open the door to see Matthew standing on the front porch and Edgar on the sidewalk straddling his bike. "Hi!" I greeted them too enthusiastically.

My sister came rushing down the stairs behind me. "Hey, sorry, I was just changing."

"No worries." Matthew smiled. "Should we just head right back?"

"Sounds good to me." Amelia stepped through the doorway, and I jumped down the steps, landing next to Edgar.

We all walked down the driveway to the back, avoiding any possible interrogation from my mom or Uncle Bobby. Matthew slung his backpack off and took out a variety of tools, an oil filter, and four quarts of oil.

Amelia's eyes widened. "You walked over here with all that? I could've picked you up."

"No, it's OK. I could've taken my mom's car but Edgar wanted to bring his bike."

"Yeah, but lugging all those tools and oil seems a little crazy."

"We go on fourteen-mile ruck marches with more. Really, it's OK."

I looked at Edgar. "What's a ruck march?"

"They have to carry these giant backpacks and march in a line, up mountains and stuff, and sometimes they sing these songs together to keep everyone going."

"That sounds fun!"

Matthew laughed and shook his head. "All right, Em, you ready to change some oil?"

"You're putting me to work, huh?"

"Well, you have to be able to do this when I'm not here, I believe that's what your mom said."

"Fine."

Matthew grinned. "All right, I hope you're OK with getting a little dirty."

Amelia's cheeks blushed a little as she laughed.

I didn't see what was funny; it sounded like a legitimate warning when working on a car.

Edgar rolled his eyes at our older siblings' interaction. "What do you wanna do?"

"We could go play catch in the church parking lot?"

"Sure!" He wheeled his bike over and leaned it against the side of the house.

I retrieved two baseball mitts and a ball from the back hall cabinet and met Edgar in the driveway. "We're going to play catch!" I hollered to Amelia.

She was kneeling next to Matthew as he explained to her how to use the car jack. "Sounds good."

* * *

Edgar and I skipped down the driveway and across the street toward the church. It was late enough in the day that all the cars had cleared out from the morning service. When we reached the sidewalk out front, we gave each other a sideways look, then broke into a full sprint. Edgar pulled ahead just as we turned into the parking lot. I willed my legs to speed up and fought against the stinging burn that accompanied every step. We didn't stop until we reached the storage shed on the back end of the lot. Edgar raised his arms in victory as I bent over huffing and puffing.

"No fair! I was carrying the baseball gloves!" I tossed one at his stomach.

He flinched as he caught it. "Jeez, don't be a sore loser."

"Whatever."

"Butthead."

We both started giggling. I grabbed the baseball from the webbing of my glove. "Go deep!"

Edgar ran about fifteen yards away and I lobbed the ball to him. For a few minutes we played catch silently, chucking the ball high into the air to practice catching pop-ups and bouncing it off the pavement to simulate grounders. I hated grounders because I could never judge where the ball was going to hop. Edgar knew that, which is why he threw me several in a row. I was able to snag the first one out of pure luck. But all the ones that followed jumped past me at the last second. After running to retrieve the fifth missed throw, I asked him to cut me a break.

"Well, you're never going to get better if you don't practice!" he shouted back.

"I'll practice more later, let's just play catch for a bit. I'm sick of running after the ball."

"Hey, you saw what happened when we raced here—maybe you need to practice running too!" He smirked.

"Shut up and get ready for my fastball."

"Bring it."

I wound up like a pitcher, stretched my arm back, and flung it forward as hard as I could, letting the ball roll off my fingertips.

Edgar leaped to the left and the ball smacked into his glove. "Not bad!"

I nodded. "A little off though."

He tossed the ball back. "What do you think about Matthew and your sister?"

"I dunno. She seems happy. And he brought her flowers at work yesterday."

"Yeah, I was there when he picked them out."

I adjusted my grip on the ball before I threw it back. "Maybe they'll get married, and then we'll be brother and sister. Then your mom can't keep us apart."

Edgar laughed. "I don't think that's how that works."

"All I'm saying is it's worth a try. And they have been spending like every free moment together."

"I know, I guess they're trying to get as much as they can in before he leaves."

A wave of sadness rushed through me. I hadn't thought about Matthew leaving. Did that mean Amelia would go back to being depressed and Edgar would go back to being banned from seeing me? I tried to ignore my worries and responded with sarcasm, "I'm sure your mom loves that your brother has been spending so much time with my family."

"I think she's been pretending to be OK with it because she knows Matthew will just get mad if she says anything, and she doesn't want to ruin his time with us."

"How was your movie night?"

"Really fun actually. It was the first time we'd gone out since everything happened." Edgar paused and looked at the baseball in his glove. "I hope she still takes me after Matthew leaves."

I nodded. "I hope so too."

He wrapped his hand around the ball and looked up. "Get ready for my fastball."

I spread my legs into a wide stance and opened my glove.

Edgar wound up and released. The ball smacked hard right into my glove; I barely needed to adjust. I took my hand out of the mitt and shook it back and forth. "Jeez! You got speed!"

"Thanks. My dad was a pitcher in high school, he tried to teach me."

I smiled, then thought about how my dad never had the chance to really teach me anything. The stinging subsided and I slid my hand back into the glove. "I sent my dad a letter last week."

"Your dad? I didn't think he was around."

"He hasn't been, since I was four." I tossed the ball back to Edgar. "But I found a letter he sent to my mom, and I think there's been more than just that one."

"Did you ask your mom about it?"

"Yeah, she said she hasn't talked to him. And I was going to talk to Amelia about it and tell her I sent our dad a letter, but she doesn't want anything to do with him."

Edgar kept the ball in his glove and walked toward me. "So they don't know you sent him a letter?"

I shook my head. "I've only told you."

We walked over to a concrete parking barrier and sat down. "So what happens if he writes back and your mom or sister get the mail? Do you think he'll even respond?"

"I hope so. I'll just have to try to get the mail before them."

Edgar looked at the ground as he rolled the ball back and forth between his hands. "Penny, I don't know about this."

"What?"

"It just seems like if your mom and sister don't want him around, it's probably for a reason, right?"

"But I never got to know him, to see if I want him around or not."

"I guess. But if he doesn't write back, I know you'll be disappointed. And if he does, well, you still might be disappointed."

"But you don't . . ." I stopped myself because I knew deep down he was right. "I just need to find out for myself."

Edgar nodded and rolled the ball toward me.

I tucked it into my glove. "I suppose we should get back."

"Yeah, they're probably almost done."

We both pushed ourselves off the blacktop and began walking. "So when does Matthew leave?"

"He got two weeks leave, so not till next Wednesday."

"I'm worried about Amelia once he leaves. He seems to make her really happy."

"Yeah, my mom too. She's been so different since he's been home, more . . . I don't know, alive I guess."

Edgar's response caught me off guard. I had been so

focused on how my sister would handle Matthew leaving that I hadn't considered how hard it would be for Edgar. He'd be losing his brother and, in a way, maybe his mom too. As we stepped onto the sidewalk, my heart felt a sudden weight. "You think she'll go back to how she's been once Matthew leaves?"

"I dunno."

"Maybe she'll be better." I grasped at anything to give Edgar hope. "She'll realize what it's like to be happy again and what she's been missing."

Edgar walked with his head drooped, staring at the ground. "Maybe."

I realized at that moment how lonely Edgar had been since his dad died. Matthew was thousands of miles away, and his mom might as well have been too. My mom and Amelia were busy with their own lives, and I didn't mind being left to my own imagination. Even if they weren't always around, I knew they were there for me when I needed them. Edgar's mom was around all the time because he wasn't allowed to go anywhere and she never left the house. But even though her body was physically present, she wasn't really there, she wasn't available. He was stuck with someone who made him feel like he was alone.

We walked the rest of the way home in silence, both of us contemplating what was to come.

CHAPTER 14

On Thursday, we had a substitute teacher. Ms. Jenkins had let us know the previous day that she would be gone, which immediately put a smile on every face in the class. Subs meant little work would be done and a high probability of watching a movie. When Mr. Thompson greeted us at the door, there was already an unruly energy bouncing around our fourth grade line. It zigged and zagged in ways that would never fly if Ms. Jenkins were there. Had Mr. Thompson put a stop to our shenanigans right then and there, he may have been able to gain some respect and authority and ensure a more orderly school day.

"All right, guys, now settle down." It was less of an instruction and more like he was asking politely.

Nobody quieted down or even acknowledged that he had said anything at all.

He waved us in with no further attempt to quell the rowdiness. The tone was set for the rest of the morning. We roared upstairs and into the coatroom to put our things away. Most of us had sweatshirts or jackets to hang up because of the crisp morning air, but by recess we'd be tossing them to the ground in a sweaty pile.

I made my way into the classroom and began the morning assignment that Ms. Jenkins had left on the chalkboard. I was one of the only ones. Half of the class was out of their seats chatting with their friends. Mr. Thompson walked to the front of the room to try to gain some control over the disorder. He was middle-aged and slightly overweight, with thinning brown hair that was combed over to the left side of his head. He wore huge square glasses that were constantly sliding down his nose, and he had a thick, wiry mustache, which may have contributed to the whistling sound he made when he breathed.

"All right, class, Ms. Jenkins left a writing assignment on the board." A paper airplane whizzed past his head and crashed into the chalkboard. "Now, take out your writing notebooks and let's get started."

A handful of students slowly made their way to their seats and took out their writing notebooks. That seemed good enough for Mr. Thompson. He retreated to Ms. Jenkins's desk, where he pulled a thermos of coffee out of his bag. The usual offenders continued to chat and throw paper airplanes, but without an audience, their efforts were pointless.

After our morning writing, we had a painful social studies lesson about the different branches of government. We were supposed to take turns reading aloud parts of the chapter in our social studies textbook. This was continuously interrupted by Kevin and Perry making fart noises, the rest of the class giggling, and Mr. Thompson telling us all to stop. It took us twenty minutes to get through two pages. Eventually, he gave up and told us we had to read the chapter and answer the questions on our own, and whatever we didn't finish was homework. That motivated most of us to get to work, but there was still the occasional *ppprrrrrtttt* that broke our concentration.

Before lunch, all of our hopes were brought to fruition. Mr. Thompson appeared from the teacher's closet wheeling the TV cart. "All right, class. For science, Ms. Jenkins left a video for us to watch, on our galaxy."

A wave of joy rushed through the room. Everyone was paying attention now.

Mr. Thompson looked down at the lesson plan. "Ms. Jenkins wants you to take notes, and then at the end, write three things that you learned."

I lifted the top of my desk and grabbed my science notebook and a pen. The VHS tape crackled with static before the title whooshed across the screen in bright yellow letters—*Outer Space and Our Solar System*. I scrambled to write it down at the top of my page, then awaited the first important fact. The video took us on a tour around the galaxy, starting with the sun. My hand scribbled furiously, trying to keep up with all the information. Usually, educational videos were boring and cheesy, and the actors spoke with a fake enthusiasm that made you try to tone them out. But this video had no actors, just a narrator who spoke in the background as we whizzed across space. We stopped at each planet to learn facts about how it was formed and what conditions were like there compared to Earth. We also stopped on moons, visited nearby stars, and flew on a satellite.

There were so many amazing facts about space, but the topic that caught my attention the most was gravity. I always thought it was just the thing that made objects fall to the ground and never realized it played a role outside of our planet. I was fascinated to learn how different planets and moons have stronger or weaker gravity based on how big they are. The reason everything rotates around the sun is because it's so huge. Gravity even controls the oceans, and it's the reason everything gets sucked into a black hole, including light! I was suddenly terrified that everything in our universe would be pulled into a black hole, including Earth, and that all life would cease to exist. The narrator reassured the viewers that the black hole in our galaxy was too far away to cause us any harm, but I remained skeptical. We took a ride on an asteroid back to

Earth, where the narrator said his farewell, and the video zoomed out, showing the rest of the planets orbiting the sun, then our entire galaxy, and finally the infinite galaxies in the universe.

Mr. Thompson bent over and pushed the stop button. "Please pass your notes to the front of your row." The VCR whined as it rewound the tape.

Ms. Jenkins insisted we always write our first and last name and the date on anything we turned in, and she would decorate the top of our papers in red pen if we forgot to. I made sure to label my notes appropriately and wondered how many other kids would remember to include the date.

As Mr. Thompson walked to the front of each row to collect the papers, Kevin snuck into the coatroom and grabbed a kickball. He emerged bouncing the ball on the classroom floor. "Hey, Mr. T, can we watch a movie after lunch too?"

Mr. Thompson pushed his glasses up on his nose. "Kevin, put the ball away and find your seat."

"But it's lunch, we're allowed to get balls for recess."

"I haven't dismissed anyone yet. Please put the ball back in the coatroom."

Kevin continued to bounce the ball at the back of the room. Mr. Thompson set the stack of notes on Ms. Jenkins's desk and debated his next move. We all watched the battle unfold before us. I felt bad for Mr. Thompson, knowing how it felt to be bullied by Kevin and other kids in the class with an audience watching. Most substitutes struggled to gain control, and we all took advantage of that to some extent. But Kevin was pushing the limits, and we all thought he had the upper hand.

Mr. Thompson surprised us all by sitting down. "I guess we'll wait for you to find your seat." He turned his attention toward the lesson plans on his desk.

"Come on, Mr. T, just let us go." Kevin bounced the ball between his legs and behind his back.

Mr. Thompson ignored him completely, not wavering on his initial demands.

Marques spoke up, "Kevin, man, come on, we wanna go."

"Then let's go, he ain't gonna stop us."

We all looked around nervously, some of us debating what to do. I knew I wasn't budging, not even if the entire class left. I wasn't one to succumb to peer pressure, and I wasn't going to risk getting called into Mr. K's office again.

Mr. Thompson picked his head up. "Ms. Jenkins instructed me to leave her a report on how the day went, and to be sure to include anyone that may need to miss out on recess for the rest of the week. So far, the only one on the list is Kevin."

"Hey, Mr. T. I'm just playin', man." Kevin quickly sunk down into his chair, sticking the ball on the floor in between his feet.

We all sat quietly, waiting for Mr. Thompson to make a move and speculating on what he was writing in Ms. Jenkins's notebook. He put the pen down and pushed his chair out to stand up. "Penny, please get the cold lunches and get in line."

It was my week to be the lunch helper. I walked to the coatroom and picked up the laundry basket of cold lunches. There were only a handful of lunches because most of the kids got hot lunch. Marques was called next to carry the basket of playground equipment, minus the ball Kevin already grabbed. Mr. Thompson proceeded to call the rest of the class by row and walked us to the lunchroom.

My stomach grumbled as I walked the lunch basket to our table in the cafeteria. The school lunch today was fish sticks, potato wedges, carrot medallions, and mixed fruit. I was happy that I had a bagged lunch. I wasn't a fan of fish sticks to begin with, and these were so soggy that they didn't deserve to have the word *stick* in their title. The potato wedges needed a whole bottle of ketchup to choke them down because they were so dry. And canned carrots and fruit are just never good. We really needed to add "food critic" to our weekly job board.

I ate quickly and escaped to the fresh air of the playground. There was a four square game going with the third graders, and the fifth graders had a kickball game on the field, but I didn't know anyone from any other grades. Since I was too shy to try to make new friends, and most of my class was still eating lunch, I grabbed a ball and began kicking it against the wall. There was a yellow square outline painted on it for a baseball strike zone, and I used it for my target. The rubber ping reverberated each time the ball hit the brick. Kick, ping, bounce, bounce. Kick, ping, bounce, bounce. I missed my target twice in a row, and I was just about to try a third attempt when a loud thud sounded from above.

I looked up in the direction of the noise, but there was nothing there. My eyes traced down the side of the building to a small dark spot on the ground, only about fifteen feet away. I walked over to investigate. As I got closer, the spot began to take shape. A wing appeared on one side, and that's when I realized it was a bird. But it wasn't chirping or fluttering like birds usually do. It wasn't moving at all. I crouched down to see its neck twisted and turned in a way that didn't look right. The bird's tiny chest heaved subtly up and down, barely noticeable, but it indicated it was still alive. A pit formed in my stomach and my heart began to beat fast with worry. The poor little bird was suffering. I had to help but didn't know how. My hand reached forward to pet the bird, to try to comfort it.

"Penny, don't!"

A voice from behind halted me right before I made contact. I pulled my hand back and turned to see Mr. K hovering over my back. My heart skipped a beat as I remembered our last encounter.

"It could be sick." He bent down next to me. "Did you just find it here?"

I relaxed a little, realizing he wasn't here to yell at me. "I heard it hit the window and then fall."

Mr. K nodded and leaned closer to examine the bird.

"Will he be OK?" I asked, fearing I already knew the answer.

"I don't know, he looks pretty bad."

I stared at the hurt animal, then at Mr. K, wishing he would do something to help it. Teachers were supposed to be able to solve any problem.

He saw the concern in my eyes. "Let me see if I can find a box. You stay here and make sure no one touches it."

"OK." A glimmer of hope rose in my heart.

Mr. K walked in through the cafeteria doors, and I sat down next to the bird. I scanned the playground back and forth, watching out for any stray balls or kids who might disturb the injured animal. A minute or two later, the cafeteria door opened, and Mr. K reemerged carrying an empty shoebox. Jasmine and Marcus were following behind him. They all crouched down next to me and the bird.

"Whoa, I've never seen a dead animal before!"

I didn't like Marcus's assumption. "He's not dead!"

"Yet . . ." Jasmine chimed in.

Mr. K ignored our bickering. He set the box on the ground and reached into his pocket to pull out a pair of plastic gloves, the kind the cafeteria workers used when they served food. We all shut up and watched him intently. He put the gloves on and carefully picked up the bird and set it in the box. The bird remained asleep, and for a moment it seemed to be completely lifeless. I stared intently. To my relief, its chest was still moving with each weak breath. Mr. K closed the lid on the box.

"We gonna bury it?" Marcus asked.

"He's still breathing!" I was overly defensive of the poor helpless animal.

Mr. K finally intervened. "Marcus, we're trying to save him."

"How we gonna do that?"

It was a question that I was also wondering the answer to.

"We're going to keep him in this box in a dark, quiet place for a few hours. Hopefully he snaps out of it and can fly away when we open it."

"I don't know, Mr. K, his neck looks all messed up." Jasmine spoke the truth I didn't want to hear.

"It does, but only time will tell."

That wasn't good enough for me. "Isn't there something else we can do?"

"I don't think so, Penny, aside from putting it out of its misery."

Marcus jumped in. "What that mean, like, shootin' it?"

"Well, nobody at school better have a gun, but yes, there are other ways."

It was a harsh reality that most teachers wouldn't approach with their students. But Mr. K was different. He believed in preparing kids for the real world, not sheltering them from it. He went on to tell us a story about a time he'd gone hunting with his cousin. His cousin took a shot at a deer, but it wasn't clean. It hit the deer through the neck and it fell instantly. However, as they approached it, they realized it was still very much alive. It huffed and snorted, angry with steam and snot shooting from its nose. It was trying to stand to charge them, but it was paralyzed. Mr. K walked up to the animal cautiously. It was still breathing heavily but seemed to accept the fact that it could no longer move. It would be hours before the animal died on its own. Mr. K told us that even though they went out that day to kill a deer, he didn't want one to suffer. He stared at the dying animal in its fear-filled eyes and then put it out of its misery.

My heart sank as he finished his story. It all sounded so cruel. I remained quiet, hoping our bird wouldn't have the same fate.

"Man, Mr. K, that sounds pretty mean, killing a helpless animal." Marcus finally shared my emotion.

"It's not easy. But I was taught if you're going to eat meat, then hunting is the most humane way to do it."

That was a concept I wouldn't even try to understand until much later in life. I just knew that right now, I didn't want to kill any animals.

Mr. K stood up with the box and began to walk toward the building. We all stood up and followed. He took the box to an entrance alcove that wouldn't be used until the end of the school day. "We can leave him here for a few hours and check on him at afternoon recess."

I was surprised at how caring Mr. K was toward the wounded animal. He tucked the box into a shadowy corner just as the recess bell rang. We were all hesitant to line up, not wanting to leave the bird alone.

Mr. K motioned for us to go line up. "It'll be fine, we'll check on him this afternoon."

We accepted his direction and raced to the cafeteria doors. Mr. Thompson met us, still chewing his last bite of ham sandwich. He wiped the mayonnaise from his mustache and ushered us inside. The threat of future missed recesses must have stuck in most of our minds because the line was much less rambunctious than earlier that morning. We made our way to our desks and took out our math workbooks. I couldn't stop thinking about the bird the entire math lesson. I even named him Bert. We were working on writing word problems and turning them into equations. All of mine were about Bert. *1) Bert has twelve berries. He eats six for lunch. How many berries does Bert have left? B = 12 – 6. 2) It takes fifteen sticks to build a nest. Bert has seven sticks. How many more does he need? 7 + S = 15.* I found a way to work him into five of my problems and then began running out of bird-related ideas. Luckily, our work time was almost up. I spent the last few minutes drawing pictures in my math notebook.

Mr. Thompson walked to the front of the room, signaling us to stop working. "All right, who wants to write one of their problems on the board for someone to solve?"

Writing on the chalkboard was a privilege not often given out, so almost every hand went up, even those who were folding paper airplanes and playing tic-tac-toe with their neighbors for the entire math lesson. I think I was called on only because Mr. Thompson was confident that I had done the work. I walked up to the board with my notebook. Taking a piece of chalk in hand, I carefully wrote out my word problem. Monique and Jessica were also at the board writing out their problems. When we finished, Mr. Thompson asked for volunteers to come write and solve the equations. This time only the confident or not easily embarrassed raised their hands. Kevin, Damon, and Jasmine were called to the board.

Kevin walked up to my problem. "Aye, who's Bert?" He began laughing.

"Just solve the problem, Kevin," Mr. Thompson instructed.

Kevin took a piece of chalk in his hand and stared at the board. Damon and Jasmine were almost done solving the equations when Kevin began writing. *S = 7 + 15, S = 26.* No part of his answer was correct. Once everyone was done writing, each student was asked to explain their thinking to the class. Jasmine and Damon went through their answers with approval from Mr. Thompson. Then it was Kevin's turn.

"See, he got seven sticks plus fifteen for the nest, so that's twenty-six sticks, S equals twenty-six." He spoke with confidence even though he knew he was wrong.

Mr. Thompson remained silent for a few seconds after Kevin stopped speaking, then nodded sympathetically. "Thank you for sharing, Kevin. Did anyone else get a different answer?"

A few kids raised their hand to share the correct answer. It was a subtle revenge, but it brought a smile to my face.

Our math lesson concluded. Next was our half hour of silent reading time. I flipped through a Choose Your Own Adventure chapter book about a pirate, skipping to all of the path diversions. It felt like an eternity because I didn't enjoy reading, and all I could think about was going to check on Bert. Finally, Mr. Thompson told us to put our books away and get ready for afternoon recess. I tossed my book into my desk and jumped up.

Mr. K was holding the outside door for my class as we filed out. He stopped me, Jasmine, and Marcus and told us to wait for him. When everyone was on the playground, he led us over to where he'd placed the box.

Suddenly, panic flooded through me. The story that Mr. K told us about the deer was still fresh in my mind, and I worried that Bert might have to suffer the same fate. We all immediately crowded around the box. For a brief moment, the bird was both alive and dead in our minds, and I wasn't sure which fate I was hoping for. I wanted more than anything for him to fly away, but if Bert was alive and severely injured, I didn't know if I could bear having to kill him. I would rather he just already be dead if that were the case.

Mr. K asked us to back up as he reached forward to lift

the lid of the box. Bert was curled in the corner with his head tucked down. Every particle in my body wished for the tiny animal to move, to chirp, to fly away. But he didn't. Jasmine and Marcus looked at Mr. K, but I refused to take my eyes off the bird. I watched intently for any sign of life. A gentle breeze ruffled his feathers, and for a second, I was hopeful that he was going to be all right. But the breeze stopped, and the bird remained still. His tiny chest was no longer moving. He was no longer breathing. The realization sent a bolt to my heart. It radiated slowly through my veins like warm molasses, then settled heavily in my stomach. Bert was dead.

"We did all we could do." Mr. K reached forward to close the lid, forcing me to break my stare.

I looked over at Jasmine and Marcus. They looked almost as pathetic as I felt. Jasmine turned to Mr. K. "What now?"

"I can take care of it from here." He looked at our faces and realized that might not be enough for a few sad fourth graders who didn't have much experience with death. "I'm sorry he didn't make it, but he died peacefully, and we did everything we could to help him. Sometimes these things happen, and it sucks."

"Too bad we can't eat him like that deer in your story," Marcus chimed in.

Jasmine rolled her eyes and shoved him on his shoulder.

"What?" Marcus shot back.

Mr. K picked up the box as he stood. I silently made one last wish that the bird would flutter to life and burst through the lid, but I was left disappointed.

"All right, you three, go try to enjoy the last few minutes of your recess." Mr. K dismissed us to the playground.

Jasmine and Marcus took off running. I took one last look at the box in Mr. K's hands and pictured Bert's lifeless body crumpled up in the corner. I hoped he knew he wasn't alone. I hoped he wasn't scared. And I hoped Mr. K was right, that he went peacefully without pain. Suddenly, a twinge of shame ran through me. I was more distraught about the death of a bird than I was when my grandma died. That seemed wrong, but I couldn't figure out why. I began to contemplate it when I saw Jasmine standing in front of me.

She had stopped her sprint and turned back toward me. "Hey, wanna play one-on-one?"

My head shot up. "OK."

"Race you to the court!"

We both dashed toward the basketball court, making it there just as the bell rang.

CHAPTER 15

My mom picked me up from school on Friday because we had plans to go to the theater. We were going to see a movie called *Braveheart*. I didn't know what it was about, I was just excited for popcorn, candy, and soda. Her car rolled to a stop at the side of the school, and I hurried over. Clouds filled the sky, but it wasn't summer storm clouds. Instead of thick humid air, these clouds were accompanied by cool autumn air with a windy bite that made you want to bring your winter coat out of hibernation. I quickly jumped into the warmth of the car.

"Hey, honey." She had an uneasy look on her face.

I sunk into the seat and closed the door. "What's up?"

"We're gonna have to skip the matinee and go to the six o'clock show."

"How come?" I turned to shove my backpack behind my seat.

"You know how Mr. Schobke is retiring at the end of the year?"

I nodded.

"Well, we're interviewing for his replacement, and the only time everyone was available is four thirty." My mom sped away from the curb. "You can sit in Mr. Schobke's office while we meet."

"OK." I wasn't terribly upset because I enjoyed going to my mom's work.

"It should only be about a half hour or so. It's all just

been a mess. Mr. Radler has been pushing for these inter-views, and Mr. Schobke has been putting up every obstacle because he wants to give his position to his nephew, Dick."

I smirked. Dick Schobke. Surely it was short for Rich-ard. But why, I would never understand.

My mom spent the rest of the drive venting about the power struggle between Schobke and Radler these past few months. Each had a different vision for how the law firm would proceed after Schobke's retirement, and neither of them was willing to concede. She also mentioned that she was looking forward to not having to deal with Mr. Schob-ke's condescending and arrogant attitude, but she worried that if his nephew got the job, he might be even worse. Last Christmas she had met Dick at an office get-together, and he'd spent the night talking over everyone and telling one terrible lawyer joke after the next. I listened silently, adding the occasional "mm-hmm" or "right." It was clear she'd had all this swirling around in her mind for a while and no one to talk to about it. The only other women at her office were the crotchety old receptionist, Patty, and the cleaning lady, who only spoke Hmong.

We pulled up in front of the law firm just as my mom was finishing her thoughts on the workplace drama. "And he acts like Dick is some hotshot lawyer, but Patty said he didn't even pass his bar exam the first time around. I know that's just office gossip, and I don't like to get caught up in that, but come on, one of our interview candidates is bound to be more qualified and less of a pain in the butt."

I nodded as she shifted the car into park.

"All right, here goes nothing." She grabbed her purse from between the seats. "Do you want to bring any school-work to keep you occupied?"

I shook my head. "No, I'll be OK." I planned on playing solitaire on Mr. Schobke's computer the entire time.

I followed my mom up the front steps of the law office

and through the front doors. As we passed the waiting room, I grabbed a *National Geographic* magazine off one of the tables. Most of the lights were off or dimmed, putting me on alert for any zombies or ghosts that might be lurking in the dark. It was only 3:30, but everyone was clearly done with clients for the day. We walked into the back reception area, where Patty was packing up her belongings and putting her jacket on. She paused as we entered.

"Patty, you remember my youngest, Penny?"

Patty responded with the raspy voice of someone who had smoked since she was thirteen. "Is she the one you're interviewing for Schobke's position?" Patty wheezed as she laughed, revealing a few missing teeth.

I knew Patty well. I had been to my mom's work a million times and had also seen her at all the Christmas and summer office parties. Her gruff and brash personality was not something I associated with a customer service position. But she had been with the law firm longer than I'd been alive, so there must have been a different side to her that I wasn't aware of.

My mom smiled and forced a laugh. "Penny's just here waiting until the interview is over."

"Shucks, she'd probably be better than Schobke's nephew." Patty grabbed her bag and reached forward to lock the sliding glass window of the reception desk. "Well, if she ain't here to interview, have her file some cases while she's just sitting around. There's a stack sitting in the back."

"Thanks for the suggestion, but I don't know how much Jack or Robert would approve of a fourth grader filing confidential client information."

"Oh, she could handle it." Patty grabbed her bag and stepped toward the door we were standing in front of.

My mom stepped aside and I shuffled behind her, trying to avoid Patty's attention.

"The interviewee's file is on my desk. Harold Turner,

must be fresh out of law school at twenty-six years old." She stepped past us, pulling a pack of cigarettes from the side pocket of her bag.

"Well, like you said, he can't be any worse than Schobke's nephew." My mom smirked. "Have a good weekend, Patty."

"You too!" The smack of the pack of cigarettes against her palm echoed through the hallway her entire walk out.

My mom turned toward me. "I have to wait here for Harold to show up; hopefully he's early. You wanna go back to Mr. Schobke's office and watch TV or play a game on the computer?"

I nodded. "OK."

"Or you could always go to the file room and take care of that stack of cases we have."

"Maybe—what are you gonna pay me?"

"Free room and board."

I rolled my eyes. I was hoping for an opportunity to get some money to spend on candy with Edgar at the convenience store by my house. I turned and headed down the back hallway, passing Mr. Radler's office on the way. The door was cracked, and I could hear Mr. Radler and Mr. Schobke talking. The conversation sounded a little heated.

"Rob, this isn't a monarchy. We need the best, most qualified candidate, not just the one who's related to you." Mr. Radler was sitting behind his desk, leaning back in his chair, but not in a relaxed position.

I could only see half of Mr. Schobke's back. He was sitting across from Mr. Radler with his fancy dress shoes propped up on the desk. "Dick is the most qualified. I vouch for him, that should be worth more than anything these other guys come in with."

"Don't play me for a fool, we both know he hasn't taken his law career seriously and there are people better suited for the job out there."

Mr. Schobke slammed his feet to the floor. "And we both

know even after I retire, I'm still part owner. How long are we going to do this, wasting time on these interviews? If we hire Dick, I can mentor him before I leave."

I was so immersed in their conversation I didn't notice my mom, who had stepped around the corner into the hallway. "Penny, I'll come and get you when the interview is over."

I jumped at the sound of her voice. "Oh, yeah, OK." I made a beeline for Mr. Schobke's office before I could get in trouble for eavesdropping.

It was pitch black when I entered. Turning the lights on did little to brighten the dark atmosphere. The walls were a deep plum color, not light enough to be purple but not dark enough to be black. He had a cream-colored sofa to the left of the doorway with frames of his accomplishments hanging above it—his doctorate, his picture on the cover of *Lawyers Today*, some type of certification, another picture of him shaking hands with some guy that looked like he belonged to a yacht club. To the left of the doorway was Mr. Schobke's desk. It was a huge, three-sided, deep red fortress. If his office was designed to intimidate any who entered, I'd say they did a pretty good job.

There was always a bowl of Jolly Ranchers sitting on the left wing of the desk. It seemed out of place, like a trick luring people in for some sort of attack. I ignored any sort of suspicions, like a kid following someone into a van with the promise of candy. The watermelon Jolly Ranchers were my favorite. I walked over to the bowl, took a glance over my shoulder to make sure nobody was watching, then proceeded to pick through the bowl and grab all the watermelon flavors. Once both of my pockets were stuffed full, I put a few in my hand, then took a seat at the desk in front of the computer. The screensaver was a 3D first-person maze that continuously turned into dead ends. It was equally frustrating as it was mesmerizing. You had no control over which direction you went, and no matter how long you stared, you would never reach the end of the maze, yet it was extremely difficult to look away. I popped one of the candies into my mouth and clicked the mouse to break the screensaver's spell.

Mr. Schobke's computer wallpaper was a picture of him holding a huge rifle and standing over the body of a lion. It made me uncomfortable because hunting a lion was something that I had never heard of. It seemed much different from hunting a deer or a turkey, but I couldn't really pinpoint why. Did people eat lions? As I pondered what it might taste like, I opened up a game of solitaire. The computer shuffled the cards and shot them onto the table quicker than any human could. After an hour of playing the card game and eating watermelon Jolly Ranchers, it began to lose its allure. I closed the game and left the keyboard and mouse untouched, trying to bring back the maze screensaver. Before I was sucked back into the endless turns and dead ends, my mom appeared in the doorway.

"Hey, sweetheart, you ready to go?"

I stood up instantly, ready to escape the dungeon.

"OK. I have all of my things; I just need to lock up on the way out."

"Should I shut the computer down?"

"Oh, yes, please. Mr. Schobke left right after the interview."

I clicked the shutdown button and followed my mom down the hallways and out of the building. As we both slid into the car, I turned and asked her a question that was weighing heavy on my mind.

"Hey, Mom?"

She started up the car and turned to face me. "Yeah?"

"Have you ever eaten a lion?"

My mom laughed at the randomness of my question. "What? No, of course not."

"Oh." I was disappointed to not get any more insight into why someone might hunt a lion. I decided to ask Mr. K the next time I saw him. He knew a lot about hunting.

* * *

We made a quick stop at home on the way to the movie. I waited in the car as my mom ran inside to change. She returned with an apple in hand and Uncle Bobby in tow. I hoped he was on his way to work, or church, or the bar, anywhere but with us.

"Here, eat this on the way so I don't feel completely like a delinquent parent." She tossed the apple at me.

"Can I get popcorn and a candy?"

My mom gave me a dubious stare. "Fine, but you have to eat all of that apple."

I bit into the apple without hesitation. "OK, let's go."

"We just have to wait for your uncle, he's grabbing something out of his truck."

My stomach dropped. "I thought it was just going to be us going."

"Bobby wanted to come along. I thought it'd be good for him to get out."

I rolled my eyes and glared out the windshield. Uncle Bobby was reaching into the driver's side door of his truck. When he appeared, he was tucking something into the inside chest pocket of his jacket. He slammed the truck door shut and slid into the back seat of my mom's Beetle. "Thanks for letting me tag along, I haven't been to a movie in years."

My anger softened slightly. Maybe my mom was right, and it really was good for Uncle Bobby to come with us.

He scooted all the way to the middle of the back seat and stretched his legs out. "So, what are we seeing?"

"*Braveheart.*" I spoke between sloppy apple bites.

"Huh. Never heard of it."

"It's about the Scottish fight for independence, it got really good reviews." My mom shifted into reverse. "And I hear it's a pretty long movie, so prepare yourselves."

"Sounds like it calls for a large popcorn with a free refill." I looked at my mom as she backed out of the driveway.

* * *

We made it to the theater with ten minutes to spare, just enough time to use the bathroom and get concessions. My mom caved and fulfilled my snack requests. The large bucket of popcorn filled both my arms, leaving my mom to carry the oversize soda and M&Ms. She justified it by saying that we could all share, even though Uncle Bobby insisted on getting his own soda. By the time we got into our movie's auditorium, the only seats left were either in the way back row or the very front. We opted for the way back. The previews began just as we sat down. I set the soda in one cup holder, my box of peanut M&Ms in the other, and rested the popcorn on my lap. There were about fifteen minutes of previews, during which I already scarfed down almost half of the tub of popcorn. As the opening movie credits began to play, my mom looked over at me stuffing my face. She shook her head and stole a handful.

I realized I'd better pace myself if I was going to make my snacks last the entire movie. If this movie ended up boring, I wanted to at least have junk food to preoccupy me. The start of the movie wasn't promising. There was weird mystical bagpipe music playing as the camera panned over hills and mountains of Scotland. I automatically reached for more popcorn and took a swig of soda. Good thing I had a free refill coming. I shoved the bucket toward my mom, and she grabbed another handful. She kept her eyes glued to the screen, as if she would be happy if the entire movie were just Scottish scenery. I rolled my eyes and extended the popcorn bucket to Uncle Bobby. He hunched forward in his seat, pouring something into his soda cup. My mom was too focused on the movie to notice or just chose to ignore it.

Bobby didn't realize I was looking at him until he sat back and returned the flask to his jacket pocket. He grabbed a handful of popcorn as he took a long sip from his drink. I retracted the bucket and sunk back into my chair. My optimism about having Uncle Bobby come along quickly faded. His drinking made me uneasy. It filled the night with uncertainty. My uncle was in a good mood at the moment, but alcohol had a way of turning things on their end. I took a deep breath and grabbed the box of peanut M&Ms. Tonight was going to be a good night, I convinced myself. I tore open the box of chocolates and focused on the movie. To my surprise, I was suddenly drawn in.

The beginning of the movie followed a young boy through the countryside. He was about my age and spying on an argument between his dad and another man, so naturally I related. There wasn't an overly cheery mood to begin with, but the atmosphere turned completely somber when it was revealed that the boy's father didn't return from war. He stood at his father's grave. A small gathering of people surrounded him for the burial, but it was clear that he was on his own now. He had no family left, and it made me think of Edgar. The movie jumped ahead, and the boy was now an adult, and he was falling in love. Just when I thought the movie was going to take a more positive turn, his wife was murdered by the government, and he started a war. The more intense the movie became, the quicker I shoved popcorn into my mouth. By the time the Scottish defeated the British, I was halfway through my second bucket and my bladder was ready to burst.

The ending credits rolled and I stood up to rush out to the bathroom. My mom and Uncle Bobby lagged behind, gathering their jackets and the remaining popcorn and soda. As I exited the bathroom, I spotted them waiting for me by the entrance doors.

My mom pushed through the door into the crisp night air. "What an amazing story."

Uncle Bobby held the door as I walked out behind him. "Yeah, that actually was pretty good."

I listened carefully for any slurring in his words. He was carrying his third "soda" in his hand, having emptied the rest of his flask into it just before the movie ended.

"Penny, what'd you think? Did you like it?" My mom put her arm around me as we made our way through the parking lot.

I shrugged. "I guess it was better than I thought it'd be."

"I'll take that." She smiled and squeezed my shoulder gently before breaking away to dig her keys from her purse.

I was relegated to the back seat for the ride home. As we drove, I thought more about the movie. I didn't understand a lot of it, but what I did understand completely captivated me. It was about love, freedom, and fighting against all odds for what you believed in and cared about. They were all things that made me feel like life was part of something bigger than just one person, and like maybe death was sometimes necessary. I wondered if I'd be brave enough to fight, to die for the things I valued, secretly worrying that I wouldn't be.

* * *

As we pulled into the driveway, I noticed Matthew's car parked out front. It was almost ten o'clock, but Amelia was eighteen and I knew my mom wouldn't care that Matthew was still there. I followed my mom up the back steps with Uncle Bobby behind me. For some reason, he continued into the kitchen with us instead of going up to the attic. Having him at the movie with us wasn't as bad as I thought, but I wasn't looking to extend my time with him. He made a beeline for the refrigerator and grabbed a beer. I hoped he would take it upstairs with him. Instead, he cracked it open and took a seat at the kitchen table. My mom set her purse on the counter and slid off her jacket.

I walked past both of them and headed to the bathroom. All that soda had gotten the best of me. As I passed my sister's bedroom, I heard soft music playing and muffled giggling. It should've set off an alarm, some sort of warning, but I was too preoccupied rushing to relieve my bladder to really pay attention. When I got out of the bathroom, my mom was headed to her bedroom.

"I'm beat. I'm going to read and head to bed."

"OK," I mumbled, disappointed that I would be stuck alone with Uncle Bobby.

"Thanks for going to the movie with me, honey, I had a really nice time." She said it like it was the first time she'd had a nice night in a long time.

"Me too." I smiled, happy that she was happy.

My mom walked to her bedroom, and I glanced over at Uncle Bobby sitting at the kitchen table cracking open another beer. He clearly wasn't going anywhere anytime soon. I debated what to do. Usually, I'd bug Amelia to play a game or watch a movie, but she seemed to be busy. I decided to write another letter to my dad, even if I wouldn't send it.

I made my way to my bedroom. Henry was cuddled on the brown recliner in the living room as I passed by, but the second my bedroom door closed, he was scratching to get in. He headbutted it until there was a crack big enough for him to slither through. He slunk over to where I was sitting on the floor, brushing his head against my hand to say hi, before he jumped on the bed and curled up on my pillow.

I retrieved a pen from my backpack, leaned back against my bed, and began writing.

"Dear Dad. . ."

Henry's purr rumbled loudly behind me. I was having trouble figuring out what to say. My dad hadn't written me back, so part of me felt like anything else I said was pointless. I looked around the room for inspiration and spotted my boom box in the corner of the room. Music always had a way of inspiring me. It also pulled out feelings that I wasn't completely aware of. The right song brought out things that I felt deep in my soul but didn't know how to put into words. It was something I realized the first time I heard Ben E. King sing "Stand by Me" on the oldies station and it gave me goose bumps.

I crawled over and pressed play on the tape deck. Earlier in the week, I recorded a song off the radio. I didn't know what it was called or who it was by, but it was about a magic carpet ride. I crawled back to my notebook as the song began, *"I like to dream! Yess yesss. Right between the sound machine, on a cloud of sound I drift in the night . . ."* It immediately made the hair on my arms stand up and a warmth spread through my chest. I grabbed my pen and began writing to the music. The song broke into the refrain just as I heard the sound of a shotgun being loaded.

It was a distinctive sound, easily recognized, even though I had only heard it in movies and on TV. This was different. Closer. Real. Some people may have jumped to the conclusion that an intruder had broken in, maybe a robber. But there was only one thought that came to my mind: Uncle Bobby. I cracked my bedroom door and peeked out. The living room was dark, just a slight shadow of furniture from the glow of the kitchen light. I listened for a moment before stepping out. There was talking that sounded like it was coming from Amelia's room. It was muffled and low, hard to distinguish.

I expected to see my mom's bedroom light flick on as she awoke to the commotion, hoping she would come to investigate so I wouldn't have to. No such luck. Her room remained dark. I crept through the living room and into the dining room. The voices became much clearer as I got closer. There was an argument unfolding. I snuck closer and peeked into the hallway.

Uncle Bobby was standing outside my sister's door holding a shotgun across his chest. "Matthew needs to leave or I'm going to make him leave."

Amelia opened the door violently. "Bobby, get out of here. Get rid of that shotgun, now!" She wasn't intimidated or scared, just pissed.

I, on the other hand, was sure someone was going to get shot. Nevertheless, I inched closer to get a better view. Amelia was face-to-face with Uncle Bobby and she wasn't backing down.

"I'll put the gun away when Matty-boy here leaves." Uncle Bobby spoke with a familiarity that he hadn't earned. It was all part of his plan to irritate my sister and try to draw a rise out of Matthew.

Amelia took a step forward. "You're acting crazy. You need to leave."

"*He* needs to leave." Bobby gripped the shotgun tighter and began to aim it past my sister at Matthew.

Amelia grabbed the gun and shoved it into my uncle, angling it back into a vertical position. They struggled for a moment, each of them fighting to gain control.

Matthew stepped out of the bedroom to try to intervene. "Amelia, stop!"

Every muscle in my body tensed as I waited for the explosion of the gun to rip through one of them.

Bobby pulled the shotgun away and took a step backward. Amelia pushed past him to pick up the phone in the kitchen.

"I'm calling the cops." She spoke as she dialed. "Yes, hello, there's a man in my house threatening me with a shotgun . . ."

This wasn't going as smoothly as Uncle Bobby had expected. I guess I'm not really sure what he expected, but his bold posture had suddenly melted away. He was visibly flustered. Amelia spoke to the 911 dispatcher, and Bobby darted out the back door carrying my mom's car keys and his shotgun.

CHAPTER 16

It took three hours before the police officer arrived. I wondered what it took to get the cops to show up in a timely manner if someone threatening you with a loaded shotgun didn't work. My mom joined us outside shortly after Bobby drove off in her car. It was becoming more and more clear that he was not mentally stable. Religion and alcohol had been his coping mechanisms his entire life, both Band-Aids over a gaping wound. And right now, alcohol was winning, creeping up and gaining control, feeding the illness in his mind. Add a loaded gun into the mix and it was a recipe for disaster. I was worried he would hurt someone, or himself. Either would be against his religion, but depression can have a stronger grip than even God.

We were all sitting on the front porch when the officer walked up. My sister and Matthew took the lead in explaining to the officer what had happened. He took notes, asking for details every now and then, like what type of car Bobby was in. The encounter ended with him flipping his notepad shut and telling us to call if Bobby showed back up. The whole thing lasted less than twenty minutes. I thought I'd feel more reassured once the police arrived, but after hours of waiting, I suppose the urgency of the situation had subsided. There really was nothing else the cop could've done at that point. I watched him drive off just as uneventfully as he came. No sirens or flashing lights.

"I'm sure Bobby will come back at some point. Do you want me to stay?" Matthew was asking all of us.

Amelia grabbed his hand. "No, it's OK, I doubt he'll show back up tonight."

"And if he does, I suppose it might be better if I'm not here spending the night." Matthew seemed to be finishing Amelia's thought, even though I knew that wasn't at all what she was thinking.

My sister wasn't one to back down in a conflict. In fact, I was surprised she didn't ask Matthew to stay just to get under Bobby's skin in case he did come back. I hoped he would just stay away for everyone's sake. It was unnerving to watch my uncle point a loaded gun at Matthew, but despite everything that had happened, I was worried about him. It was a confusing feeling. I had felt the wrath of Bobby's temper firsthand and imagined how terribly this night could have ended. But I had also seen a different side of him, a side I genuinely enjoyed, and that made me realize he wasn't all bad. Things were never as black-and-white as I wished; shades of gray muddled the simplicity.

Amelia said goodnight to Matthew, then followed us upstairs. We were all exhausted to the point of silence. My mom hadn't said much since she'd met us outside anyway. I know she didn't approve of Uncle Bobby's behavior, but she also did little to take charge and prevent it.

As I lay in bed, I wondered if I was the only one having a hard time turning my thoughts off. An hour went by, maybe more, and I lay there restless, staring at the back of my eyelids. Finally, I decided to just get up. I reached under my bed to retrieve my notebook. The page was still open with "Dear Dad," written on top. I'd forgotten I was even writing to him. That would have to wait for now. I flipped to a new blank page. A letter to Uncle Theo seemed like a good way to sort through everything swirling around in my head. My hand spilled the events of the night onto the page, as well as all my thoughts and emotions that came with them. I wrote until my mind was empty. Three messy scribbled pages later, I tucked the pen in the metal spiral of the notebook, then curled up on my side with my head nestled in the pillow.

* * *

Morning came quickly, and for a moment, I wondered if the whole thing was a crazy dream. I opened my eyes and blinked away the sunlight. As my vision adjusted, reality quickly faded in. Uncle Bobby, the shotgun, Amelia, the cop—it wasn't just something I'd worked up in my imagination. I sat up and threw off the blanket. My notebook sat open on the floor with the letter I'd written to Uncle Theo staring up at me. It more resembled a journal entry, truthful in a way that a completely sound and well-rested mind couldn't be. A raw honesty brought on by a lack of sleep. Now that I was fully awake, I second-guessed sending it. Uncle Theo might see a side of me that he didn't know existed. The only people I really let in were Amelia and Edgar, and my letter talked about things that I may not even say to them. What if Uncle Theo thought I was weird or stupid? I glanced over what I'd written one more time and decided that it was better to keep this to myself, for now.

I pulled on a pair of shorts and opened my bedroom door. Amelia was sitting on the couch eating a peanut butter sandwich with Henry in her lap. "Do you work early today?" I asked. She wasn't an early riser, so I was surprised that she was awake before me.

She shook her head. "It's already eleven thirty, I'm just waiting for Matthew to pick me up."

I glanced up at the clock, skeptical that I had really slept that late. The little hand was almost on the 12. "Oh."

Amelia set her plate on the coffee table. Henry jumped to follow and began licking up the crumbs.

"Did Uncle Bobby come home yet?" I sank into the couch next to my sister.

"No, Mom's been trying to get ahold of him all morning. He still has her car."

My stomach churned with anxiety. I didn't necessarily want Uncle Bobby to be home, but I was worried that no one knew where he was. "Do you think we should call the cops?"

"Again? For what?" Amelia didn't seem to share my concern.

I shrugged, not willing to admit that I cared about Uncle Bobby.

A car pulled into the driveway and we both peeked out the window to see if it was our mom's green Beetle. It wasn't. Instead, we saw Tomas's maroon Toyota Tercel. Matthew was in the front passenger's seat.

Our mom came racing out from the kitchen. "Is that Bobby?"

Amelia stood and slung her backpack over her shoulder. "No, it's my ride to work."

"Oh. Are you coming home when you get off or do you have plans?" My mom walked over and peeked out the window, like she was making sure it really wasn't Bobby.

"I'm not sure. If I do anything, I'll let you know." Amelia disappeared into the hallway.

I waited to hear the front door close, then kneeled on the couch to peer out the window. Amelia walked up the driveway and greeted Matthew with a short kiss. His hand fell to the small of her back as he opened the passenger door for her. She slid into the front seat next to Tomas. Matthew closed Amelia's door, then climbed into the back. I sunk away from the window and rolled to a seated position on the couch.

My mom looked down at the cordless phone in her

hand, wishing it to ring. Silence. She peeked out the window one more time before pacing back into the kitchen.

I grabbed the remote and flipped through the TV channels. The Saturday morning cartoons were already over. It was all infomercials and religious sermons. I paused on one of the sermons, thinking of Uncle Bobby. The man on the TV was speaking with an intensity that made me uncomfortable. He was shouting about how Jesus had died for our sins, and that it is only through the power of God that we can be forgiven. I didn't get why anyone would want to listen to a show that seemed to be yelling at you. It didn't make me feel comforted or uplifted, the way Edgar talked about his belief in God. I flipped the TV off just as the doorbell rang.

Was it Bobby? Why would he ring the doorbell? Maybe it was the police because he'd done something terrible with the gun. I raced into the front hall and peeked from the top of the steps. A bright floral headscarf peeked through the top of the window. Edgar's mom. She must have found out my uncle pulled a shotgun on her eldest son and was coming to completely ban our family from seeing her sons. I refused to answer it, hoping she would go away.

"Who is it? Is it Bobby?" My mom rushed past me.

"No, it's Mrs. Gonzalez." I watched my mom walk down the steps and open the front door.

"Hi, Louanne. I'm sorry to stop by unannounced. I'm not interrupting anything, am I?"

"No, not at all. Is everything OK?"

"Yes, I've just noticed that Matthew seems to be spending a lot of time with Amelia." She paused for a moment.

"Yeah, they do seem quite taken with each other," my mom jumped in, sounding just as unsure about where this was going as me.

"Well, the reason I bring it up is because Matthew

is leaving in a few days to go back to his base, and I was thinking we should plan a surprise going-away party for him. And, well, Leo—" She paused again, swallowing hard at the mention of her late husband. "He was always so much better at those things than me, so I was wondering if you could help me plan it?"

My mom's shoulders dropped with relief. "Oh, Evelyn, of course!" Her back was to me, but I could hear the smile in her voice. "Would you and Edgar like to come in? We could talk in the kitchen."

My chest rose at the mention of Edgar. I didn't realize he was outside too.

"Sure, that would be nice."

My mom stepped back to let Edgar and his mom through the doorway. Edgar spotted me at the top of the stairs and squeezed past his mom.

"Hey!" he huffed, out of breath from sprinting up the stairs.

* * *

Edgar and I sat on my bedroom floor counting change. I had emptied my piggy bank so we could get candy and Icees from Open Pantry. As we counted, Edgar noticed my notebook tucked under my bed. The letter to my uncle sat open. "Is that your diary or something?"

"No!" I said, embarrassed. "It's a letter to my uncle Theo."

"Oh, cool." He continued separating out the quarters. "About what?"

I looked at him, and at the letter, and then down to the floor. "I'll tell you, but not here."

I was worried either of our mothers would overhear. Edgar nodded and we finished counting. Ten dollars and forty-two cents. That should be enough for a good sugar fix. We headed toward the back door. Our moms were settled in the kitchen. Notebooks, the yellow pages, and mugs of steaming coffee were spread out before them on the table.

"Where are you two off to?" my mom questioned.

"Walking to Open Pantry."

"OK, we'll be here planning." My mom took a sip of her coffee.

I waited for Edgar's mom to say something, to try to stop him. She peeked up from the yellow pages. "Edgar, what do you think Matthew would like better, barbecue or tacos? I just can't decide."

Edgar shrugged. "Probably barbecue. He likes your pulled pork with the homemade barbecue sauce, like you used to make for Dad's birthday."

His mom shifted her eyes away from her son. Everyone was silent, worried about saying the wrong thing. Just when I was about to skip down the back stairs to escape the awkwardness, she looked back at Edgar. "Well then, I think it's decided. Pulled pork it is!"

My mom smiled. "I can make potato salad and a few other sides."

"And we can get an ice cream cake for dessert!" I saw my opportunity and seized it.

"Nice try, Penny. Weren't you leaving?" My mom knew my tricks and shooed me out the door.

Apparently, I wasn't involved in the planning. "Oh fine, we're going."

Edgar and I hopped down the back stairs and out the back door, relieved to finally be able to talk freely.

"So, what the heck happened?" Edgar was unusually inquisitive.

I was just as eager to tell him. "My uncle went crazy last night."

"Like crazier than normal?"

"Way worse."

We turned into the alley.

"So, what happened?"

"Well, I was sitting in my room trying to write a letter to my dad—"

Edgar interrupted, "Wait. I thought this letter was for your Uncle Theo. Did your dad respond?"

"It *is* for Uncle Theo, and no, my dad didn't respond."

"Oh." There was a lot of weight behind Edgar's single-syllable answer. He wanted to say more about my dad, but I didn't give him the chance.

"So I was trying to figure out what to write, and all of a sudden I heard a shotgun."

Edgar's eyes widened. "Like someone was shooting?"

"No, it was being loaded."

"Your uncle?"

I nodded. "He was standing outside my sister's bedroom demanding that Matthew leave."

"Oh man."

"Yeah." I nodded.

We crossed the street and headed down the second alley.

"So, what happened?"

"Luckily nothing. Amelia called the cops and my uncle left in my mom's car. He hasn't come back yet, and we can't get ahold of him."

Edgar took a deep breath and exhaled as he looked at me. "That's really bad."

"I know."

We approached Open Pantry and Edgar turned toward me. "What'd your mom do? Is she going to kick him out?"

"I doubt it. Right now she's just worried about finding him."

Edgar stopped before opening the door. "Are you scared for him to come back?"

"Sometimes, a little." I tried to step forward and push through the door, but Edgar stopped me.

"Penny, you gotta tell your mom how you feel." His arm was blocking the doorway.

"It'll be OK." I lowered his arm out of my way. "Come on, let's go."

I wanted to believe that everything was going to be OK, and if I admitted to my mom that I was afraid of Uncle Bobby, I felt like I would be making things worse. Edgar paused before following me into the store. He was worried about me, but he knew I was stubborn and that anything else he said right now would be futile. We skimmed the candy aisle, deciding what we each wanted. He ended up choosing a Reese's and I got a Kit Kat, both king-size. Then we walked over and filled up two Icee cups, one red, one blue. When we checked out, we had two cents left over that I left in the penny cup.

* * *

The walk home was much quieter, only because we were both trying to balance eating our candy bars and drinking our Icees without spilling either. We turned out of the alley and onto my block just as my mom's Beetle flew past. Edgar and I stopped midstride and looked at each other. He read my mind, and we both took off running toward my house, still trying to keep our snacks intact.

My mind raced with questions about what my mom was going to do and worries about what Edgar's mom would do if she found out. We sprinted as fast as we could, not wanting to miss any of the action. Uncle Bobby was just turning into the driveway as we approached. We slowed to a walk so he wouldn't see us. The car door slammed shut and I heard my mom at the back door.

"Bobby! Where have you been? Are you OK?"

I peeked down the driveway and saw my uncle standing by the driver's side door. His shoulders were slightly hunched, and his clothes were wrinkled. My mom appeared from the back of the house and I jumped back, plowing into Edgar. He grabbed me as we both stumbled backward but somehow managed not to fall. I knocked his cup from his hand, but luckily, it landed standing up. We steadied ourselves and tried to swallow the urge to laugh. Edgar picked up the cup and we resumed our snooping position.

"I gotta get some sleep. Here's your keys." Bobby's words were just barely loud enough for me to make out.

I waited for my mom to respond, to demand an explanation or apology. She said nothing. My uncle pushed past her and retreated into the house. He had no emotion and showed no remorse. My mom stood in the driveway clutching her car keys. I wondered where the shotgun was. I wondered what Edgar's mom was doing, and if she was watching. But mostly, I wondered how my mom said nothing, and how she just let him back in our house. But I knew that would be the end of it.

CHAPTER 17

The morning of Matthew's party didn't hold the excitement of celebration that I was hoping for. His mom planned the party for the day before he left, which meant it was on a Tuesday and I still had to go to school. I stood in the kitchen pleading with my mom to let me have the day off, an argument that began the night before and continued the second I saw her in the morning.

"But you and Amelia both are off—it's not fair!"

"I'm helping Evelyn set up for the party, and your sister is spending the day with Matthew. She talked with her teachers to get it excused."

"I could help set up."

"We don't need any help." She crossed her arms as the coffee maker gurgled to life behind her.

"I could clean the house." I was second-guessing the words as they came out of my mouth. Was cleaning really better than school? It was too late to retract it now, so I dug in deeper. "You're always saying how this place is full of dust and clutter."

My mom stared at me as if she were almost contemplating it, then firmly replied, "No, and I'm done talking about this. Go get ready."

"But you could talk to my teacher to get it excused."

Her glare spoke louder than any words. It was like a dormant superpower that was brought to life the second you had a kid. I didn't stand a chance. I hung my head as I sulked back to my bedroom to get my backpack, accepting my defeat. When I made my way back to the kitchen, I almost ran right into my sister. She looked like a zombie, half asleep and on a mission to get something to eat.

I jumped back, startled. "Jeez, I thought you were still asleep."

Amelia yawned and took a few steps into the kitchen before acknowledging me with a grunt and shrug of the shoulders. It led me to believe maybe she was still asleep. She reached for a coffee cup and poured it full to the brim, then turned toward me. "Me and Matthew are going to Bender Lake State Park for the day so he's not around when they're setting up for the party."

"Isn't that like three hours away?"

"A little over two, which is why I'm up so early." She took a sip from her mug. "I gotta pick him up at eight and we're stopping to grab food for a picnic, and we gotta be back here by three to shower and be ready for the party."

"I wish me and Edgar could come."

"You guys have school, and besides, I kinda want to just be with Matthew` before he leaves. It's going to be so busy at the party. I want some time with just him."

I nodded. As much as I didn't like it, I understood.

My worry about how Amelia would react to Matthew leaving returned. She was so heartbroken over Jimmy. I didn't want to see her upset like that again. So far, she seemed to be handling it OK, but it probably wouldn't really sink in until after he left. They only had a little over a week together, which they had spent every possible moment together. It was already obvious to me that she was in love. I didn't know how that all worked or how long it was supposed to take, but I knew my sister. She didn't think someone like Matthew existed. He was exactly what she needed when she needed it, and I wasn't sure how she would handle having all that taken away.

I walked over to the pantry to grab a granola bar. "What time does he leave tomorrow?"

"In the evening. I think his flight is at 7:49 or something."

"Then how long till you get to see him again?" I was already running late for school, but this seemed more important.

Amelia shrugged. "I dunno. We haven't talked about that yet."

The reality of the situation hung heavy in her voice. Their relationship was barely just starting, and long distance was hard. I didn't know how to respond.

Luckily, my mom came in to shoo me off to school. "Penny, I'm not driving you, you better hustle."

"Fine," I huffed as I grabbed my backpack and headed for the door. "Have fun with Matthew, see you guys later."

"Thanks, see you at the party."

* * *

School seemed to take forever. It was one of those days where time seemed to stand still or almost move backward. We were halfway through our social studies lesson as I watched the second hand creep around the clock and listened to Ms. Jenkins explain the different features of a map. It was an injustice that I had to sit here learning about maps when there was a party being set up. I wished for a fire, or a gas leak, anything to shut school down. But unfortunately, I was stuck in the present, learning about longitude and latitude.

My mind began to wander, wondering what Amelia and Matthew were doing. We had gone to Bender Lake State Park with our mom every year since I could remember; it was a fall tradition. We'd hike around the miles of trails and stop for custard at Kitt's drive-up on the way home. This year was the first year we hadn't made it there. I could picture the blazing colors, hear the crunch of the leaves beneath our feet, feel the crisp fall air on my cheeks, and smell that earthy, comforting aroma of change. It was something Amelia would only share with someone she trusted, someone she loved. I felt a mix of jealousy and happiness. Besides Edgar, Amelia was my other best friend, and I wished I was there with her.

I spent the rest of the social studies lesson daydreaming and was brought back to reality when Ms. Jenkins handed out homework—a worksheet about finding locations on a map using longitude and latitude. I wondered when I would ever use longitude and latitude in real life. Maybe if I was a pilot like Amelia Earhart, or a soldier out on a mission in uncharted territories. Was professional map reading a job? My mom always kept a few different maps tucked in the door compartment of the car in case of emergencies. On a few road trips, we had gotten lost, and she asked me to pull out the map to figure out where we were and get us back on track. Every time, I'd unfold the map and spread it across my lap and attempt to find our location and what route we needed to take. And every time, I was unsuccessful. My mom would try to help, but it was clear that she was where I got my sense of direction from. We would always end up at the nearest gas station asking for directions. I thought about my social studies lesson, but I still didn't see how it would help in a situation like that. Maybe I was destined to be lost forever.

I tucked the worksheet into the crease of my social studies book, marking the section on maps that I had just completely daydreamed through. The rest of the day, I tried to pay attention to avoid playing catch-up on any more assignments. Luckily, the second half of the day was mostly nonacademic. We had music after lunch and, after that, an all-school assembly on fire safety. They brought in real firefighters, which to a nine-year-old was basically the same as bringing in superheroes. They asked for a volunteer to demonstrate stop, drop, and roll, but I was too shy to even raise my hand. One of the firefighters dressed up in all his gear so we would know what it looked like and wouldn't be afraid if we ever had to be rescued by them. The assembly went right up to school dismissal. At the end, we all got sticker Fire Chief badges. Normally, I would be beyond excited about any sort of sticker, but I was too focused on getting to the party, to Amelia and Edgar.

The second we were dismissed, I began running and didn't stop until I reached our front steps. I unlocked the front door and raced upstairs. To my surprise, my mom was at the doorway just outside of her bedroom having a heated conversation with Uncle Bobby. Neither of them realized I was at the top of the steps. The front hall door was closed just enough to conceal my arrival.

"I don't think it's a good idea, Bobby, not after what happened the other night." That was the first time my mom had directly brought up the shotgun incident since it happened.

Bobby shrugged his shoulders. "I think it would make things better if I went."

"If you want to make things better, you won't go."

"It's not really your decision what I do. You're making this a big deal."

My mom's hands clenched with frustration. "Why don't you ask Matthew and Amelia if they want you there?"

I was honestly surprised that Bobby was putting up such a fight to go to the party. It didn't seem like something he would really want to be a part of.

"Louanne, come on. I'll have a bit to eat, a few drinks, apologize to Matthew, and call it a night."

Drinks. It was then that I realized my uncle must be out of booze, and that was his motivation.

My mom narrowed her gaze on her brother. It was quiet for a few seconds, then she put her hands on her hips and shook her head. "No, Bobby. I'm sorry, you're not invited."

I waited for my uncle to explode in a fit of rage. Instead,

he just nodded silently and turned away, retreating to the attic. My mom took a step to follow him, then paused and retreated into her bedroom. It was one of the only times I saw her stand up to her brother, and I knew it had to be hard on her. She may stand firm when it came to making me go to school, but overall, she had a very soft heart.

As I stepped out of the front hall and into the living room, I could hear sniffles coming from my mom's room. My chest suddenly felt like it was filled with lead. Hearing a parent cry was something kids weren't equipped to deal with, no matter how old they were. It was unnatural. The parents were meant to be the strong ones, the protectors, there to wipe away their children's tears. I felt awful that my mom was so sad, but it also scared me. I didn't know what to do. Before I could make a move, Henry jumped onto the scene. He scampered past my feet and into her room, letting out a loud "Mrrrreow!" as he jumped onto her bed.

"Hey there, buddy." My mom's voice was light and nasally. I could picture Henry headbutting her, trying to make her feel better. He was more empathetic than most people were.

Relieved that my mom was in good hands, I dropped my backpack and headed to the kitchen to get a snack. To my delight, there was a whole tray of deviled eggs in the refrigerator and a plate of brownies on the table. I pulled out the tray of eggs. They were perfect. Each one had golden-yellow yolk filling with sprinkles of red paprika on the top. My mouth watered in anticipation as I peeled the plastic wrap from the tray. First, I'd have a few eggs, and then follow it up with three or four chocolatey, powdered sugar–dusted brownies. I reached to grab an egg and popped it into my mouth.

"Hey!" My mother's voice reached out and my hand jerked away from the tray of eggs.

I jumped back, whipping my head around to see her standing in the hallway.

"Get your hands off those, they're for the party!" Henry had apparently done quick work at improving her spirits. She didn't seem like she had just been crying minutes earlier.

"Oh," I conceded, my mouth still watering. "Well, maybe I should try them, to make sure they're good before we give them to other people?"

"They're good. Put them back in the refrigerator, please."

"Fine." I reluctantly re-covered the eggs and slid them back onto the refrigerator shelf. "When are we leaving? Can I ride my bike over there early?"

"It's almost three thirty; we should get going in a few minutes to make sure we beat Amelia and Matthew there."

"But can I take my bike, in case me and Edgar want to ride around?"

My mom nodded. "Sure, that's fine with me, but dress warm, it's getting chilly out."

"OK!" I darted to my room to grab a sweatshirt, then quickly raced out the back door. No matter what happened, I knew tonight would be good because I'd be with Edgar.

* * *

There were already several cars parked in front of the house. I pedaled down the driveway to see Edgar and his uncle standing over the firepit, adding newspaper and twigs. His uncle sparked a match and gray smoke danced up, followed by a small orange flame as the newspaper ignited.

"Hey, Penny!" Edgar lit up when he noticed me standing at the edge of the driveway.

I walked my bike over and leaned it against the fence. "My mom is on her way, I wanted to ride my bike."

"Come on over, me and my uncle are trying to get this fire going."

I stepped next to him by the fire, which was slowly dwindling out.

He turned to introduce me. "Uncle George, this is my best friend, Penny."

Hearing Edgar call me his best friend made me feel invincible. He could've just said "friend," but he chose to add the word "best." It was a distinction that didn't go unnoticed.

His uncle extended his hand toward me. "Well, Penny, it is a pleasure to meet you."

"Nice to meet you too." I reached out to shake his hand.

We all stood silently for a few seconds staring at the firepit. The smoke had dissipated. All that was left was gray ashy newspaper. The sticks that lay across the top were untouched.

I looked up at Edgar's uncle. "Need some help starting this fire?"

A huge grin spread across George's face. "I like her, she's got spunk."

Edgar laughed and shook his head.

His uncle rearranged the sticks and newspaper and struck another match as he looked at me. "So, what do you think this fire needs?"

I scanned the backyard and saw a bottle of citronella oil sitting next to a tiki torch. A memory of my Uncle Theo flashed through my mind. I looked back at the firepit and saw that the flaming twigs were trying with all their might to light the larger piece of wood, but it was a losing battle. The flames quickly fizzled out.

"Well, it's an ancient Indian secret."

Edgar and his uncle looked at me like I was crazy.

I remembered a similar look on my mom's face when Uncle Theo used that line. I smiled as I replayed the memory in my mind:

He was in town for Christmas one year and talked us all into getting bundled up and having a fire after dinner. The only problem was the little wood that we had was damp from sitting outside uncovered. That didn't deter Uncle Theo though. My mom, Amelia, and I sat around shivering as he tried everything to get a fire going. He used paper, leaves, dryer lint, and even leftover turkey scraps. Each attempt left us even colder and more pessimistic. After the last match died out, Uncle Theo took a sip of his beer and threw up his hands. We all felt relieved that he had finally given up and we could retreat to the warmth of the house.

But we were wrong. Just as my mom turned to shuffle us inside, my uncle protested, "You can't abandon ship now! I still have one last trick up my sleeve."

Amelia groaned. My mom shook her head. I planted my feet, waiting to see what he'd try next. We all watched as he disappeared into the shed and reappeared with a bottle. It was too dark to make out what he had grabbed, which added to the suspense.

"This is an ancient Indian secret." Uncle Theo raised the bottle of mystery juice toward us as he began his story. "I had a brief stint in my thirties working on an oil rig in North Dakota, where I met this beautiful Lakota girl, Chante. Her name meant 'heart,' and she had sure stolen mine."

Like most of my uncle's stories, this one began with a girl.

"I first laid eyes on her on her family's bison ranch. Chante's long, silky black hair was blowing in the wind. The setting sun illuminated her strong cheekbones and made her caramel skin glow." My uncle took one more swig from his can of beer. "She was standing at the fence line, watching the bison graze in the distance. I was there to try to talk the owner of the ranch, Chante's father, into selling two acres on the north of his property to the oil company. It was a proposition I didn't really care to propose, but when the boss man gives you an order, you gotta at least pretend to comply. When I saw Chante standing at that fence in the sunlight, my attitude changed. I stepped toward her, my cowboy boot crunching into the gravel driveway. The noise pulled her attention away from the bison and she turned toward me. I turned on my charm, and I think she turned on her sympathy, laughing at all my dumb jokes and over-the-top pickup lines. It wasn't long before I was inside at the dinner table with her and her father. We feasted on bison steaks, roasted sweet potatoes, and red wine. When we finished eating, we took the party outside. Chante's father, Mato, brought out a case of red wine and handed us each a bottle.

"Chante set her bottle down, unopened, and went to grab firewood from a pile along the fence line. I set my bottle down and rushed over to help her. By the time I got to her, her arms were already loaded with logs. I motioned to help relieve her of some of the load, but she shook her head and told me to grab more. Mato dug the cork out of his bottle with a knife and tipped it into his mouth. Chante stacked the wood in the firepit. No kindling or nothing, just thick hunks of wood. I never thought it'd light. Mato reached behind him and emptied the contents of a bottle of citronella oil onto the fire. He then lit a match and tossed it into the pit. And that, my dears, is the origin of the ancient Indian secret to lighting a fire."

Uncle Theo popped the top on the can of citronella from the shed and soaked the already damp wood. It took a little more finesse than in his story, but within a few minutes, there were flames and we were no longer freezing. It didn't involve chanting or ritual dances like I had imagined. It was simple and I was confident that I could recreate its success.

* * *

Edgar and his uncle were waiting for me to explain myself. I left them in suspense. After a few adjustments to the contents of the firepit, I walked over to grab the bottle of citronella oil. I returned and emptied it onto the firepit.

George looked at me. "Well, that's cheating."

"No, it's an ancient Indian secret."

Edgar shook his head. "So, what, if we tell someone, you gonna have to kill us?"

"Mm-hmm." I crossed my arms and nodded my head.

They both stared at me suspiciously. Then we all burst out chuckling at the thought.

George lit a match and held it to the paper that rested underneath the twigs and larger pieces of wood. It ignited almost immediately and didn't fizzle out this time.

My mouth curved into a smirk.

"Shut up." Edgar shoved me in the shoulder.

"I didn't say anything, jeez!"

"You were thinking it."

I smiled and shrugged. He was right, the words *I told you so* were running through my head. I shoved him back just for fun.

George disappeared and returned with a beer for himself and two sodas for me and Edgar. "Cheers to the Indians and their secrets."

We stood around the fire sipping our drinks when my sister and Matthew walked up the driveway.

"What's everyone doing here?" Matthew looked at us, then turned toward Amelia.

My sister shrugged her shoulders. "Surprise?"

Edgar's mom stepped out of the back door, her hands full with a huge aluminum pan of BBQ pork. "Amelia, you two are early!" she shrieked, nearly dropping the food.

Matthew rushed to help his mother. "Let me take that."

He reached to grab the pan, but Ms. Gonzalez protested, "I got it. This was supposed to be all set up before you got here."

"And I appreciate that, but I also think everyone would appreciate eating their pork off a bun instead of the concrete."

His mom arched her eyebrows and pursed her lips. "Watch it or the pork won't be the only thing on the ground." The corner of her mouth curved into a smile, and she winked as she stepped down off the stoop.

I'd never seen her tease anyone before—she was always so serious. And in that moment, I saw the person that Edgar told me about when their father was still alive. A strong, confident, playful, loving mother. For the first time, I could see her beauty.

Matthew put his hands up to surrender. "Apparently it's my party, so no violence." He stepped back with a smile to let his mother pass.

A second later, my mom pushed through the back door holding an equally large tray of buns. She stopped abruptly at the sight of Matthew. "Amelia! You're early!"

My sister rolled her eyes. "The *one* time I'm early and everyone has a problem with it. This is why I'm always late. I get crap no matter what I do . . ."

"It's a surprise party, the one thing it's OK to be late to," my mom replied.

Matthew stepped in, attempting to defend my sister. "Ms. Marques, it's OK. I'm plenty surprised. Let me help you with that."

"Don't you dare. Now go have fun."

Once again, Matthew was defeated. He retreated to Amelia.

They both walked over to join us at the fire.

Edgar looked at me with a smirk and glanced over at his brother. I knew exactly what he was thinking. I nonchalantly slid to the other side of Matthew, so he was in between Edgar and me. We gave each other one last look to confirm the plan, then turned up toward Matthew. "SURPRISE!" we shouted at the top of our lungs.

It was immediately met with a shove from both of our siblings.

Before we could retaliate, George appeared behind us and handed Matthew a beer. "If you're old enough to fight for your country, you're old enough to have a drink."

Matthew accepted the beer. "Thanks, Uncle George, just don't let my mom see."

"Hey, it's your party, don't let those old ladies boss you around."

They clinked bottles and each took a sip.

"Hey now, careful who you call old ladies." Aunt Theresa appeared across from us at the fire. She was holding an oversize wineglass filled to the brim. Her dark hair was tucked under a maroon knit cap that matched the color of her wine almost perfectly.

"Who invited this one?" George motioned to Theresa. "Somebody call security."

"I would think twice about what you say, I have our freshman yearbook and I *will* bring it out. I'm sure everyone would love to see your marching band picture." Aunt Teri seemed to have the dirt on everyone.

"What, do you just drive around with it in your car in case you need to embarrass people?"

She shrugged and smiled as she took a sip of her wine.

George shook his head, then looked at Amelia. "Your aunt is a crazy lady."

Amelia shrugged, smiled, and stole the beer out of Matthew's hand to take a sip.

"Matthew, are you sure you know what kinda family you're getting yourself into here?"

Matthew slid his arm around my sister and pulled her to his side. "I don't know, Uncle George, I think you reap what you sow."

"Huh, give the kid a beer and this is how he repays me." George tipped his beer back to finish it. "See, you all are driving me to drinking."

Aunt Theresa rolled her eyes. "What's your excuse the other three hundred and sixty-four days of the year?"

"See what I mean, these old ladies are ruthless." George stepped over to the coolers to grab another beer.

"Hey, while you're over there?" Matthew raised his bottle, motioning that he needed a refill.

"Increíble!" George gruffed, but he returned with a smile and two beers.

Edgar's mom appeared again on the stoop by the back door, this time with a bottle of beer for herself in one hand and a fork in the other. She began tapping the fork on the bottle and everyone quieted. She froze for a moment, seeming overwhelmed. My mom appeared next to her with a full wineglass and gave her a playful nudge. They both took a sip from their beverages, then Edgar's mom began to speak.

"First, I want to thank everyone for showing up. I know a Tuesday evening isn't ideal for a party, so I wanted to make sure you know how much it means to us that you came. Having Matthew home this past week, well, it's put some things into perspective for me. I'm sure most of you . . ."

She paused for a moment. Her fingers wrapped tightly around her beer bottle as her eyes darted to the ground. My mom stepped forward and placed her hand gently on Mrs. Gonzalez's shoulder.

Edgar's mom cleared her throat and continued, "I'm sure you know I've been kind of lost since Leo died. This past year or so hasn't been my finest, and I want to apologize. I'm sorry to you all for how withdrawn I've been, most of all to Matthew and Edgar. You both deserve so much more, and I have let you down as your mother."

Her sadness dripped down her cheeks. I looked at Edgar. Tears formed at the corners of his eyes. I quickly looked away, knowing he would be embarrassed if I saw him cry. But my heart ached seeing him so sad. I knew this sorrow had been hiding somewhere deep within him for a while. He just never saw a point in letting it out until now. Silently, and without looking, I reached my hand over to find his. His fingers immediately tightened around mine. We had been close since the day we met but had never held hands. It didn't feel as awkward as I thought it might. It was actually sort of nice; it felt natural.

I was so preoccupied worrying about Edgar that I hadn't noticed Matthew standing next to his mother. He draped his arm around her as he began talking. "My mother, while well intentioned, doesn't know what she is talking about. She is a wonderful parent."

Everyone laughed briefly, and he continued, "If you knew my father, you know he was one of a kind. Irreplaceable. And if you knew my mother and father together, you know they were hopelessly in love till the day he died."

Edgar squeezed my hand tighter. We both continued to stare straight ahead as his brother spoke. "When my dad died, we all suffered an emptiness that is unable to be filled. But my mother lost her soulmate. I want to thank her for throwing me this incredibly thoughtful party. And thank you all for helping to make it happen. Let's raise a toast: to my dad and my mom, and to the love they created that will be forever present in our lives. Cheers! Let's party!"

Everyone raised their drinks and cheered loudly before taking a sip.

Edgar finally turned toward me. I didn't look at first,

unsure of what to say or do. Our hands remained clasped as I shifted my eyes to him. He nodded his head toward the front yard. I nodded back with a smile. We let go of each other's hands and sprinted down the driveway.

CHAPTER 18

We collapsed onto our hands and knees, huffing and puffing. The music and chatter of the party buzzed in the background. I turned to look at Edgar and was pleased to see a smile across his face. We took a seat on the front stoop.

"Your mom seems happy." Almost immediately as the words left my lips the smile disappeared from Edgar's face.

He stared down at the ground. I was unsure of what I said wrong, and I didn't want to risk saying anything else that might make it worse. Neither of us spoke for a few minutes. Usually I thought of the quiet as being peaceful, but this wasn't. There was a tension that saturated the silence and put a wedge between me and my friend. I didn't know why he was upset, but I felt like it was my fault. After what felt like an hour, Edgar spoke.

"I feel guilty." Tears formed in the corners of his eyes again. He clenched his jaw, trying to hold them back.

"Why?" I was confused. This was clearly bigger than anything I said.

He kept his focus on the ground and didn't respond right away. I joined him in staring down at the pavement, giving him time to think. Usually Edgar was the strong one. He seemed so self-assured and resolved. Even when his dad died, he kept such a positive perspective. Everything happens for a reason, he'd say, there are no coincidences, God has a plan. He seemed wise beyond his years, like he had lived before. I often looked to Edgar for answers and reassurance when things were bad. Now that the tables had turned, I wasn't sure I could fill his shoes.

"I let him down." He raised his stare toward the sky, blinking long and hard forcing the surplus of tears to stream down his cheeks.

"What do you mean?"

"My dad. He would be so disappointed in me." He dropped his head and looked back at the ground.

I turned toward him. My best friend. He had been holding in something big for so long and I never knew. How could I have never noticed? I felt like a bad friend. Edgar's tears fell onto the pavement, leaving little splotches beneath him. I wished I could make them stop. Maybe all he needed was someone to listen. I waited for him to continue.

"I blamed my mom for the way she was. I blamed her for being a bad mom." He closed his eyes and shook his head. "Sometimes I was so angry with her. But it wasn't her fault. And I should've been a better son. I should've seen that she just missed my dad so much. I should've been there more for her instead of being upset with her. My dad . . ."

Edgar paused to wipe his cheeks. "My dad would've expected better from me; he would've expected me to comfort her. Instead I pushed her away."

I thought of how my mom was upset earlier, and how helpless I felt wanting to take care of her but not knowing how. And how angry I was with her for hiding the truth about my dad. Nothing was clear-cut. Nobody was all good or all bad. A flood of emotion washed over me. Edgar had been carrying this for so long. I didn't know how to make him feel better, but I had to try.

"That's not how it works, Edgar. Whether you realize it or not, you are just a kid. We're nine years old. It's not your job to take care of your mom. She was sad, and that doesn't make her a bad mom, but you also aren't a bad son for how you felt. You're my best friend—I know you, and I know your dad would be proud of you."

Usually I struggled to find the right words in situations like this, or in any situation really. Talking wasn't my strong suit. But this was different. I didn't think, I just spoke. Edgar raised his head and turned toward me. We'd had plenty of conversations, some heart-to-heart, most just fun. But this felt different; it was beyond our years.

Edgar's eyes were still glossy, but he was no longer crying. "Do you really mean that?"

"You callin' me a liar?" I smirked.

"Well, maybe." The corner of his mouth curved into a smile.

"Of course I mean it. I'm proud to be your friend, and I know your dad would be proud of you."

"Thanks, Penny."

I looked back up at the stars. "Besides, he's probably up there looking down at all this and smiling."

"That's not how it works, Penny. Heaven isn't up in the stars."

"How do you know?"

"Because I'm smarter than you." We both laughed.

We lay back on the front stoop staring up at the twinkling sky.

"I've never seen a shooting star." I brought my hands up and rested them behind my head.

Edgar followed my adjustment and linked his fingers behind his head. "I've seen one when I was camping with my dad, up by Pike Lake. We caught a huge muskie that day, and we weren't even trying. It almost bit my dad's finger off!"

"My Uncle Theo told me we're all born from the stars."

"Like he thinks the stars are alive?" Edgar was genuinely

asking; I knew he wouldn't make fun of me or my uncle. I could tell him anything, that's how our friendship worked.

"No. I don't know. I think like we're made of the same material or something. I didn't really understand what he was talking about."

"Huh."

It was quiet for a moment as we watched for the sparse twinkles in the dark void.

"Edgar, if Heaven isn't in the sky, where is it?"

"I don't know." He paused for a moment. "I suppose it could be."

For some reason, that comforted me. "I like to think that it is up there, and everyone that's died is watching over us. And maybe shooting stars are people traveling to Heaven. I wonder if my grandma was a shooting star." I sighed. "But I know that's not what you believe."

He turned toward me. "Yeah, but it's OK if we don't believe in the same thing. My dad's best friend was an atheist."

"What's that?"

"A person that doesn't believe in anything."

"Oh." I looked back at the sky. "That sounds depressing."

Edgar laughed. "Yeah."

"Hey, you two!" a voice shouted from behind us. It was Matthew. "What, are you trying to ditch my party?"

Edgar and I sat up straight and whipped our heads around.

Tomas ran up behind Matthew laughing hysterically.

"What's so funny?" Matthew asked, suspicious of his friend.

"I just chucked a handful of bottle rockets in the fire!" Tomas answered, obviously pleased with himself.

"You idiot!"

A loud series of pops immediately followed. Edgar and I began laughing as hysterically as Tomas. Matthew rolled his eyes, not surprised by his friend's actions, and started pounding him in the shoulder repeatedly. Tomas scrambled around the driveway trying to dodge the blows.

Just then, Amelia appeared from the shadows. "Matt, your mom is asking to have a word with whichever friend it is of yours who put fireworks in the fire."

Tomas immediately put his hands up and began pleading, "Please don't tell her it was me, please! She scares me!"

Matthew grabbed him by the collar and dragged him up the driveway. Edgar and I followed, giggling at the show.

Tomas pleaded with Matthew the entire way but was shown no mercy. Mrs. Gonzalez was waiting at the back stoop with her arms crossed. Matthew shoved his friend forward like a sacrificial lamb.

"Mrs. Gonzalez, I'm sorry, it was just a prank. I didn't mean to upset you." Tomas began frantically apologizing but was quickly cut off.

"Save it. That was incredibly reckless. You could've hurt someone! Fireworks aren't toys, Tomas. I have half a mind to call your mother and have her come pick you up because I don't trust that you're in the right state of mind to drive, and clearly you aren't capable of making responsible decisions." Her words shot out like a rapid-fire assault, and she wasn't letting up.

Tomas couldn't get a word in even if he tried, so he just stared down at the ground pitifully, taking the barrage. Mrs. Gonzalez paused to take a breath and reload, and that's when Tomas was granted some reinforcement in the form of Edgar's uncle George.

"Woah, slow down there, Evelyn. Cut the kid a break, he was just having a little fun." He stepped in front of Tomas like a shield.

"I don't wanna hear it, George, that wasn't fun. It was dangerous and stupid."

George cracked open a beer and extended it toward her as a peace offering. "Nobody's arguing with that. He's a nineteen-year-old kid, dangerous and stupid is his default."

Evelyn rolled her eyes but let him continue.

"Let's not let it ruin Matthew's party. Here, take this beer and go relax by the fire. I'll keep an eye on mister firecracker here and make sure he doesn't do anything else that stupid."

She sighed loudly and clutched the beer. "Fine. Only because I don't have the energy to deal with this any further. He's your responsibility." She took a sip of beer and sauntered over to the fire without another word.

The second she was out of earshot, Tomas shoved Matthew in the shoulder. "Thanks for the backup," he said sarcastically.

Matthew laughed. "Don't blame me for your mess. You know my mom—like I'm gonna defend you after that stunt."

"Well, I got a whole trunkful of Roman candles with your name on it and one five-hundred-gram megablaster, guaranteed to last three minutes."

"Well, that's definitely a record for you." Matthew, Amelia, and Gorge all burst out laughing.

I didn't understand the joke but chuckled to feel included.

Edgar turned toward me. "I'm thirsty. You want a soda?"

"Sure, I can grab 'em. What do you want?"

"Root beer."

I nodded and headed to the coolers by the back porch. One was filled with beer and the other with sodas and water. I dug through the second one searching for root beer. All that was left was 7-Up and ginger ale, beverages only the sick wanted. I slammed the cooler shut and headed inside to check the fridge. Bowls of chips and other various snacks were spread across the table. I grabbed a handful of pretzels and shoved them into my mouth, then opened the refrigerator. As I scanned the shelves for root beer, I heard a voice coming from the other room. It sounded like my mom's, but it was hushed, like she was trying to not be heard. I gently shut the refrigerator door and tiptoed toward the hallway to get a better listen.

"I told you. I can't talk about this right now. I can't believe you called Teri's cell phone. That is way out of line."

Who called Aunt Theresa's phone? I listened intently for clues.

"Yeah, I know she wrote to you, that doesn't mean you should come see her . . . Why not!? Because—" My mom stuttered for a moment, like she didn't know what to say. "Because, Loren, she's nine. She wants a lot of things that she shouldn't have."

It was my dad. He had gotten my letter and was trying even harder to be a part of my life now. And my mom wouldn't let him. Resentment burned in my chest. I wanted to run in there and rip the phone out of her hand and talk to my dad. Instead, I forced myself to listen a little longer.

"No, I didn't give her the ones you wrote back to her. I don't think it's a good idea right now . . . No, I don't know when or even if I will . . . This is not about me or us! It's about protecting Penny . . ."

I'd heard all I needed. A lump swelled in my throat, but my veins coursed with anger. I turned toward the back door, shoving a kitchen chair into the table on my way. It shifted the whole table backward and knocked a bowl of chips onto the floor. The bang was surely heard by my mom and probably most of the people outside. I pushed through the screen door and made a beeline to my bike. I didn't stop until I got home.

* * *

I chucked my bike onto the back lawn and ran upstairs. It wasn't until I got upstairs that I realized I was crying.

Betrayal and disappointment overwhelmed me. How could my mom do this to me, to my dad? I wasn't a little kid that needed protection. I wanted to know my dad, and he wanted to know me. Who was she to stand in the way? I stormed to my bedroom, determined to do something. Maybe I'd run away to go visit my dad. I knew where he lived. I could pack a bag tonight and empty my piggy bank. It seemed like a plan. A plan that was abruptly cut short when I arrived at my bedroom and saw Uncle Bobby standing in my room.

He hovered over a pile of my *Cat Fancy* magazines, clutching my grandmother's Bible in his hands, the one he had given me that day in the driveway. I'd buried it under my magazines, and now the cover and first few pages were bent and torn. I froze in the doorway. His head whipped in my direction. I was like a deer in headlights. His eyes glared at me.

"This is how you treat your grandmother's Bible!"

My mouth opened to speak but no sound came out.

"What do you have to say for this?" He held up the tattered Bible. "How are you going to fix this?"

His screaming made the hair on my neck stand up. I suddenly realized that I was alone with him. My mom and sister were at the party, and who knew when they'd be home.

Uncle Bobby charged toward me, shoving the Bible in my face. "Look at what you did!"

"I . . . I didn't mean to," I squeaked.

"You didn't mean to. Well, that just makes it all better."

Even at nine I understood sarcasm, but I didn't know how to respond.

"And what's this!?" He motioned at the dream catcher hanging above my bed. "You destroy the word of God, and you have this sacrilegious symbol hanging over you."

"I didn't . . . it's not . . ."

Henry was lying on the bed, and I wished more than anything that I could run over and hug him.

"This unholy thing doesn't belong under this roof!" Uncle Bobby ripped the dream catcher down and shook it toward me. "This is garbage!"

Just then, Henry awoke and saw the dangling feathers in the air. It activated his hunting instinct. He sprung up and batted playfully at the feathers. His paw accidentally caught Uncle Bobby on the hand, drawing blood. Bobby flinched, dropping the dream catcher.

"Agghhhh!" He yelled with anger, then reached down to grab Henry by the back of the neck. Henry hissed and swatted but couldn't reach Bobby.

"Stop! Put him down!" I screamed and lunged toward them, trying to free Henry. Bobby reached his arm out and flung me across the room. I landed by my dresser. My mind raced, trying to think of how to save Henry. He hung helpless in Bobby's grasp. I turned and saw my slingshot resting behind my dresser. My hand quickly reached to retrieve it. A basket of marbles sat under my bed. I scrambled to grab a handful and loaded the slingshot. Without thinking, I began to fire. My first couple of shots did little but grab his attention. But as I adjusted my aim, I began to hit him. My last two marbles hit him directly in the forehead. He threw Henry into the wall and lunged at me. I rolled out of the way and stared at Henry's lifeless body lying on the floor. I knew cats could survive falling from great heights, but being thrown into a wall was a completely different story. I scrambled toward Henry, but Bobby was there to stop me. He grabbed my foot and dragged me backward. I kicked uncontrollably, screaming for help at the top of my lungs.

After what seemed like forever, my mom and Amelia appeared in the doorway to my rescue.

"Let go of her!" Amelia yelled.

Bobby's head whipped up. It was like he was in a trance, and my sister's voice snapped him out of it. He let go of my foot and took a step backward.

"Bobby, what are you doing?" My mom's voice sounded more concerned than angry.

I rushed over to Henry. He was motionless.

"Penny, are you OK?" My sister crouched down next to me.

"He threw Henry into the wall," I sobbed.

Amelia was already furious, but when she saw what Uncle Bobby did to Henry, she lost it. "Get out of here!" She sprung to her feet and started toward him.

My mom stepped in between them. "Amelia, calm down."

"Calm down? He's a violent drunk who attacked your daughter and Henry. Get him out of here!"

My mom glanced over at me and saw Henry lying on the floor. "Is he OK?"

"He's not moving." I reached my hand out to gently pet his side, hoping it would wake him. It didn't.

"Bobby, you need to go." My mom spoke quietly and calmly, but her voice was firm. Without another word, she turned away from her brother and knelt beside me.

Bobby slunk past us to leave, clutching Grandma Margery's Bible at his side. Amelia watched him leave, then positioned herself next to the doorway. "Is Henry breathing?

I looked closely for any movement. His side was rising and falling, faintly. My mom reached her hand out to pet his face; still no response. "Amelia, honey, can you go check the yellow pages for emergency vets?"

Amelia nodded and rushed out of the room. My mom turned toward me. "Penny, can you grab a sheet from the closet? We're gonna try to gently slide Henry on it so we can move him without jostling him too much."

"OK." I jumped to my feet.

That's when we heard the can opener going off in the kitchen. I looked at my mom, and she was just as perplexed as me. Before either of us could say anything, Henry's eyes squinted open and he wiggled to his feet. He quickly trotted out of the room toward the sound. My mom and I leaped to our feet and hurried to follow. When we arrived in the kitchen, we saw Amelia bent down with a can of tuna fish and Henry ravenously scarfing down as much as he could.

My mom shook her head and smiled. "Well, I guess that saved us a vet bill."

"I figured it was worth a try." Amelia shrugged. I bent down and scratched Henry behind the ears, one of his favorite spots. He responded with a low purr as he continued eating. The amazing Henry, brought back to life by food.

CHAPTER 19

I was so happy that Henry was OK I'd forgotten the whole reason I fled the party. Now that the chaos had subsided, my memory began to return. I looked over at my mom, who was giving Henry a pat-down from head to tail to make sure he wasn't injured anywhere. A twinge of anger sparked in my chest, but I let it pass. On top of being emotionally drained, I was too relieved that my sister and mom had come to my rescue to be mad at the moment. However, me leaving the party in such a dramatic fashion was something that would not be ignored.

"Penny, why did you storm out of the party?" My mom was the one who broached the subject, not realizing what she was stepping into.

The words crept up my throat. Maybe it would be better just to confront her about what I'd overheard. But I was more like my mother than I realized, and I decided it would be easier to avoid an argument for now. I cleared my throat, trying to figure out what to say.

Luckily, Amelia sensed my hesitation and jumped in to save me. "Yeah, what happened with Bobby? Are you OK?"

"He got mad because some pages in Grandma Margery's Bible got bent underneath my magazines."

"What an asshole."

"Amelia Grace, watch your language." Our mother tried to scold her, but we both knew it was in vain. What Bobby did was way worse than any word we could say.

"When he grabbed Henry, I was so scared. I got my slingshot and popped him right between the eyes! It was just like David and Goliath!"

Talking about it all gave me a little rush of adrenaline and the words just kept spilling out. "That's when he came after me. I got him twice in the forehead with a marble and he threw Henry and grabbed me. It all happened so fast; I was trying to get to Henry to see if he was OK but Uncle Bobby dragged me back. I thought for sure he was gonna throw me into the wall too. But then you guys came to save me."

I paused to take a breath. My mom and sister weren't used to me talking so much. They both stared at me, waiting to see if I was done. I wasn't. "I don't know what would've happened if you didn't come. Uncle Bobby was so mad. How did you guys know to come get me?"

"We came to make sure you were OK. You left the party without saying anything to anybody."

It was at that moment, when I looked at Amelia, that I realized what I had dragged her away from. It was her last night with Matthew, and she had to leave him because of me. And then I thought about Edgar and how worried he probably was as well. When you're a kid, I guess you don't always realize how your actions affect other people. My mouth opened, but the stream of words that had gushed out just moments earlier was severed. All I could come up with was "Oh."

My mother, seemingly oblivious to my attitude change, picked up on the one detail of my story that only a mother would. "Slingshot? What slingshot? Where in the world did you get a slingshot?"

My eyes met my sister's. I didn't want to tell my mom it was her that got me the slingshot, so I just froze. Luckily, my sister was better on her feet than me. "Who cares where she got it? I'm just glad she had it. Uncle Bobby deserves that and worse. Where is he anyway? Penny is probably scared to fall asleep knowing he is still under this roof."

My mom looked at me and I nodded sheepishly, trying to look as pathetic as possible. She fell for it. "You girls stay here and watch over Henry, I'll see if I can find Bobby and talk to him." She stepped toward the back door, then paused. "Penny, are you OK?"

"Yeah, I'm OK."

The corner of her mouth curved into a sympathetic look of acknowledgment and sorrow for what I had just been through. With a small nod, she turned and headed out the back door.

I gave Henry a hug and looked up at Amelia. "I'm sorry I made you leave Matthew's party."

"It's OK, I'm glad I did. Who knows what would've happened if we didn't follow you."

"Yeah, but I ruined your last night with Matthew."

"The party was winding down anyway. Matthew's helping his mom clean up and then he's coming over here. You didn't ruin anything."

"OK." I still felt bad, but my sister's words helped.

"Why *did* you storm out of the party like that?"

I knew I had to tell her. Despite what I thought her reaction might be, I couldn't keep it a secret any longer. "Mom was talking to Dad. She was on the phone with him at the party and I overheard it all."

Amelia looked at me quizzically. "What would she be talking to Dad about?"

This was the part I was dreading telling her. I closed my eyes and swallowed hard, like I was gagging down medicine. With a long exhale, I began explaining, "I wrote him a letter. Well, you know how I found out he had been writing to Mom, and us? I copied down his address and wrote him back. He's been reaching out, wanting to see us, and Mom has been hiding it. And he even wrote a letter back to me and she didn't tell me. That's what I overheard at the party. He called her on Aunt Theresa's phone, and she was arguing with him about my letter and about seeing us."

My sister's silence was unbearable. Was she angry with me for reaching out to our dad, or for hiding it from her? Or was she upset with our mom for withholding the letters? Or maybe she was sad about our dad? My mind raced, trying to figure out what she was thinking. I stared down at Henry, afraid to look at her.

"Wow."

Her response didn't give me any more insight, but at least she wasn't yelling at me.

"When did you write Dad?"

I continued staring down at Henry as I spoke. "A few weeks ago. He'd been sending letters for Mom to Aunt Theresa's house."

"Why didn't you tell me?"

"I thought you'd be mad or think I was dumb for reaching out to him. You said you didn't want to see him again after he left. But maybe he's changed—he really wants to see us. And I hardly have any memories of him, and what I can remember isn't bad. I just really want to meet him and see what he's like, what it's like to have a dad." I rambled on, hoping if I could get her to understand my side of things, she wouldn't be upset with me.

"I can't believe Mom's been keeping this from us."

Relief flooded over me like a warm blanket. "You're not mad at me?"

"No, Penny. I mean, yeah, I don't really have much of a desire to see Dad, but I understand that it's different for you. And if he's been reaching out . . . I don't know, it's been a while, maybe he's gotten better."

I felt stupid for not telling my sister sooner. Of course she would understand. "So, what do we do?"

"We have to confront Mom. It's not just her choice to make, and she needs to realize that."

I nodded. My sister was a force to be reckoned with, and now that I had her on my side, I felt confident that I would get to see my dad, one way or another.

We heard footsteps coming up the back hall, and our focus shifted toward the door as we waited to see who it was. My heart pounded beneath my chest in anticipation, hoping it wasn't my uncle. The door cracked and Matthew stepped through. I exhaled and felt my muscles relax. I hadn't even realized I was tensing them.

"Hey, you two, is everything OK?"

I watched as my sister's face lit up just at the sight of him. She stood to greet him. "Yeah, sort of."

Matthew looked from Amelia to me, then back to Amelia, waiting for one of us to explain. My sister took his hand and guided him to a chair at the table. "You might wanna sit down, there's a lot . . ."

As she began filling Matthew in, my mind wandered to Edgar. He was the person I always talked these things through with. I wondered if he was still up; maybe I could ride back over there. I looked at the clock: 9:30 p.m. It was too late, even if we both didn't have school tomorrow. I would have to find a way to meet up with him tomorrow. Now that his mom had lightened up a little, maybe we'd get to hang out more often. I shifted my attention back to the conversation. Amelia was just finishing up the part about Uncle Bobby. Matthew's hands slowly tensed into fists as my sister described how our uncle had dragged me across the carpet. Before she could finish, Matthew's chair shot out backward and he was standing.

"Where is he? I don't want you guys to stay here if he's here, he's getting worse. I don't like this at all."

"It'll be OK, our mom went to talk to him. She actually

seemed like she was going to do something about it this time, and Bobby is mostly talk."

Amelia's words did little to reassure Matthew, but there was little he could do, and he realized that. He relaxed his fist and took my sister's hand as he sat back down. "Promise me that if he even threatens to lay a hand on you or Penny again, you'll go stay with my mom until he's gone."

It was an argument my sister didn't want to have, especially on Matthew's last night. She nodded. "I promise we will be OK."

I wondered if Matthew noticed how she changed his words. He looked over at me and Henry sitting on the floor like he was silently asking us to hold Amelia to her promise. I knew she would protect us the best she could, but Uncle Bobby scared me. I didn't trust him when he was drinking, which seemed to be more and more lately. I tried to picture what it would be like to stay with Edgar and his mom. Living with my best friend seemed like it could be pretty cool. But what about Henry, and my mom, and all of my stuff? I shook the image out of my mind. Amelia was right, we would be fine. I retreated to my bedroom, ignoring the doubt that ached in the pit of my stomach.

* * *

The next afternoon, we said goodbye to Matthew. I was surprised by how sad I felt. Matthew had become a consistent presence since he came home. He'd brought so much happiness and excitement that I was worried he'd take it with him when he left. I stood in Edgar's driveway with my bike between my legs and watched as he said goodbye to his family. His mother wiped her eyes and hugged her eldest son tight. Despite the tears, she still seemed happy. The fog that was lifted with Matthew's arrival would hopefully never return. Edgar didn't cry. To an outside observer, it might not even appear that he was upset at all.

But I saw the way his chest rose and fell with each shallow breath, and how he fidgeted with his fingers. I saw the way he stared his brother up and down intently, trying to memorize every piece of him. And when Matthew bent to give him a hug, Edgar collapsed into his arms as if his legs had just given out. He pressed his head into Matthew's chest and clung to his uniform like he was trying to absorb this moment into his soul. With the holidays coming up in a few months, it probably wouldn't be that long before they saw each other again. But something about that hug made it feel like this was the last time.

Matthew broke away and squeezed Edgar on the shoulder. With one last wave to me and his mom, he turned and followed Amelia into our mom's car. She was taking him to the airport to say goodbye there. After they drove off, I was scared to look at Edgar. I wanted to be there for him, but I wasn't good at handling my own emotions, let alone someone else's. I stared down the empty road, pretending I was still watching the car.

"Hey!" Edgar's voice startled me.

My head whipped around to face him.

"Race ya to the river?"

"You're on!" I gripped my handlebar like I was revving the engine on a motorcycle.

Edgar ran to the backyard and returned on his bike. He stopped next to his mom. "I'll be home before dark."

"*Well* before dark," she said sternly, still drying her eyes.

"OK."

I shuffled to turn my bike around as Edgar began pedaling. By the time I was facing the right direction, he was turning out of the driveway. "Hey! Cheater!"

I pedaled furiously to catch up. It was close, but I never took the lead. Edgar skidded to a stop at the river a few seconds before me.

"You . . . are such . . . a cheater," I shouted between gasps.

"You are such a sore loser." Edgar wasn't even out of breath.

We ditched our bikes on the bank and headed toward the water. It was too chilly to wade in, so we scoured the ground for any debris to throw.

I spotted a huge stick and bent to pick it up. "So, did your mom get abducted by aliens or something?"

Edgar let out a sound that was a mix between a laugh and a cough. "What?"

"Come on, she's like a completely different person. She's letting us hang out. She didn't even give you a hard time about biking with me. You didn't even wear your helmet!"

Edgar reached one hand up and brushed the top of his head, double-checking that I was correct. "Oh no, I'm gonna hear about that."

"She saw you leave and didn't say anything."

"Yeah. I'm still gonna hear about it."

"Do you think she'll stay like this?" Hope rose in my voice.

Edgar bent down to pick up a stick. "Maybe. I told you she used to be like this all the time."

"I know, it's just weird to actually see it for myself."

Edgar nodded and changed the subject. "Bet I can hit that log." He motioned to a log on the other side of the river that extended into the water a few feet.

"No way."

He cocked his arm back and released the stick into the air. It landed with a splash only halfway across, nowhere near the log. We both laughed.

"Well, even I can do better than that."

"Come on, Penny, haven't you heard the saying 'you throw like a girl'?"

He knew that would get under my skin. I glared. "Yeah, well, I am a girl. And we both know that saying doesn't apply to me."

I chucked the stick as hard as I could and made it within one to two feet of the log. "Ha!" I wiggled my shoulders back and forth in a celebratory dance.

Edgar shook his head and smiled. "You dork."

I shrugged and continued looking for things to throw.

"My mom said we're going to visit Matthew over Thanksgiving. She already bought the plane tickets to Arizona. I can't wait. I've never been on a plane!" Excitement reverberated through Edgar's voice.

"Aww, that's so cool!"

"I think it'll help my mom too, giving her something to look forward to."

I nodded. I couldn't get over how different Edgar's mom was. Grief and sadness have a way of bringing things out of people that you didn't know were there. Edgar's mom had retreated inside of herself, trying to bring Edgar with her because she was afraid to lose anyone else. Her heart was broken, but it still fought to protect the ones she loved. Maybe she didn't really change. She was the same person at her core, but it was the despair in her life that had brought out a version of her that lay dormant. It was a version that seemed unrecognizable to those who thought they knew her. As I grew older, I began to learn that a person's heart is unwavering. Who you are is who you are, but how you behave is heavily influenced by your environment and things that happen to you—good or bad. I'd learn not to fully trust anyone who I didn't see struggle. It's your worst moments that define you.

The setting sun twinkled on the water, creating a magical lighting. My eyes shifted to Edgar. He was staring across the river watching for fish to jump. In just a few weeks, this spot would look drastically different. The leaves were already starting to fall from the trees. Soon they would blanket the ground and the trees would be bare for winter. It seemed to me like it should be the other way around, but sometimes the world just doesn't make sense the way you think it should.

"I better get home soon. If I'm late, it's guaranteed that my mom will never let me out again." Edgar was still staring out over the water.

"Do you think she will if you're on time?"

Edgar nodded. "Yeah, I think so."

A cool breeze danced through the trees, nudging a few leaves to the ground and raising goose bumps on my arms. The sudden chill reminded me that Halloween was coming up. It usually didn't matter what costume you chose because there was a 90 percent chance it'd be covered up with a winter coat. But that didn't diminish any of the fun of getting a sackful of free candy. I was excited. "Hey! We have to go trick-or-treating together! I'm totally gonna be an X-Man. I don't know which one yet, probably Wolverine."

Edgar's focus shifted from the water to me. "That's like a month away."

"So?"

"So how do you already know what you're gonna be?"

"How do you not?"

Edgar laughed. "Because it's a whole month away!"

"Well, I like to be prepared. Now, are we going together or not? I'll help you pick your costume because you clearly need some ideas."

"Yeah, yeah, yeah, I'll go with you."

"Good."

Edgar crouched down and started digging in the dirt with a stick. "You know, I did have one costume idea that I've been planning for a while."

"What!"

"Wolverine."

"Shut up, I'm Wolverine!" I shoved him in the shoulder, almost knocking his butt to the ground.

"We can both be Wolverine."

"No! There's only *one* Wolverine!"

Edgar looked up at me and shrugged. "Fine. Then you can be Rogue."

"No. You can be Cyclops."

"Never!" he shouted. We both hated Cyclops and thought he was the most whiny of all the X-Men.

"Well then, I don't know what to tell you. I am Wolverine." I was resolved. To be honest, I was wavering back and forth between Rogue and Wolverine up until that very moment.

Satisfied that I had won, I crouched down next to Edgar and helped him dig. He reached to his left and grabbed two more sticks. "See, this proves it."

When I glanced over at him, he had positioned each of his three sticks in between his fingers like Wolverine's claws and was holding his hand up to my face.

"I. Am. Wolverine." He whispered for dramatic effect.

I rolled my eyes and shoved him to the ground. It didn't take much because he was already squatting.

"Hey!" He quickly pushed himself up but not before the butt of his pants was covered in dirt.

I started giggling in anticipation of the obvious and childish joke I was about to make. "You pooped your pants!" I put one hand to my stomach as it heaved with laughter.

Edgar immediately took that opportunity to shove me back, knocking me into the dirt and leaving me in the same state that he was in. "Now who pooped their pants!"

We both collapsed in hysteria. It was uncontrollable. The more I laughed, the more Edgar laughed, and vice versa. It was an endless cycle until we were both left lying on our sides gasping for air. A wave of pure joy spread through my body. There was nothing on my mind except being there in that exact moment with my best friend. It was a rare thing to feel nothing but pure happiness, and it got rarer and rarer with each year. That memory of laughing with Edgar on that riverbank would forever be in my mind as one of the happiest moments of my life.

The sun was nearly under the trees across the river, leaving our side in the shadows. Edgar pushed himself to his feet. "We should go, it's getting dark."

"OK." I took a deep breath and sat up.

Edgar brushed off his pants and extended his hand down to me. We hopped on our bikes and hurried down the trail. Soon we were at the split-off.

"I'll see you later!" I called as I turned off to the left.

"See you later," Edgar called back.

"I'm Wolverine!" I shouted one last time. He shouted something back, but I was already too far away to hear him. His voice drifted off into the trees, the sound waves scattering and dissolving before they reached my ears.

* * *

When I got home, Amelia was in the kitchen arguing with my mom. I got to the top of the back steps and heard them. They were talking about Bobby. I paused and sat down quietly, pretending to fix my shoelace.

"There's nothing to explain. He should not be here."

I heard my mom sigh, and I pictured her sitting at the table with her hand to her forehead. "It's more complicated than you realize. If you would give me a chance to explain, then maybe you'll understand."

"Fine. What is the reason that your drunk, abusive, self-righteous, hypocrite brother should be allowed to stay under this roof?" There was a sharpness to Amelia's voice that I wasn't sure my mom deserved.

It was quiet for a moment. "Something happened . . ." My mom's voice cracked, and she was quiet again. I felt bad for her, like my sister was being too harsh. It wasn't my mom's fault that Bobby was the way he was. I had to do something to ease the conversation. Just as I was about to burst through the back door, my mom cleared her throat and continued, "After I moved out to be with your father, something happened to Bobby."

"Yeah, he went nuts under your mom's religious rule."

"No, Amelia." My mom's voice was soft and somber.

I heard a chair being pulled out as Amelia sat down at the table. "OK, what happened?" She wasn't arguing anymore.

"Your uncle was only eight when I moved out. I had taken care of him while I lived there, so when I left, he was mostly on his own. Grandma Margery was so involved in the church and had so many different groups she ran. If Bobby didn't go with her, he was alone." My mom cleared her throat again. "One afternoon, he was walking home from the church, and one of the neighbors saw him. The neighbor asked if Bobby wanted to go fishing at a nearby creek, said he knew the best spot but that it was a secret. Bobby knew better than to get in a car with a stranger, but this was a neighbor, so Bobby went with. It took him almost two years to tell anyone what happened to him at that creek. Two years he kept that inside of him, and I was living my life oblivious to his pain. And when he finally told me, all I could think was if I hadn't moved out, I could've been there for him. I would've been with him, and that guy would've never thought about approaching him." Her voice was heavy with years of hidden regret.

I had watched enough *Dateline* and *America's Most Wanted* to fill in the awful details that my mom had left out. My thoughts spiraled, trying to make sense of what I'd just overheard. That could've been me; I walk home alone all the time. Would Bobby be nicer if that hadn't happened to him? How could I blame him for anything after what he had been through? I looked from the back door to the door to the attic where Bobby stayed, then down to my feet. Maybe my uncle deserved a break.

Amelia seemed to disagree. "Mom, that's terrible. Really, really terrible." She took a breath. "But it's not your fault, and it doesn't excuse his behavior. Yes, Bobby needs help, but he can't get it here. It's not safe for him to be here. Think about Penny."

"I'm not leaving him again. He knows what he did was wrong, and it won't happen again. He promised he wouldn't come down here again without our permission."

"You can't really believe that." My sister was very good at not letting her emotions cloud logic.

"He's staying in the attic and that's the end of the discussion."

Amelia knew there was nothing she could say to change our mother's mind, so she changed the subject. "Fine. So why won't you give us the letters Dad's been writing? Penny said he wants to see us. If you let Bobby around, I don't see why Dad shouldn't be allowed too."

That was my cue to enter the conversation. I stood up and pushed through the back door. My mom's eyes darted toward me, filled with worry. She turned back toward Amelia. "Not now." She spoke quietly and shook her head.

"Hey, what's going on?" My voice was unnaturally high pitched. I was trying too hard to cover up the fact that I had been listening.

"Nothing, honey. How was your time with Edgar?"

Amelia cut off my answer, not letting our mom ignore the topic at hand. "Mom, you have to let Dad be part of our lives. Penny wants to see him."

I froze, debating whether to say something. Just as I opened my mouth to speak, my mom cut me off.

"Now is not the time for this. I'm going to bed." She stood and walked out of the room without another glance in my direction.

Looking back on it, I could see where my mother was coming from. That was not the right time for Amelia to bring up our father. And that's exactly why my sister did. She was trying to get back at my mom for continuing to allow Bobby to stay with us, for putting him before her own children. They were both right to feel the way they did. But feelings didn't affect the truth. Bobby needed help, and it was only a matter of time before something else happened.

CHAPTER 20

The next few weeks went by without any interactions with Uncle Bobby. It seemed like he was taking my mother's words seriously. I'd see his truck pull in or out of the driveway and could sometimes hear his television sermons blasting from the attic, but he was doing a good job at staying away. I wondered how he was filling his time outside of work, until I saw the recycling bin overflowing with beer cans. I didn't care though; as long as he wasn't around me, he could drink all he wanted. It didn't seem to fit with his religious obsession, but if God forgave all who believed in Him, then maybe that's how Uncle Bobby justified his weakness.

Amelia was spending her days working and studying and most of her nights talking with Matthew. Our mom hadn't brought up our father since Amelia interrogated her about it. I was so preoccupied with school and hanging out with Edgar that I didn't bring it up either. But I hadn't forgotten, and it was made clear on the first Friday in October that Amelia hadn't either.

The school bell rang and I raced out the door toward freedom. Edgar was going to a movie with his mom, so I wasn't going to see him, but that didn't make me any less excited for the weekend. I stepped out onto the playground and the crisp air filled my lungs. It was a perfect cloudy and cold autumn day. The kind that made you want to carve pumpkins and watch scary movies. We'd already covered the Freddy Krueger series, so this year we'd have to move on to Michael Myers. Edgar would have to sneak over to watch them with me and Amelia, but it wouldn't be the first time. I scanned the sky for any signs of snowflakes, but it wasn't quite cold enough. My hands reached back, struggling to pull my hood out from under my backpack. I lifted it over my head and began to walk home.

"Penny!" a voice called from behind me.

I turned around to see Jane's car. Amelia was in the passenger's seat with the window rolled down. I walked over. "What are you doing here?"

"You wanna go see Dad?"

"What? How? Did you talk to Mom?" It seemed too good to be true, but I knew my sister wouldn't ask unless she was serious.

"I got his address, he's only a two-hour drive away. I already told Mom we were taking you to see a movie, so we have plenty of time."

I hesitated. "Are you sure?"

"It's worth a try, right?"

I nodded and hopped into the back seat. Jane pulled away from the curb and excitement fluttered in my stomach. I was finally going to see my dad! Suddenly, my mind was flooded with all different scenarios and questions. Did he live in a house or an apartment? Was he tall or short? Did he have a beard? Where did he work? Did I look like him? I imagined us pulling up and him standing out front waiting to greet us. A warmth spread through my chest as I pictured him hugging us and welcoming us inside. I couldn't believe that in less than two hours I'd be with my dad!

About halfway there, we pulled into a gas station. We each made a trip to the bathroom and Amelia let me pick out a snack. I got a soda and a pack of Dubble Bubble and set them on the counter. Amelia looked at my choice and then at me. "Are you sure that's all you want?"

I nodded. I wanted to save room because I thought once we met up with our father, we might all have dinner together. Maybe I could even talk him into getting ice cream! We walked back to the car as I pondered what his favorite ice cream flavor was. I spent the rest of the drive popping bubbles in the back seat and dancing to the radio. Amelia and Jane took turns picking different radio stations and talking about their boyfriends. Jane swore that she and Tomas weren't dating. I had seen enough of their interactions to know that she was lying, even if she didn't realize it. It didn't matter what she wanted to call it, her and Tomas were not just friends. I stared out the window trying to decide whether a lie was still a lie if the person telling it was too oblivious to realize that they weren't being honest. It seemed like a question for Edgar. He had an answer for everything. I couldn't wait to tell him about my father.

We turned off the two-lane highway and onto a dirt road. The car tires stirred up a thick red dust that trailed behind us. I sat forward, trying to get a glimpse of my dad's house as we approached. At first there was nothing, just dirt road as far as I could see. Then a tree appeared with a tire swing hanging from the largest branch. Then a garage with a bike lying on the ground in front. It was a child's bike, with training wheels and a pink ribbon hanging from the handlebars. Did my dad know we were coming? Did he get me a bike? I'd have to break it to him that he missed my training wheel years. Finally, his house appeared in full view. It had a huge front porch with two large potted plants on either side of the steps.

We pulled up and parked in front of the bike. Amelia turned to look back at me. "You ready?"

I nodded. My hand reached to open the door, and I took

a step out. A figure appeared on the porch. He was tall, dark-haired, with a bronze complexion and dark stubble on his face. His eyes were what stood out the most. They were piercing blue, so bright that they were almost glowing. The flutter in my stomach rose to my chest and pounded through my heart. It was him, my dad! I slammed the car door shut, ready to sprint to give him a hug. But before I could take a step, my body froze. A small figure appeared behind him. My mind raced, trying to figure out what was going on. Were we at the wrong house?

The figure pawed at his side, then pointed in our direction. "Who that?"

"Honey, go back inside for now." The man turned and ushered the girl through the front door of the house.

Amelia looked at me with concern in her eyes. "Penny, hold on. I'm going to go talk to him first."

I nodded and watched her head up the path. I wanted to ask her if that was really our dad, but she would've told me if it wasn't. He walked down the steps to meet her. I watched them talk, trying to figure out what was being said. He looked in my direction, then back at Amelia. A smile rose on his face and he called out, "Penny?"

He motioned for me to come over, but my sister stepped in his way, pushing his arm down. My curiosity was too strong to stand still. I took a few hesitant steps forward. I could barely make out their words.

"Let me talk to her first." Amelia was still blocking him from me.

I took a few more steps forward.

My dad peered around her to get another glimpse of me. "She's still my daughter—you are both still my daughters. Nothing has changed that."

"I don't know." Amelia sounded sad.

I took a few more steps forward until I was standing

only a few feet from them. My dad nodded for Amelia to turn around.

"Penny, I told you to wait." She sounded upset, but I didn't think it was with me.

"What's going on?"

Amelia looked from me to my dad. He waited for her to explain.

"Penny, it's my fault, I'm so sorry. I shouldn't have brought you here like this."

"What are you talking about?" Her explanation did little to help me understand. I looked up at the towering figure before me. "Are . . . are you my dad?"

He collapsed to his knees and extended his arms. "Yes, my little Penny-pot, I am."

I leaned into him, and his arms wrapped around me like a warm blanket. It was just as I had imagined. He was perfect. My mom was wrong—he had changed. He was a good dad. He was a good man. Maybe she would see that and want him back and we could all live together. I pictured us playing catch in the driveway and basketball in the backyard, and having family dinners at the kitchen table. My heart beamed.

Then I heard a yell from the front door; it was the tiny figure again, a little girl. "Papa! Mommy wants you!"

I immediately recoiled from the hug. My dad turned toward the girl. "OK, Addy, tell her just a minute."

"Mommy said now."

I stared at the little girl standing behind the screen door. She looked about three years old, not much younger than I was when my dad left. Her blond curls bunched messily around her head, a stark contrast from my and Amelia's dark hair. She glanced at me, then back to her father. Our father. My eyes welled with disappointment. This wasn't how it was supposed to go. How could he rejoin our family if he had a whole other family here? I felt replaced and betrayed.

Someone appeared behind the girl, her mother. I saw where the blond curls came from. She also shared my father's dark complexion, but the uneven lines on her shoulders suggested it was a leftover tan from summer. She was beautiful. "Loren, what's going on? Dinner is getting cold."

"Holly, these are my daughters."

I glared at my father, swallowing my tears and turning them into anger. This was his family now. I didn't belong here. He ushered his new wife and daughter out to the porch. I didn't give him the chance to introduce me. I turned and sprinted back down the path and jumped in the back seat of the car. Jane looked through the rearview mirror at me. "You OK?"

I clenched my teeth and watched out the window. My father started after me, but my sister stopped him. She argued with him for a moment until he nodded and took a step back. Her hand rose to give a subtle wave goodbye to the wife and daughter, then she walked to the car and slid into the front seat. "Let's go, Jane."

Jane looked at my father and his family watching us from the front porch. "Are you sure?"

"Yeah, it was a mistake to come here like this." Amelia looked back at me, but I kept my eyes fixed out of the window.

My dad waved as we pulled away. Sadness hung on his face. We drove back down the dirt road, and I fought the urge to look back. The trip home was much quieter. I pictured my dad sitting at his kitchen table eating dinner with his new family. Laughing and talking about their day while they passed the peas and mashed potatoes around the table. His wife smiling and dancing as they did the dishes together, his daughter and her curly hair bouncing around the kitchen behind them. Then I imagined him tucking her in and reading her a bedtime story, then kissing her goodnight on the forehead. I wondered if he helped her hang a galaxy pull cord for her light. A twinge of jealousy shot through me. I propped my arm up on the window and leaned my head onto it like a pillow. My eyes shut hard, tears leaking out of the corners. I pretended to sleep the rest of the way home so my sister didn't try to talk to me.

Jane pulled into our driveway, and the second the car stopped, I flung my door open and raced upstairs. I darted to my bedroom and shut the door. Images of the little girl and her mother replayed through my mind like an endless loop of torture. I crawled over to my boom box and flipped the radio on. Otis Redding sang through the speakers, "*I left my home in Georgia, headed for the Frisco Bay. Cause I had nothing to live for, it looked like nothing's gonna come my way...*" I lay on my bed and buried my head. With each word he sang, I felt my pain ease a little.

I listened to a few more songs and then was interrupted by a loud grumble. My stomach. I forgot that I hadn't eaten anything since lunch. A sharp pain shot through my side. My stomach must be eating itself. I pushed myself up and headed to the kitchen. Maybe there were leftovers in the fridge. I opened the door and searched. Eggs, milk, carrots, peppers, cheese, ground beef, and a ton of condiments. But nothing was already prepared. I opened the freezer and searched for anything that I could microwave.

"Hey, kiddo, how was your movie?" My mom's voice startled me.

I peeked out from behind the freezer door. I didn't know what to say, so I just shrugged.

"You hungry?"

I nodded.

"French toast?"

I nodded again, shutting the freezer door.

My mom began gathering the ingredients, and I took

a seat at the table. We were both quiet as she prepared the French toast. After she placed the sloppy, egg-soaked bread into the pan, she broke the silence.

"Penny, is everything OK?"

"Did you know Dad had another family?" The words exited my mouth before I even had a chance to think about what I was saying.

My mom's mouth dropped. "How did you—" She paused. "Yes, I knew."

It was quiet again as we both thought. The French toast sizzled in the background.

"How did you find out?"

I stared down at the table, afraid to tell her the truth. I could say that he wrote me a letter and I found it before my mom got the mail, but the idea of telling another lie made my stomach hurt. Or maybe it was the hunger. Either way, I decided to go with the truth. "Amelia picked me up after school and we drove to his house, their house."

"Oh, Penny." She turned the burner off and sat next to me. "I'm so sorry. I know I haven't handled this whole situation very well. Your dad, well, it's all been very tough for me . . . but I know it hasn't been easy on you or your sister either."

I shrugged, unsure of how to respond.

My mom continued, "He told me about two years ago. We were in contact after he left. It started out just as business, then he gradually started asking more and more about you girls, and eventually he was asking to see you. I was thinking about setting it up. He seemed better, like he wasn't drinking, and he had a steady job not at a bar. But right before I agreed to it, he told me he had met someone else, at his AA class or something, a year after he had moved out. He said that they had a baby. It wasn't planned, but he'd fallen in love and married her. After that . . ."

She paused and looked away for a moment. When she

turned back, I could see the pain in her eyes. She swallowed hard, then continued, "After that, I decided it was better to hold off on letting him see you both. I'm so sorry, Penny, you shouldn't have found out like that."

The way she told it made it seem like she was trying to protect me and my sister, and maybe she was. But there was more to it than that. She was trying to protect herself. She couldn't bring herself to face our father knowing that he'd fallen in love with another woman and started another family. All the hurt and betrayal that I had felt was painted across my mother's face. He had broken her heart all over again.

"It's OK, Mom. I'm sorry we lied to you." I wished I had something better to say, something to make her feel better.

My stomach gurgled loudly. She looked down at it and laughed. "Let's get this French toast on a plate."

Amelia appeared in the doorway. "Hey, I want some French toast."

"Have a seat," my mother instructed, setting a plate in front of each of us. She plopped a piece of French toast down for both of us, then began making more.

My sister looked at me. "You OK?"

I nodded and took a bite.

Our mom finished cooking and joined us at the table. She set a stack of French toast in the middle and we all grabbed a piece.

"So, Amelia, how was the movie?" My mother's eyebrows were raised, and her lips curled into a smirk.

Amelia looked at me, and my eyes widened full of guilt. She caught on immediately. "Penny! You told her?"

"Well . . ." I stuttered. "I had to."

"Well, am I in trouble? What's my punishment this time?"

Our mom chuckled. "Hmm. I sentence you to dishes, and then you have to watch any movie of my choice."

It was nice to see her smile. We finished eating, filling

Amelia in on our previous conversation in between bites. I helped my sister wash the dishes, and then we all moved to the living room. We spent the rest of the night curled up under blankets watching *Kramer vs. Kramer*. I glanced from Amelia, who was sitting next to me with Henry on her lap, to my mom in the recliner. Maybe this was all the family I needed.

* * *

The next morning, there was a knock at our back door. Amelia and I looked at each other, eyes wide. We were both thinking the same thing—it was Uncle Bobby. Amelia stood up and walked to the back door. I watched her turn the knob and crack it open.

"Hey, we were just wondering if someone could move the truck? Your mom said we could park in the driveway last night."

It was our downstairs tenants. I breathed a sigh of relief.

"Oh, sure." Amelia sounded relieved too. "Let me just get my mom."

He smiled. "Great, thanks so much. We're running late to our frolfing tournament."

"Frolfing?" I could tell my sister was holding in a laugh.

"Yeah, Frisbee golf."

She cleared her throat. "Oh. OK, we'll get the truck moved, just give me a minute."

"Thanks again." He turned and headed back downstairs.

Amelia closed the door and looked at me. "What the heck is frolfing?"

"It sounds like when Henry pukes, he frolfs!"

We both started laughing.

"I better go get Mom." Amelia walked toward my mom's room, then returned a few moments later. "Do you know where she went?"

I shook my head and took a bite of cereal.

"Was she here when you got up?"

I shook my head again and slurped down the last of the milk from my cereal bowl. "Wait, didn't she say something about getting brunch with Aunt Teri?"

"Ugh, you're right, I bet Teri picked her up." My sister sighed. "Great, what are we gonna do about Uncle Bobby's truck?"

I shrugged. "We could just wait for Mom to come home."

"They have to get to their tournament, we can't wait. We're gonna have to go ask Bobby ourselves."

The idea of talking to Uncle Bobby made me nervous. We hadn't seen him since the night of Matthew's party, and I wasn't sure how he'd react. I rinsed my bowl in the sink, then turned toward my sister. "What if he gets angry?"

"It'll be fine. We'll go together."

I was still hesitant, and Amelia could tell.

"I can do it by myself if you really don't want to go up there."

I stared down at my feet, trying to muster up the courage. My sister could do it on her own, but it would be better if there were two of us in case something did happen. I shook my head. "No, I'll go with."

Amelia nodded. "It'll be quick, come on."

I followed her out the back door and up the attic steps. It felt like we were marching into battle. I pictured my slingshot tucked behind my dresser and wished that I had grabbed it. As we reached the top of the steps, my palms grew sweaty. There was no gospel music or sermon blasting, but I wasn't sure whether to take that as a good sign or not. A garbage bag full of empty beer cans sat outside the door to his room. I looked at Amelia and whispered, "What if he's drunk?"

She shrugged and lifted her hand to knock on the door.

We waited a few seconds. Nothing. She knocked again, this time a little harder. "Uncle Bobby?"

After a few more seconds, we heard rustling. Uncle Bobby cracked the door and peered at us through bloodshot eyes.

Amelia took a step back. "We need you to move your truck, the downstairs tenants have to go somewhere."

Bobby scratched his head and turned around without a word. A moment later he reappeared, shoving his truck keys through the crack into Amelia's hand. "I'm taking a nap, you do it." His voice was gruff and mumbly.

"Umm . . ." My sister was about to protest, but Bobby pushed the door closed. A beer can prevented it from latching. He kicked it out of the way and shut the door without another word.

We both stood there for a second, stunned. Bobby looked awful. He sounded awful. I looked up at my sister for direction. She motioned toward the steps, and I followed her all the way downstairs to the backyard. Now that we were out of earshot, I voiced my concern. "That didn't seem good. Do you think we should tell Mom?"

"We can try." Amelia didn't sound very optimistic, and I didn't blame her. Our mom had done little about all of Bobby's previous concerning behaviors, so this would probably be no different.

I followed her to the edge of the driveway and watched her back the truck out. The downstairs tenants were waiting on the front porch. They each had a mesh bag with an assortment of different-colored Frisbees inside. The second Bobby's truck was out of the way, they hopped in their car and backed out, waving one more time to say thanks.

I met Amelia at the end of the driveway.

She shook her head as I approached. "He had more empty beer cans in his truck. We should tell Mom."

Almost on cue, Aunt Teri pulled up in front of the house. Our mom hopped out with a to-go box in hand. "Thanks again for picking me up, I'll talk to you soon!"

She shut the car door and waved as Teri drove off. Amelia began to walk toward her, and I followed.

Our mom turned and greeted us with a smile. "Well hi, what are you two doing? Headed somewhere?"

"No, we had to move Uncle Bobby's truck because the tenants had to go somewhere."

Our mom's smile faded at the thought of us having to talk to our uncle. "Oh, I'm sorry, I should've been here to handle that."

"Mom, he has a real problem. There were beer cans all over the attic and his truck. He could barely get up to give us the keys."

Our mom nodded. "OK, I'll talk to him."

"That's what you always say, and nothing changes. It just gets worse."

"Amelia, I said I'll handle it."

I watched silently as my mom and sister argued. Amelia was right, Bobby had consistently gotten worse since he'd moved in. But it wasn't all my mom's fault. You can't force someone to change their behavior if they don't want to. Uncle Bobby had been struggling since he was my age, and now he was rapidly spiraling down. His life was like a coin in one of those wishing well funnels, spinning out of control at an increasing rate. I closed my eyes and secretly made a wish that he would get better, that he would be a good uncle. Hopefully there was still time. I knew once the coin fell into the dark center hole of the funnel, you never got it back.

CHAPTER 21

I went for an early bike ride on Sunday morning and met Edgar outside of his church. It was one of the oldest churches in our city. I didn't care much for religion, but the building itself was breathtaking. It was all Cream City brick with huge stained-glass windows and ornate gold trim that sparkled in the sunlight. In the center rose a tall steeple with a bell tower and a shiny gold cross at the top. If there really was a God, it made sense that he would live in a place like that. I watched from the sidewalk as dozens of churchgoers began streaming out of the huge arched wooden doors. Edgar and his mom were toward the back of the crowd. I waved as they approached.

"Hey, Penny!" Edgar ran ahead as his mom talked with an older woman in a flowery blue dress with a matching hat. Everyone was wearing their Sunday best. Edgar had on khaki dress pants and a plaid button-up shirt.

I was in athletic pants and my favorite Smokey Bear T-shirt. For a moment I felt out of place, but as Edgar approached, the rest of the people and any of their imagined judgments faded to the background. "How was church?"

"Good." Edgar unbuttoned his shirt collar and looked at me. "Did you know his original name was Hotfoot Teddy?"

"Oh. Is that because he walked through the desert?"

Edgar looked at me, puzzled. "What?"

"Didn't he have to walk a long time in the desert or something?"

"Who are you talking about?"

I squinted and raised my eyebrows. "Jesus, who are you talking about?"

Edgar burst out laughing. "Your T-shirt!"

I looked down at what I was wearing and joined him in laughter. "Oh! Hotfoot Teddy is a way cooler name than Smokey Bear."

Edgar's mom met us on the sidewalk. "Hello, Penny, how are you?"

"Hi, Mrs. Gonzalez. I'm good."

"Well, it's nice to see you here. You should come a little earlier next time and join us for the service."

I smiled uncomfortably and looked down at my feet. "OK, maybe."

Edgar quickly changed the subject for me. "Mom, can we go play baseball by Penny's house?"

"There's a yard full of leaves that needs to be raked first."

"I can help," I offered eagerly.

"All right." Mrs. Gonzalez tucked her purse under her arm. "Well, let's get going then."

It was about a thirty-minute walk to their house, and halfway through I wondered why they didn't drive. When we finally made it, Edgar ran inside to get changed while his mom went to the basement and brought up two rakes. She leaned them against the house next to my bike. Edgar flew out the back door and jumped down the steps.

"Just rake them into a pile by the curb but be careful by the street. Drivers around here don't always pay attention," Mrs. Gonzalez instructed.

We both nodded and she turned to go inside.

Edgar and I each grabbed a rake and marched down the driveway to the front yard. The entire lawn was blanketed in orange and brown leaves, not a speck of grass showing through. We had our work cut out for us, and I was already tired from our walk. Edgar began raking and I followed suit.

"How come your mom doesn't drive to church?"

"She does in the winter, usually. But she says the fresh air brings her closer to God."

"Oh." I nodded. Even though I didn't really believe in God, it made sense to me. Being outside in the fresh air always made me feel more at peace.

We continued raking in silence for a few minutes. The swooshing sound of the leaves being dragged into a pile was almost hypnotizing. My mind wandered to a variety of random subjects—an upcoming math test that I had to study for, Amelia graduating in December, Halloween coming up in two weeks, my father. I paused for a moment, caught off guard by the thought of my father taking his daughter trick-or-treating. Something I had never gotten to do with him.

Edgar noticed me staring at the pile of leaves in front of me and knew something was up. "Hey, you OK?"

His voice broke my trance, and I looked up at him and shrugged. "I met my dad on Friday."

Edgar's face lit up with excitement. "Really? That's great!"

"I dunno, I don't think I'll see him again."

Edgar's shoulders dropped and he leaned against his rake. "What do you mean? What happened?"

"He has a whole 'nother family. A little daughter, and a wife. It's like he completely replaced us."

"Oh, man. Your mom didn't tell you?"

"No, she didn't know we were going to see him."

"Was he upset that you were there?"

"No. He acted like nothing was the matter, like we could still be part of his life, like we could still be his daughters."

Edgar looked at me, then threw the rake forward into the leaves and swept a pile back. "Hmm."

"What do you mean *hmm*?" I stood still in protest, waiting for him to explain himself.

Edgar shoved a pile of leaves toward me. "Here, you look like you need some."

I rolled my eyes and began raking again, reluctantly. "I just can't believe he did that to us, to our mom. And then he acts like nothing is wrong. I never want to see him again."

Edgar stared down at his accumulating pile of leaves. "Why can't you still be a part of his life?"

"Because." I stopped and thought for a second. I wasn't expecting Edgar to question me. "Because he has a new family."

"But didn't you say he's been writing to you and trying to see you for a while?"

"Well . . . yeah."

"So, it seems like even though he has another daughter, he still really wants to be a part of your life?"

I shrugged. "I guess."

"And now the only thing stopping it from happening is you?"

Edgar's logic made me angry. I threw my rake forward and dragged it back furiously, ignoring his question. My face grew hot with a mix of frustration and exhaustion.

Edgar ignored my tantrum and continued talking. "I get why you're upset, but all I'm saying is that if I had another chance at seeing my dad, I wouldn't let anything get in the way."

My body halted under the weight of his words. He wasn't trying to make me feel guilty, but I did. Here I was complaining about my dad, and Edgar didn't have a dad to complain about anymore. I held the rake in between my hands and looked up at him sheepishly. "Maybe you're right."

"You know I am." He smiled.

I kicked my foot through the leaf pile, shooting them in his direction.

He threw his hands out to the side. "Hey! All my hard work!"

"What do you mean all *your* hard work? I did over half the lawn!"

"Yeah right, you were over there pouting."

He knew those were fighting words. I dropped my rake and scooped up an armful of leaves.

"Don't you dare."

Before he could say another word, I dumped them over his head. We immediately began wrestling. He threw his rake aside and tackled me into the pile of leaves. We rolled around back and forth, taking turns shoving leaves down each other's backs. It only took a few minutes before we both completely ran out of steam. We flipped onto our backs in the bed of leaves, huffing and puffing.

I tilted my head toward Edgar. "Maybe you could come with me to meet my dad next time."

I wasn't sure if I was saying it more for me or for Edgar. Having him with me would make me feel more comfortable, and maybe he could share my dad, since I already had to.

"Sure, I'll come with."

A small weight lifted that I didn't even realize I was carrying. We lay there for a few more minutes catching our breath. The sun softened the brisk fall air and made me want to close my eyes and take a nap. But we had undone all our previous work, and we needed to get the rest of the leaves to the curb. There was no time for naps.

Edgar nudged me. "We better finish this before my mom comes out here."

I nodded. We both stood up, shook the leaves out of our clothes, and got to work. By the time we got the lawn cleared, my arms ached, and my hands had developed tiny blisters from holding the rake. I didn't mind it though. It felt good to do some hard work.

Edgar's mom appeared in the driveway. "Are you two hungry for lunch? I made up some sandwiches and lemonade."

"Yes!" Edgar and I shouted in unison, ready for a break.

We skipped down the driveway and up the back steps. I spent the rest of the afternoon with Edgar and his mom. We were too tired for baseball after lunch, so instead we played video games and helped Mrs. Gonzalez bake chocolate chip cookies. I was surprised at how much I enjoyed spending time with her. She let us sneak some cookie dough from the bowl and served us gooey hot cookies right from the oven with big glasses of ice-cold milk. We sat at the table eating our fill of cookies and watching her bake. She floated around the kitchen like she was dancing, her polka-dot apron swaying with each step. The whole time, she was talking about how happy she was for Matthew and my sister, and about her and Edgar's trip to see him in November, and how Edgar's father was probably smiling down on us from Heaven. The more she talked, the more comfortable I felt around her. I even brought up the incident with my dad. She agreed with Edgar that I should give him another chance. "Forgiveness is the only way to cleanse the heart of pain," she said, and it made sense to me. It was an unexpectedly perfect day.

* * *

By the time I left Edgar's house, I had eaten two turkey sandwiches, a bowl of apple slices, and five chocolate chip cookies, plus a few spoonsful of dough. I hopped on my bike and pedaled home slowly to avoid barfing. It was close to four o'clock when I turned into our driveway. My uncle's truck was gone. He must be at work. I ditched my bike in the grass and headed up the back steps. My mom was in the kitchen starting dinner. I grimaced at the thought of more food. Hopefully my stomach would settle down by the time she was done cooking. I briefly said hello, then headed to my room to write my Uncle Theo a letter. It had been a while since I'd received his letter about the sailfish, and I'm sure he was wondering what was taking me so long to respond since I never did send the "letter" I wrote after the shotgun incident. I grabbed my notebook and curled up under a blanket on my bedroom floor.

Dear Uncle Theo,

I'm sorry it took so long for me to write you back. There has been a lot going on here. Well, first I should tell you about Amelia's new boyfriend! It's Edgar's brother! His name is Matthew and he's in the army. I really like him. He makes Amelia happy, and he is a good big brother to Edgar. He was home visiting and we got to spend a lot of time with their family. It seems like their mom is finally doing better. I didn't realize how sad she was, and Edgar too. Does that make me a bad friend? I don't always know how to talk about serious things. Edgar is so good at being my best friend, he always knows what to say. He even said he was gonna come with me to meet my dad next time. Oh yeah, that's another big thing that happened. Amelia took me to see our dad and he has another family. A daughter and a wife. I was so upset at first. I cried the whole way home (don't tell Amelia). Edgar and his mom told me to give him another chance. I guess it feels like the right thing to do, but I don't know. What do you think?

You knew my dad, do you think I should see him again? Just the thought of it turns my stomach into knots, but with Edgar by my side I think I could do anything. Uncle Bobby is still staying with us, but he's been sticking to his space up in the attic. I don't really like having him here, but my mom thinks he needs our help, and I do feel bad thinking about throwing him out. I guess we're all he has. Sometimes he's OK, but not very often, and I don't like when he drinks. He's been doing that a lot. I loved your picture of the sailfish, that thing looked as big as me! Have you caught any more? The next time you're here we should go fishing by the river. Edgar used to fish there with his dad. Maybe all three of us could go. I hope to see you soon!

Love,

Penny (a.k.a. One-Cent)

I folded the letter and hopped up to find an envelope. The second I stepped out of my bedroom, the sweet and smoky aroma of bacon caught my nose. I followed the scent through the house all the way to the kitchen. My mouth watered out of instinct, but my stomach was still trying to digest lunch.

My mom stood at the stove dodging the sizzling grease popping out of the pan as she turned the bacon. "Penny, perfect timing. Can you wash the lettuce and cut up those tomatoes?"

"OK." I set my letter on the kitchen counter. "Can you mail this to Uncle Theo tomorrow?"

"Oh, that's nice. He's been asking when you were going to write him back." She returned the grease shield to the pan. "I'll give you an envelope and a stamp. We can drop it off on the way to school tomorrow."

"OK, thanks." I turned on the faucet and grabbed the head of lettuce with both hands. I never liked that term, *head* of lettuce. It made me imagine that I was holding a human head. It was about the same size as my own. I shuddered and then began to separate some of the leaves to make it more resemble a vegetable. Once it was thoroughly rinsed, I set it on the cutting board next to the tomatoes.

My mom lined a plate with paper towels and began to extract the bacon from the pan. Once it was all on the plate, she put another paper towel over the top to blot the grease. I finished cutting up the tomatoes, then took a seat at the table. "Are we waiting for Amelia?"

My mom set the plate of bacon on the table. "She's working until eight o'clock tonight, it's just you and me."

"Oh." I nodded. Even if my sister wasn't at work, I had a feeling she wouldn't join us for dinner. She was still upset with my mom about Uncle Bobby. I grabbed a plate and began assembling my sandwich: first the mayonnaise, evenly spread on each slice of bread, then the bacon, the crispiest pieces I could find, placed in a crisscrossed pattern, then a thick slice of tomato, and finished with a big crunchy piece of lettuce. It was a very specific assembly. Once it was complete, I placed the top piece of bread on and took a bite.

My mom set her sandwich on her plate and grabbed a napkin. "I just bought some Halloween candy at the store today. Did you decide what you're going as this year?"

I nodded. "Wolverine. Me and Edgar are going together. He said he wants to be Wolverine too, but I think he was just kidding. Or we can both be Wolverine. Can you help me with my costume?"

"That's great, I'm glad he's able to go this year. I know his mom didn't let him last year."

"Yeah. She's been really nice lately."

My mom smiled. "Well, I'll try to help you with your costume, but I'm not very creative."

I nodded and took another big bite of my sandwich. My mind wandered to my conversation with Edgar and his mom, about my dad. If I could talk to them about it, I should be able to talk to my own mom. I swallowed. "I think I want to see Dad again."

Her face immediately tensed with worry. I stared at my sandwich, waiting for her to try to talk me out of it. "Well, if that's what you really want, we can set something up."

My eyes darted up at her; I couldn't believe what she said. "Wait, really?"

"He's your father, and if you want to see him, I want to help you do it the right way."

"I can't wait to tell Edgar. What day should we pick?"

"Hold on, Penny, slow down. I want you to really think about it, you were so upset the last time. Do you think you're ready for this?" It was almost like she was asking herself.

I already knew the second visit with my dad would be light-years better than the first. This time there wouldn't be any surprises, and Edgar and my mom would be there with me. "I'm sure, Mom, I'm ready."

"All right." She sighed. "I'll call him this week."

"Thanks, Mom!"

I gulped down the rest of my sandwich and set my plate in the sink. Now that I knew what my dad's house looked like, I could better picture how the next visit would go. Edgar and I in the driveway with my new sister trying to teach her how to ride her bike, my dad watching from the porch with his wife. Us all having dinner together and then going out for ice cream. The idea of having a second family was growing on me. I snatched my letter to Uncle Theo off the counter and grabbed a pen from the cup by the telephone.

> *P.S. I just talked to my mom about it, and she said I could see my dad again! She's going to call him this week to set it up. I'll let you know how it goes!*

I refolded the letter and went to find an envelope. My mom sat at the table alone. Her half-eaten sandwich remained untouched on her plate. I was so caught up in the moment I didn't realize the sacrifice that she was making for me. I didn't realize how she didn't fit into the scenario in my head. She wasn't gaining a second family but losing a part of her first. To her, it felt like the final nail in the coffin of her failed life with my father.

I sealed the envelope and danced back into the kitchen. "My letter's all ready to go, I just need Uncle Theo's address and a stamp!"

"OK, honey, just let me get cleaned up here." She stood up and walked to the garbage.

"I can't wait for him to get it. I told him all about seeing Dad!"

She forced a smile and set her plate in the sink. "I'm sure he'll be happy to hear it."

I wouldn't understand until I was older, once I realized that I was a lot like my mom. When she fell in love, she fell in love completely. She loved unconditionally no matter what happened, which isn't always an easy way to live after things dissolve and both parties move on. Even if she found someone else, a part of her would love my father forever. It turns out love isn't as clear-cut as the movies make it seem.

CHAPTER 22

My mom called my dad on Thursday, after almost a week of me incessantly asking her if she had set anything up yet. I watched from the living room as she grabbed the phone off the receiver and began to dial. Anticipation pulsed through my veins. She smiled nervously when he answered and began wrapping the phone cord around her index finger. I looked down at my own hands and realized I was weaving my hair tie in between each of my fingers. Apparently, excitement and anxiety looked very similar.

"Hi, Loren, it's Louanne." She paused.

My mind struggled to fill in his end of the conversation.

"No, no, that's not why I'm calling. They told me all about that, I'm sorry that it was such a surprise . . . Mm-hmm, mm-hmm . . . Well, I was hoping we could set up something a little more planned. Penny wants her friend Edgar to come along too . . . No, it was her idea . . . Well, yes, she was, apparently, she wants to give it another try . . . Yeah, I suppose it's time to let them make some of their own choices . . . Uh-huh, I heard . . . Oh, I'm not sure about that, Loren, I think it'd be better if I just stayed home . . ."

I tried to keep listening, but my mom turned away and her voice became quiet. I wasn't sure if she was still talking or if she was listening to my dad. My attention was so focused on the phone call that I hadn't noticed my sister standing in the front doorway.

"Penny, what's going on?"

I turned around to face her. "Oh, hey."

"I said hi like three times, what are you looking at?"

"Mom's on the phone with Dad, setting up a time for us to all meet again."

Her face wrinkled. "Are you sure that's a good idea? Last time didn't go so well."

I nodded. "Yeah, I wanna try again, now that I know about everything. Edgar said he'd come with too."

"Well, that's nice of him." She slipped off her shoes and sat down next to me on the couch. "I just talked to his brother earlier."

"How's he doing?"

"Good. He keeps talking about his mom and Edgar flying out there for Thanksgiving, he can't wait."

"Yeah, Edgar is really excited too."

Amelia put her feet up on the table and flipped on the TV. "Do you know if Mom's making anything for dinner?"

I shrugged. "She didn't say."

Amelia leaned over to investigate the kitchen. My mom's back was still toward us. "Well, I'm not going to interrupt that." She began flipping through the channels.

I stared at the TV, hoping for something other than the evening news. "Are you gonna see Matthew soon?"

"Yeah, we were talking about it. I should finish my diploma in December, so we're trying to plan something around then."

"Oh, cool!" My voice rose with surprise. I didn't know my sister would be done with school so soon. "We should have a graduation party!"

"Yeah, maybe." She shrugged, not sharing in my enthusiasm. She liked parties, but not when they were for her. I, on the other hand, jumped at any opportunity for presents and cake.

Before we could settle on a show, my mom called to us from the kitchen, "You girls hungry? I'm going to heat up some leftovers."

"Ugggghhh," we both responded in unison. We had meat loaf the night before and weren't fans of it when it was fresh.

"Well, suit yourselves. You can make sandwiches if you want." She turned around and disappeared into the kitchen.

Amelia looked at me and rolled her eyes. "No, we're coming!"

She flipped off the TV and I followed her into the kitchen. The pan of meat loaf sat on the table next to the leftover mashed potatoes. My mom took out three plates from the cabinet and set them on the kitchen counter. We each took turns dishing up what we wanted and warming it in the microwave. I grabbed the ketchup from the fridge and squeezed almost half the bottle onto my hunk of meat loaf. It was the only way to make it edible. Amelia gagged. "Penny, that's disgusting."

I rolled my eyes and dug in. "So, what did Dad say? Are we meeting him?"

"He'll be out of town for work for a couple weeks, but after that he said he'd love to have you over for dinner, and Edgar too."

"For work? What does he do for work?" I talked as I chewed. "Amelia, are you going to come?"

My mom took a long sip of wine before she answered, "He's a woodworker, I guess he specializes in custom home bars. Go figure."

I realized my mom hadn't put any food on her plate yet, and the bottle of wine in front of her was half empty. She rarely drank on a work night unless it was a special occasion. But this was no celebration.

Amelia looked at me sideways, then responded, "That sounds like a cool job. His place looked pretty nice; he must make decent money."

I could tell my sister was trying to put a positive spin

on the situation, and it made me hopeful that she would come along. "Do you think you'll go to see him again too?"

"Yeah." She nodded as she took a sip of her soda. "Probably."

"Well, that's great," my mom said, refilling her wineglass. "It'll be a family reunion. Amelia can just drive, and I won't have to be a part of any of it."

My sister narrowed her eyes. "Mom, come on."

I sensed the tension and watched silently, using the last bite of my meat loaf as a spoon for my mashed potatoes. My mom looked at Amelia, then to me. Her gaze softened. "I'm sorry. Of course I'll drive you, if that's what you want. I know how important it is to both of you."

I recognized my mom's change in attitude and felt grateful the tension had eased. "Thanks, Mom," I responded softly.

Amelia relaxed back in her chair and continued eating. "This meat loaf kinda tastes better the second day around."

"What was wrong with it yesterday?" my mom questioned, setting her wineglass on the table.

Amelia and I knew better than to answer. We looked at each other, then down at our plates.

"Huh. Well, you two are welcome to cook dinner any time you'd like." She plopped a hunk of meat loaf onto her plate and took a bite of it cold. "Will you pass me the ketchup?"

Amelia grimaced. "Ew, you're not going to heat it up?"

"It tastes fine just like this." She took a sip of wine and smiled.

"Gross." Amelia stood to clear her plate.

I followed and set my plate in the sink. "Is the driveway clear for me to play basketball?"

"Yeah, I think I parked far enough back."

I looked at my sister. "Em, you wanna play?"

"No, I gotta study. I have some midterms coming up."

My mom looked at me. "Penny, are you sure you don't have any studying to do?"

I shook my head. "I already did all of my homework."

My mom nodded and squirted more ketchup onto her plate. Thinking about the cold meat loaf and watching her slather it in ketchup was starting to gross me out too. I turned and headed out the back door before I had to watch her take another bite.

There was just enough daylight left for me to get at least a half hour of playing in. I grabbed the basketball from the back hall and stepped outside. I made it about one step before I halted in place. Uncle Bobby was sitting on the back stoop smoking a cigarette. My first reaction was to run back inside, but it was too late. He'd already turned and seen me. I tried to act normal.

"Excuse me, Uncle Bobby." I slunk past him, trying to keep as much distance as possible.

He scooted over to let me pass. He was silent at first, which almost made me more uncomfortable. I tried to ignore him and began dribbling. He took a drag off his cigarette and watched. I walked to the free-throw line and took a shot. The ball hit the rim and bounced back to me. I glanced at Uncle Bobby out of the corner of my eye, trying not to make it obvious. He was still staring in my direction; whether or not he was looking at me was unclear. I dribbled the ball to the right side of the court and took another shot. This time it missed the hoop completely and bounced over to my uncle. He put one foot on it and guided it to his hand. I hesitated, hoping he would just toss it back to me. He didn't. My palms grew sweaty as I approached. I stopped a few feet away and held my hands up for him to throw it to me. He lifted his arm and bounced the ball in my direction.

"Thanks," I mumbled shyly, relieved to have avoided any close interaction.

He nodded.

I walked to the free-throw line again, figuring it was a safer shot. I dribbled as I lined up my shot, then lifted my arms to throw. Swish. The ball fell clean through the net. I smiled as I walked over to retrieve it.

Uncle Bobby flicked his cigarette to the ground and stepped on it. "Penny, c'mere a moment."

I clutched the ball between my hands and didn't move.

"I'm not gonna bite, I promise."

His promise did little to reassure me, but I slowly made my way toward him, stopping just out of reach.

He looked at me and slid his hand into his jacket pocket. "Here, you should have this back."

His arm extended toward me. My grandmother's Bible rested in his palm. I stared at it, unsure what to do. Why would he give me the Bible back after I'd ruined it? Was this some kind of trick? Or a test? He continued to hold it out until I finally took it. I was hoping he'd offer some sort of explanation. My hand lightly clutched the Bible, not fully committed to accepting it. Uncle Bobby waited until my eyes met his, then stood up and went inside without another word.

I stood motionless, trying to figure out what exactly just happened and what to do with my grandmother's heirloom. After how angry Uncle Bobby had gotten with me before, it was a responsibility I didn't want. The sun was already beginning to set, meaning my mom would expect me inside at any moment. I rolled the basketball under the back porch and headed up the steps.

Later that night, I rolled around restless in my bed. The interaction with my uncle replayed in my head, only this time I noticed something I hadn't earlier. Misery.

It clouded his eyes and sank in his face. His whole body seemed to be pulled down, drooping, from the weight of his sorrow. It made me uneasy to think of how sad he was. Before I fell asleep, I did something I had never done in my entire life. I prayed. I asked for Uncle Bobby's pain to go away.

* * *

I wasn't sure how religion worked, but I was pretty certain my message didn't go through. The next afternoon when I got home from school, my mom told me that Uncle Bobby had lost his job. She didn't go into the details, but my sister and I had filled in enough blanks to guess that it was due to his drinking. He was supposed to go in on Monday to turn in all of his company uniforms and pick up his last paycheck.

Amelia wasn't reserved when it came to expressing her concern. "Mom, staying here isn't helping him. He's just getting worse."

My mom stood at the kitchen sink with her back to us. "I'm not throwing him out on the street, Amelia. He's kept to himself; I don't see why you care so much."

"Because he's like a ticking time bomb waiting to go off at any moment!"

My mom turned to dry her hands on a dish towel. "You're overreacting."

"You're underreacting!" My sister's body tensed with frustration.

My mom remained calm and matter-of-fact. "It's not up for debate. He's staying here, at least until he finds another job."

Amelia looked to me for support. "Penny, how do you feel about him staying here?"

Usually in any situation, but especially when it came to

Uncle Bobby, I would have my sister's back. I should've told my mom that I feared my uncle; it would've been the truth. But my empathy clouded my judgment. The image of him holding out my grandmother's Bible flashed through my head. Suffering stained his face, and I didn't want to add to it. I looked at my sister, then my mom. "I dunno, maybe just a little longer is OK."

Amelia stared at me in disbelief. "Fine. I'm going to study." She retreated to her bedroom, defeated.

Guilt welled in the pit of my stomach. Deep down I knew she was right. Uncle Bobby was destructive and unpredictable, and he wasn't getting the help he needed by staying with us. But it was hard to push aside my feelings. Logic and truth often lost the battle with emotion. I was tempted to go into my sister's room and try to apologize, but before I could make it to the hallway, the doorbell rang. Edgar was coming over to work on our costumes and carve pumpkins. I'd almost forgotten!

I raced to the front door and pulled it open. Edgar had his arms clasped around a huge pumpkin. His mom stood behind him, carrying a paper grocery bag in one hand and another pumpkin in the other.

"Come on in!" I stepped aside to make room.

When we got upstairs, my mom was waiting in the living room. "Hi, Edgar, Evelyn, welcome!"

Edgar's mom set the bag and pumpkin on the coffee table. "Louanne, thanks for having us over. I didn't realize how much I missed getting out of the house!"

"Of course, anytime." My mom smiled. "What's in the bag?"

Mrs. Gonzalez reached inside and pulled out Edgar's costume along with a few scraps of extra fabric and accessories. "The project of the night," she said, handing the items to her son.

"Looks like he doesn't have much more to go," my mom commented.

"And this"—Mrs. Gonzalez reached into the bag again, this time retrieving a bottle of red wine—"is for us."

"I like the way you travel!" My mom laughed. "I'll get the wineglasses."

They both disappeared into the kitchen. Edgar held up his costume. "What do you think? I even got playing cards to carry around and throw!"

He ended up going as Gambit, letting me have Wolverine all to myself. "It looks great! I'll go grab mine." I darted into my bedroom and reappeared with my costume. "I just gotta sew on the X and figure out what to use as claws."

"Hmm, what about chopsticks? You could tape them to your gloves?"

"Ooooh, yeah, I wonder if we have any."

We got to work adding the last details to our uniforms. I grabbed my mom's sewing kit and checked the kitchen drawer for chopsticks. Luckily, my mom had a habit of saving all sorts of odds and ends, just for moments like this. "You never know when you're going to need that," she'd always say when Amelia and I would look at her sideways for adding a random button or screw to the drawer. I grabbed three sets of chopsticks and rejoined Edgar in the living room.

"Here, put your gloves on and I'll try to tape them to your knuckles." He grabbed the roll of duct tape from the table.

"My mom set up a date for us to go see my dad!" I slid the gloves on, and Edgar began taping. "We're going to go the second Friday in November. He wants to have dinner with us!"

Edgar paused. "That's perfect, it'll be right before we go see Matthew!"

"Yeah, I'm glad you can come. I'm sorta nervous."

The tape wasn't holding, so he tried to reposition the chopstick. "How come? It sounds like he's excited to see you."

"I dunno, I'm excited. But I don't really know him. What if he doesn't like me as much as his other daughter?" My mind flashed to the time my mom surprised me with a little stuffed bunny in a pink flowery dress for Easter. I was so upset because it wasn't as cute as my favorite stuffed hippopotamus that I had spilled milk all over and didn't tell anyone about until it grew too sour to ignore. I remember thinking there was nothing that I would love as much as that hippo, and I hated anything that tried to compete with it. What if that's how my dad would feel about me?

Edgar shook his head. "You're his daughter. He will love you just as much as Amelia and his other daughter."

"Addy."

"What?" he questioned.

"Her name is Addy, I heard him call her that when I was there."

"OK, well, he will love you as much as Amelia and Addy. You have nothing to worry about."

I nodded. "But . . . how do you know?"

Edgar thought for a moment, still trying to get the first chopstick to stick to my hand. "Do you know why me and Matthew are so far apart?"

"I figured you were a surprise, like me."

He shook his head. "My mom and dad started trying to have another child when my brother was three. She got pregnant a few times. Some made it a few weeks, one even made it a few months, but eventually she lost them. She told me that even after I was born, she was so scared of losing me, like it wasn't real, or it wasn't what God wanted. But she also told me that she loved every one of those babies just as much as Matthew and me. And that she still prays for them every night before she goes to sleep. That's how I know. If your dad is really a good dad, one worth having, he'll love you as much as any of his other children."

I looked up at my best friend and a warmth flooded my heart. All my worries had vanished. "Wow, I had no idea."

"Yeah, not many people do." He'd secured one of the chopsticks to my hand and moved on to a second.

"I prayed last night."

Edgar's jaw dropped in disbelief. "You what?"

"Well, I dunno if I did it right, it didn't seem to work."

"Hold still." He fumbled with the tape. "What did you pray about?"

"My uncle. But it didn't work. I found out he lost his job today."

Edgar sighed. "That's not how it works, it's not like a genie in a lamp that grants your wishes."

I rolled my eyes. "Well, why not?"

"God doesn't just give you what you ask for, he has a plan. You have to have faith in his plan even if it doesn't make sense."

"Well, that doesn't make sense." I fidgeted and both chopsticks fell to the floor.

"Ugh, Penny! This isn't working."

"That's exactly my point!" I threw my hands up.

"No, not you praying. The tape."

"Oh, right." I hopped to my feet and headed toward the kitchen. "Mom! Do we have any super glue?"

It took a little convincing, but with the help of a few glasses of wine, my mom handed over the super glue. Edgar and I managed to glue three chopsticks to each glove without attaching any of our own body parts. By the time we finished our costumes, our moms were on their second bottle of wine. We carved the pumpkins in the kitchen, separating the seeds for baking. Amelia even made an appearance, at the request of Mrs. Gonzalez. We spent the rest of the night eating popcorn, pumpkin seeds, and licorice and watching *Ernest Scared Stupid*.

When the movie was over, Edgar and I raced downstairs to get one last look at our glowing pumpkins on the front porch. The candles flickered, making the faces dance in the darkness. We watched them in silence until our moms appeared through the front door.

"Time to get home, mi milagro." Edgar's mom motioned toward her car.

I looked at Edgar. "Milagro?"

"It means 'miracle,'" Edgar mumbled bashfully. It was the first time I had ever seen him embarrassed.

His mom put her arm around his shoulders. "Louanne, thank you so much for everything. This means more than you could possibly know."

My mom put her hand to her heart. "Oh, Evelyn, of course. We'll have to do it again soon."

I waved as they pulled away, then turned to head inside. My mom was waiting at the front door. "Penny, can you get the candles on your way in?"

"Sure." I stepped onto the porch and took the lids off the pumpkins. With a quick exhale, the flames were extinguished. I watched as the smoke swirled up, like a spirit dancing through the night air. It quickly vanished, and I followed my mom upstairs.

CHAPTER 23

The next afternoon, I was sitting on the couch watching a nature show about bees when I heard the mail drop through the slot. The narrator was in the middle of explaining how bees communicate. He described how they use the angle of the sun to point their sisters in the direction of food through something called a waggle dance. The videos of them shaking their butts were so cute it made me want a pet bee. He went on to say that they also communicate distances through other movements and wing vibrations, and they can alert the hive to a threat by emitting different odors. It was all so fascinating that I couldn't turn away. I waited for a commercial break, then raced downstairs to retrieve the mail.

I paged through the pile. There was a stack of ads to various stores and a few envelopes addressed to my mom that looked like bills. Then I saw the corner of a letter peeking out from the bottom; the return address was my Uncle Theo! I skipped upstairs and tore it open. I unfolded it and began reading.

"Annie,

I got Penny's letter . . ."

I paused and took a second look at the envelope. It was addressed to my mother, not me. I thought about folding the letter back up and handing it to my mom, but my curiosity forced me to keep reading.

I got Penny's letter. First, I wanted to tell you how proud I am of you for setting up that meeting with her father. I know that is still an open wound for you, and how difficult it was for you to reach out to him. He moved on, and I'm sorry about that. But hopefully this will help you finally come to terms with everything. You often learn more about a person at the end of a relationship than at the beginning, and in this case, this just proves you were right all along. Loren is a good man, and a good father. It just wasn't meant to be with you two kids. I hope you realize that it ain't too late for you. Look at me, sixty-five years old and I'm still out there picking up the chicks. They're more like hens now, I suppose, but my point is the same.

Anyway, the other reason I'm writing is Bobby. Penny says he's been staying with you, and that he's been drinking. Annie, I know you feel like you need to take care of him, and I understand why. What happened in his past is horrible, and it ain't his fault, but it ain't yours either. Your brother has a lot to overcome, but only he can do it. You can't make him better; it's his responsibility. I get that it ain't fair, but it's the only way. I don't like him there when he's drinking. He's unstable. I've seen it before firsthand. He should've been arrested for what he pulled at your 30th birthday party, pulling a knife on Loren. Penny and Amelia shouldn't be around that, and it worries me having him there. I want to help. Hell, he can even come stay with me if that's what it takes. I'm asking you to really think about it and think about your girls. Let me know what you decide, I'll be waiting. Give Penny and Amelia my best and tell Penny I'll write soon.

Take care,
Theo

I folded the letter back up and slid it into the envelope. My mind tried to process what I just read. Everything Uncle Theo wrote filled in blanks that I was unaware existed. His words made me wish he were here. I knew he could make my mom feel better because that's just what he did. He had a straightforward way about him that didn't tip-toe around the truth while also making it a little easier to accept.

I put the letter on the top of the pile of mail and headed to the kitchen. My mom sat at the table with a cup of coffee and the weekend crossword puzzle.

"I grabbed the mail," I said, setting it down on the table next to her coffee. "I accidentally opened the letter from Uncle Theo. I thought it was for me."

My mother looked up. "Oh, OK, honey, thanks for grabbing it."

She went back to her crossword. I paused, wanting to say something but unable to find the words. My mom was stronger than I realized, and I probably should have told her that. Instead, I turned and walked back to the living room to finish the bee program. The narrator was now talking about honeybee swarms. The screen showed a huge cluster of bees attached to the side of a house. It looked terrifying, but the narrator explained that they weren't harmful if you left them alone. He said they stayed there temporarily while scout bees went out to find a new home. I imagined bees in little army uniforms flying around looking for a safe place to move their family.

The screen focused on one hive in a tree, and then panned out slowly to show the individual bees flying around from flower to flower collecting pollen and nectar. The credits began to roll across the screen. I sat and watched, quietly reflecting on what I'd just learned. The life of bees seemed so honorable and selfless. They lived every day for the survival of their colony, even sacrificing themselves if needed. It was almost as if they were one big life force made up of individual bees. I vowed silently to never kill another bee again, even if I was still a little scared of them.

Amelia got home from work around 8:30 that night. She hadn't really talked to me since the conversation about Uncle Bobby, and I was worried she was still mad at me. I ducked into my bedroom trying to avoid her.

"Hey, Penny?" She cracked open my door and poked her head in. "Me and Jane are going to George Webb, you wanna come?"

I looked up from the magazine I was pretending to read. "Oh, sure!"

Apparently, I had misjudged her demeanor the past few days. I hopped to my feet and followed her out to Jane's car. We both hopped in, and Jane quickly pulled away.

"What's Tomas doing tonight? I thought you guys hung out every Saturday." Amelia reached forward and began scanning the radio stations.

Jane let out a sigh of frustration. "I'm not talking to him right now."

"Why, what'd he do this time?" My sister implied this wasn't the first time Jane and Tomas weren't speaking.

"That jerk invited me to his friend's birthday party out on some farm near East Mills, so I got a new dress and shoes and was all excited to go. And the day before, he tells me he wants to just go with his friends and have a guy's night." Jane tightened her grip around the steering wheel as she talked.

"Ugh, that's annoying."

"Yeah. That's not even the end of it," Jane continued. "He had the nerve to ask me to still drive him there because his car needs new brakes or something. Can you believe it!"

My sister let out a muffled laugh. "That's bold. I

woulda let him take his car and hoped the brakes stopped working altogether."

"Yeah, that would've been good."

"So, how'd he get there?" Amelia questioned.

Jane was silent.

"Wait, you didn't drive him, did you?"

Jane shrugged.

"What is wrong with you? I can't believe after all that you still drove an hour to take him there!"

"Well, I figured if I didn't take him, he'd do something stupid and get himself hurt, and then I'd have that hanging over my head." She tried desperately to defend her decision. "And I didn't talk to him the entire way, so he knows that I'm still furious with him."

Amelia shook her head. "You're ridiculous."

I laughed quietly to myself in the back seat, enjoying the entertainment.

Within a few minutes, we were at the restaurant. The hostess seated us at a booth and set a menu in front of each of us. I pushed mine away, already knowing what I was getting—French toast, French fries, and a chocolate milk. She came back with waters, and we took turns ordering. The second she walked away, I grabbed a handful of the coffee creamer pods from the bowl on the table. I peeled off the tops and knocked them back one after another. Jane looked at me like I had spiders crawling across my face. Amelia was used to my tradition and hardly noticed. She fidgeted with the straw in her water. "Are you going to Anna's Halloween party next weekend?"

"Probably. Hopefully Tomas makes it up to me by then. We were supposed to go as Bonnie and Clyde." Jane took a sip of water. "What about you?"

"I might stop by. I dunno if I'll have a costume."

My excitement burst into the conversation. "Me and

Edgar are dressing up as X-Men, you could be Rogue! Or Storm!"

Amelia smiled. "Yeah, maybe." She looked down and began tracing the lines on the table with her finger. She didn't say it, but I had a feeling she was thinking about Matthew. She missed him more than she admitted.

"Does Matthew get to do anything for Halloween?" I asked, hoping to make her feel a little better.

"No, I don't think so, I'm pretty sure he has to work."

"Oh, that stinks, his costume would be so easy. He could just go as a soldier."

Jane looked at me and rolled her eyes. "That wouldn't really be a costume."

I made a face at her and mocked what she said in a silly voice, pretending that's what she sounded like. She responded by shooting her straw wrapper at me from across the table. There wasn't really any animosity between us. Jane was like a second big sister to me. She had even babysat me a few times when Amelia was going through her more troublesome phase. We picked on each other like siblings, me going out of my way to annoy her and her telling me I was the reason she never wanted children. It was all in good fun and we both knew it.

The waitress brought my chocolate milk out and set it in front of me. "There ya go, hun. Your meals will be out shortly. Anything else y'all need?"

We shook our heads. A group of rowdy college-aged guys at the next booth over called out loudly for her to come take their order. They seemed too drunk for how early it was. We looked over at them and then back at our waitress. "It's the remnants of the Pumpkin Pub Crawl. We see a lot of their type in here, just usually not till much later." She smiled and headed to take their order.

Amelia shook her head. "I don't think I could deal with that on a daily basis."

Jane nodded. "Yeah, you have it bad enough with your uncle at home."

"Don't even get me started on that."

I drank my chocolate milk and hoped the topic of conversation would change. My sister was still angry about Bobby living with us, and I didn't want to get pulled into the conflict again.

Jane didn't let it go. "Why, what'd he do now?"

"Well, he's now our unemployed uncle who lives in our attic. He got fired."

"Seriously? Hasn't he had like six jobs in the past two years? Was it for being a Bible-thumper again?"

Amelia smirked at Jane's choice of words. "No, this time I'm pretty sure he was drunk on the job."

"Wow. What a loser."

"No kidding."

I knew better than to stick up for Uncle Bobby again, but that didn't mean I had to stay silent. "Uncle Theo offered to let Bobby stay with him."

Amelia looked at me skeptically. "What? Where'd you hear that?"

"He wrote a letter to Mom and I accidentally read it."

"You accidentally read it, huh?" My sister knew better than to believe that. "What did Mom say? Is he gonna go?"

"I dunno, Mom doesn't know I read it."

Amelia was on the edge of her seat. "That would be so perfect. Uncle Theo wouldn't take any of Bobby's crap. We gotta convince Mom to make him go. Will you talk to her with me tonight?"

I nodded hesitantly. Even though I agreed that it was a good idea for Uncle Bobby to move out, I didn't think our mom would feel the same. My sister was clearly on a mission and wouldn't back down easily. I worried I would be walking into a huge argument.

The waitress brought out our food, offering a temporary

distraction from my concerns. We ate quickly. The drunk college kids were getting increasingly disorderly as they waited, and we were trying to avoid any unnecessary confrontations. As soon as we finished, Amelia asked for the check. We made it out the door just in time. As we exited, we heard one of the guys barf all over the floor. I thought of our poor waitress who was probably stuck cleaning it up and hoped we left a big tip.

* * *

It was 9:45 when Jane pulled up in front of our house. I secretly hoped our mom would be in bed by the time we got upstairs, but it was a weekend, so the chances were slim. We stepped into the living room, and she was waiting for us.

"Penny, Amelia, I have something I want to talk to you about." She ushered us over to the couch and we sat down.

Amelia and I looked at each other wearily. It usually wasn't good news when someone sat you down to talk. Either we were in trouble, or somebody had died.

Our mom took a seat in the recliner and continued, "I've talked to your uncle Bobby, and he's agreed that it's best for everyone if he goes to live with Uncle Theo for a little while."

My muscles were tense with anticipation but instantly relaxed with my mother's words. There wouldn't be an argument after all. Amelia couldn't contain her elation. "That's great news. I mean, I think that's a good idea. I could see Uncle Theo being a good mentor."

"That's what I'm hoping." My mom seemed disheartened, like she had once again failed her brother.

I wanted her to know that she hadn't, but I wasn't sure what to say. I went with the first thing that came into my mind. "I think Uncle Theo will really help him. He always knows how to make things better."

My mom smiled. "He does have a way about him, doesn't he."

"When does Uncle Bobby leave?" Amelia pressed for details, probably not fully believing it would happen.

"Well, Uncle Theo has a room all set up for him. He's just working on getting him into the AA group at one of the local churches and finding a few job possibilities for him. I got him a flight booked for November seventh."

That was only two weeks away! I couldn't believe that my mom had taken Uncle Theo's advice, and that Uncle Bobby had agreed to it. Things finally seemed like they were going to work out for him, if he was willing to put in the effort. Maybe God was listening to my prayer.

CHAPTER 24

Thursday was the first real cold snap of the season. The grass was coated in sparkling white frost that crunched when I stepped on it. My mom had to drive to the airport to pick up Mr. Radler, so I was stuck walking to school. The wind whipped across my face, turning my cheeks the same rosy color as my jacket. It pushed me to keep moving forward. I'd much rather be tucked in my warm bed with Henry curled up at my side, but if I missed school, there was no way my mom would let me go trick-or-treating. I pulled the hood tight around my head and shoved my hands in my pockets. Within a few minutes, I was at the playground. The bell rang and Ms. Jenkins appeared to welcome us inside. The warmth of the building was inviting, and my face immediately began to thaw.

There were only two days until Halloween, and every kid in my class was planning how to get the most candy in the few short hours of trick-or-treating. Some kids had their parents drive them from house to house, and they didn't even wear costumes. I knew that would never fly with my mom. My plan was to go to the rich neighborhoods, where they handed out full-sized candy bars. Edgar and I had already talked it through. His mom agreed to drop us off if my mom picked us up. We'd have three straight hours to load as much candy into our bags as possible. The anticipation made me want to jump out of my seat.

I tried to stay focused on Ms. Jenkins's lessons. She knew all we were thinking about was the upcoming holiday, so she tried to incorporate it into most of our assignments.

It made the day go by surprisingly fast. Before I knew it, there was only an hour and a half to go. I just had to get through English. For the end of day writing assignment, Ms. Jenkins stuck to her Halloween theme. We could either write a story about what would happen if we turned into our costume for a day or write about what superpower we would choose and why.

I went with the superpower theme. There were so many options to choose from: invisibility, superspeed, superstrength, telepathy, X-ray vision—the list went on and on. I narrowed it down to either flying or time travel. Flying would be more fun; I imagined floating through the clouds, looking down on the cities and laughing at the ant-sized people. It would be so peaceful and free. Time travel, on the other hand, would be more useful, being able to zip to the future to see what happens or revisit the past to reverse mistakes. It would mean I had complete control over what happened in my life. After close consideration, I settled on time travel.

Just as I began to write, Mr. K appeared at the front of the classroom. Ms. Jenkins met him at the doorway, and they talked quietly for a moment. Then she turned toward the class. "Penny, can you come here a moment?"

I felt my face flush. My heart began to pound. Why me? Was I in trouble? The memory of Mr. K screaming at me outside of his office made me want to run away. I stood up and walked timidly to the front of the room. With every step, I could feel the eyes of my classmates like lasers burning my back. Ms. Jenkins put her hand on my shoulder. "Honey, go grab your things from the coatroom. Your mother is here. Mr. K will walk you down."

Why was my mom here? She was supposed to be at work. Did I have a doctor's appointment she forgot to tell me about? My mind swirled with questions, but I didn't have the resolve to ask. Instead, I nodded obediently and headed to the coatroom. I returned with my jacket and backpack slung over my shoulder. Mr. K put his arm around me and ushered me out of the classroom. He was being too gentle for me to be in trouble. My heart slowed a bit as I reassured myself that everything was OK. I bet my mom just forgot to tell me about an appointment.

Mr. K walked beside me as we headed downstairs. I looked up at him, regaining some courage. "Why is my mom here? I didn't know she was going to pick me up early."

He smiled, but it wasn't a happy smile. It was more like a placeholder for something he didn't want to say. "She'll explain everything. She's waiting for you in the principal's office."

Something didn't seem right. They didn't usually bring you into the principal's office for early pickups. Uneasiness returned to my stomach. I followed Mr. K into the office and saw my mom standing in front of the desk. One hand tapped nervously on the shiny maple wood, the other grasped a crumpled tissue. She turned to face me, and it was clear she had been crying. I froze in the doorway, afraid to take another step forward.

"Oh, Penny." She collapsed to her knees and engulfed me in a hug.

I stood still, waiting for it to end. When she pulled away, she guided me to a chair.

I sat. "Mom, what's going on?"

"Honey, something happened." She rested her hand on top of mine. "Edgar was in an accident, honey. He didn't make it."

I pulled my hand back and stared blankly at my mother.

I understood what she meant, but I didn't believe her. Edgar and I were trick-or-treating in two days, we had our costumes all ready and our route planned out. As my mom spoke, the words bounced off my consciousness like a stone skipping across the water. I heard them, but they didn't sink in. She gently described what had happened while I tried desperately to focus on anything else. If she was telling the truth and this was reality, then I didn't want anything to do with it. My eyes fixed on a coffee stain on the desk. It vaguely resembled a duck. I smirked at the memory of when Edgar and I were down by the river and were competing to see who had the best duck call. Neither of us succeeded at making an actual duck appear, but it didn't matter. We were having too much fun making fools of ourselves.

"Penny. Did you hear me?" My mom's voice snapped me back from my thoughts.

I shifted my focus from the duck stain to my lap. My brain struggled to piece together what my mom had said. Edgar was on his bike. Uncle Bobby had just picked up his last check from work. Edgar wasn't wearing his helmet. Uncle Bobby was drinking and didn't see him in time. Edgar flew from his bike and hit his head, and he was rushed to the hospital. Uncle Bobby was taken by the police. Edgar never woke up. I slowly lifted my head to face my mother. "So . . . Edgar's dead."

My mom nodded.

There were moments in my life when time seemed to move so slowly I could swear I aged a whole year in a single minute. There were also moments when it sped by faster than I could catch it. This was neither. Time ceased to exist. The clock on the wall ticked, but my life wasn't moving forward. It seemed I would be stuck in this spot for eternity. Even when I left this office, and the school building, no matter where I went, my heart would live forever in these few minutes. An emptiness ached in my gut and gnawed at my chest. Despite feeling hollow, the room suddenly felt very crowded, like the walls were sinking in and suffocating me. I had to get out.

I shot up and pushed past Mr. K standing in the doorway. He didn't have time to react. Voices yelling for me to come back echoed in the background, slowly fading to silence. I ran as fast as I could, with no idea where I was going. The cold air stung my lungs, and I welcomed the pain. By the time I stopped, my shirt was drenched in sweat and my legs were trembling. I crumpled to the ground and began heaving uncontrollably. Tears poured from my eyes and my chest spasmed in a mix of gasps and moans. I don't know how long I lay there. It could've been ten minutes or a few hours. When I finally cried myself into exhaustion and there were no tears left, I pushed myself up and realized where I was. The river.

I sat in the dirt, hugging my knees and listening to the flowing water. Memories of Edgar bombarded my mind. Things I had completely forgotten about or that seemed inconsequential clawed their way to the surface as if to say, *"This is all you have left, you better not lose it."* It started with small details—the way he always turned the tab of his soda can to the side, the way his dark hair poked out of his baseball cap when he wore it backward, the way he said my name right before he was going to tell me I was being ridiculous. More significant memories slowly crept in, and it became too much to handle. I felt panic rising in my chest. It was the same feeling I got when I was lying in bed at night trying to fall asleep. I tried to focus on my surroundings—the sway of the trees, the smooth stones rolling through my fingertips, the smell of the autumn leaves in the crisp air. It didn't work. Everywhere I looked reminded me of Edgar.

Dread and anxiety swelled in my stomach and exploded out through my mouth. "No!" I shouted angrily. I hadn't realized that I was now standing at the edge of the river. The tips of my feet dipped into the icy water. I considered jumping in. It was forty degrees out, and the water wasn't much warmer, but it seemed inviting. As I contemplated my next move, I noticed a large dark shadow zipping through the air. It startled me back to sanity for a moment. The shadow swooped and rose, zigged and zagged, all at an incredible pace. It took a moment for me to recognize that it wasn't one giant being but hundreds of tiny black starlings. They moved in such smooth unison that it looked like one huge ominous wave crashing through the sky. I was mesmerized. How did they all know to turn and dive at the exact same time? It was like they all shared the same brain. I watched the birds in awe for a few minutes until they eventually dispersed and disappeared. It made me think of the show I'd watched about bees, and of the monarch's journey. Nature had a way of manifesting organization in a universe that was destined for chaos.

For a moment, I had forgotten about everything. Once the distraction was gone, the weight of reality sunk back in. A cold gust of air tousled my hair and sent shivers down my back. My sweaty, damp shirt was like a vacuum sucking out all my body heat. I stepped away from the water and onto dry land. My body convulsed, trying to get warm, devouring any energy I had left. How would I make it home? My mom was probably sick with worry. I wrapped my arms around myself and stumbled up the path. A figure appeared at the opening. "Penny! *Dios mio.* Come here!"

It was Mrs. Gonzalez. What was she doing here? She

rushed over to me and smothered me in her arms. Her warmth soaked into my body. I clung to her and buried my head in her side, never wanting to let go.

"Your mother has the entire police force out looking for you. We need to get you home."

I squeezed her tighter, tears returning to my eyes. She didn't pull away, seeming to need the embrace just as much as me. Finally, I loosened my grasp and peered up at her. Her eyes were red and puffy. Guilt immersed me. "It's my fault . . ." I sobbed. "If Edgar had never met me, he'd still be alive."

I buried my head again and wept uncontrollably. Mrs. Gonzalez held me. "Oh, honey, don't you ever think that again. Edgar loved you, and there was no keeping you two apart."

She was right; even when she was afraid to let him play with me, we found a way. But something deep down still made me question if he would've been better off without me. I tried to swallow my sadness, but I couldn't muster the strength.

She caressed my head and continued talking. "After his father died, I could tell he'd changed. There used to be a spark in his eyes, the innocence and carefree spirit that a child should have. It vanished."

The vibration of her chest as she talked was soothing. I leaned in, trying to get closer.

"He was only seven years old; he didn't understand how to deal with never seeing his father again. He didn't deserve to feel such pain, and I was too broken to comfort him the way a mother should." Her voice was low and raspy from crying. She paused to clear her throat.

"But when he started spending more time with you, Penny, that spark came back. He was my miracle, and you were his. You hear me?"

I nodded, tears still streaming from my eyes.

Mrs. Gonzalez broke the hug but kept one arm around me. "Now let's get you home and warmed up."

"OK," I whimpered.

We walked up the path, still clutching each other. I remained heavy with guilt. It was my uncle who killed her son. It was me who always helped Edgar ditch his helmet. I didn't understand how Mrs. Gonzalez didn't hate me, but I was grateful that she didn't. I clung to her the whole way home, replaying her words in my head. Was I really Edgar's miracle? The thought rested softly in my chest, filling in a little piece of the void.

***

Two days after the accident, Amelia drove with Mrs. Gonzalez to pick Matthew up from the airport. They were all coming back to our house to finalize the funeral arrangements. I stayed home with my mom, helping to bake homemade sugar cookies for them. As I scooped the dough and rolled it into balls, my mother put on a pot of coffee. It was a pleasant distraction, and for a few moments I felt normal.

"Penny, if you eat any more of that dough there won't be any cookies left to bake," my mom scolded me.

I snuck one more scoop and then agreed it would be the last. My stomach was starting to hurt from all the sugar and butter anyway. "When does Uncle Theo get in?"

"He's not coming until Monday."

"Oh. Are we picking him up?" I put one last dough ball on the tray, then slid it into the oven.

"Depending on the time, I might just send your sister. There are some things I have to take care of at the courthouse."

"With Uncle Bobby?" His name burned my throat. I hoped he would stay locked up forever.

"Yes. I'm meeting Mr. Radler to talk things over Monday morning."

"Why, what are you talking about?" Suspicion rose in my voice.

"I don't want you to worry about it, not until I have some solid answers." My mom tried to change the topic. "Make sure to keep an eye on those cookies so they don't burn."

I didn't care about the cookies anymore. "Are you trying to help him?"

"Penny, I don't think we should talk about this right now."

"Please, Mom, I just want to know what's going on."

She stared at me and took a deep breath, deciding what to do. I tried to look just pitiful enough to gain her sympathy but not so fragile that she wouldn't want to tell me.

"All right, but first you need to understand that whatever happens, Bobby has accepted all guilt and isn't going to fight the charges."

"OK." I nodded.

"Your uncle has asked that he be released on bail before his arraignment."

I felt a pressure building in my head, like a teakettle on the verge of blowing its top. I swallowed hard. "What's an arraignment?"

"It's where your uncle is formally charged and enters a plea. He has already agreed that he is going to plead guilty."

"So why does he want out? Where is he going to go?" The thought of having to see my uncle again made me nauseous. I sat down and bunched my knees up on the chair.

"He asked to stay here for a night, in the attic, so he could gather his things. And then he would go to a hotel."

My body was a squall of anger and sadness. I stared daggers into the mixing bowl on the table, pretending it was my uncle, wishing I could make him suffer. "I don't want him here."

My mom brushed my back. "I know, honey. I promise

you won't see him, and it will only be for a night. Then he will be gone."

* * *

The days that followed were a blur. I welcomed sleep. Nightmares were my favorite type of dreams because of how happy and relieved I felt when I awoke to real life. Now that reality was a nightmare, I tried to spend as little time awake as possible. I tried going to school a few days a week. My mom hoped the routine would help take my mind off things. Some days it did. I'd get so caught up in a game of basketball with Jasmine or an art project that I didn't think about the fact that my best friend was dead. Other times I would stare off into space or break down crying over an untied shoe, and Mr. K would call my mom to come pick me up.

Uncle Bobby was released from jail that Monday, with the help of Mr. Radler and my mom's bail money. He stayed in the attic one night, as promised, and I never saw him. I didn't ask what hotel he was staying at, but I saw a number for the Red Roof Inn on a notepad in the kitchen, room 213. Uncle Theo came that same Monday. I drove to the airport with Amelia to pick him up. He kept me busy with presents and stories and a trip to Herman's Custard Stand. I was so happy to see him I temporarily forgot why he was here.

The funeral was planned for November 10. It was the same week I was supposed to meet my father again, with Edgar. I wondered if my mom told him about what happened. The thought of Edgar's body sitting all alone in the morgue for days suffocated me. He shouldn't be there, he needed company, he needed his best friend. I forced myself to take deep breaths and push the image to the back of my mind. My Uncle Theo told me to focus on getting through one day at a time. It seemed like good advice, so any time I felt the panic rising, I just repeated his words to myself. *"One day at a time."*

CHAPTER 25

Edgar's funeral was different from my grandma Margery's. My grandma's was filled with countless people from different periods in her life, all sharing stories and reminiscing about the past. It was a celebration of a full life lived, complete with cake. Here, the parlor was mostly filled with family and friends of Mrs. Gonzalez, and nobody was in the mood for cake. Edgar hadn't had enough time to accumulate the same abundance of friends and acquaintances. He hadn't had a chance to find love or get a job or go to college. A few kids from his Catholic school made an appearance, but I was his only friend there. All the adults tiptoed around awkwardly, unsure of what to say or how to act. A parent outliving their child wasn't the natural order of things. It made people uncomfortable.

Amelia checked in on me every now and then, but she was mostly stuck to Matthew's side like a support beam holding him up. He wore his army service uniform and gripped my sister's hand so tightly his knuckles were turning white. It was an odd juxtaposition—someone who on the surface looked so commanding and strong but, upon closer examination, was on the verge of breaking into a million pieces.

Edgar's mom sat at the front, near the casket. She had a black shawl with bright red rose petals draped around her shoulders. Her head was buried in her hands. Edgar's uncle George slid his arm around her as she rocked back and forth. I didn't have the nerve to approach her. She was too close to the body. It was an open casket, and I refused to go near it. I watched from the back of the room as people walked up to pay their respects. The coffin was so tiny. I wondered if it cost as much as an adult one.

My mom was playing hostess and cleaning crew, walking around making sure everyone had what they needed and picking up the garbage. It was the same thing she did at her mother's funeral. When she saw me standing at the back of the room by myself, she came to make sure I was OK.

"How are you doing, sweetheart?"

My eyes darted to the front of the room where my best friend's body was sitting in a wooden box. My mind flashed to him being buried in the ground, where he would spend eternity alone, decaying into nothing. But I knew better than to tell my mother that. "I'm fine," I lied.

She ran her fingers through my hair. "OK. Do you want me to grab you a water or soda?"

I shook my head no.

"Well, let me know if you need anything, baby. I love you." She gave me a side hug and went on to clear more end tables.

Matthew and Amelia walked down the aisle and took a seat next to Mrs. Gonzalez. After a few moments, my sister stood up and walked toward me. "Hey, do you want me to go with you up to the casket to say goodbye?"

Anxiety fluttered in my stomach. "I don't want to."

Amelia lowered her gaze. "Penny, I know how hard this is, but I think you'll regret it if you don't."

I stood silently; my eyes fixed on the tiny coffin. Fear coursed through my veins. I didn't want to go up there to see him for the last time. The thought of saying goodbye to Edgar forever was too much to bear.

My sister held out her hand. "Come on, it'll be OK." Another lie. Nothing was OK about any of this.

I shifted my stare to my sister's outstretched hand. She refused to take no for an answer. I lifted my hand into hers and followed her up to the front of the room. The first thing I saw were Edgar's feet. His shiny black shoes poked out from the edge of the coffin. I followed them up to his black dress pants and jacket. His hands were folded together at his waist. He wore a red tie that matched the roses on his mother's shawl. Finally, my eyes rested on his face. It didn't look like him. He looked like a wax figure that would cave in if you touched it. As I got closer, I grew more uneasy. The energetic friend who used to challenge me at any chance was gone. What lay before me was a vacant shell. My eyes darted to the ground. I worried if I looked any longer the image would be stained in my mind, and I didn't want to remember Edgar this way.

Amelia turned toward me. "Do you want to say anything?"

I shook my head and continued staring at the ground. That wasn't Edgar anymore. It didn't feel right for me to say goodbye like this.

Amelia squeezed my hand tighter and looked down into the coffin. "Edgar, thank you for being such a good friend to Penny. I hope you continue to watch over her from Heaven and find a way to cheer her up. We all miss you."

Amelia ushered me back down the aisle and to my spot at the back of the room. I was relieved to have some distance from the coffin. I looked up at my sister. "Do you really believe in Heaven?"

"I dunno, but Edgar did." My sister's answer was honest, but I was looking for something more comforting.

"Do you think it's up in the stars? It seems like that would be a good place for it." My voice rose with hope.

"Maybe. I'm sure wherever Edgar is, it's someplace good."

I nodded, satisfied with the reassurance that Edgar's being still existed somewhere. The thought of him being completely erased from the universe was too terrifying to acknowledge. "How is Matthew doing?"

Amelia sighed. "About as good as can be expected. He's trying to stay strong for his mom."

I glanced up to the row where Mrs. Gonzalez sat. Matthew was next to her on one side and his uncle George was still on the other with his arm around her. In one week, she and Edgar would have been on their way to see Matthew for Thanksgiving. It was going to be Edgar's first time on a plane. I thought of how excited he was and shut my eyes tight. Tears squeezed out of the corners, and I quickly wiped them away, hoping my sister didn't see.

Luckily, her attention wasn't on me. She was looking at our mom, who was escorting a new guest in. It was our father. His gray striped suit made him look taller than I remembered, especially next to my mother. They were both headed in our direction. I looked up at my sister. "What's Dad doing here?"

She shrugged. "Mom must've told him."

As they approached, my heart began to pound. What would I say? Should I hug him? Were his wife and daughter here too? I wished for Edgar; he would know what to do.

"Loren, it's been a while." A booming voice emerged from behind me. My uncle Theo stepped forward and extended his hand to my father.

My heart rate slowed. Uncle Theo's presence immediately put me at ease.

"Theo, it's great to see you." My dad shook his hand firmly. "You still fishing?"

"As long as my old ticker is beating." Theo smiled.

"I hear you got yourself a wife and another daughter. Congratulations."

"Yes, yes, thank you. It's strange the way life works out."

It was at that remark that my mother grabbed a glass of wine off an end table. I was pretty sure it wasn't hers, but she didn't seem to care.

Theo eyed her up and down but refrained from commenting. "It surely is. Are they here with you?"

My father shook his head. "No, they stayed home, figured it was better that way."

"Well, I'll have to meet them another time then." Uncle Theo stepped toward my mother. "Annie, come show me where the refreshments are."

After they departed, my dad turned toward me. "How you holding up there, kiddo?"

He spoke with a familiarity that made it feel like he hadn't been missing from my life for the past four years. "I'm OK," I mumbled.

My dad looked at Amelia, then back at me. "Edgar sounded like a great friend. I wish I could've met him."

"He was."

"Well, maybe you could tell me about him sometime?"

My dad's request brought a twinkle of light to the darkness that engulfed me. There was so much I could tell him about Edgar. An opportunity to talk about my best friend meant the door wasn't completely closed on his life. I stepped toward my father and wrapped my arms around his side. He bent to one knee so he could hug me back properly. A tiny smile curved on my lips, the first to appear in days.

My father stood back up and looked at Amelia. "I can't get over how grown-up you are, Amelia. What have you been up to? Did you graduate yet?"

Almost on cue, Matthew stepped next to my sister and handed her a soda. "Here, Em. Sorry, I got caught up talking to my cousins."

"Thanks." Amelia grabbed the soda from his hand. "Matt, this is my father."

Matthew smiled and immediately extended his hand. "Nice to meet you, sir."

"Please, call me Loren." My dad reached out to grab Matthew's hand. "I wish we were meeting under better circumstances. My deepest condolences about your brother."

"Thank you." Matthew broke the handshake and put his arm around Amelia.

"So, you're in the armed forces? Where are you stationed?"

I watched my sister as they spoke. Peace glowed on her face. She had been waiting just as long as me for this moment. We finally had a dad again.

I spent the rest of the funeral walking around looking at the picture boards of Edgar's life. They were organized by age, a couple of years crammed onto each one. I scanned his earlier years, looking at him as a pudgy baby with fuzzy black hair blanketing his head. He had the same smile even back then. When I got to the ones of him as a toddler, I could really start to recognize him as the Edgar I knew. It was just a miniature version of him. I scanned through the phases of his life, trying to memorize every detail. There was him learning to ride a bike in the driveway, him building a tower of Legos with Matthew that almost touched their living room ceiling, his mom teaching him to fly a kite, and various holidays and birthdays. There were so many things I never knew about his life, so many things he didn't have time to tell me about.

One of my favorites was him standing next to his father down at our spot by the river. He was holding a net that was just about as big as him. His father stood next to him with outstretched arms, helping to support the net. Edgar was staring down at a huge trout poking out from the aluminum rim. His mouth opened wide, and amazement shone across his face. That was how I wanted to remember my friend—happy, full of wonder.

* * *

I woke up in bed the next morning to Henry licking my face. His whiskers tickled my cheeks while his rough tongue scraped across my eyebrow. I reached up to gently push him away and tuck him into my side. He instantly began purring. I smiled and scratched behind his ears, one of his favorite spots. Then it hit me like a brick. Every morning since Edgar died, I had woken up thinking about him, missing him—every morning except today. Worry spread through me. What if I stopped thinking about him, stopped missing him? What if that lingering pain eventually faded and then he was truly gone forever? I shot out of bed and raced to my dresser. Mrs. Gonzalez had let me keep a few pictures from the funeral. I pulled open the top drawer and grabbed them, studying each one closely. A longing ached through me. I embraced it, clinging to the pain because it was all I had left. After a few moments, I tucked the pictures back into the drawer, relieved that my heart hadn't forgotten my friend.

Amelia was taking Matthew back to the airport that afternoon. I wished he could stay longer, but the army only gave him a limited number of days for a death in the family. He said he'd already used up the rest of his leave to come home before the funeral. I thought of Mrs. Gonzalez all alone in her home. She had lost two of the most important people in her life, and now the third was about to fly over a thousand miles away. I silently made a promise to Edgar that I would check in on her. It didn't matter that he was gone; I was still his best friend, and that was what a best friend would do.

I pulled a sweatshirt over my head and opened my bedroom door. The living room was quiet. Uncle Theo had insisted on sleeping on the couch so I wouldn't have to give up the privacy of my bedroom. His blankets were folded neatly over the armrest. I headed to the kitchen. Henry followed behind closely at my feet, almost tripping me.

My uncle Theo's voice reverberated through the dining room as I approached. "Bobby made his own choices, it's just a shame that boy had to suffer the blowback."

My mom answered, "Theo, I saw how much he was drinking. I should've done something."

I slowed my pace and paused at the edge of the dining room, so I didn't interrupt.

"You tried. Things like this are never simple. You need to cut yourself a break."

Henry raced around my feet meowing loudly. My cover was blown. I stepped into the kitchen and my mom immediately changed the subject. "Hey there, honey, you want some breakfast?"

Uncle Theo sat at the table with a plate of poached eggs and toast in front of him. My mom sat across from him with a mug of steaming coffee. I grabbed a cup from the cupboard and sat down next to them. "Can I have poached eggs too?"

My mom sprang up. "Sure, coming right up!" Her voice was overly cheery, like she was trying to compensate for the morose atmosphere.

I grabbed the carton of orange juice from the center of the table and poured it into my cup. Uncle Theo broke open one of his poached eggs and the yellow yoke oozed out across his plate. He cut off a piece of toast to sop it up. He looked at me as he finished chewing. "What do you say you and me do some fishing today?"

My face lit up. I had been living vicariously for years through all of Uncle Theo's fantastic fishing stories. I couldn't wait to have one of my own! "Yeah! I could show you our spot by the river."

The word "our" tugged at my heart. Our, as in mine and Edgar's. Now it was just my spot. I didn't like having it all to myself.

"I would love that." Theo took a sip of orange juice. "I've been hearing so much about that spot, I bet it's even more magical in person."

My mom plopped two eggs into the metal egg cups and headed to the sink to wash her hands. "Theo, you want any coffee before I turn it off?"

"No thanks, dear, doc says caffeine ain't good for this old heart." He patted his chest and took another bite of toast and eggs.

My mind raced with excitement. "You think we could catch dinner? Edgar used to with his dad all the time, but that was a while ago. You think there's still any good fish in there to eat?"

"I reckon if there are, we're gonna catch 'em." Uncle Theo winked at me.

My mom lifted the cover on the eggs and let it boil for another minute. "I have some fishing gear stored in the attic. We can take a look after you eat."

My stomach soured at the thought of going up where Bobby used to live. A hate this strong felt too big to be contained in my nine-year-old body. My hand shook as I reached for my orange juice. I was glad nobody else noticed.

"I'll take a look up there once my food settles." Uncle Theo rubbed his stomach. "Usually, I have at least one pole with me wherever I go, but they don't fit in my gosh darn carry-on."

My mom set a plate in front of me and wiggled the two poached eggs onto it. "You want white toast or wheat?"

"White please."

She stuck two pieces of bread in the toaster. It popped up a minute later, and she put it on my plate. Just as she turned toward the sink, the phone rang.

"Hello?" she answered, tucking the phone into her shoulder so she could still scrub the dishes. "Yes, this is."

It was silent for a moment. I watched as my mom slowly stopped scrubbing and lowered the pan into the sink. She dried her hands and walked into the dining room to continue the conversation. When she returned, her face was as pale as the egg whites on my plate. She saw me looking at her and forced a smile. "Theo, will you come run an errand with me? I need your help."

Uncle Theo turned. "Well, sure, I suppose. What's this all about, Annie? Who was on the phone?"

"Oh, um, I forgot I told Theresa I'd pick up her car from the shop for her, and it's been sitting there all week while she's been out of town for work."

My aunt Theresa worked as a flight attendant, so she was gone a lot. I always thought it was such a glamorous life, traveling all over the country and staying in hotels. It suited her perfectly, staying in New York one night and San Francisco the next. She didn't like to be tied down. I liked being close to home too much to ever dream of a job like that, but I envied her sense of adventure.

Uncle Theo pushed his chair out and stood. "Well, I suppose duty calls." He set his plate in the sink and turned back toward me. "Don't you go anywhere; we have some dinner to catch when I get back."

I nodded and stuffed a bite of toast in my mouth. My mom was already standing at the back door with her purse and keys in hand, urging Theo along. I ate the rest of my breakfast in silence. Henry jumped onto the table, and I let him lick the remaining crumbs off my plate before setting it in the sink. I stood for a moment, contemplating what to do. Amelia's bedroom door was wide open, meaning she had already gotten up and was gone to Matthew's. She'd offered to bring me along, but I wasn't sure if I was ready to confront Edgar's house and all the memories that went with it quite yet. Now that I was home alone with nothing but those memories swirling around my head anyway, I was rethinking my decision.

My mind wandered to the last time I was there, after we raked the whole front lawn, twice, and then he convinced me to give my dad another chance. Who would be there to talk sense into me now? Edgar was always my voice of reason. When I thought of a future without him, a wrench clamped around my heart. Scenarios flashed through my mind, images where I once saw Edgar by my side and now it was just me, alone. With each thought, the wrench tightened until my chest felt like it was on the verge of bursting. I needed a distraction.

Uncle Theo should be home soon. I decided to go to the attic to find the fishing gear so we would be ready to go as soon as he got back. I stepped into the back hall and the tension in my chest eased. I focused on the task at hand. Excitement rose with each step I climbed. I had never caught a fish before, and just the thought got my adrenaline pumping. When I reached the top of the attic steps, a twinge of panic returned. My eyes darted to my uncle Bobby's old room. The door was cracked, taunting me to peer inside. I inched forward, afraid that he was going to somehow appear. My uncle's presence would haunt my memory of the attic for the rest of my life unless I proved to myself that he was really gone.

I made it a few feet from the door and stopped, trying to summon the courage to go in. I held my breath as I reached forward to pull the door open. The room was empty;

Uncle Bobby really was gone. A gust of relief rushed from my lungs. There were a few pieces of furniture left behind, but I was pretty sure they were my mom's to begin with. A dresser sat against the side wall with its drawers pulled open and emptied. A clunky box TV indented the carpet at the front of the room. It was so old it had two huge bunny-ear antennae and a dial to change the channels. I took a step further into the room. It reeked of my uncle—stale beer and cigarettes, with a hint of church incense. I inhaled and the image of him materialized before me. It was so vivid it made my skin crawl. I closed my eyes tight and shook my head like an Etch A Sketch, trying to erase him from my mind.

When I opened my eyes, I noticed his mattress against the back wall. There were a few crushed Bud Light cans next to it in the corner. The bedsheets were bunched in a ball at the foot of the mattress, and a rectangular outline rested on top of the pillow. I moved closer to investigate. It was a folded piece of paper, and on the front was my name. My hand instinctively reached forward but my mind yanked it back. It felt as if Bobby was inside of that letter, and if I unfolded it, I'd be letting him out. It'd be like he was right here in this room with me. My palms grew clammy at the thought. But could I really just leave it there untouched? I was stuck in place with indecision. The letter stared at me. I stared back. My hand reached forward again, cautiously. I ran my fingertips along the letters in my name. Curiosity gnawed at me, nudging my other hand forward to grab the paper. I unfolded it and began to read:

> *Penny,*
>
> *I don't expect you to forgive me, I don't even ask for God's forgiveness. You deserved more time on this earth with your friend. But Edgar was a good*

kid and I know he's in Heaven. I pray that you get to see him again. Keep your grandma Margery's Bible close, it'll show you the way. I am ready to pay for my sins. May God always be with you.

Bobby

My uncle's words reached through the paper and closed around my neck. I threw the paper to the floor and folded my hands on the top of my head, struggling to catch my breath. Once I did, I realized it wasn't fear or sadness that had overcome me, it was anger. How dare he say Edgar's name. I pictured my uncle sitting in his hotel room reading the Bible, at peace now that he'd apologized to me. He probably thought he could serve his time, confess his sins to God, and all would be forgiven. I could never believe in a God that would allow Bobby to rest in Heaven alongside my best friend, who he killed.

I grabbed the letter from the floor and raced back downstairs. The name and number to my uncle's hotel was still sitting next to the phone—the Red Roof Inn, room 213. I had seen that hotel before. It was on Cass Street, only a few miles away. I crammed the letter into my back pocket and raced down the back steps to grab my bike. My uncle couldn't get the last word and think all was OK between us. He needed to know I hated him, that I would hate him for eternity. I was determined to throw the letter back in his face and tell him that he deserved to suffer in Hell, and that God would make sure of it.

Rage powered my legs. They pumped furiously, and with each push I felt more invigorated and steadfast. Before I knew it, I was only a couple of blocks away. A strange sense of calm flooded over me as I approached. I was ready to face my uncle. I turned into the parking lot and was met with a flash of ambulance and cop car lights. Curiosity slowed my stride. I suddenly became a detective with a case to investigate. There were two officers in the lobby talking to the lady at the front desk. I peeked inside to see what was going on. The lady looked young, maybe just a few years older than Amelia. She had headphones pulled down around her neck and a variety of body piercings that I could see. The two police officers were standing across from her, each with a notepad out. I watched them talk for a few seconds, but I was too far away to hear what was going on. This was a dead end.

I hopped off my bike and slowly guided it down the walkway. A handful of people in different types of uniforms was concentrated outside of one of the rooms. I watched from a distance as they swarmed in and out. It reminded me of a beehive, everyone with a different task but working toward the same goal. They were all too focused on their jobs to notice me, so I decided to get a little closer. I stopped outside of the room that was two doors down. My eyes glanced up at the number on the door, 211. I looked back down at the flurry of people. An officer appeared at the doorway carrying a shotgun. A little evidence tag dangled from the trigger guard. I immediately recognized it as my uncle Bobby's.

Everything clicked all at once. That was his room. That was his shotgun. Where was he? I inched closer, and that's when I saw my mom. She was talking with one of the officers, her face even paler than when she left. Uncle Theo stood at her side, his elbows out with his hands on his hips.

I should've figured it out sooner, but it wasn't until they wheeled out the gurney that I understood what happened. The figure of a body was outlined by a huge sheet. It was my uncle Bobby. He had shot himself. He was dead. I would never get to tell him how much I hated him. I wondered if my mom would get her bail money back now that he was unable to appear in court. My hand reached back to feel the note in my pocket. This was why he wanted to get out on bail—to write this letter, and to kill himself. His last words replayed through my mind: *"I'm ready to pay for my sins."* This is what he was talking about. Wasn't suicide a sin? Edgar said anyone who has truly accepted God into their heart would never consider taking their life.

I wanted to make my uncle suffer, but it turns out he had already been suffering, almost his entire life. If there really was a Heaven and Hell, where did that leave him? The scorching anger that had driven me here diminished ever so slightly. I still hated my uncle for what he did, but it seemed he hated himself even more. I hopped back on my bike and took the long way home. My mom and Theo wouldn't be home for a while, and I needed the fresh air to sort out the storm of emotions that spiraled inside of me.

CHAPTER 26

To my surprise, my mom's car was sitting in the driveway when I turned in. I parked my bike in the back and headed upstairs. My mom was sitting at the kitchen table with her head in her hands. She didn't even look up when I walked in.

"Mom?" I closed the back door and stepped into the kitchen.

She looked up; defeat shrouded her face. I thought about her having to plan yet another funeral, now for her little brother. At some point, there was only so much a person could take before they became numb. I was so angry with Uncle Bobby for what he did to Edgar that I thought this is what I wanted. I thought that him being gone would make me feel better. But it didn't. I felt even worse now. I wished I could take this burden from my mom. As much as I hated my uncle for what he did, my mom didn't deserve to suffer too. I stepped closer, waiting for her to say something.

She lowered her hands to her lap. "Penny. Hi."

She didn't even ask where I'd been. Usually, those'd be the first words out of her mouth. I took another step closer and paused.

"Penny, there's something I need to tell you." Her eyes were swelling with anguish.

Before she could say another word, I rushed forward and threw my arms around her, squeezing so tight my muscles stung. It was all I could do. I couldn't stand seeing her so distraught, and I didn't want her to have to speak the words.

She froze at first, accepting the hug but not returning it. "Honey, your uncle—"

"I know. I saw what happened," I murmured.

Her arms instantly wrapped around me so tight I could barely breathe. I didn't pull away. Her chest heaved even though she tried to stop it. When the embrace finally broke, my shoulder was soaked with her tears.

"I'm sorry." She lifted her head and wiped her eyes dry. "You shouldn't see me like this."

I took a step back. "It's OK."

"I don't know that it is but thank you." She brushed my shoulder. "Oh, look what I've done. You need a new shirt."

"It's OK," I repeated.

My mom's mouth curved downward. "How did you know?"

I reached back to retrieve the letter from my pocket but paused. Something kept me from pulling it out. I brought my hand back to my side. "I went to the hotel to confront him, and I saw the cops and ambulance, and the stretcher."

"Oh, honey, I'm so sorry you had to see that." She shook her head. "I'm so sorry about everything."

I nodded. It was quiet for a moment, and I tried to think of something to say to break the silence. "Where's Uncle Theo?"

"He walked over to Benji's Deli to pick up lunch. He wouldn't take no for an answer."

I nodded again. "Is it OK if I go to my room for a little bit?"

"Of course. Are you OK?"

"Yeah, I just want to write in my journal."

My mom put her hand on mine. "OK, I'll come get you when Theo is back. He got you your usual, turkey club and matzo ball soup."

"Thanks." I turned and headed for my room.

Henry was sleeping on my pillow when I pushed the door open. I crawled onto the bed and folded my arm around him. He tried to wiggle out at first, but he quickly gave up and nuzzled in next to me. His purring was like magic, lulling my worries into submission. I lay next to him as long as he allowed. After a few minutes, he grew restless and hopped off to head to another room. I sat up. The corner of my grandma Margery's Bible peered out from beneath my bed. I reached down to grab it and opened the cover, and inside was a handwritten inscription.

> *Dear Margie,*
>
> *This has helped me through my darkest days. I've outlined some of my favorite passages and I hope they bring you comfort after I am gone. We've had our differences, but none of that really matters anymore. You brought me the two greatest gifts in this world I could ever ask for, and I will always love you for that. Please take care of Annie and Bobby after I'm gone. Those kids are my heart and soul. God Bless.*
>
> *—L*

It was from my grandpa. He died of lung cancer before Amelia and I were born. I didn't know very much about him, only bits and pieces from my mom and Uncle Theo. He had fought in World War II, and it sounded like he was a real hero, liberating a concentration camp and earning several accolades. After the war, he worked in a tannery turning animal hides into leather. He developed cancer when my mom was in high school. That was pretty much all I knew. I wish I had gotten a chance to meet him. He must've left this Bible for my grandmother, and then she gave it to Bobby. I should've opened it sooner. Remorse hung in my heart. This Bible meant more to Bobby than I realized. It was the last connection he had to his father, and he gave it to me.

I paged through the book and saw several highlighted passages. On the side of one of the pages was my grandfather's handwriting—"Hatred only brings strife, love heals all, you must forgive even if it seems impossible." I ran my fingers over his words, trying to bring myself closer to him. It was a strange feeling to miss someone I had never met. I reread the notation again, and it made me think of Edgar. It sounded like something he would tell me during one of our long talks. I reached into my back pocket and pulled out Uncle Bobby's letter. It still made my veins course with anger when I thought about him. He took my best friend from me, erased Edgar from the face of the earth forever. No matter how much I tried to force myself, I couldn't forgive him yet. I tucked the letter into the pages of the Bible. It belonged there, holding that spot until my heart was ready.

* * *

Amelia returned from the airport around 4:00 p.m. We were all in the living room when she walked through the front door. My mom was in the recliner taking a nap, and Uncle Theo and I were on the couch playing Go Fish. A mindless sitcom played on the TV in the background. My sister slipped her shoes off and joined us on the couch.

"Did Matthew get out OK?" Theo asked, putting our game on hold.

"Yeah. It was hard for him to leave. He's worried about his mom."

"It is a shame he couldn't stay longer. I suppose the army ain't too flexible with most things though."

"No, they're not." Amelia's voice was low and sullen.

"That's what kept me out. Well, that and my bad patellar tendon." Uncle Theo reached down to rub his knee. "I wasn't against fighting for my country, but I don't think I'd have taken very well to all them orders and rules. Your grandfather never hesitated; he would've forged medical documents if he had to in order to fight them Germans."

I smiled at the mention of my grandpa. The urge to ask Uncle Theo about him gnawed at the base of my throat. But Amelia continued before I had the chance.

"I'm thinking of trying to talk Mrs. Gonzalez into still using her plane ticket to go see Matt, maybe over Christmas. It'd be good for both of them."

"You should go with too!" The words shot out of my mouth like a cork under pressure. It was the perfect opportunity for Edgar's mom and Amelia to get to know each other, and that way Mrs. Gonzalez wouldn't have to travel alone.

Amelia shook her head. "I don't think so, Penny."

"Why not?" Theo jumped in to tag-team.

"Because. I don't know. It's expensive, and Matthew didn't invite me—he probably would just want to spend time with his mom."

"You know dang well that boy wants you there. He would pay for your ticket in a heartbeat if that's what it took." Uncle Theo narrowed his eyes at my sister. "What's the real reason?"

I watched with eyes wide open, enjoying the chance to interfere with my sister's love life. It was a pleasant distraction.

Amelia crossed her arms. "Well. I don't know. I just don't like the idea of having to spend that much time alone with Mrs. Gonzalez. I'm still not sure she likes me all that much."

"Aha, I see." Theo nodded, pleased with the truth. "I reckon if you love him, you're gonna have to work that out eventually. I've always found that sooner is better than later with matters of the heart."

"I never said I loved him." Amelia looked down, blushing with embarrassment. It wasn't often that happened.

"Well, maybe you haven't said it with words yet, but it ain't a secret to those who pay attention." Uncle Theo held his stare. "But don't you worry, he feels the same way."

A small smile appeared on my sister's face. "Maybe." She shrugged. "But Mrs. Gonzalez is a different story. She probably sees me as a delinquent high school dropout."

"No, she doesn't." I sat forward. "She likes you."

Amelia's eyebrows arched. "What? How do you know?"

"The last time I was at Edgar's, she kept talking about how happy she was that you and Matthew are together. She wouldn't shut up about it." The memory tugged at my chest.

The smile on my sister's face grew. "Thanks, Penny."

Just then, my mom stirred in the recliner. We all looked in her direction as she sat up. Her eyes were puffy from crying. Amelia's smile faded. "Mom, are you OK?"

Reality returned, cloaking the room like a shadow.

* * *

Amelia took the news about Uncle Bobby just about as I expected. She wasn't sad about it; she was just concerned for our mother. She agreed to keep her company so Uncle Theo could take me fishing. It was almost five o'clock and the sun was already beginning to set, but he said sometimes night fishing is the best. I was just excited to go with him. If there was anyone who could help me catch my first fish, it was Uncle Theo. We drove to Riverside Park and lugged our fishing gear down the path. I lit the way with a flashlight and rested the fishing poles on my shoulder. My uncle followed at my side, carrying the tackle box in one hand and a thermos and net in the other.

Before we left, my mom stuffed our jacket pockets with hand warmers and filled the thermos with hot chocolate. She also tried to layer me with long johns and sweatpants, but Uncle Theo stepped in to prevent me from looking like the Marshmallow Man. He agreed to take some extra clothes and blankets in the car in case we got cold. I usually hated when she tried to baby me, but I knew better than to get upset with her right now. My mom was a caretaker; it was her way of coping, or maybe distracting herself from her sadness. I swallowed my frustration and gave her a big hug before we left.

We were silent as we walked, each of us taking in the sounds of nature. There was much less activity now that it was November. Most of the life had retreated into the background, preparing for winter. The only animal we heard was an owl hooting in the distance. A gust of wind rustled through the trees, causing the thick branches to squeak as they swayed under the pressure. I looked up wearily, afraid that one of them might come crashing down. Uncle Theo noticed my concern and patted me on the back. "Those trees sure do sound ominous."

"Mm-hmm," I answered.

The sound of the rushing water grew louder as we approached. Goose bumps rose on the back of my neck, and I wasn't sure if it was from the chill or my excitement. The path opened up and we made our way to the river's edge. Uncle Theo set the tackle box and Thermos down in the dirt, then turned toward me. "All right, One-Cent, hand me one of them poles and shine that light down here."

I extended a pole to my uncle and tilted the beam from the flashlight onto the tackle box. He opened the lid and dug around the various lures. It almost looked like a toy box. There were all different shapes and colors, shiny metal keychain-looking things, some with feathers and some with spiral tails. My favorite were the floppy rubber worms. I watched attentively. "How do you know which kind to pick?"

"Well, the bait you choose depends on two things: what you're trying to catch and what the fish are in the mood for."

"How do you know what the fish are in the mood for?"

"Good question." He retrieved a shiny metal one that had frilly shreds of rubber on one end and began tying it to the fishing line. "You don't. You can only guess. Now, since it's fall, and we're fishing the river, I'm gonna set you up with a spinner. The trout tend to go for these later in the season."

I watched as he looped the line through the bait and tied it off with a knot all in one fluid motion. His stubby fingers didn't look like they could move so gracefully. He extended the pole toward me and kept his hand out as I handed him the other one. "Are you going to use the same kind of bait?"

"I'll try a spoon. That way we can test out a couple different kinds and narrow down what they're hungry for."

With both poles set, he stepped toward the river. I followed behind eagerly. He extended his pole backward and flung the bait forward into the middle of the river. I stared at the reel of my pole, trying to figure out how to cast it. Uncle Theo saw my confusion and offered a hand. He reeled his in and walked me through what to do. I followed along carefully. My finger reached to hold the line as my other hand flipped the reel over. Then I extended the pole back and threw the lure forward. It flew out into the water and was carried downstream. The line unraveled rapidly. Theo reached over and flipped the reel back over, locking it into place.

"Now wind that in slowly," he instructed.

I nodded and began cranking, paying close attention to how the line felt and hoping for a bite.

After a few more shots, I was able to do it all on my own. We both stood on the edge of the river casting and reeling. It was tedious and repetitive, but I enjoyed the practice. If I had gotten a fish right away, I wouldn't have any idea how to even get it to shore. Being out in nature often caused my mind to wander to deeper things. The topic that rose to the surface first was my grandfather. His notes in the Bible offered some insight, but I wanted to know more.

"Uncle Theo, did you go fishing with my grandpa?"

He chuckled loudly. "Every chance we got. It was always a race to see who could catch the biggest fish, or the most fish, or the ugliest fish. We turned just about everything into a competition."

I stared out into the darkness as the memory of my dead friend stirred in my head. That sounded just like me and Edgar, competing any chance we got. I blinked it away and continued, "Was he really a war hero?"

"Oh yeah. He would never say so; he hardly ever even talked about the war. I think when you see the types of things that he saw, you do everything you can to try to forget them. But he helped a lot of people over there."

"Did he see a lot of people die?"

Theo paused his cranking and looked down at me. "This conversation is taking a rather dark turn, little One-Cent."

I kept reeling. "Well, I was just wondering."

"I suppose just about every man over there saw people die," my uncle appeased me. "But thankfully, your grandad wasn't one of them."

"Yeah." I looked up at the sky. The moon was only a tiny sliver, giving the stars the stage to shine. I wondered if my grandpa was up there with Edgar. And then I wondered where Uncle Bobby was. "Uncle Theo, do you believe in Heaven?"

Before he could answer, I felt a tug on my line. At first, I thought I'd just gotten caught on a log, but then my pole was nearly yanked out of my hand. I clenched the rod and stared at the water. Adrenaline surged through my body.

"Keep your tip up! You got one!" Uncle Theo shouted. "Keep reeling!"

I cranked the line as fast as I could. The fish fought with all its might, and I worried it would slip off before I got it to shore. My uncle had already reeled his bait in and set his pole on the bank so his hands were free to help me.

"It feels like a big one!" I grunted.

"It's definitely got some spunk—keep it steady!"

As the fish was pulled closer, its tail began to splash on the surface of the water. Once I got it to the shore, it was flailing out of control. "He doesn't seem very happy."

Uncle Theo bent down and lowered the net toward the water. "I reckon you wouldn't be either."

He scooped the fish in and dragged it on shore. It was as long as my arm and flopped around wildly. I took a step back, afraid to get close. "I told you it felt big!"

"Yep, you got a doozy, maybe eleven inches! I think it's a keeper." I watched in amazement as he grabbed the fish in his bare hands, putting one gently around its midsection and another by its mouth. That's when I noticed the hook. The barb had pierced right through the lower lip. My uncle tried to wiggle it out while the fish resisted, struggling to flee his grasp. There was a stiff popping sound as the hook finally broke free through the skin. I breathed a sigh of relief, glad to not have that job. Uncle Theo pulled the net further back onto the shore so the fish had less temptation to jump for the water.

"What do we do now?" My voice was light with exhilaration.

Uncle Theo sat down in the dirt, exhausted from the skirmish. "Well, it's your catch, so it's up to you. But if we ain't gonna keep him, we better return him to that river mighty quick."

The burden of decision was heavier than I anticipated. I always viewed animals as friends, as something to love and admire. My emotional detachment from the food I ate was something I took for granted. Now my ignorance could no longer be pushed to the outskirts of my mind. I had a choice to make, and this fish's life was held in the balance. It struggled in the net, using every ounce of energy it had left fighting for freedom. I wondered if it knew it was dying. Did animals know what death was? My heart sank as I thought of it suffering. But I came here to become a fisherman, and this is something fishermen had to do.

I turned to my uncle. "Is there a way to put it out of its misery quicker?"

"There is, but it ain't pretty."

I looked at the fish once more. Panic flared in its eyes as its body gasped for oxygen. My heart ached from its pain. "What do we have to do?"

"Go grab me that big stick over there." Uncle Theo motioned to my left.

I scurried over to retrieve the stick and hand it to him.

He moved over to the net. "It's OK if you want to look away."

I shook my head, feeling it was my duty to watch. My uncle put one hand on the fish's body to hold it still. He brought the stick back behind his head, then struck it down hard behind the fish's eye with two powerful blows. It immediately became motionless. My head dropped and I said a silent prayer, thanking the fish for its sacrifice.

My uncle Theo set the stick down and looked at me. "It's pretty chilly out here; we shouldn't have to worry about getting it home on ice. What do you say to a cup of hot chocolate?"

I grabbed the thermos and sat down next to him. "Sure."

He unscrewed the first lid and flipped it over into a cup. "You were brave today, that's not an easy thing to do."

I nodded.

He unscrewed the second lid and poured the steaming chocolatey liquid into the cup. "So, you were asking me if I believe in Heaven?" He extended the cup toward me.

"Yeah." I reached my hand to grab it and took a sip. The warmth immediately radiated through my body. I hadn't realized how cold I was. I soaked it up and continued, "Edgar believed in Heaven. He talked about it a lot. I wanna believe he's up there, with his dad and Grandpa Louie, but I don't know."

"Well"—Uncle Theo took a swig of hot chocolate right from the thermos before continuing—"what don't you know?"

"It just seems like a fairy tale, or like, I don't know, a trick to make kids behave."

My uncle nodded. "I know what you mean."

"So, you don't believe in it?"

He leaned back onto his elbow and looked up at the sky. "I'm still figuring that out, I guess. But from what I've gathered so far, there's no one right answer."

I looked down at my cup of hot chocolate, disappointed in my uncle's lack of clarity. "But doesn't that scare you? Not knowing?"

"Penny, nobody knows. You just have to believe. And it's up to you what you believe."

I took another sip of hot chocolate and looked up at the sky. A streak of light shot across the sky so fast I wasn't even sure it was real. "Whoa! Did you see that? I think it was a shooting star!"

I gazed up at the sky and thought of Edgar and that night we lay out on his front lawn watching the sky. Was Heaven in the stars? I wanted more than anything now to believe that it was. That the shooting star was his soul finding its way there. But I wasn't convinced. I thought about how I used to wish I could control time so I could speed it up to get to hang out with him. But now I didn't want to speed it up. There would be no point. Now, I wished with every particle of my being that I could slow it down and reverse it so I could live in the memories of Edgar, or just have the chance to make one more new one. I wished I could tell him not to go home that way, or to stay at school for just a few more minutes, so he'd be here with me when I caught my first fish. But that was impossible. He was gone, and there was nothing I could do about it. I was so lost in thought I'd forgotten my uncle Theo was sitting next to me.

"I saw it." He smiled, staring up at the sky. "You know, we all came from the stars."

"You've told me that before. But I don't really know what you mean."

"Well, the particles in our bodies have been in existence for billions of years. Have you learned about the big bang yet?"

"Sort of. I dunno."

He continued, "Outer space was in all sorts of turmoil. Things smashing together and exploding into new elements, stars becoming supernovas and collapsing in on themselves. All that chaos created the material that made Earth, and that made us."

I was still confused. "But I thought I was made of cells and atoms."

"You are, but those cells and atoms are made up of

elements, and those elements were created from the stars imploding. Therefore, you and everything else on Earth were born from the stars. Does that make sense?"

"Sort of, I guess. So, we're just like recycled material?"

Uncle Theo laughed. "I suppose you could put it that way."

I stared up at the sky, trying to make sense of what my uncle told me. I still didn't fully understand what he was talking about. If my body was made up of stuff from billions of years ago, did that mean I wasn't really nine years old? If our particles had been around since before I was even alive, then that meant they'd still be around after I wasn't, and that meant Edgar wasn't completely gone forever. The more I thought about what my uncle said, the better I felt. Maybe Heaven really was in the stars. It brought me peace to think that the shooting star was Edgar's soul finding its way there. The material that made up his body would be reabsorbed into the earth, but his soul, his energy, still existed in the universe. I wasn't sure if that's really what I believed, but in the moment, it felt right, and I clung to it. If he was up there in Heaven waiting for me, then death didn't seem so scary.

I looked at Uncle Theo. "How do you know all that stuff?"

He turned toward me. "When I was in college, there was this pretty little physics TA in one of my classes."

I listened intently. I always enjoyed my uncle's love stories.

"She was smart well beyond what I was capable of, and I knew if I wanted any kind of chance with her, I'd have to study. I checked out every physics book I could carry and read for hours in the library. After a week straight of learning about particles and theories and all types of things that seemed like a whole lot of nonsense, I decided I was ready to ask her out. I walked up to her after class one day and told her I thought that our particles were quantumly entangled."

My eyes scrunched in a bewildered fashion as I tried to figure out what my uncle meant.

He looked at me and laughed. "That look on your face is just about the exact look she had on hers. Turns out I spent all that time studying quantum physics, and the class I was in was classical physics. No wonder it made no sense to either of us. To top it off, she was a microbiology major who was only helping out grading papers because she was dating the professor. I had no chance from the start."

I chuckled at yet another of Uncle Theo's relationship blunders. "Well, at least you learned something."

"Yeah, the hard way." He chuckled along with me.

We sat watching the sky and sipping our hot chocolate for what felt like hours. I thought about the fish, and how he would soon be cooked and eaten and become part of me, giving me energy to continue living. Maybe everything was connected in that way. Everything was just energy, transferring from one form to another. Is that what a soul is? I thought of the bees working as one, the monarchs traveling from generation to generation, the starlings moving as one huge monster, and the elephants that shared happiness and mourned with their families that were so similar to mine. Maybe it was all the same, one energy force grasping at survival. God and nature intertwined. Death wasn't the end. It wasn't lonely. It was the opposite. Everyone had to return to the stars to continue the harmony of life.

ACKNOWLEDGMENTS

Thank you to my husband, Eric, whose love, support, and encouragement motivated me to see this through to the end.

Thank you to my mom, Marti, and my sister, Kristin, for their time and efforts in providing me with valuable feedback and editing.

ABOUT THE AUTHOR

Kate Radtke is a first-time author from Oak Creek, Wisconsin. She has always enjoyed writing in her free time but never considered it as a profession. She graduated from UW–Milwaukee with a bachelor's degree in criminal justice and intentions of becoming a police officer. However, her experience as a swim coach made her realize her passion for working with children. She went back to obtain a teaching certificate and pursued a profession in childcare. For seven years, she ran a before- and after-school program for an elementary school in Whitefish Bay, Wisconsin, then shifted to part-time work once she and her husband expanded their family and welcomed a baby boy. When she's not writing, she enjoys spending time with her family, including their two dogs and two cats, exploring nature, and studying health and fitness topics.